THE SAINT
OF THE HILL

Published in the United States of America
ISBN   Paperback: 978-1-966012-09-2
ISBN   Hardback: 978-1-966012-10-8
ISBN   eBook: 978-1-966012-11-5

The opinions expressed by the author are not necessarily those of ReadersMagnet, LLC.

ReadersMagnet, LLC
10620 Treena Street, Suite 230 | San Diego, California, 92131 USA
1.619. 354. 2643 | www.readersmagnet.com

Interior design by Don De Guzman

THE SAINT
OF THE HILL

LUIS ZAENSI

CHAPTER ONE

DON FRANCO

It was 1956, and on the small but charming Italian island called Ischia, Mr. Vittorio opened his business, which had been in the family for three generations. It was a repair shop for fishing boats and medium yachts. It was a great surprise when he saw a car arrive at the front of his business, since in those days, not everyone could afford a car. Vittorio thought this car was lost, but was surprised when the driver got out and opened the rear door. This meant that someone important was arriving.

Vittorio thought they must be lost, but the stranger was getting closer and closer, and suddenly, he heard.

"What's wrong Vito? You don't recognize me?"

Vittorio was speechless when he recognized the voice of his friend Franco, with whom he had conspired as a partisan during the Second World War. Vittorio spread his arms and ran toward Franco, but the driver got in the way.

"Take it easy Luigi. Vito is more than a friend." Franco told him.

The driver returned to the car and kept a safe distance, but always watching for any strange movement.

"I knew I would find you here. I will never forget your stories and your passion for the sea and boats. Your parents did not lose money by sending you to study naval mechanics in Naples."

"Yes, this has been the pride of our family for three generations. I remember when my grandfather sat me on his lap and told me to pay attention to my father, because one day I would have to take charge of the business and here I am, just as my grandfather prophesied."

Vittorio looked at Franco and saw he had changed physically, but not in his way of being. Franco was only twenty-four years old, medium height, and looked older than he was. Gray hair filled his head, he did not have good health since his childhood and had to fend for himself to survive since the age of fourteen. He was still observant, with a strong and confident character.

"I can see that you have done very well." Vittorio said.

Franco was slow to answer. He only stared at Vittorio as he did before during the times of partisan collaboration. It was as if he could read with his eyes what people were thinking, and thanks to that quality, Franco discovered many traitors and saved Vittorio's life twice. Vittorio felt somewhat uncomfortable because his friend Franco hardly spoke to him, but if he had come, it was for something, and it was evident that it wasn't money.

"That's enough, Franco. What do you want from me?"

Finally, Franco spoke. He had convinced himself Vittorio had not changed, and he could trust him.

"Vito, you haven't changed, but I have. I had to survive, and I did it my way. I have bought the resort on the hill, and I have thought of you as my right hand. You are honest, brave and you are a native."

Vittorio stared at him and said.

"You were orphaned. We were your family, and when the war ended, the family that united us also ended. We went our separate ways and I understand you have done some illegal things to survive. I do not judge you or applaud you. I understand you. You do not have to explain how you accumulate such wealth in a short amount of time. I will only ask you one question and I know you will tell me the truth and with that I will put my life in your hands as I have done before. You saved my life twice and you are still carrying the bullet you took for me. Tell me about this job offer. Will I work for my partisan boss or the Don Franco of today?"

Franco looked at him and was silent for a while.

"I never lied to you, nor will I lie to you now. In this case, you would not work for the partisan, you would work for Don Franco."

Vittorio looked at Franco in the face and said.

"I'm sorry, friend, but I cannot accept your offer. I appreciate you consider me as someone to trust, but there is no money in the world that can buy the peace of my family. I sleep tired, but calm. My only ambition is to see my son grow up and educate him as my parents did. I always listen to your advice, but this time, listen to me, please. You have enough to live comfortably for the rest of your life. Make a family, have children, build a future, and forget the past. Material needs have a price, so you can buy them or live without them, but the needs of the soul can never be bought and without them life is incomplete, that is why God gives them to us for free, because he knows that there is no money in the world that can buy the laughter of a child."

Franco was speechless. It was the first time someone had rejected him, and even more, he had given him advice. Franco knew his friend was right, that for the first time he could not find an argument to defend his position.

Franco tried to compose himself and he said to Vittorio.

"Thank you, Vito, I know you are sincere and that you speak from the heart. I just want to tell you that my health is not good. The bullet I took for you has never stopped annoying me. My life will be sedentary from now on. I have plans to get married next month and I want you by my side in a moment so special."

Vittorio hugged Franco tightly and told him.

"Of course, I would not miss it for anything in the world. I just have one question for you."

Vittorio looked Franco straight in his eyes.

"Does she know who she is marrying? Is she marrying Franco or The Don Franco you have become?"

Franco once again felt helpless. For the first time, he could not look into the eyes of the person who spoke to him. Franco lowered his head, unable to look at Vittorio, and answered.

"No, she knows the Franco you know, she doesn't deserve a Don Franco."

Vittorio placed his hand on Franco's shoulder and told him.

"Franco, you need more loyalty from her than from me. A relationship as important as that cannot begin with deception. She should know with whom she is going to start a family. I am sure you know everything about her, and you do not expect surprises. It's not fair to her, and don't expect loyalty if you start off with a hoax."

Franco, without even being able to look at Vito's face, answered him.

"You are absolutely right. Thank you for opening my eyes about my fiancé. This weekend she will come with her parents to Ischia, and I will introduce her to the Don Franco that she does not know."

Victtorio responds. "It would be much better if Don Franco ceased to exist, and not to expose your relationship to rejection by an undeserving Don Franco. You have not dared to introduce him to her because he is not worthy of it."

Franco could not take it anymore. Every word from Vittorio was a dagger to his chest. He never imagined he would receive such a moral beating.

"I'm sorry friend, Don Franco is a monster that I can't control. He is out of my hands. Only God can help me, but every time, I get further away from God."

Franco turned and left without being able to look Vittorio in the face. The driver saw him coming and went quickly to open the door, but Franco yelled at him,

"I don't need you to open the door. I can do it."

It was obvious he was terribly upset, and he had to take his anger out on someone. The driver was shocked. That was not the Don Franco he knew.

"Excuse me, Don Franco, I was just....."

Franco did not let him finish; he interrupted with a yell.

"Just nothing. Let's go home."

All the way back, Franco did not say a word, which was unusual. His mind went back to 1944 during the Nazi occupation; when on a cold, rainy morning, he was meeting with Vittorio and two other young men on a second-story balcony. From the balcony you could see the narrow street, which was the only entrance wide enough for a truck of soldiers to enter. One of the young men in charge of watching yells at them.

"The Nazis are coming."

They all look down and see a military truck creeping slowly, with about a dozen heavily armed soldiers. Suddenly, the truck stopped, and the soldiers got out. Vittorio said.

"Franco, they stopped in front of your house. Someone must have seen you and betrayed you. You have to be careful. It is the third time they searched your house this month."

The youths continued to watch as the soldiers shouted. They could hear what the soldiers were shouting because they were only 50 meters away. The soldiers had forcibly extracted Franco's parents and held them on their knees in the middle of the street.

"Where is Franco? We know he was here ten minutes ago."

One soldier gives Franco's father a whack on the back of the neck with his rifle, throwing him face down on the ground. Another soldier kicks him and yells at Franco's mother.

"We will kill him. Is that what you want?"

The sergeant in charge fired two shots into the air, scaring the children who were watching the macabre scene.

"I want this to serve as an example for those who collaborate or cover up anyone who conspires against us."

The sergeant ordered a soldier to pick up Franco's father, who was still lying on the ground. As the soldier tried to pick him up, he realized he was dead. The blow he received had fractured his neck.

"This man is dead." Yelled the soldier.

A group of about thirty neighbors had gathered around and several women shouted in horror when they heard what the soldier said. Those screams prevented Franco's scream of pain from being discovered by the Germans and gave time for the young men to throw themselves at Franco and immobilize him. Vittorio put his bandana in Franco's mouth to prevent him from screaming. The sergeant looked at the soldiers and ordered them to lift the body of Franco's father and put it on his wife's lap. Franco's mother was on her knees, hugging her husband against her chest tightly as she screamed.

"You will not make it out of Italy alive."

The sergeant ordered three soldiers to stand in front of Franco's parents as a firing squad. He raised his right arm and yelled.

"Prepare!" There was the synchronized sound of the rifle mechanism.

"Aim!" Silence and terrified faces could be seen among the neighbors.

Then the sergeant lowered his arm and yelled. "Fire!"

The sound of three shots in unison echoed in the place. That sound haunted Franco until the day he die. Franco could not see the execution of his parents because he had three young men literally on top of him. Franco stopped resisting. He knew everything was over, but the young men did not let go of him until the soldiers left. Franco composed himself and with tears in his eyes with a firm voice said.

"I promise you that my mother's words will be fulfilled! Those bastards won't make it out of Italy alive."

Crying uncontrollably, Vito hugged Franco and told him.

"I want to take part in that. I also feel like an orphan."

Franco wiped his tears away and answered him.

"Tomorrow I will kill those bastards along with that traitor, Marco. He was the one who gave me away."

"How do you know it was Marcos?" Vittorio asked.

"Because he was the only one who has seen me all three times the Nazis have come for me."

"How will you kill them all tomorrow?"

"You don't have to come. I will do it myself, but they die tomorrow!"

Vittorio answered firmly. "I'm going. This is my business too. What should I do?"

"I will be at the abandoned mill located ten kilometers north of the city at nine in the morning. I need you to bring me a roll of fifty-pound transparent fishing line of at least 500 meters. I also need brown colored cardboard. Take the broom that is leaning against the wall, cut the broom handle into three pieces five centimeters long and make a small hole in each stick to pass the fishing line through. Finally, I need nine horseshoes and a handful of nails. Make sure the nails are long and pass through the holes in the horseshoes."

"Is that it?" Vittorio asked, confused.

"No, I need a wagon at four in the afternoon to collect the soldiers' weapons."

Franco did not say anything else and left, everyone was looking at each other confused, they could not understand Franco's plan, it was impossible to kill sixteen heavily armed soldiers with a fishing line, cardboard and three pieces of wood, nine horseshoes and a handful of nails, surely, he had lost his mind with the loss of his parents. But the next day at 9 a.m. Vittorio was delivering the order to Franco.

"Let me help you, Franco. You are making a big mistake. You always told me it is not good to act under your emotions." Vittorio said, almost begging Franco.

"Thank you, Vittorio, but this is personal, I will just kill them all, I need you to go back to town and tell Marcos I will be at the abandoned mill at five in the afternoon, that I will be recruiting neighbors to avenge the death of my parents."

"Are you crazy? He will give you away and they will kill you!"

"Don't ask me and just do what I tell you. After talking to Marcos, get the wagon and come to get the weapons. Stop halfway and wait. When you see the truck coming, follow your path towards me. They will surely pass you and because you are going alone with no load, they will not stop you because you do not present any threat to them."

Vittorio shook his head and said. "My God, you lost your mind."

Vittorio returned to the town and contacted Marcos two hours later, as Marcos was leaving his house.

"Hi Marcos." Vittorio says.

Marcos is scared and nervous, his dirty hair and disgusting appearance left much to be desired.

"I have a message for the neighbors." Vittorio continues,

"I'm in a hurry. I can't help you."

Marcos thought they had discovered him and was trying to escape, but Vittorio tells him.

"It's from your friend Franco. He needs a favor from you.

Marcos took a deep breath, stopped and sighed as he thought they hadn't discovered him.

"Of course, if it is coming from Franco, everything else can wait. Franco is like a brother to me. I feel very hurt by what happened."

Vittorio answers him. "I know he trusts you, that's why he wants you to convey to the neighbors that today, at four o'clock in the afternoon in the abandoned mill north of the city, we will plan revenge for the death of Franco's parents."

"I will take care of that. You can count on me. I will leave now and tell the neighbors. I will see you this afternoon." Marcos replied and left in a hurry."

Vittorio was tempted to follow him to see if Marcos was going to give him away, but the order was to find a wagon and wait on the side of the road. Vittorio got a wagon and set off for the mill. Marcos went straight to see the sergeant.

"I know where Franco will be today at four in the afternoon."

The sergeant looked at him with contempt and grabbed him by the neck, pushing him against the wall.

"You made me waste my time yesterday again, and I will play none of your games. You will not receive another penny."

Marcos, almost out of breath, answers him. "He is preparing revenge; he wants to gather the neighbors in the abandoned mill north of the city."

The sergeant lets go of him. He knows that the road is flat, and it is not possible to ambush without being seen.

"At what time will he be there?"

"At four in the afternoon, sir."

"Then we must go earlier to surprise him, but you go with us and if Franco does not die, you will die in his place."

"My source is safe. I can also give it to you, but that's extra."

The sergeant looks at him with contempt. "You are a traitor, son of a bitch. You will sell your mother if they offer you money."

"You are wrong, and you offend me. I am loyal to Mussolini, who was an ally and may God save his soul."

The sergeant felt a deep disgust for Marcos, spit in his face and told him.

"I want to kill Franco. It is not personal. I am a soldier, and we are on opposite sides. That makes us mortal enemies. Franco is a stone in my shoe I have to eliminate, otherwise I would not mind being his friend and deep down I have admiration for him, but you have no side, values or principles, so try to find Franco today, because I don't trust you or need you anymore."

Two hours later, Vittorio sees a truck approaching in the distance and set off as agreed. A few minutes later, he stands aside to let the military truck pass. The truck stops for a moment. The sergeant who was in the cabin next to the door looks at Vittorio, but he does not see any danger and orders the driver to continue. Marcos was sitting in the cabin between the driver and the sergeant. He recognized Vittorio, but he was afraid to say something, thinking the sergeant would think it was an ambush and he would be the first to be killed.

Five minutes later, Vittorio hears explosions and sees black smoke rising into the sky. Vittorio exclaimed.

"He did it! Long live Italy! Death to fascism!"

Then shots began to be heard and Vittorio's face changed completely, his tears flowed, and he screamed.

"No, my God! Why did you allow it?"

He knew Franco could not fight alone against so many soldiers. He was pulling the rein and screaming desperately.

"Damn donkey! Hurry up, run!"

The shots stopped, and Vittorio quit pulling on the reins. There was nothing else that could be done except to continue to see his friend's corpse and give him a last goodbye. The next few minutes felt like an eternity. He could see in the distance a truck that was still on fire. Vittorio kept getting closer, and suddenly, he could not believe what he was seeing. Franco was in the middle of the road and had a pile of weapons on the side of the road. Franco yells at him.

"Hurry, Vittorio, we have to collect these weapons and get out of here as soon as possible."

Vittorio gets out of the cart and begins to inspect the scene. All the soldiers are dead. The driver, Marcos and the sergeant, are also dead in the cabin.

"How did you do it?"

Franco responds. "We don't have time. Let's get the weapons and get out of here as quickly as possible. I'll explain on the way."

Along the way, Franco explains to Vittorio.

"I took the nine horseshoes and tied a grenade tightly to each one, then nailed three horseshoes in the center of the path at a distance of ten meters with the detonation rings, all facing in the same direction to the rear. Then I tied the detonation rings with the fishing line so that when the line is pulled, all three would be activated at the same time, from the last grenade I ran the line about eighty meters and passed the fishing line through the hole of the broom stick, so that it would serve as the handle of the detonator. I covered the grenades with the cardboard as rocks so that they would not be noticed, and the fishing line was transparent, so it was undetectable."

Franco pauses and looks at Vittorio, whose mouth is open in astonishment. He continues.

"Then I repeated the same thing on both sides of the road."

Vittorio, still in amazement, asks him.

But how did you do it so that the truck was in the center of the grenades?"

"I just calculate the following. On this road, a truck can go at a speed of thirty to forty kilometers per hour."

"That does not tell me anything." Vittorio answers.

"So, I took the average speed of thirty-five kilometers per hour, that is 35000 meters per hour and one hour has 3600 seconds, which gives a speed of 9.7 meters per second."

"I still don't understand." Vittorio answers.

"I calculated the time it took me to get off the side of the road and pull the grenade's detonator in the center of the road and it was three seconds. That meant that I had to get out of my hiding place when the truck was thirty meters before reaching the first grenade."

"Why then the other grenades?" Vittorio asks.

"That was in case the driver sped up, and if the truck was disabled, the inertia would keep pushing it forward. I took reference points for the distance by observing them from my hiding place. I stood on the side of the road and when I saw them coming in the distance, I covered myself with dry grass and bushes looking at the grenades."

"They never saw you?"

"Yes, but it was too late. I had the element of surprise. From the moment they saw me to the moment they reacted, it was a matter of seconds, but the grenades exploded. The truck continued forward because of inertia about fifteen meters, so it is in the center of the three grenades' craters."

"But they shot at you. I heard the shots."

"Many soldiers were injured and jumped from the truck, some to the right and another to the left. Then I pulled the side detonators and killed them all."

"Does that mean nobody survived?"

"No, only Marcos was left unharmed. He was in the center of the cabin, so the driver's body sheltered him on the right and the sergeant's body on the left."

"But the shots, explain the shots to me?"

"I was making sure that everyone died because some were still alive. Upon reaching the cab of the truck, I opened the door and saw that the sergeant was seriously wounded, but not dead. He had the pistol in his hand. He could have killed me if he had wanted to. Marcos was petrified. He told me they forced him to betray me or else they will kill his parents. So, the sergeant who was pointing the gun at me congratulated me. He told me he was sorry for killing my parents, but that he would do it a thousand times more if he had to, then he asked me for a favor."

"A favor! What could that bastard ask for?"

"I thought that if he had wanted to kill me, he would have done it without a problem. I said yes, I would grant it to him. He told me he knew I wanted to kill Marcos because he was a traitor, but that he wanted to do it himself because he hated traitors."

"What did you answer?"

"I told him yes, kill him and if he didn't kill him, I would."

"What did he answer you?"

"That if he had wanted to kill me, he would have already done it, that this was not personal, that his life was over, that he had never killed for satisfaction or senselessness. So, he shot Marcos in the head and then asked me to kill him."

"What did you do?"

"I could not kill him. It was the first time I had seen a criminal with principles and honor. I told him I could not kill him, but I was going to make sure that he dies. He took his pistol by the barrel, gave it to me, and said.

"Take it and don't be afraid to use it. Then he died."

Franco shook his head from side to side as if to return to reality, he had been transported back in time remembering the experiences lived with his faithful and unconditional friend Vittorio, but the reality was totally different. When he got home, the driver opened the door for him, and Franco apologized for the unfair way he had treated him.

"There is no problem, Don Franco. We all lose control sometime in life and if I can help you with something, you know I am at your command as always."

Franco took a deep breath.

"No Luigi, thank you. There is nothing you can do. Have a good night. See you tomorrow at 10 a.m."

Luigi, despite being ten years older than Franco, admired him and he was loyal. Luigi was a giant of enormous strength, but with a great sense of humor. Franco had recruited him in the second year of starting his criminal career and he had been his right hand all these years, for that reason he had been jealous of Vittorio when Franco told him he wanted to recruit Vittorio and that Vittorio would be on the same level as him. However, he was even more surprised by Vittorio's refusal to accept Franco's offer. He felt mixed feelings, because he was glad he would not have competition, but he felt anger that someone had rejected his boss. He felt it as an insult, and more so because he was the one who received the backlash for Vittorio's refusal.

CHAPTER TWO

SALVATORE & VICENTE

Rome.

At the office of the organized crime investigation department, Umberto has a meeting with his two best detectives. Sitting in front of the bureau is Detective Salvatore, recognized for his great successes against organized crime. Salvatore, with nine years of experience, is a graduate in political science, psychology, and criminal science. He had a sixth sense to tie up loose ends and, thanks to this, he had solved several cold cases. He was tall, handsome, and loved to be sarcastic to show that his intelligence and lexicon were superior to anyone else's.

Vicente was the other detective. He has got all his experience from almost nineteen years of work and his results have been surprising. He had nerves of steel, which allowed him to infiltrate criminal groups in different parts of Italy on more than one occasion. He was a tall man with black hair, a beard, and glasses. A man of few words, just his presence, inspired respect.

Umberto, known as the boss, oversaw the organized crime unit. He was an elderly man with wavy white hair, wore thick glasses and always dressed impeccably. Umberto took two thick files and put them on his desk.

"Gentlemen, you are my best detectives. I have sent for you because something is happening on the Island of Ischia. Our informants told us that Don Franco settled on the island and bought a tourist complex on top of a hill overlooking the sea. It makes little sense to buy an economically bankrupt tourist complex, since tourists prefer the beaches. We have been informed that members of organized crime have visited him. Don Franco is a very smart man. We have been after him for three years, but we have not been able to associate him with any criminal activity to arrest him. He is considered a hero by many. He was the head of the resistance intelligence groups in Naples and the leader of a partisan cell during the war at age seventeen. When he was fifteen years old, he was already collaborating with the resistance. This reached the ears of the Nazis who went for him, but when they did not find him, they shot his parents. He spent all the time in Naples under the nose of the Nazis, who thought he had gone to the mountains. He was always one step ahead of the Gestapo. He is an educated man, despite not having attended school, as his parents were extremely poor. He has a photographic memory and reads voraciously. He has a high concept of honor for actions and words as well. It is a pity that he is on the other side."

"We have also been able to infiltrate Don Marcelo's group. He will travel to Ischia next week to put an end to the alleged weapon smuggling. He does not know that one of you will be the alleged smuggler. Don Marcelo is a charismatic man, capable of selling you the Tower of Pisa and presenting the proof it is his. He is brave, has more life than a cat and all the tricks of a wizard. Marcelo is a born survivor, but he makes mistakes. Those mistakes led to his arrest twice. The first time, he incredibly convinced the detective that the person they were looking for was not him, but his bodyguard. When the detective hesitated, he disappeared in front of his nose. The second time, he escaped from the police station jail. He changed clothes with a stinking drunk and the same police threw him out of jail. This time, there is no escape. We have reinforcement and he will be surrounded."

Salvatore interrupted, saying. "That means this case is already solved. From what I have seen, they all make mistakes sooner or later. I prefer Don Franco. Let's see how smart he is. I promise it won't take me three years to put him behind bars."

Umberto looked at him and said.

"I think you are underestimating Franco. This case may not be as easy as you think. I wish I was wrong; I would love to see him in prison. It would be a triumph for our department."

Salvatore stood up and told his boss. "Then start preparing the party, because next week we will bring you two presents for your birthday."

Vicente had not said a word. He only looked at Salvatore and kept silent. He knew Salvatore was exceptionally good at his work, but he never underestimated a case. His experience had taught him this mistake could cost a lot.

Umberto tells Salvatore.

"Well, Salvatore, you have Franco, and Vicente has Marcelo. Salvatore, you can leave whenever you want, but Vicente will leave the day of the meeting with Marcelo. The two of you will go to the police station and present your credentials. You will inform only the chief of police about the cases; I repeat once again, only the police chief and nobody else. Also, on the day of the meeting with Marcelo, you must have at least three undercover police in the area. This time, he could not escape. As soon as the transaction has been made, you arrest him and transfer him straight to Rome. You will always be with him. Any questions?"

"No, Sir." They both replied and left the office.

As they leave, Salvatore asks Vicente.

"When will you leave for Ischia?"

"On Friday morning, I have my meeting at 8 p.m."

Salvatore laughs and tells Vicente.

"Then I will leave on Thursday morning so we can come back together on Saturday."

Vicente stopped and looked at him.

"I think you are taking this lightly. Do not play with fire. You could get burned."

"It's a joke. Don't take it so seriously, relax. A little humor will make our work more pleasant."

"I hope that is the case." Vicente replied.

It was obvious there was no chemistry between Vicente and Salvatore, and the arrogance of Salvatore did not please Vicente.

Salvatore arrived in Ischia on Thursday at 11:00 a.m. He went straight to the police station and with an arrogant attitude, presented his credentials and asked for the chief of police. The police officer on duty told him.

"The boss is busy right now. Can I help you?"

"I would not have asked for the boss if you could help me. I come directly from Rome. I am not a tourist."

The police officer picked up the phone and called the chief to give him the message.

"Just wait a minute. He will be with you shortly."

Salvatore, arrogantly, answered him.

"Well, I hope so. I have things to do."

Two minutes later, the Ischia chief of police comes out to meet Salvatore. He shakes his hand, says respectfully.

"Nice to meet you, I am chief Raffaelle. How can I help?"

"I'm not a tourist, as I told the previous officer. We need to be more professional and not speak here in public."

The chief was a person the same age as Umberto, and they even looked alike physically except that Raffaelle did not wear glasses. Raffaelle was surprised by the way Salvatore had spoken to him, but he decided to ignore the comment.

"Oh! Of course, come to my office, please."

Salvatore walks into the office and sits down, crossing his legs. The boss looks at him in amazement and says.

"Wait a minute, I'm going to ask that no one interrupt us."

"Sounds like an excellent idea." Salvatore replied.

The chief closes the door and goes to the police officer on duty.

"Who's that fucking ass in my office?"

"I don't know. He just presented me his credentials and said he was on a special mission."

This island has remained trouble free. We don't need crap from Rome, let alone a clown like this." Raffaelle grumbled.

Once inside the office, the boss asks Salvatore.

"How can I help you?"

Salvatore presents his credentials, and with an arrogant attitude, once again responds.

"I am Detective Salvatore from the Special Organized Crime Investigation Unit. I have been sent by the commander of said unit to solve a case of one of these criminals who is on this island. His name is Franco, and that is all you need to know and keep quiet. You will provide me with the logistics and the necessary help if I need it. Another thing, Detective Vicente arrives tomorrow for a special mission. I need three officers dressed in civilian clothes to reinforce the arrest of a smuggler. I want these men ready tomorrow at 9:00 a.m. I will come to look for them, but not a word to them about what is happening, only that they come to work dressed in civilian clothes. If you want to confirm what has been said, just call the head of the central organized crime investigation office. His name is Umberto and tell him it is from Salvatore. Is everything clear?"

Salvatore stands up from the seat and asks again.

"Dou you understand me? I'm counting on your collaboration."

Raffaelle was stunned.

"Yes clearly, we are all at your disposal."

"Thank you very much." Salvatore replied and left.

Raffaelle turned to the officer on duty and said,

"I want you to call three police officers, tell them I want them here tomorrow at 8:30 a.m. in civilian clothes, but armed."

"But there are only five officers on the island per shift." Replied the officer on duty.

"I don't care. Do as I tell you."

"If they ask me what they are going to do, what do I tell them?" Asked the duty officer.

"I don't know, nor do I care. All I know is that this jerk came to take away our peace on the island."

The officer on duty was speechless. His boss was a kind man and never yelled at them. It was clear this Salvatore was a stone in the shoe for everyone.

Salvatore stops a taxi and asks the driver to take him to Franco's complex called Monte Santo. Just by the taxi driver's look, Salvatore understood this complex was not for tourists, much less for those who came out of a police station. The taxi driver drove Salvatore to the compound and left. Salvatore entered the reception and was assisted quickly.

"Good afternoon, sir. My name is Guido. How can I help you?"

"Yes, good afternoon. I'm passing through and would like a room for the weekend." Salvatore replied.

Franco was in a corner and looked sideways, as if he was not paying attention to what was happening. Salvatore saw Franco as well, concealing that he noticed him.

"Of course, sir. What is your reservation number?"

"I don't have a reservation; I'm just passing through."

"I'm sorry, sir, but we are completely booked. If you like, we can call a taxi to take you to another hotel."

"The humidity near the sea is not good for my health."

"That is the main reason our clients come to our complex. We have a wonderful view of the sea, but not its humidity and if you add our thermal water pool, it is the perfect combination to improve your health. If you wish, you can take our phone number and call later in case there is a cancellation."

Salvatore took the pamphlet and left in the taxi.

Guido was Franco's man at the reception. He kept control of who entered and left the complex. Guido was small and chubby; you could tell he lived at that front desk, accompanied by a plate of food and a drink.

"Excellent Guido, excellent job. Franco said, patting him on the back.

"My pleasure, Don Franco, my pleasure."

"Remember that tomorrow morning my fiancée will come with her parents. Please don't ask for a reservation." Franco joked.

"Of course, sir," Guido replied.

"All of you have been hand selected to form, not a team, not a cell, but a family. I know I count on you unconditionally, as you can count on me as well. The only thing that cannot be forgotten is that in this family, I am the father."

"That is more than clear, Don Franco. It is not necessary to mention it."

Luigi approaches Franco and tells him.

"The taxi driver informed us he picked up that man in front of the police station, and we must alert everyone. We have already taken pictures of him and in two hours we will distribute them."

"Good job Luigi." Franco responds and retires to his office.

About thirty minutes later, Luigi knocks on Franco's door.

"Excuse me, Don Franco. The man did not leave at all. He is in a tree looking here with binoculars."

"Very well. Let him look at all he wants. Don't bother him, but keep him under surveillance. Find out where he stays as well."

Franco's complex was surrounded by exceptionally large trees that were hundreds of years old. That was the only part that was not developed on the hill, since the entire back of the complex had several farms which ran from the beginning of the hill to the very top adjoining Franco's complex.

CHAPTER THREE

MARCELO

The next day, Salvatore showed up at 9 a.m. at the police station, and as if he were the boss, he told Raffaelle.

"Good morning. Do you have my men already?"

"Yes." The chief answered.

"Well, bring them to me. I want to talk to them and inspect them."

Raffaelle bit his lip, trying to control himself; he took a deep breath, counted to three, and told him.

"Follow me, please."

Salvatore knew he annoyed Raffaelle with his arrogance, but he enjoyed it. He felt in control and superior to everyone. He entered the office and saw the three police sitting at a table, talking.

"Are you tired already? Let's see, stand up."

The carabinieri looked at each other in amazement and rose to their feet.

"Are you armed?"

"Yes, sir."

"I just want to make sure you haven't forgotten. Listen to me. You are going with me to the port to meet a person. You will stay close, but not more than six meters and you will not speak to him. You will follow him when I leave. He will have a meeting today at 8:00 p.m. We do not know where yet. Your job will be to stay outside and cover the exits so that the subject does not escape."

Salvatore sarcastically asks them.

"Do you think you can do this, or is it exceedingly difficult for you?"

The carabineros look at each other again and Salvatore breaks the silence.

"I can't hear you. Do I have to repeat everything again?"

Everyone responds at the same time.

"No, sir."

Salvatore says nothing and leaves without even looking at Raffaelle. The chief punches his desk to vent his anger and one police officer asks him.

"Who is this guy?"

Raffaelle, biting his lips, tells him.

"That is the biggest idiot I have seen in my life. Do what he told you, so he gets out of here for good."

Vicente disembarked in Ischia and is received by Salvatore.

"I didn't know you would come to greet me." Vicente said.

"Don't worry, everything is done for you."

"What did you say?" Vicente asked.

"Yes, I think the less visible you are, the better. I don't want someone to recognize you by any chance."

Salvatore points at the undercover officers and says.

"Those three men talking there will be your reinforcement. They will surround the place of your meeting and will not communicate with you unless you decide differently. I hope you do not take it the wrong way. I did it to prevent you from taking the trip to the police station and for your own safety. We cannot fail. If you see that police station, you will have a heart attack. The chief is a stupid old man and behind the time. You haven't missed a thing."

Vicente felt uncomfortable, but he did not want to argue. It was better to go to the hotel and wait for Marcelo's call as they had planned for. He knew Salvatore wanted to impress and make them believe he was important, but this was not the time to put him in his place, as it would be to start the operation on the wrong foot. Vicente made eye contact with the policers to make sure they were alert.

"Yes, I'd better go to the hotel." Vicente exclaimed.

"I'm not accompanying you. You are well protected. I made sure they are vigilant and well-armed to protect you. You should have seen their faces when I told them their life depends on yours. I forgot to tell you; I went to see Don Franco. We made believe we did not see each other. I know I made him very nervous. I then pretended I was leaving and watched the place. I don't think he's as smart as the boss says. He's on the top of a hill. When it comes the time to arrest him, I just surround the hill, and he has no escape."

Vicente did not want to hear more. It was torture for him, and he was relieved to take a taxi. The police officers followed the taxi in their car without raising suspicion.

Franco's fiancée and her parents had disembarked and as they walked towards the exit, Maria remembered how one cold morning she met the one who would soon be her husband. That day the snow was falling, Maria and Franco were walking on the same sidewalk, but in the opposite direction, Franco was walking and reading the newspaper without paying much attention. The snow had fallen on a layer of ice, making it dangerous and undetectable. Franco slips and falls, his newspaper flies and his scared face is fully visible. Maria was walking towards Franco. She was about three meters from where Franco was still sitting on the ground, looking at Maria. Maria cannot help laughing and Franco catches the laughter from her and starts laughing at himself. Maria, without realizing the danger, enters the ice covered by snow and slides, falling next to Franco, who gets on his knees and holds her, cushioning her fall.

Maria and Franco were almost embracing, on the ground, and laughing like children. Franco helps her get up and when he is face to face with her stops laughing. He feels an attraction towards the young woman that goes beyond his control. Maria blushes, realizes that Cupid has shot not one but two arrows.

Franco tells her. "I have the pretext of the snow, but I would have fallen at your feet anyway. It's hard not to fall before so much beauty."

Maria smiles and answers him. "I'm sorry, but I can't say the same."

Franco smiles too. "I know, but God is so wise that to compensate, he gave us, the ugly, the chance to dream and hope in miracles."

"I did not mean ugly. Never stop trying or lose hope." Maria responds.

Franco kisses Maria's hand and tells her.

"I thought this was a cold gray morning, that I shouldn't leave the house, but you have changed everything in a moment." Franco points to the cafe in front of them.

"I invite you to have a coffee. It will be good for both of us. Better yet, we need it. A meeting like ours is worth celebrating."

Maria felt haunted. She never spoke to strangers, but this time she felt free, as if she had known Franco for many years. Maria accepted Franco's invitation and as she entered the cafe the snow began to fall even harder. They both sat with their eyes towards the street. The heat from the fireplace and the smell of coffee helped to relax the atmosphere, and both engaged in a conversation as if they were old friends. It was a coffee, cakes, then another coffee and with the help of the weather that invited them to stay inside and not go out. Maria suddenly looks at the coffee clock and exclaims.

"My God, it's been an hour and a half. I must go. My parents are waiting for me."

Franco takes Maria's hand and says. "My dream has already come true when met you, now I hope to see you again."

Maria answers. "I come every Monday to the textile store on the corner to bring my father's business order."

Maria is awakened from her thoughts when she hears Luigi calling her. Maria is surprised to see Luigi. She knew Franco and Luigi were great friends and that they worked together.

"Luigi, I did not expect to see you here. I thought you were in Naples."

"You know Franco is like a brother to me and I would not miss his wedding for anything in the world." Luigi responds.

Luigi greets Maria's parents and takes them to the complex where Franco was waiting to surprise them in style. They did not know about Franco's wealth. He had always been simple and wanted his future wife to love him for love, not for his money. Franco had told them that his parents were sick and that he had to take over the farm. Maria had accepted and her parents were very fond of it. Franco had invited her to meet his parents and celebrate a simple wedding with friends in town. What a surprise, when they were received in style by Franco and hearing everyone referring to him as Don Franco.

Maria, Franco's fiancée, was a young woman in her twenties, slim with long black hair, of a sweet character, and she never raised her voice. Maria took Franco's arm and said.

"You have deceived us by pretending to be a simple person."

"I did not deceive you. I am a simple person. I prefer the woman who accepts me as a simple man rather than for my money, and that is why I love you much more."

The three of them were speechless. It seemed like a fairy tale, which was interrupted by Pedro's question, Maria's father.

"Please, introduce us to your parents. We want to meet them."

Franco looked at them sadly and said.

"You are my parents. I am orphan, so you already know them."

Tears ran down everyone's cheeks and they sought comfort in a strong mutual hug.

Franco yelled. "Boys, today is a holiday. I promised my future wife I would introduce her to my parents, and I already fulfilled that. Now I have to introduce her to the rest of the family, so after lunch you all go home. I want you here at 5: P.M. with your whole family, which is my family to make a toast."

After lunch, Franco showed the complex to his future family. The gardens were beautiful, with all kinds of roses. They had thermal pools that fell as a waterfall. The ocean view was spectacular, the breeze was nice and constant. Luigi interrupted the walk.

"Excuse me, Don Franco, you have a phone call. I think is important."

"Luigi, today is a special day. I am not here for anyone. I explained it to you yesterday."

"Yes sir, I will communicate."

A few minutes later, Luigi interrupts again.

"Don Franco, I apologize, but it's Marcelo, and he says it's important."

Pedro, Maria's father, tells Franco,

"Go, son. If it is important, answer it. Anyway, we'll be here long enough to see everything."

Franco apologizes to them, goes to his office, and picks up the phone.

"Hello Marcelo, you are always so inopportune, but I'm glad to hear you, anyway."

"I need to see you today before 8:00 p.m., it is especially important."

"It will have to be tomorrow. I can't today."

"No, it has to be today before eight."

"What do you want? Just tell me." Franco asks.

"I can't explain it to you. It must be in person."

Franco thinks that this has to do with the person investigating him and it must be important when Marcelo has come personally to speak with him.

"Okay, see you at 6:00 p.m."

Marcelo responds. "I'll wait for you at the tavern on Florence Street."

Franco meets Maria and her parents again, apologizes to them, to which Pedro responds.

"No apologies necessary. I don't know how you manage to have time for us."

"There will be always time for you, otherwise, what good is all this to me? The party starts at five o'clock, but I have to leave for a moment due to an unforeseen event. It will not take me long. I will return, and we will continue until tomorrow."

Maria takes him by the arm and separates him to the side and Franco says.

"We are not married yet. Do not fight or hit me now. There will be time for you to do so later."

Maria looks at him and says. "I want to know everything about you, because this is not the Franco that I know."

"I promise you that tonight, you will know everything about Don Franco. The only thing I can tell you is that both Franco and Don Franco would give their lives for you without a second thought."

Maria hugs Franco and tells him. "Do you remember the last time we were together in Naples before you left to Ischia?"

Franco keeps holding her hands. His mind goes back to the day that Maria gave herself entirely to him before his departure. Starting with breakfast in the cafe where they met in a harsh winter. The cafe where they religiously met every week since that day. When leaving the cafe, Maria asked him.

"Why have you never wanted to take me to your home?"

"I'm hardly ever at home. Men are messy and I'm ashamed." Franco responds.

"You are hiding something from me. You have never wanted to take me to your home, and you always avoid the conversation when I ask you what you do."

Franco feels pressured, knows he has not been sincere, and fears a negative reaction that could ruin his relationship with Maria.

"I have told you I work on whatever comes up. Luigi and I have been working in a furniture warehouse lately, but I will take you to my apartment this afternoon so you can see I have nothing to hide."

Franco remembers how Maria, when entering his apartment that afternoon, exclaimed.

"This apartment is cleaner and tidier than my house. Why didn't you want to invite me earlier? Tell me the truth."

Franco lived in a modest apartment, which he kept immaculate, and many books were visible. Franco sits on the bed and tells her.

"I cleaned and fixed it yesterday to check it out tomorrow. Luigi will send me the books later."

Franco was still sitting on the bed while Maria inspected the apartment with amazement. She did not expect to see everything orderly. Most men pay little attention to cleaning and need to be attended to. Maria stops in front of Franco, puts her hands on his shoulders and says.

"You are hiding something from me. I cannot resist lies. I always told you I will be with you through thick and thin, but not in deception."

"My love, I would never cheat on you. You are everything I have and want in life. It's only that my friends make fun of me saying I am an old housewife just because I like to keep my apartment clean. I did not want you to make fun of me too, that is all."

Maria laughs and pushes him back.

"Fool. How are you going to think that of me?"

Franco remains semi-lying on the bed. Maria leans on him and kisses him.

"You are not strange, you are different, and that is why I love you."

Both kiss passionately, between fiery sighs and kisses and hugs, Maria repeated to him.

"Promise me you will be my faithful companion, without secrets, that we will be one person, always united in good and bad times."

Maria had heatedly unbuttoned Franco's shirt and was kissing him wildly, who in turn responded.

"It is more than a promise, it is a fact. My life without you has no meaning."

Both young people lost control and gave free rein to their passions. They made love, leaving aside the prejudices of the time, not even thinking about the consequences. They loved each other, and in a few days, they would be husband and wife. It was a happy afternoon in every way. Maria had become a woman. Franco was her first love and her first experience. For Franco, it was the first time he had been with someone for love. The memory had hypnotized Franco, but suddenly he comes back to reality when Maria moves him and tells him.

"What's up, love, don't you hear me?"

"Sorry, you asked me if I remembered that day, and for me, that day is like a movie that goes through my mind constantly. I never tire of watching it. That is the most beautiful memory I have in my life."

Maria answers him. "I know what you remember, but what I want you to remember is that I told you we will be together in good times and in bad times, but not in lies."

Franco responds sweetly. "Love, there are no lies, but an explanation is necessary, which you will get and you will understand everything and the why of everything."

Salvatore had found a huge and lush tree from which he could see the entrance and the gardens of the complex. Salvatore had climbed up the tree and was taking notes of all the movements in the complex. He thought there must be a party according to what he saw. When he sees Luigi accompanying Franco to the car, he gets off the tree and follows them. Upon reaching the tavern, Franco gets out of the car and tells Luigi.

"Park far away and see if that man is following us. If you see him, just come in and tell me that everything is fine."

Franco enters and sees Marcelo sitting at a table in the middle of the tavern. Marcelo gets up and hugs him.

"I've missed you so much. I miss your scolding." Says Marcelo.

"Oh, Marcelo, you don't change. Are you coming to bring me information about the man who follows me?"

"What man? I do not know what you are talking about."

"Luckily, he follows me and not you." Franco responds.

"How many times did I tell you never to sit exposed to anybody? That you must take a position as if you always have to escape, but your lack of attention to details has brought me problems."

Franco and Marcelo wore almost identical black capes. Marcelo takes off his cape and puts it on the chair. Franco takes off his cape and does the same.

"I have drunk a lot and need to go to the bathroom. I'll be back in a minute." Franco gets up and goes to the bathroom."

Marcelo asked his bodyguard, Patricio, who was seated at a separate table, to change the table to the back corner next to the emergency exit door. Marcelo takes the opportunity to call Vicente and give him the meeting point. When Franco returns, Patricio tells him that Marcelo had ordered him to move to the corner table. Franco smiles and goes to sit in the new place. Since the capes were remarkably similar, Franco did not realize that he was sitting in the chair that had Marcelo's cape. Marcelo comes back and says.

"Excuse me Franco, I went to make a call for today's appointment at 8:00 pm, to which I would like you to come with me."

"No, I can't today. I came because I thought it had to do with the stupid man who follows me."

Marcelo looks around as if to verify that he can speak without problems and says.

"Franco listen, today I will have a meeting with an arms smuggler. I have worked on this project for six months. The profit is enough to quadruple your wealth. Nobody knows about this. I have only shared it with you because you are more than a friend to me, and I owe you many favors. You will not regret it."

Franco shook his head and asked Marcelo.

"No one else has worked this with you."

"NO!"

"Nobody else knows about this project."

"No! Just you." Marcelo replied.

"In that case, my answer is no."

"Why? What happens?" Marcelo asked.

"One: I do not trust the work of others without me having had enough time to verify that it is not flawed."

"Two: You have worked this alone, and I know you. You leave many loose ends, and you are very easy to penetrate. It is not the first time that this has happened. It has happened twice before."

"Three. My life is going to change totally. I will work from here, from my home. I will be everyone's meeting point. I will ensure all contracts made between the groups are respected. I will act as a mediator and enforce their compliance. This leaves me a large commission. You see, no more risks of going anywhere or exposing myself to someone betraying me. I have a legitimate business that protects me. Also, my health is not what it used to be."

"For those three points, I do not take your offer, but I thank you. I would like to ask you to cancel the appointment. I let me investigate if your contact is legitimate. It is an extremely large business transaction, and I want to make sure no one else knows about it."

At that moment Luigi entered the tavern, passing without stopping by Franco's table, and said.

"Everything is fine, sir."

Marcelo looked at Franco puzzled and says.

"Nobody knows about it because I did it myself. I have been working on this for six months; a delay can raise suspicions. I will also lose my buyer and the seller will look for a new buyer. I have money and time invested in this. I know I have made mistakes. But I made my living out of this for over ten years? Do you think I have learned nothing all this time?"

Franco answers him.

"Don't take it wrong, I only want the best for you and if it turns out well, I'll be thrilled, but if something happens, I will feel terrible for not having warned you of the danger I am seeing in this operation. I must go. I have an important party at home. I would like you to come, so I would know everything went well for you and I would celebrate this party twice."

"I'll be there." Answered Marcelo.

They both got up and said goodbye with a big hug. Without realizing it, Franco put on Marcelo's cape and left the tavern with Luigi. Salvatore followed Franco from a safe distance, parked his vehicle and climbed the tree to keep watch.

Franco entered the complex and was greeted by his girlfriend. There was music, food, drinks, the children ran and played in the gardens, everyone was screaming.

"Don Franco is here, long live the couple!"

The employees ran and sat each of them in a chair and picked them up, walking them through the gardens while they shouted.

"Long live the couple."

Maria's parents could not believe their eyes. That young man whom they met, humble, was a rich man loved by his employees whom he treated like family. There was no doubt the Don Franco they had just met was humble and simple as Franco had said.

CHAPTER FOUR

VICENTE

Marcelo had summoned Vicente to a very popular restaurant for tourists and locals. He was prepared in case something could go wrong. He carried a briefcase with two tear gas grenades and two smoke grenades. He also had a gun hidden where no one would imagine. In addition, he had his bodyguard, Patricio, outside as a lookout. Patricio would fire a shot in the air to warn Marcelo in case of any danger. Finally, he had made the appointment at 8:00 p.m., but he would arrive at 7:30 to make sure everything was safe.

Vicente entered the restaurant wearing a black overcoat and dark glasses. He looked around and saw Marcelo. He pretended not to see Marcelo, so no one would know he knew him. He would wait for Marcelo to contact him. Vicente had given him the description of the clothes he would be wearing. He noticed Marcelo was carrying a black leather briefcase and thought the briefcase must have valuable information.

Vicente sat down and ordered a coffee. Marcelo observed him for thirty minutes to make sure Vicente was alone. Vicente drank his coffee, waited for about twenty-five minutes, then got up and left the restaurant. Marcelo thought his plan had worked. If the smuggler was a police officer, someone would have contacted him, but he arrived alone and left alone. When Vicente opened the car door, Patricio stopped him.

"Sir don't go. Marcelo is waiting for you."

Vicente looked at him with a suspicious face and told him.

"I don't know what you are talking about. I don't know any Marcelo."

"Please understand, sir, it's a matter of security."

Vicente calmly responds. "I understand."

Patricio tried to frisk Vicente, who pushed him away and yelled at him.

"What are you doing? Of course, I'm armed and so are you."

Patricio stopped short, not expecting such an answer.

"You are a bandit, Marcelo is a bandit, and I am also a bandit. We bandits are armed. I will not negotiate with the POPE."

"Yes, sir, excuse me." Replied Patricio.

Vicente was an expert. He had made Patricio and Marcelo swallow the hook completely and was interested not only in Marcelo, but also in the loot in the briefcase. Vicente returned to the restaurant and sat at the same table he had previously. Marcelo made him wait another fifteen minutes and then he approached him. He greeted Vicente. He took off his coat and put it on onto the back of his chair, then apologized for making him wait.

"Can I offer you something? The food here is good."

Marcelo was trying to break the ice, and Vicente, pretending to be annoyed, responded.

"Let us get to the point. I've wasted enough time."

"All right, show me your catalog and price list."

Vicente took a magazine out of his coat pocket and handed it to Marcelo. Vicente had positioned himself with his back towards the front door as the police covered his back. Vicente negotiated prices for a long time, making sure there was no one else but Marcelo. When Vicente was sure Marcelo was alone, he got up from the chair, pulled out his revolver, and spoke.

"Marcelo, you are under arrest for arms smuggling, prison break, people smuggling, and prostitution of minors."

Marcelo was speechless. His mind handled a thousand pieces of information per microsecond, and the main question was. What went wrong here? But he came back to reality. He had a detective in front of him, pointing a revolver at him. Since Vicente was standing in front of Marcelo, he could not see Patricio and Patricio could not see him. The police officers could not see what was going on either because Vicente was very tall and completely covered Marcelo. Plan "A" had failed. It was time for plan "B".

Marcelo raised his hands while he was saying Vicente.

"We can negotiate. I have enough money. I can give you all the information you want. I am more valuable to you more as an informant than as a prisoner."

At the same time, he harmlessly lowered his hands with his fingers crossed, as prisoners of war do.

"There is no negotiation. It is over. You are finished. This was your last transaction."

Marcelo kept a terrified facer, as not raising suspicion he had lowered his hands to get the revolver he had hidden behind his neck. Marcelo thought it was now or never. He told Vicente.

"Here's your loot, that's what you want."

Marcelo kicked the briefcase, throwing it towards Vicente, who for a thousandth of a second, looked at the briefcase, but it was enough time for Marcelo, like a magician, to draw his gun behind his neck and shoot Vicente in the chest. Vicente fell onto the table and then rolled onto Marcelo's chair. In a split second, Marcelo opened the briefcase and detonated the four grenades. He threw two to the front and two to the rear.

It was a fantastic plan. He created panic and confusion. Everyone had to run out of the restaurant so they would not suffocate. When the police heard the shot, they could see nothing. When they tried to run inside, they had to run back out for air. The third police officer, who was further away, saw Patricio draw his weapon, and he disarmed him without incident. Marcelo came out among the group of people fleeing and coughing for air. Marcelo had escaped again, but this time he was on an island, and they would turn every stone, searching for him.

Franco was enjoying his party when Luigi interrupted him.

"I'm sorry Don Franco, you have a call from Marcelo."

Franco thinks if Marcelo calls him on the phone, it means that everything is fine, and he was not in prison. It must be to tell him he is on his way to celebrate. Franco tells Maria to come with him to answer a call from a friend at the office and show her the projects he had in mind. When Franco picked up the phone, Marcelo did not let Franco speak.

"You were absolutely right. I did not listen to you. I am in big trouble now."

Franco asks Luigi to get Maria out of the office. Maria could not believe it. Why should she go out? What is going on?

Franco picks up the phone again and Marcelo yells.

"Get me off the island now, please I have killed a detective. This happened five minutes ago. If I do not leave in the next fifteen minutes, I am a dead man."

Franco gave him the address of Vittorio's business and told him to go there immediately. Franco called Vittorio, who was closing the business.

"Hello Vittorio, I have to ask you for a favor. I need you to get a person off the island right now. That person will die if you don't."

"I don't do favors for Don Franco. I don't belong to that family. See you later."

"Please don't hang up, you're not doing me a favor, you're saving the life of a fellow partisan of yours."

Vittorio was paralyzed. "What did you say?"

"Yes, it's not for me. Do it for him. I don't know if he deserves it, but he was one of us."

"Where is he?" Vittorio asked.

"He is on his way to your business." Franco replied.

Vittorio ran to the dock. He had a boat full of fuel ready to be delivered the next day. He was releasing the last rope when he saw a man running towards him. Marcelo yelled at Vittorio.

"Don Franco sent me."

"I don't know that man, but come here."

When they were close enough, Marcelo said.

"Vittorio, I know you. I'm Marcelo. Do you remember me?"

Marcelo extended his hand to Vittorio, but Vittorio did not shake his hand or answer him, he only told him.

"Move quickly!"

Marcelo jumped into the boat, and in seconds, they were underway to Naples. In just nineteen minutes, Marcelo was about to flee the island.

"Can we go a little faster, please?"

"You are fleeing because you must have done something stupid and now you want me to do the same. If I go fast, I will raise suspicions."

Those were the only words Vittorio said to Marcelo during the entire trip. Marcelo tried to start a conversation several times, but Vittorio never responded.

Vittorio docks at the refueling point at the port of Naples and asks the pump operator to fill up the tank. Marcelo takes out a roll of money, and Vittorio, without looking at him, says.

"Save your money. I don't need it."

Marcelo asks the operator.

"How much is the bill?" But Vittorio yells at the operator.

"Don't take that money. It's dirty money, cursed and almost certainly stained with blood."

In another situation, Marcelo would have split Vittorio's face, but he had no time to lose, nor was he going to fight with the man who had just saved his life, so he left immediately.

The smoke and toxic gas took about ten minutes to dissipate because of the few windows of the restaurant. When the smoke cleared and the place was ventilated, all the police officers entered the restaurant. They saw a body on the chair clinging to the cape Marcelo was wearing, which in fact was Don Franco's cape. When turning the corpse, a police officer says.

"Oh, my god! It's Vicente, the detective."

Upon reviewing the bloodstained cape that Vicente was still holding, they discovered Franco's documents. The police officers never saw Marcelo because Vicente blocked Marcelo's face all the time. They went to arrest Franco immediately. Salvatore was up in his tree watching Franco's party when he heard sirens. He looked down and saw the lights of approaching police units. Salvatore quickly got down and stood in the middle of the street as he realized they were going to Don Franco's place. He stopped the police units, and one of the undercover officers recognized him.

"Where are you going?" Salvatore asked.

"We are going to arrest Don Franco for the murder of Detective Vicente."

"When did this happen?" Asked Salvatore.

"About fifteen minutes ago in the restaurant, Vicente had Franco's cape in his hand, and it was stained with his blood."

Salvatore knew Franco had not murdered Vicente, as he followed Franco from the restaurant to his house and Franco was at the party. He quickly saw an opportunity to have a motive to arrest Franco and took charge of the situation.

"I should arrest Franco. You know this is my case. I am guarding his residence, and I just saw him enter his house at full speed about five minutes ago. He was fleeing the crime scene, but he forgot his coat. What a surprise he will get! Listen carefully, no one speaks a word. You will be there in case he resists the arrest. I give you the authority to use whatever force is necessary to arrest him and anyone who interferes with the arrest."

Salvatore got into his car and led the police caravan. The three cars arrived at the entrance of the complex and burst into the party.

"Stop the music. The party is over." Shouted Salvatore.

Franco came out front and told Salvatore.

"On what authority do you enter private property to stop a party?"

"With the same authority I have to arrest you for murdering Detective Vicente, the organized crime detective, who has been a stone in your shoe, and you got rid of him the only way you know how, by killing him."

"I am not a murderer; I have killed no one." Answered Franco.

"Are you really going to deny you went out to meet him? I followed you and saw you running away from the scene to your house. But you forgot your cape at the crime scene. Are you going to deny that this belongs to you? It has your documents, cigarette case and the detective's blood."

"Arrest him!" Yells Salvatore.

The police, without saying a word, arrested Franco. He did not resist and asked his employees not to interfere with the arrest, trusting he would clarify that it was not him. Maria was crying inconsolably and since none of the police officers said that the crime had just happened, she believed the story since Franco had previously acted strange.

She fell apart in the fairy tale moment. She was the fiancée of a murderer who had lied all along. He himself had told her that there was a Don Franco that she did not know. Maria ran to Franco and told him.

"You have lied to us all the time. You are a monster. You not only kill people but also hearts. May the justice of men fall on you with all the weight and may the justice of God not forget to condemn you, too. I will do everything possible and impossible to tear you out of my life."

Franco just replied.

"Do not blindly trust the justice of men. It is imperfect and if there is the justice of God, then one day you will be convinced of my innocence."

The police took Franco away in a hurry to the police station. Salvatore calls his boss and informs him of Vicente's death. He tells him Marcelo had met with Franco before the meeting with Vicente, and then Marcelo and Franco met with Vicente. Salvatore tells there were only Marcelo's fingerprints, because Franco had used gloves since he was prepared to kill and leave no prints. However, Vicente held down Franco's cape so he would not escape punishment. That he had seen it all, because he did not lose track of Franco for two days. Umberto could not believe he had lost one of his best men and had to admit Salvatore had closed a case in two days, which they could not advance a step in three years.

After calling Rome, Salvatore went to Franco's cell and asked the jailer to leave him alone with Franco because he had to interrogate him. Salvatore was happier than ever. He felt great. He thought he was unstoppable. He knew he would be in all the newspapers and the photo of him taking Franco to prison would travel all over Italy.

"I'm sorry, I spoiled your party Franco or Don Franco. How would you like me to call you?"

Franco did not answer.

"What happens? Your file says you are communicative and intelligent, but this must be a mistake. I do not see any of these qualities."

Franco kept silent.

"I marvel at your intelligence, your cape in the hands of a murdered detective, and then not even a resistance to arrest. I have heard comments about your bravery during the war, but so far, I am not impressed."

Salvatore tried to provoke Franco to see if he would bring out something he could use. He knew that an angry person does not think when speaking and that was one of his techniques.

"You are such a coward, you don't even respond, and the two bullets that you got during the war were hit in the back. That means fleeing, not fighting."

Those words were a dagger to the heart of Franco who stood up and grabbed onto the bars.

"Tell me, what did you do during the war?" Franco asked.

"I was a thirteen-year-old boy. My parents sent me to Switzerland to study."

"Bravo! That means your parents were rich." Franco replied,

"Yes, they are rich. Or is being rich a crime?"

"No, being rich is not a crime, but being a traitor is. While others gave their lives and their children defending their homeland, traitors like your parents sent their children to Switzerland to keep them safe and remain indifferent to the situation in the country. When we pressed them, they collaborated with us and, at the same time, collaborated with the Germans. Their loyalty was to money, not to the country. I was a ten-year-old kid who collaborated and had more courage and honesty than you and your whole family put together. You are not worthy of your organization, because you lie miserably. You know well that I did not kill the detective. You better than anyone knows it."

Salvatore had managed to make Franco furious, but he had not achieved his goal, so he tried one more time. He approached him and laughed in his face.

"Yes, I know, but I also know no one else knows about that. As you can see, I have you in my hands. In the end, as the saying goes; THE END JUSTIFIES THE MEANS. On the other hand, if you give me Marcelo and the rest of those who go to your tourist complex, which is more than a tourist complex, is a nest of bandits, I promise you I will testify you were only at the meeting, that Marcelo was the one who shot Vicente. This way, your sentence would be for conspiracy, not murder. It is a considerable discount. When you add the collaboration to arrest the rest of the group, I can get you witness protection. Cheer up! Not everything is lost, nor is it I have it with you. It is that to fight you, I must think and act like you."

Franco, this time calmer, answered him.

"If I were in your place and you in mine, I would have hit you three times for you to shut up, not to force you to talk. You are a born traitor and coward. I am a man of honor, loyalty, and word. My honor does not allow me to make alliances with traitors, because you betray the principles of your own institution. My loyalty to my friends will never allow me to expose them and I always keep my word. I give you my word you are going to exonerate me of the charges. You are going to agonize at my feet, and I will spit in your face."

Salvatore laughed and said. "Oh, I forgot to tell you, I captured Patricio."

Franco was surprised; he did not expect that.

"He offered to testify against you in exchange for the witness protection plan."

Now Salvatore had really hit the nail on the head since Franco had always doubted Patricio's loyalty. Patricio had made a deal to talk about Marcelo, not about Franco. Franco knew that Patricio was not a danger to him, because he had no way to implicate him in anything, but he could expose Marcelo's entire organization. There was no other way out other than to eliminate Patricio, who the police had in custody in a hotel. Before leaving the police station, Salvatore asked the chief of police he needed two police officers to guard Patricio twenty-four hours. The angry boss replied.

"We only have twelve police officers on the island to cover twenty-four hours, 365 days. You asked me for three officers for one day and now you want two for a twenty-four-hour detail. How long is this going to be?"

"Until it is necessary, or you are going to take responsibility if something happens to the witness?"

The chief took a deep breath, counted to three, and said.

"Fine but try to take your witness to Rome and bring him back for the trial, because I just don't have the staff."

Salvatore totally ignored him. He knew he had risen to fame and felt untouchable.

The next day, Luigi shows up at the police station with Franco's medications and gets permission to see him for a minute. Franco immediately asks him about Maria. Luigi answers him.

"I'm sorry, Don Franco, but they left the complex that same night to go to a hotel and today they departed for Naples early in the morning. She left all the gifts you gave her and tore all the photos."

"I understand her and do not judge her. I only ask that without contacting her, keep me informed in case I can help her."

"That will be done. I'll get in touch with someone in Naples."

Franco looks Luigi in the eye and speaks.

"You will be in command of the complex until I return. Please call Marcelo's lieutenant organization and tell him that starting today he is the new boss, that Marcelo left the country and will never return."

Franco also tells him that Patricio is in the police's custody, ready to collaborate with the police, and he must be eliminated.

Luigi promises to follow Franco's orders. He goes out to find a good lawyer and to contact Marcelo's lieutenant. Luigi traveled to Palermo to contact Carlos, Marcelo's lieutenant. He explained to him the serious situation in which they all are if Patricio betrays them.

Carlos, now the new boss, promised to send someone trusted to eliminate Patricio, who was not to his liking either. Luigi used his contacts and money to get Patricio's whereabouts. He was just waiting for Carlos's hitman to arrive.

That same night, Carlos's hitman arrived in Ischia. He was a man of medium height with a terrifying face and few words, who did not even say his name. He arrived at the complex and when Guido went to greet him, he just said.

"I come from Carlos; I need Luigi."

"One moment, please." Replied Guido. He took the last bite of his cookie and called Luigi.

Luigi went to the reception, and invited him to come inside, but he bluntly answered.

"No thanks, I come from Carlos. Give me the address."

Luigi took a piece of paper out of his pocket and handed it to him.

"I only have the hotel, but not the room."

The man turned around and left without saying goodbye. Luigi looked at Guido and commented.

"With that face, who needs a gun." They both laughed.

The hitman went to the hotel, presented a fake ID to the receptionist, and told him.

"I am Detective Zambrano from the organized crime investigation unit. Only Detective Salvatore knows I am here. No one else can know about it. The police are guarding the witness Patricio. My job is to make sure that all of them do their job. We do not want surprises. First, I need to know if the safety rules were followed. Are the rooms on the right and left adjoining the witness room empty? Yes, or no?"

The young man at the reception, nervous, looks up and says.

"Yes, they are, sir."

"Excellent! The three rooms in front of the witness must also be empty."

The stuttering young man responds.

"Sir, the one in front is occupied."

"Morons. How can they do a thing like that? This is a high-profile case; I cannot believe it."

The young man answers. "I was working last night and Salvatore himself told me not to move it, so as not to raise suspicion."

"Of course, they should not have moved him last night, but today in the morning they should have moved him to another room with the excuse of any repair. That was clearly told to the chief of police, but they are all inept. That is the reason Salvatore sent me. You can't trust these fools."

"Excuse me, sir, it's not my fault." Said the young man.

"I know, don't worry. Don't tell anyone about this, but tomorrow morning you move that person to another room, otherwise it will be your fault." Is that understood?"

"Yes sir, I promise you."

"Damn!" said the hitman.

"What happens now, sir?" Asked the young man.

"What happens is that now, because of these idiots, I will have to stay all night, and I will only be able to leave when you change that person's room. They have spoiled all my plans."

Once again, the young man says." I'm sorry, sir."

"Well, there is no other way. Give me the keys to one of the empty rooms and not a word of this to anyone. This case is so big, we have to watch even those who are watching."

The young man gave him the key to the room and told him.

"Count on my silence, sir."

"If you talk, you will pay for the years in prison instead of the witness."

The hitman, without having asked for Patricio's room number, had obtained everything he needed. His plan was simple, but effective. He would start knocking on the front door and create a scene until someone opened the door to stop the commotion. The hitman banged on the door loudly and yelled.

"I know you are in there, you son of a bitch. Open the door."

The banging and screaming were loud enough to be heard in the room across the hall. Patricio was guarded for by two police officers. One of them opened the door to see what was happening. The hitman continues screaming and banging on the door. A man opened the door and said.

"Hey, you are wrong."

The hitman gave the man a powerful punch and kicked him while screaming.

"I'm going to kill you son of a bitch so that you learn to respect women."

The police officer knew the room was occupied, and his police instincts took control of him. The last thing they wanted was for the floor to be filled with curious people. The police officer opened the door, and revolver in hand, yelled.

"Stop in the law's name."

The hitman turned around and told him.

"What would you do if a monster like this rape your daughter?"

The man was lying on the ground, almost unconscious; everything had been so real that the police officer believed it.

"That's what we, the authorities, are for; you can't take justice into your own hands."

The hitman put his two hands in front of the officer.

"Well, arrest me then. I did what I had to do."

The police officer was convinced this was a totally foreign problem, and he holstered his gun to speak with the supposed father. That was his fatal mistake. The hitman took out his revolver and shot him in the head. The hitman burst into the room and shot Patricio three times in the chest, but he did not notice the second officer who shot him fatally.

Salvatore receives a call to inform him of the fatal incident. Salvatore responds.

"Nobody touches anything, or says anything,. Close the room. I am on my way there."

When Salvatore arrived, the press was waiting. He had become the figure of the moment. Salvatore turned to them and said.

"I promise you when I come out, I will give you all the information about what happened. The only thing the press knew was that several shots had been fired and that entry to the hotel was prohibited."

Salvatore enters the room and sees the three corpses.

The police officer tells him. "We lost the witness, sir."

"No, idiot, the witness is alive. Do you understand? Alive! Help me change his clothes."

The police officer, confused, asked, "What did you say?"

"Get moving, come on, help."

Salvatore and the officer cleaned Patricio's body, changed his clothes and posed him as if he was sitting on a chair, they put the body of the bloody hitman on the floor in front of the chair and next to him the police officer posed with the gun in one hand and the other hand on Patricio's shoulder. Salvatore took several photos of the scene. When Salvatore finished, he told the officer.

"Remember not a word of this to anyone. If they find out from you that Patricio is dead, you will be accused of divulging confidential information and you will end up in jail."

Salvatore ordered him to remove the body of the hitman and to leave the police officer's body uncovered. His goal was for journalists to take photos. He knew this would make the case more popular. When Salvatore left the hotel, once again the journalists surrounded him. He increased his popularity by making comments like.

"If Franco bought himself a cell with the murder of Vicente, now he threw away the key to the cell with the murder of the police officer guarding the witness, plus the assassination attempt against the witness, Patricio. Thank God he could not murder the witness. Now, the witness's testimony, will put him behind bars for the rest of his life."

CHAPTER FIVE

THE TRAIL

Rome.

Salvatore shows up in Umberto's office and receives a hero's welcome. In three days, he accomplished what they couldn't in three years. Salvatore, putting Franco's folder on the table, tells Umberto.

"I can fill this desk with his files if you allow me to carry out a plan. Umberto surprised asks him. "What the hell did you say?"

"It is amazingly simple. Franco is a sick man. He enjoys a certain sympathy for his past as a partisan because his parents were shot by the Nazis and for his help to the people. We could offer him thirty years of house arrest."

"Are you crazy? Are you asking me to let the bastard loose as if nothing had happened? That will never happen!"

Salvatore puts both of his hands on the desk and answers.

"You think Vicente's death doesn't hurt me? I want to see all of them behind bars in the memory of Vicente."

Umberto leans back in his chair and answers.

"Explain yourself because something is not clear. What do you have in mind?"

"As you can see, Franco bought a resort on the top of a hill. Since then, my contacts tell me there have been several meetings of organized crime at that location. He does not let anyone stay in his complex he does not trust, and he is selective with every guest. It is just a matter of time. I will catch them all. Besides, Franco thinks he is very smart, but it only took me three days to put him behind bars. If he puts one foot out of the complex, he goes straight to jail for the rest of the sentence. Franco is arrogant, he thinks he is very smart.

He is going to continue committing crimes. I have a tree from where I can take all the pictures of those who enter and leave the complex. He is so stupid to be on top of a hill because there is no escape possible. I think I have proved to you I can do the job. Imagine an operation where four or more criminals fall in one hit."

Umberto was thoughtful. He knew they had just delivered a great punch and another one would lead him to retirement as one of the best directors of all time.

"Well, this does not depend on me alone. I must convince my superiors. Remember, you are asking me to send a criminal to his house and keeping him there may be risky."

"Just present the records of what you have spent in three years going after Franco and then what you spent with me in three days. I think the difference will prove you right."

Umberto shook his head and said.

"Not a bad idea. Tomorrow, you will be awarded a medal for your work, but before that, we will have a meeting with my superiors. I will talk to them about your plan. You must return to Ischia for the trial. If the bosses accept your plan, you must take a letter to the prosecutor and another to the judge. They must know why they are offering him a house arrest."

Salvatore smiled and told him.

"They will not regret it. I assure you that from the next blow, they will never recover."

That afternoon, Salvatore was decorated and applauded by his superiors. He was the man of the moment, and he enjoyed it to the fullest. At the end of the decoration ceremony, Umberto called Salvatore to his office. Once in the office, Umberto told Salvatore.

"It was an uphill battle to convince the bosses, but we reached an agreement to give you a chance. Tomorrow, you will leave for Ischia with a letter for the judge and another for the prosecutor. If they have questions, they can call us. Please do not talk to them. If you have no results in five months, you come back to Rome and forget about the project. Is that clear?"

"More than clear, sir. I don't think it will take me five months. Three months is enough time for Franco to relax and make another mistake." Salvatore replied.

Salvatore returned to the island and went straight to the jail to see Franco. Franco was still in isolation and did not know about Patricio's death. Franco is taken to an interrogation room where Salvatore awaits him with a folder. Franco sits handcuffed in front of Salvatore, who mockingly laughs and tells him.

"Hello partisan. How have you been treated at your new resort?"

Franco does not respond.

"Sorry to give you some more bad news, but lately all your moves are going backwards. What's wrong? Is intelligence failing? You are no longer the same partisan."

Franco does not respond or flinch.

Salvatore opening the folder, takes out the photos taken in the hotel where the hitman appeared next to the dead police officer and another photo of Patricio who posed as if he were alive next to the police officer.

"Well, maybe these photos will change your mood."

Salvatore puts the photos in front of Franco and tells him.

"What a disaster, Franco. The hitman you sent to eliminate Patricio ended up killing a police officer. As you can see, Patricio is alive, and now after this, he is more than determined to cooperate with us. He will say whatever I want if we give him protection. Now you have the killing of a detective and are implicated in the death of a police officer, which translates into entering the cell and throwing away the keys. Brilliant Franco! Brilliant! Oh, I forgot, here it is in the newspaper for that day. It is all about you."

Salvatore takes out the newspaper where on the front page shows the photos of the corpses of the hitman and the police officer and a headline that said, "FRANCO HAS FAILED AGAIN."

Franco was pale and without words. He recognized the hitman. He was one of the best he had ever met. Believing Patricio was still alive, he feared Patricio will give them all away. Franco looked at Salvatore, and in a very calm tone, said.

"You have won a battle, but not the war."

"Seriously! When is the war over, then?" Salvatore laughed.

Franco stared at him and answered.

"I can't tell you when, but I can tell you how it ends."

"Don't leave me with the intrigue, please. Tell me how it ends?"

"You see Salva, you don't pay attention when I speak to you, because I already told you."

Salvatore was shocked that Franco had called him Salva. He felt it as diminishing, disrespectful and as if Franco believed he was still in control.

"Well, please repeat it to me. This time I will pay more attention, DON FRANCO."

Salvatore put emphasis on DON FRANCO to counter when Franco called him Salva.

"As I told you before. You will exonerate me of all charges while dying at my feet and I will spit on your face."

"Oh, my God! In your file there are many qualities, but I miss that one. I will need to add it. I am missing the fantasy one, yes that one is missing. Tomorrow you can call a lawyer or Luigi to find one for you. Nothing is going to change, but the procedure requires it. I am leaving you the photos and the newspaper as a gift. See you tomorrow O BELLA CIAO, O BELLA CIAO, CIAO, CIAO."

Franco felt a rage and helplessness like never in his life. He knew he was at a dead end and only a miracle could change his situation. The police officer escorted Franco to his cell and asked him.

"Are you going to take the photos and the diary?"

"No thanks. Remember that the reporter writes the stories from his point of view or interest and the photographers take the pictures showing you what they want you to see. I advise you to only believe in what you see and, when reading, draw your own conclusions, because the truth is often between the lines."

The officer had more sympathy for Franco than for Salvatore. Franco's simplicity inspired confidence and Salvatore's arrogance was repugnance. Franco asked the officer if he could make a phone call to contact a defense attorney. The police officer accepted with no problem, and Franco called Luigi, entrusting him with that task.

Salvatore went directly to meet with the prosecutor and the judge in charge of the case. He presented the letters he brought from Rome. Then, in an imposing way, he made them believe it was necessary to give Franco house arrest because it was part of a plan that would put all the criminals in jail. If they refused, they would take the wrong side or perhaps help the criminals. Salvatore achieved his objective and told them that during the trial they would ask for the maximum sentence, so that way it would be easier for Franco to accept the house arrest.

Franco receives a visit from his lawyer, who was a well-known man among them, especially because he spoke clearly and wasted no time. Franco explains to him the precarious situation in which he finds himself. Franco tells him he did not kill Vicente, that everything is a setup. The lawyer takes notes and tells him.

"I will go out to see what I can do, but this doesn't look good. If it is entrapment, it is very well done and if they move the trail to Rome, we are lost. Let's not lose hope. I'll see you in two days."

The next day, Salvatore sees Franco again and when he enters the interrogation room, he sees the photos and the newspaper are on the table. Salvatore smiles and says.

"So, you want to portray yourself as a lion, but let's see how the little mouse suit looks on you."

Franco enters the room and sits across from Salvatore without saying a word.

"Well, I know you are a man of few words, and I don't have much time to waste with you. I admire you, Franco. Please do not think I hate you, but the end justifies the means. I've put you behind bars and you have no escape. However, to prove to you I am not as bad as you think, I will try to compensate by asking that, based on your valuable history and that you had never been convicted of a crime before, plus your health that is not good, to make an exception and offer you house arrest. About thirty years, not in a penitential but in your complex. Remember, if you put a foot out of the complex, you break the deal and you would go straight to the dungeon. Look at it this way. That will compensate for the murder of Vicente that you did not do, but you are involved in the murder of a police officer. As you can see, neither you nor I are holy, but I'm not that bad."

Franco looked at him and replied.

"In the first place, you don't have the authority to ask for a house arrest. Second, I do not pretend to be an honest person. You do, and you are not. You present yourself as a man of law, when in fact you lie and fabricate serious charges to frame innocent people. That is to be a false and unscrupulous person, not worthy of your own institution. When the truth comes out, your name will be erased, and my name will be vindicated."

"There is no doubt you are arrogant and believe in fairy tales that always end happily. Remember this proposal and present it to your lawyer. He will make you understand it is the best gift you can receive, thanks to me, although you do not appreciate it, partisan."

Salvatore got up and said to the police officer. "Take him away. He has a lot to think about."

That night Franco could not sleep. He was waiting for the appointment with his lawyer, hoping that some news would allow him to see the light at the end of the tunnel. At eleven in the morning, Franco was taken to the interrogation room where his lawyer was waiting for him.

"What do you bring me? "Franco asks him.

"Nothing worthwhile, with Patricio alive we are lost."

They all thought that Patricio was alive and had been transferred to Rome.

"The prosecution is asking for maximum penalty and the judge does not seem friendly at all."

Franco shook his head and sighed deeply.

"Yesterday Salvatore was here, and he was commenting to me he could propose house arrest. I think it is another of his tricks. Something is up." Franco commented to his lawyer.

"Salvatore has no power to do something like that, it must be a trick, but I'll talk to him anyway. We cannot lose anything when everything is lost."

"Thank you for lifting my spirits with those words," Franco replied sarcastically.

Franco's lawyer went to see Salvatore, who made him wait an hour outside the office. Salvatore apologized for the delay and offered him something to drink. The lawyer thanked him and without waiting any longer told him.

"I need you to explain what you told to my client, because I do not believe you have the authority to make that offer. I find it quite cruel you try to excite my client with something like that."

Salvatore, trying to ingratiate himself with the lawyer, responds.

"I know Franco hates me and believes I cause all his ills, but it is not like that. I am just doing my job. Also, I have sympathy for him and his past. It must be terrible to have your parents shot and to be totally without a family. I know he is a sick man and in prison he would not survive for more than three years. As you said, I cannot promise you that, but I can use all my influence to achieve it. Of course, if Franco accepts it."

The lawyer replied. "Very well, I'll talk to him, and I really appreciate your help. Please keep me informed if the judge and the prosecution accept your proposal."

"I will do so. Have a good day." Salvatore replied kindly.

Salvatore kept secret Patricio's dead. He led the press to believe that Patricio had been transferred to Rome for his safety. After a week of negotiation with the prosecution, Salvatore's dream came true. Franco was going to be offered house arrest. Salvatore right away contacted the lawyer and told him that if Franco accepted the charges and pleaded guilty, there would be no trial and he would be sentenced to thirty years of house arrest, which he would have to spend inside his complex. Salvatore added the offer should be accepted immediately, because if it is not accepted, the trial will begin next week, and this offer will not be repeated.

The lawyer went to visit Franco immediately and informed him what was happening.

Franco said. "I think there is something behind this."

"The offer is real. I saw the documents and contacted the prosecution. This is not Salvatore's word."

Franco shakes his head and says.

"If they were sure of winning the trial, they would not make such an offer."

"I agree, but I can't quite find a solid defense, and if Patricio testifies, then we are finished."

Franco is silent for a while and then asks." What would you do in my place?"

"I would accept the offer; I would not take the risk."

Franco stares at him and replies.

"I also believe the same, but it would also be easier for me to prove my innocence from outside the jail than from within. I also want you to know that I did not kill Vicente and Salvatore knows it. I give you my word that all this will one day come to light."

On the day of the trial, there were more journalists than inhabitants on the island. Everyone was looking for the perfect photo on the front page. Before the judge, Franco accepted the charges and pled guilty, but his soul returned to his body only when the judge reaffirmed the house arrest thirty-year sentence.

The journalists were speechless. Many asked themselves what had happened in this trial? Why such a sentence against a criminal? Many newspapers commented Franco had intimidated or bought the judge. Outside the court during a press conference, Salvatore dropped the bomb, revealing that Patricio had been killed that night.

Franco was immediately taken to his compound, where he was greeted by Luigi and the employees. Franco could not believe that he was home, and his life had changed 360 degrees.

Franco went to his office with Luigi and asked him.

"What news do you have about Maria?"

"She is with her parents in Naples. She hardly leaves her house because everyone refers to her as the mafioso's fiancée. She works in her father's factory, and they are almost bankrupt, since nobody wants to associate with them."

Franco answers. "Make sure that business does not close. Create a company to buy from them. Don't enrich them, but keep them afloat."

"I will do so, Don Franco," Luigi responds.

Franco turned on the television and they were interviewing Salvatore.

"Look Luigi, the hero of the moment." Franco says.

At that moment, the journalist asks Salvatore.

"Why did you make us believe Patricio was in Rome if he was actually killed in the hotel?"

Salvatore answers him. "The fact that Patricio was dead did not make Franco innocent of the three deaths, as you can see, he pled guilty. It would be a waste to have a long and expensive trial that would end up with the same result. I do things my way, doing nothing illegal, and my results are beneficial for everyone."

Franco sat in his chair and closed his eyes. Salvatore had tricked him again. Franco asked Luigi to leave him alone and kept his eyes closed, trying to contain his helplessness for about forty minutes.

CHAPTER SIX

DETECTIVE PABLO

It took three months for Franco to recover emotionally. The blow had been extremely hard, but life had to go on. His fiancée refused any messages from him. She wanted to move to an unknown place, because in her neighborhood, everyone called her the mobster's girlfriend. Franco sent Luigi to contact the other organizations and tell them everything was still the same. The Monte Santo tourist complex was ready for business.

Franco felt much better when he heard the news Marcelo was able to escape Italy and had settled in the city of Chicago in the United States. Salvatore had gone back to Rome, but as soon as he received news the organized crime families were meeting in Ischia, he moved to the island to finish his work.

Salvatore returned to his tree, but this time he was more prepared. He turned the tree into his office. He had a military camouflage net covering the area. He had a chair, which was rigidly attached to two branches. Also had a pulley system that allowed him to climb up and down the tree with ease. Salvatore kept a detailed logbook of those entering and leaving Franco's complex. He passed the reports to Umberto to find out if there was an arrest warrant for those individuals.

At the first meeting held at the complex, they discussed the need for an emergency exit to the sea. Marcelo's lightning flight revealed that Vittorio's business was of vital importance to the organization because of its geographical position. Franco was entrusted with taking possession of that property at any cost. Franco kept silent for a moment and then responded.

"This will not be a simple task. Vittorio is a person of high principles and great pride. That business was founded by his grandfather and has belonged to his family for three generations."

Faustino, one of the participants, answered.

"Everything in life has its price. Offer him a good price, but if he does not accept, then he will have to choose between his business or his son. I am sure that your answer will be positive."

Franco agreed to mediate for the purchase of Vittorio's business, but warned them it would not be immediate, since his priority was the underground construction of a safe house large enough to house all of them in case of an emergency. This refuge would be located under the wine fermentation cellar, which adjoined Augusto's estate. It would take care of them for as long as necessary if needed and then allow them to get out when the police were convinced they had escaped. They all agreed to the plan, as it was safer to hide there than to flee to the sea.

"I want to clarify that this work will take a minimum of four to five years, so that it does not raise any suspicion. After being safe on land, we will establish a naval mechanic's workshop for young people in Vittorio's business. This way we will not raise suspicions." Franco explained to the group.

Franco prepared for war. He knew Salvatore was constantly spying on him. Franco made him believe he did not know it and at the same time he was spying on Salvatore. Franco had bought all the properties on the hill, but he did not put them in his name. They were still in the name of the previous owners who continued to occupy them. The property bordering the rear of Franco's compound was occupied by his only remaining relative. He was a distant cousin on his mother's side. A man nine years older than Franco named Augusto.

Augusto had two children, his eldest son named Donato, had a wife named Marta, and they had a son named Venancio. His youngest son named Carlos, had a wife named Vera, and they had a daughter named Laura. Augusto was a grateful and faithful man. He knew nobody could know there was a relationship between him and Franco. Franco provided all the means for Augusto to establish a tomato plantation, which soon gained fame as the best tomato in Ischia.

Franco's hill had only two ways to get to the complex. Through the main entrance, there was a paved road in good condition that led to the complex, which had a stone entrance in the medieval style. The other road was a narrow dirt road that led to Augusto's farm, which adjoined the rear of Franco's complex. The hill was about eighty meters high. At the dirt road entrance, Franco had three safety rings exactly thirty meters apart. The first defense was a tanker truck business to transport drinking water located thirty meters high from the bottom of the hill. An old crazy man named Ronaldo operated the second line of defense. He herded fife hundred goats to produce cheese and finally Augusto with his tomato's farm. He had also installed a communication system based on rings and bells, so that messages could not be intercepted.

Franco had built a fermentation cellar in the back of his complex adjoining Augusto's farm. All these farms were rectangular, about thirty meters wide but exceptionally long, ending in a dense forest of ancient trees that faced the front of the complex.

At the back of the complex adjoining the Augusto estate, in the fermentation cellar, were ten enormous barrels to ferment wine. All those barrels were mounted on rails, but one barrel was not secure to the ground, which easily allowed it to roll forward. This allowed access to tunnel's door that led to Augusto's estate. Franco had already started to build an underground shelter that would serve for multiple operations.

Salvatore knew of a detective named Pablo, who had infiltrated an organized crime group in Naples. His boss was Vertuchi. Salvatore called Umberto and asked him for permission to use Detective Pablo to infiltrate Franco's complex.

Umberto refused. "Franco will not accept an unknown person. We can expose him."

Salvatore hardly let Umberto finish. "No, boss, I have thought of everything. He must say he works for Vertuchi, but that Vertuchi does not send him. He should say he needs a vacation, because his boss has not appreciated his full potential, so a break is not bad for him and maybe he could open new horizons."

"I don't think it will work." Umberto replied.

"It doesn't work if we don't try. The only thing Franco could think of is that a Vertuchi member is looking for a better future."

Umberto responds. "I'll give you the answer tomorrow. I must speak to my superiors."

The next day, Salvatore received a call from Umberto giving the green light for his plan.

Umberto said. "Detective Pablo will call you and you will tell him everything he has to do, but you will never have contact with him in Ischia. If Pablo enters the complex and four hours pass without giving a sign of life, you will enter with the police with an arrest warrant for Pablo. This way, we can save him in case he is in trouble. He will always wear something white, which means everything is fine, and if he is wearing something red, it means you should rescue him."

Salvatore was happy. He would give a blow to the organized crime families, since several members of different organizations were in the complex and, if he could infiltrate Pablo, victory was certain. When Detective Pablo contacted Salvatore, he explains the whole plan to him.

Pablo answered. "I don't like this plan. They can discover me or kick me out of the Vertuchi organization. It would spoil years of work."

"These are orders, not proposals. It comes from the above. Are you going to refuse?" Salvatore arrogantly told him.

"I am not refusing. I'm just giving my opinion." Pablo replied.

"Well, your opinion has been heard. Now I need you here as soon as possible. Understood?"

Pablo, annoyed by the way Salvatore treated him, simply hung up the phone. This upset Salvatore a lot and he considered it a lack of respect towards him.

Pablo arrived in Ischia in the morning and went straight to Franco's complex. Salvatore had been in his tree since early in the morning. Salvatore saw Pablo arrive at the complex and marked down the time Pablo entered the complex. Pablo enters the compound's lobby and is greeted by Guido and Franco, who were having coffee. Guido kindly says.

"Good day, sir. How can I help you?"

"I have good references for this place. I work for a very irregular company. Sometimes I have a job and other times I don't. This gives me time to rest or perhaps look for new options."

"Guido knew the man was talking with double meaning."

"I understand, sir. It must be very stressful for you to work that way because the payments are consistent. They don't come and go. What company do you work for if I can ask?" Guido asked.

"For the Vertuchi company in Naples." Pablo replied.

"I don't know about that company, but I am sympathetic to your situation. Tell me, sir. What is your reservation number?"

"Oh sorry, I don't have a reservation. Can you please do something for me?"

"Of course. Let me check our reservations. Maybe we have a cancellation."

Guido looks at the book and tells him.

"I'm very sorry, sir. I have nothing available now, but I have a reservation for next week."

"Well, a friend told me there are hot springs here. I heard they are the best."

"That's true, you will come out like new." Responded Guido.

"Well, I will take it." Pablo responds.

"You must pay in advance. We will give you the reservation number."

Guido gives him a sheet of paper to fill out with the price at the end of the form. Pablo looks at the price and says.

"Excuse me, this must be a mistake. This is a lot of money."

"Good things cost dear sir. You are reserving in a place which hardly has a vacancy. It so happened the man that reserved that week has a daughter who is going to have a baby. It is his first grandchild. Tell me if you want it because I assure you it will not last."

"Yes, I am interested. I can give you some money now and tomorrow I'll pay the rest."

"Sir, we do not take half a payment. If you wish, I will hold the reservation until tomorrow at 11:00, but I guarantee nothing after 11:00."

"Perfect, totally reasonable. I will see you tomorrow. Thanks a lot and have a good day."

Pablo went to a hotel and contacted Salvatore. He told him not everything was negative, but the amount they were asking for a week was totally excessive. It was done on purpose, so he would not go. Salvatore immediately replied.

"No, by no means! We will ask Rome for funds. We cannot miss this opportunity."

"The fact I arrive tomorrow with such a sum will arouse more suspicions. Vertuchi knows me as an average thief who cannot afford such a luxury." Pablo responds.

"That's why you must go tomorrow, so as not to give them time to find out with Vertuchi. I will put the money out of my pocket and then Rome will reimburse me later. We don't have time to wait for Rome to send us the funds. That would take at least five days."

Pablo asks him. "How will you give me the money if I cannot have contact with you?"

"I'll send it to you with an undercover police officer this afternoon. Don't go anywhere until you get the money."

Salvatore orders Pablo, who did not like very much. Pablo hung up the phone without even saying goodbye, it was obvious that he was a bit upset.

Salvatore came from a wealthy family and did not think twice about going to the local bank to get the cash. From the bank, he went straight to the police station. He went to the chief's office without even saying good morning to the duty officer as if he was the new boss. Salvatore opened the office door without even knocking on the door. Raffaelle was talking on the phone and glared at him.

"What changed in Rome that they do not knock on the door before entering, or do you have special powers?"

"Excuse me, but the timing is so critical that there is no time for protocols."

Raffaelle excused himself to the person he was talking to on the phone and told him he would call him later.

"What happened now?" Raffaelle asked.

"I need an officer dressed in civilian clothes to take money immediately to Detective Pablo."

"Just a moment! Who the hell is Pablo? Since when has he been here? What is he doing on this island? Or is it you are the new chief and I have not found out about it yet?"

Salvatore lowers his arrogance a bit and responds.

"Excuse me boss, there are things that go above you and me. I am just following orders, and the situation is extremely urgent."

Raffaelle is not entirely convinced, but responds more calmly.

"That doesn't answer any of my questions. Do I have to repeat?"

Salvatore realized this time the boss would not budge, and his authority was being questioned for the first time. Salvatore had to explain everything. Raffaelle took the phone and ordered one of his police officers to dress in civilian clothes and to meet Salvatore in the plaza for a mission. Then he hung up and asked Salvatore.

"Do you need anything else, sir?"

"No thanks, that is all." Salvatore replied.

"Well, go do your thing and I have to do mine. Have a good day."

Salvatore realized opening the door without knocking first had been the last straw and he should be more careful from now on, but it bothered him the old man had treated him as if he was one of his police officers.

Two hours later, a police officer contacted Salvatore in the plaza and Salvatore took out all his frustration on the poor police officer.

"Here you have an envelope to be delivered to this address. Don't even think about opening it. You have twenty-five minutes to do it. You should be back by then."

"But to whom?" Asked the officer..

"Well, there must be only one person in the room. If there are two, you just say you knocked at the wrong room."

"But what is that person's name?" Asked the officer.

"Why? Does the name matter to you? Your job is to deliver a package, not to ask questions."

The angry police officer took the package, turned around and between his teeth to vent his anger said, "Stupid shit head".

Salvatore heard the police officer murmur, but he couldn't understand it. However, he knew that after he had humiliated him, the murmur was not a compliment.

"What did you say?" Salvatore asked defiantly.

"I'm talking to myself. I don't think that's your business."

Salvatore was left with his mouth open. First Raffaelle and now a police officer had treated him without the respect he thought he deserved. He thought to himself. "All that is going to change. I am going to bring them all to their knees. They will fight to take a picture with me."

The police officer arrived at the indicated address in twenty minutes and knocked on the door. Pablo opened the door and kindly told him.

"Good morning, sir. How can I help you?"

Pablo noticed the envelope, but he wanted to make sure he was the right person.

The police officer did not know what to answer because he did not know if Pablo was alone.

"Excuse me sir, but I have a message a friend gave me to give it to his friend, but I forgot the name and now I do not know if it is for you or the other person who is you."

Pablo laughs and says. "There is no one here but me, by chance. Tell me, is this friend of yours named Salvatore?"

"YES!" Replied the police officer.

Pablo shook his head and said. "Stupid."

The officer, without thinking twice, said.

"Yes, that stupid one you mentioned treated me like trash. He gave me this to give to someone and gave me no name, description of the person, or at least password and believes he is the king of the world."

Pablo could not hold back laughing and said to the police officer, please come in.

"Well, this conversation remains between us," Pablo said

"Do not worry, sir, that's how it will be. It's a pleasure to meet a colleague who is down to earth like you, but your friend brought out the worst of me. Here is your package."

The police officer gives the envelope to Pablo and tells him.

"If you need something else, please, you can count on me for whatever it might be."

"Thank you, and you are truly kind. This is a lovely place. I am retiring in two years, and I think we will see each other again."

The police officer shook Pablo's hand tightly and told him.

"My name is Giovani and here you will have a friend waiting for you when that moment arrives. Good luck with your mission."

Pablo went immediately to Franco's complex, and, upon arrival, he met Guido at the front desk.

"Good morning, sir, good to see you again, and excuse me, but you never told me your name."

"It's true, my name is Pablo to serve you and when I say to serve, the meaning is quite broad." Pablo smiles.

"Good, I'll keep it in mind," Guido replies.

Pablo puts the money on the table and says.

"I hope this vacation is worth it, because here are all my savings."

Guido takes a big bite of a ham and cheese sandwich while he is counting the money and then tells Pablo in a low voice.

"Look, if my boss hears me, he will kick me out of work. With this money you can have three vacations at another hotel, but this is the best of all. As the saying goes, what is good is also expensive."

"Thanks for your advice, friend, but as the other saying goes, if you want to eat fish, you have to wet your buttocks." Pablo replied.

They both start laughing and Guido says.

"You are tremendous. That's the way to do it, my friend. We are going to reserve that week for you right now and I'll wait for you next Monday morning."

"You are exceedingly kind and efficient. Today I am going back to Naples. Is there something you would like from over there? I'd love to bring you a gift."

"No, thank you. The boss wants us to only have professional relationships with clients. He thinks if we make friends with someone, we will give them things for free or at a better price. In other words, he is a miserable miser. But on this island, jobs are not plentiful."

When Pablo left, Guido went directly to Franco's office to inform him of what had happened. Franco laughed and told him.

"Thank you, Guido."

"Why, Don Franco?"

"For making me laugh. I had not laughed for over four months, and you don't know how necessary laughter is. You already know what you must do and don't worry about the expenses. Those are paid courtesy of Salvatore."

"Yes, Don Franco, just like you said."

Pablo returned to Naples that same night. From Naples, he informed Salvatore that he had made friends with Guido, who was not thrilled with Franco, and that his reservation was confirmed for next week, starting Monday. Salvatore replied.

"Now you see I was right. We already penetrated them. It's a matter of time and you will not regret having taken part in this. When this is over, you will retire with more honors and medals than you can imagine."

Salvatore calls. Umberto, who is uncomfortable with the time.

"How can you call me at 8:30 p.m.? These are not business hours."

"The news is so good, it can't wait. Imagine that we just infiltrated Pablo into Franco's complex." Salvatore replied.

"What did you say?" Umberto said, totally surprised.

"I told you this Franco is not a big deal. Now do you believe me? Pablo will stay for a week starting on Monday and has made friends with Guido, the one who works at the reception. We already know he is not a total friend of Franco. The week at the compound will cost us ten times more in expenses than any other hotel."

"It's a lot of money!" Umberto replied.

"I paid it out of my pocket because if we wait for the money approval, we lose the week they offered Pablo. As you know, in three years, they spent a hundred times more and got nothing out of it, but in two days I gave Franco for free. Now that we can arrest several leaders of the organized crime families, are they going to make a big deal about the reimbursement of something that I paid out of my pocket for this cause?"

Umberto almost without words answer.

"You are absolutely right. This news will be a bomb tomorrow when I tell the bosses. I don't think they can object to the refund. Just make sure Pablo brings the receipt. I don't regret having recommended you. Excellent job!"

Franco was resting in his room when there was a knock on the door.

"Who is it?" Franco asks.

"Marina." Replies a lady.

"Please, Marina, I need to rest."

Marina opens the door and enters with a tray of food.

"Marina, did you forget I am your boss?" Franco tells her.

"And you forgot that you have not had breakfast, nor have you had lunch?" Marina answers.

"So, get out of that bed right now and eat."

Marina was in charge of the kitchen, and she treated Franco like a son. She even gave him orders, was strong-willed and inspired respect.

"I will not argue with you."

"Well then, eat and there will be no arguments."

Franco got up and ate. Luigi saw the open door. He enters and sees Franco sitting and eating, with Marina in front of him, hands on her waist, telling him.

"Until the last bite."

Luigi smiled at Franco and made fun of him.

"I do not think it is funny." Franco tells Luigi.

Luigi gives Franco two packages and tells him.

"In this one, are the original pictures Maria turned in and in the other, are the ones the photographer reproduced."

"What else do you know about her?"

"Well, she stopped going to work at her father's factory. She does not leave her house and only from time to time can you see her face through the window. Just as you requested, her father's business remains afloat, but without knowing it is because of us."

"Thanks Luigi. I don't know what I would do without you." Franco replied.

CHAPTER SEVEN

PABLO RUNS FOR HIS LIFE

On Monday at 8:00 a.m., Salvatore is in his tree with his camera filming Pablo's arrival at the Resort. Exactly at 9:30 a.m., Pablo arrives wearing a white jacket and carrying a medium suitcase with enough clothes for a week. Guido and Franco welcomed Pablo with a toast at the reception where they also took a picture. Guido gave the room keys to Pablo and ordered one of the employees to carry the suitcase to the room. Pablo said.

"It is unnecessary. I will carry it."

Franco intervened, telling him.

"No, my friend, our guests come to rest, not to carry suitcases."

Franco turns to Guido and tells him.

"Please make sure our guest is not missing anything."

"This is how it will be, Don Franco."

Pablo followed the boy, who was carrying his suitcase. He still could not believe he would be a week inside Franco's complex and he thought Franco himself had approved of it because he had taken an interest in him, and everything was going as planned. Pablo had to admit thanks to Salvatore he would make history.

When Pablo entered the garden area, he saw several children playing and a small puppet theater. Pablo asked the boy with great curiosity.

"Where did these children come from?"

"Oh! This week is a special week for orphaned and disabled children. We have a week for them every year. Don Franco was an orphan and has always felt protective of children. Imagine he does not charge them anything, and this is very expensive. He says that it doesn't matter how much it costs him, because just seeing them laugh and run is enough payment for him."

Pablo tried to stay calm, but he thought this was not looking good. He did not see any adults except the workers of the complex.

"When did this kids' week start?" Pablo asked.

"Saturday, sir, and they finish on Friday. It is a crazy. They don't stop running and screaming. We can't even complain if they misbehave, because Don Franco spoils them and pleases them in every way possible."

Pablo thought, this is another employee not very satisfied with his boss, maybe all is not lost. The boy opened the door to Pablo's room and put the suitcase inside. The room was very cozy with a wonderful view.

"Enjoy it sir, if you want something please let us know immediately."

Pablo thanked him and gave him a generous tip to win over the boy.

Pablo organized his clothes and realized almost three hours had passed. He had to go out to the agreed place with something white on so Salvatore would know everything was okay. Pablo went out to the garden with a white hat and played with the children. He would throw his hat up, trying to get it to fall on his head. The children laughed and made a chorus around him. Every time Pablo threw his hat, he said to himself. "I hope you see that, asshole."

Pablo had to give a sign of life three times a day in the garden, always wearing something white, and if he used something red, it was the signal for him to be arrested. That day, Pablo used the resort's amenities to familiarize himself with it. He took several pictures with the children, but his purpose was to take photos of the complex interior and then make a map.

Franco had his own photographer, who was to shoot the photos for the supposed tourists. Franco had ordered him to take photos from the same angles Pablo was using to take photos. This way he would know what Pablo had photographed and would make changes if necessary, in case security could be compromised.

Pablo tried to make friends with all the workers in the complex, who were kind, simple and might have some dissatisfaction with

Franco for different reasons. This kept Pablo hoping to make some kind of contact or alliance with someone. What Pablo did not know was Franco planned everything, since his employees were totally unconditional.

On the third day, Pablo despaired, he had not advanced in anything, and he was convinced he had to be more aggressive if he wanted any results. The next day, a five-year-old boy was missing. Pablo heard noises and screams from the employees. He went out to see what was happening. He saw Don Franco telling employees.

"That child must be found. Look for him, turn over every stone."

Pablo approached Franco and asked.

"What happened, Don Franco?"

"We are missing a child. We must find him."

Pablo saw the opportunity to offer his help.

"I have more experience in making people disappear than looking for them, but I will join the search and help. I could not sleep if something happens to an innocent child."

Pablo wanted to have access to all the places in the complex under the pretext of looking for the missing child, but Franco responded immediately.

"No, thank you. The guests are here to rest and have no worries. I assure you we will find the child. I will let you know myself, so that you can sleep peacefully."

"I would appreciate it, Don Franco. For me, children are sacred, but adults are another issue."

Pablo wasted no time sending his messages in a double meaning. Franco did not respond and continued organizing a search party.

Thirty minutes later, Franco approached Pablo, who was reading a newspaper in the garden, and told him.

"Don Pablo, thanks for your kindness in offering your help. We found the child. He fell asleep in the stable with the horses."

"Thank God. As I told you, Don Franco, children are a blessing from God. It is a pity we have to eliminate some of them when they grow up."

Franco stared at Pablo for a while, as if he wanted to say something, but he did not dare. Pablo thought he already had Franco on his side, and it was only a matter of time. What Pablo didn't know was that was exactly what Franco wanted Pablo to believe. Franco put a hand on Pablo's shoulder and said.

"You're absolutely right. It is better if some of them never grow up to be an adult and even I eliminated some of those."

Pablo was excited. He finally achieved his goal. Franco had opened to him. They would surely talk about business now. Then Franco told him.

"That happened during the war. I saw many innocents die, and I saw others die who should never have been born."

Pablo felt as if a bucket of cold water had been poured on him. He had returned to his starting point. Something is failing, and he had four more days to achieve his goal.

The next day, Pablo dressed in white like a sailor. The children were all in the garden, enjoying a puppet theater. Pablo sat reading the newspaper in the garden so Salvatore would see there was no danger. Franco approached him and greeted him kindly.

"Good morning, Don Pablo. Are we going fishing today or did you get a job as a sailor?"

"Oh no, Don Franco, today I plan to walk through the Island marinas. Have you ever thought of owning a marina? That would be a great business. You can offer fishing trips to the tourist. The other important thing is, if someone gets lost on the boat, you won't have to look for so long, or maybe it's the best place for them to get lost."

Franco smiled and answers.

"What good is it to me if I can't leave this complex for the next thirty years?"

"Well, in that case, what you need is someone who, on paper, appears as the owner, but you control the business. You don't even have to get your feet wet." Replied Pablo.

"I have not thought about that. It is difficult to find an honest person to give control of such an expensive investment. I also do not see why I should put it in the name of another person. I am prohibited from leaving this complex, but I can buy properties outside the complex. It's a good idea, thank you. I'll keep it in mind for the future."

"It would be a pleasure for me to work for you. If you want, you can put me to the test. You will not regret it."

"Thanks, Pablo. Please leave me all your work and personal information. Here we are all a family, and we have certain rules, but you have shown to have business acumen. It would not be a bad idea to have your file for the future."

Pablo was in trouble. He had to produce a work and personal file. He only had two days left, and it was impossible for him to do so because he would be discovered easily.

"Tonight, I will work on that as soon as I return from my walk through the ports. Thank you very much, Don Franco, for taking me into account. The truth is that I have spent some wonderful days in this place. These children take me back to my childhood."

"You will always be welcome here. The difficult thing is the reservation, but anything can happen."

Pablo took a taxi in front of the complex and went to the center of Ischia. Pablo visited several shipyards and fishing businesses. He fell in love with the island and in two years he was retiring. He was sure if someone followed him, it would reaffirm what he had told Franco. Pablo did not use the phone, and he was always visible. In total, he visited four businesses and in all of them he spoke with the owners inquiring about prices. Pablo returned to the complex around 7:00 p.m. and gave candy to the children who were playing at the reception. Guido thanked Pablo for his action, to which he responded.

"It's nothing. I love children and I've had a lovely time here. Unfortunately, I must cut my vacation two days short. I have to leave early tomorrow, so I want to say goodbye to you and Don Franco."

Guido looked at him with a surprised face, picked up the phone and called Franco's office. Franco came out of the office and went to the reception where Guido and Pablo were talking.

"Good evening, Don Franco." Said Pablo.

"Good evening." Replied Franco.

Guido interrupts and says. "Don Franco, Pablo is leaving us tomorrow."

"But how? What happened? Is there something we can help you with, Don Pablo?" Franco asks.

"No Don Franco, you are the best hosts I have had in my life. I have had a pleasant time, but as I told you before, my work is irregular. I have unexpectedly got a job which I cannot pass up."

"Are you going back to Vertuchi?" Franco asks him.

"Don Franco, do not take it as an offense, but discretion and loyalty is the fundamental basis of my profession, so I cannot disclose any details." Pablo replied.

Franco gave him a handshake and told him.

"You are a true gentleman and a great professional. It is a pity you are leaving us so quickly."

"Thank you, Don Franco. I think the same of all of you and forgive me for not being able to leave you the resume you asked for because of this unforeseen event." Pablo replied.

"Don't worry Don Pablo. I'll be here for many more years."

Franco went to his office, where Luigi was waiting for him. Franco asked Luigi.

"What do you have about this, Pablo?"

"Don Franco, he did not contact Salvatore, who is in his tree every day. He never used the hotel phone. He only went out today and spoke with the owners of four businesses. Finally, he has done some minor jobs for Vertuchi. So, I don't know what to say about him."

"Well, maybe you don't know, but I do." Franco replied.

"But how do you know? How can you come to that conclusion?" Luigi asks.

"Very easy Luigi:

First: He agreed to pay an exorbitant amount of money to be here for a week.

Second: The jobs he has done for Vertuchi are minor, Vertuchi does not consider him a member of his organization

Third: He didn't have the money, but the next day he did. Only a rich man or the government can come up with that amount from one day to another. That tells me he is a detective infiltrated in the Vertuchi organization.

Fourth: He was always offering his service to us.

Fifth: When I told him to give me his work and personal references in writing for a job, he left us the next day with the excuse of an alleged job. He does not have them because to make such a reference takes a long time.

Last, he was always in contact with Salvatore."

"No, Don Franco, he never contacted Salvatore. I am sure about that." Luigi replied.

Franco hits Luigi's forehead with his index finger three times while saying.

"Think Luigi. You didn't realize that during the four days he was here, he always wore something white. Whether it was a shirt, a hat, or a pair of pants, it was a signal for our bird in the tree to know he was not in danger."

Luigi was amazed at Franco's power of observation.

"Don Franco, you never cease to amaze me. How easily you can see these things."

"Each one in his field Luigi, I depend on you for many things too. Now you must go to Naples, contact Vertuchi, and tell him that Pablo is a detective or an informant. If the information about the organization is not critical, simply put him aside and never let him get close to the organization again, but if it is otherwise, eliminate him immediately."

"I will do so, sir. I leave this afternoon for Naples."

The next day, Salvatore sees Pablo leaving the complex with his suitcase. Salvatore does not understand what is happening. He keeps asking himself, why Pablo was leaving if he had two more days left, and he is dressed in white pants? His curiosity leads him to get down from the tree and follow the taxi, but without making contact. Salvatore sees the taxi has taken Pablo to the port. Salvatore cannot contain his happiness. If he leaves early, it is because he finished and if he is wearing white; it is because he is not in danger. Salvatore immediately called Umberto and informed him of what had happened. Everything showed that in just five days, they had already infiltrated Franco and would confirm it after he spoke with

Pablo. Umberto congratulated Salvatore but refused to give the news to his superiors until Pablo confirmed the news.

Luigi walks into Franco's office and tells Franco.

"Don Franco, your theory is confirmed. Our bird got off the tree and followed Pablo to the port and has not returned to the nest. He must be waiting for Pablo's phone call."

"Perfect Luigi, let's not waste time. As soon as Pablo leaves, then you leave on the next ferry to Naples."

When Pablo arrived in Naples, he waited an hour to call Salvatore, who had been waiting for the call for more than an hour. When the phone rang, Salvatore took it quickly and asked.

"Pablo, is that you?"

"Yes, it's me." Pablo replied.

"All the time in white and you finished before the week, you are my hero. I already informed Umberto; he is waiting for you to call him to confirm your success in this operation."

Pablo took about a minute to answer, Salvatore asks.

"Pablo, are you there? Do you hear me?"

"Yes, I hear you. I'm sure they discovered me and now I must disappear from Naples. I'm calling you from the train station and am going to Rome. I'm in danger here."

"It can't be. If they had discovered you, then you would be sleeping with the fish. You are not in danger, and you are running away. That is what you will have to explain to Umberto." Salvatore yells.

"From the beginning, I told you your plan was not good, but you think you are smarter than everyone else. When in reality, they are running circles around you. Pablo threw the phone at him."

Salvatore could not believe what he had heard.

"I will go to Rome to put this Pablo in his place, who is not only a coward but also disrespect me."

Vertuchi received Luigi at his restaurant. Vertuchi thanked Franco for the information and assured him Pablo had not passed more than the first ring of the organization. He had no evidence that could directly implicate him, but at the same time, they did not know they were being infiltrated by Pablo. Vertuchi tells Luigi that if they found him, they will eliminate him as an example to others.

Luigi asked. "Don Vertuchi, you do what you think is necessary. Don Franco just wanted to inform you of the danger."

Two days later in Rome, Salvatore and Pablo met in Umberto's office. It was time to clarify what had happened.

Umberto began by setting the rules. Salvatore would speak first and then Pablo. No one could interrupt and if in the end Umberto had a question he would ask. Then he would write his report and the bosses would make the final decision.

Salvatore began by saying.

"Before starting the mission, he said that it was going to fail. That's not the way to work with a negative attitude. He spent four days in the complex, was never in danger, and fled on the fifth day directly to Rome. When he finally contacted me, he insulted me and said that those bandits are smarter than us. Then he threw the phone at me. That is all I know, but I can tell you he is not professional, nor worthy of an organization like ours. I believed in this operation, and I put my own money without thinking twice because I believed in it. I know we can beat them. We only need people with pants on right and that's all I have to say."

Pablo was red and was biting his lips. When it was his turn, firm, but without raising his voice, he said.

"When Salvatore told me about his plan, I told him it would not work. I had not passed the first ring of the Vertuchi organization, and they would never consider me as Vertuchi's man. When I went to make the reservation, they asked me for such an exaggerated amount of money that no one would accept it. When I accepted and brought the money the next day, they gave me the reservation within a week, which gave them time to investigate me. When I arrived, the complex was full of children. I did what I could. I pretended to be someone who wanted to belong to another organization, because I did not see a future with Vertuchi and that made me pass the first test. All the employees spoke badly of Franco. What they really wanted was to know about me. I took as many pictures as I could to make a map. I spoke with Franco several times, hinting I wanted to work for him, and every time I thought I had him, it would drain like water through my fingers. To make my last point, he pretended to give me a job at the complex. He told me the only people he trusts worked there, that I should give my job resume plus my personal history to Guido. As you will see, I cannot prepare that document in two days because it would be very easy to discover that it is a lie. That's why I told him I had to go urgently to do a job that came out suddenly and unfortunately, I couldn't leave my resume due to lack of time. I came straight to Rome because you ruin my work in Naples, Salvatore. If I return to Naples, I am a dead man. Finally, I have more than enough pants to give to you. What I lack is your arrogance and, in case you don't know it, you are not my boss."

Umberto said. "Enough, enough. You both can leave now."

Pablo got up and left, but Salvatore remained seated.

"I said you can leave.". Umberto repeated in a stronger tone.

"Boss, I need to tell you something."

"I was very clear. You should have said it during your turn. Get out of my office."

"No sir, it has nothing to do with Pablo. I have to go back to Ischia because I have an informant at the port. He can tell me when these mobsters arrive on the island and his price is very cheap."

"Listen Salvatore, I don't want Franco to become an obsession for you and a problem for me. I'll give you the answer tomorrow. Now please get out."

CHAPTER EIGHT

MANINO

Umberto gives Salvatore another chance, because his bosses had divided opinions about what happened with Pablo and, at the same time, they demanded results. Umberto called Salvatore and informed him he would give him another chance, but this would be the last, because until now the result of his investigations had been three dead and a mobster living like a king in a tourist complex. Salvatore felt offended, but he preferred to remain silent, because he did not want to risk the return to the island.

After two weeks in Rome, Salvatore returned to Ischia and, as usual, he went to the police station. Salvatore asked the duty officer if the chief was in his office. The duty officer answered.

"Yes, he is, sir. I have already informed him of your arrival, but the boss is busy and cannot see you now. You can wait or return in two hours."

Salvatore couldn't believe what was happening. He didn't want to risk any more trouble either, so he answers.

"I was just stopping by to greet him and tell him I will be in contact with him only if necessary."

The duty officer only shook his head and did not respond. Salvatore left the station more humiliated than ever. Even the duty officer had ignored him. Salvatore rented an apartment near the hill and prepared to show everyone he was above them and he would regain respect and popularity.

With the help of his new contact, Salvatore did not have to peek from the tree every day and was trying to make friends in town, trying to get information, no matter how insignificant. Benito was Salvatore's contact at the port. Benito was only faithful to money, and everyone knew he was not a man to trust, but that did not matter to Salvatore. He would pay him only if his information could be verified. A month had passed, and Salvatore had not heard from Benito. One afternoon, Benito called him to inform him five people from the intense list Salvatore had given him were scheduled to arrive the next day in the afternoon. Benito told Salvatore he had to give him his money that night. Salvatore replied.

"No problem, a deal is a deal and I keep my word."

When Benito showed Salvatore the amount the information would cost, Salvatore responded angrily.

"That's five times more than what you told me."

"No sir, it is the correct amount. I gave you the information of five people and each one is different. I do not give discounts or wholesale packages. You pay me as agreed or we do not do more business."

Salvatore never thought Benito would charge him for each person separately. That is why it seemed cheap. He convinced his bosses with the wrong budget, but now the cost was five times higher. He knew if he asked Umberto for more money, that would be the end of his stay in Ischia. Salvatore paid the difference out of his own pocket. He was sure he would regain his investment and prestige with the arrest of several criminals who seemed untouchable. Salvatore went back to his tree and wrote all the information on the individuals who had entered and left the complex. Salvatore sent a full report to Umberto, who, after reading it, told him.

"This tells me nothing, only that they went and after four days, they left."

"No sir, we will connect the dots, and something will come to light eventually."

"You better be right." Umberto said and hung up the phone.

Salvatore continues to pay out of his pocket for the difference in the information Benito gave him and kept sending it to Umberto, who after the third report, told him bluntly.

"This is of no use to me. I don't need to pay a detective to tell me where they meet. Meeting is not a crime. If your next report is the same as the others, you can save it and return to Rome."

Five months passed without Benito contacting Salvatore, but this time, Benito tells him.

"I have good news for you, but prepare your pocket or there is no deal."

"Are you going to raise my price?"

"No, but there are twelve coming this time."

Salvatore thought this is a great thing and worth paying for.

"Deal, I will see you tonight to get the list from you." Salvatore replied.

Franco already had information Salvatore was not always in his tree, but every time he had an important meeting, Salvatore was in the tree. It was obvious someone was supplying him with that information, so he asked his people to watch Salvatore to find out who provided the information. Salvatore took data and photos of everyone who attended the meeting. He had provisions in his tree for a week and he knew his was his last chance. Luigi approaches Franco and tells him.

"Don Franco, our bird returned to the nest. What do we do?"

"Nothing Luigi, leave it like that."

Salvatore spent three days in the tree. On the third day, eleven of the twelve people who had entered the complex left. There was no doubt if he had not seen him in two days. It was because he was eliminated. Salvatore immediately called Umberto and told him what was happening. It was necessary to get a search warrant signed by the judge and search the complex. Perhaps they were still torturing him, or he would find the body. This would be a great blow. Salvatore had the photos of everyone who entered the complex and the photos when they came out, except one.

"This time I catch them all." Salvatore yelled.

Salvatore broke into the police station, went straight to the chief's office, opened the door and told him.

"I am very sorry, Raffaelle, but it is an emergency. We need a search warrant signed by a judge."

Salvatore explained to the chief what had happened in Franco's complex and that he needed three or four police officers to secure the crime scene and reporters to spread the big news. Raffaelle did not refuse Salvatore's requests. They seemed logical, and he tried to get the search warrant as soon as possible. He also would take part in the arrest. This was great publicity for him as well. Within two hours, Salvatore had developed the photos as evidence to show to the press and everything was ready for the big operation. This time, Raffaelle was leading in the caravan of three police cars.

Raffaelle and a police officer were in the first vehicle. In the second vehicle were Salvatore and two police officers. In the third vehicle, there was a police officer and two reporters. The three vehicles blocked the entrance to the complex. Rafaelle left three officers outside and ordered the fourth officer to come inside with them. Upon entering the reception area, Salvatore stepped forward, completely ignoring Raffaelle, and yelled at Guido.

"Nobody leaves here. I have a search warrant signed by the judge. I need the entry and exit records of the last seven days for this complex, and I want you to call Franco right now."

Guido calmly finishes chewing the cake he was eating, drinks his coffee and responds.

"Good afternoon, sir. It will be done as you say. No one will leave the complex and I will give you the registration in a moment, if you allow me."

Salvatore angrily tells him.

"I told you to call Franco."

"It is unnecessary to call him. Don Franco is in his office and you screaming like that makes it impossible he has not heard you. He must already be on his way here."

Guido looks at Raffaelle and respectfully says. "Good afternoon, Don Raffaelle. Can I help you with something?"

Raffaelle, ashamed by Salvatore's attitude, responds.

"No thanks Guido, I'm fine."

Guido's calm demeanor made Raffaelle realize the operation was on its way to failure. Salvatore was walking around the reception with the search warrant in hand. Suddenly he stops and yells at Guido.

"I told you to call Franco."

"It is unnecessary for him to call me. With those screams, I can hear you from Rome, Franco replied calmly, leaving his office."

Franco ignores Salvatore. He turns to Raffaelle and tells him.

"Good afternoon, Don Raffaelle. Please tell me, how can we help you?"

Salvatore feels humiliated by Franco, who has totally ignored him. He stands in front of Franco with the search warrant in his right hand and a photo in his left hand and yells at him.

"Do you see this? Do you know what it is?"

"Yes, a search warrant and a photo." Franco responds calmly.

Salvatore yells at him again. "No, you're wrong. This is your final sentence. You played with fire and burned yourself."

Reporters took the perfect photo of Salvatore yelling angrily with both hands up. He was holding the warrant in one hand and a picture of Manino on the other. Franco was calm, with his arms crossed and a smile on his face. At that moment, Guido arrived with the logbook.

"Here's the record. Who do I show it to?"

Salvatore goes to Guido and shows him the photo and asked him.

"Do you know who this man is?"

"Yes, he's Don Manino." Guido responds.

"Well, this man arrived here three days ago at 10:30 a.m. and he never left this complex."

Guido pauses as if trying to remember and replies.

"I do not remember the time of entry or departure, but he left with the rest of his friends who entered the same day."

Guido opens the book and with an astonished face says.

"You are absolutely right. Don Manino checked in three days ago at 10:30 a.m., as you say, but he left at 11:40 a.m. two days ago.

Salvatore screams. "That's a lie!"

Salvatore orders the officers to search the complex and, after four hours of searching, an officer tells Raffaelle.

"Chief, we have nothing. There is no sign of violence, there are no traces of blood and not even disturbed earth to indicate they have buried a body."

"Inept! How can they say that?" Shouted Salvatore.

"No Salva, you are the inept. You don't need a search warrant. I would have allowed you to search. I have nothing to hide, and I do not blame innocent people for murder like you do."

"My name is Salvatore, not Salva. You better respect me. You better retract everything you said, right now." Salvatore responded furiously.

Franco, undeterred, answered him.

"Respect is earned, not demanded. I will not retract what I said."

Franco goes to Raffaelle and tells him.

"I apologize, Don Raffaelle, but I wanted to show these reporters that our business is legitimate and that I am constantly and unfairly harassed by Salvatore."

Franco asks Guido to bring all the welcome and farewell photos of all the guests. Guido brings a photo album and hands it to Franco. Franco approaches Raffaelle and the reporters and tells them.

"We have a photographer in charge of taking professional photos of our guests during their stay, which they can choose to buy if they wish. We always take a complimentary photo totally free on arrival and departure. These copies remain in our files. Here are the pictures of Don Manino on arrival and the other at departure. As you can see, it is the same man dressed differently. Even more, you can see the day they were taken because the reception calendar is visible in the background. We have three taxi drivers working in the complex, and I have sent for them."

The three taxi drivers enter, and Franco shows them the photo and asks. "Do any of you remember transporting this person two days ago?"

The taxi drivers pass the photo around and one speaks.

"Yes, I took that man with me. I don't remember his name, but I remember his face. That was in the morning. He asked me to take him to the port. There he got off, and I didn't see him anymore."

Raffaelle was furious, but not at Franco.

"Excuse me Don Franco, we are leaving."

"There is nothing to forgive Don Raffaelle. You have done your job. It is Salva who has not done his and has involved you in this. You have done the right thing."

Raffaelle told the officers, without even looking at Salvatore.

"We are leaving now. Let's go!"

Salvatore was left with his mouth open, totally paralyzed and that was the other photo the reporter took.

The next day, the two photos taken at the complex were on the front page. The first photo showed a defiant Salvatore facing Franco with both hands raised and an immutable Franco with his arms crossed. The second photo was the face of a puzzled Salvatore like the one who just lost a football game at the last second and a Franco with a smile on his face that showed he was enjoying the moment. The famous police operation had become a publicity saga with headlines like "This time Salvatore loses, " "Salvatore and Franco tie the series," "Who will win next?" With headlines like these, public opinion had a 360 degrees turned, as Franco represented the local team.

Salvatore called Umberto and told him the operation had failed, and he needed time to give him a detailed report about what happened and why it had failed. Umberto answered him.

"Take as long as you need." The truth was that Umberto was so mad he didn't want to see Salvatore's face.

Salvatore spent three days without leaving his apartment, only thinking about the failed operation. On the third day, Salvatore had a detailed answer as to why the operation failed and the future remedy. Salvatore recovered, and looking at his picture in the newspaper, he said. "Next time is checkmate Franco."

Salvatore stopped by the police station to tell Raffaelle he had discovered the mistake and that he was prepared for next time. The officer on duty saw Salvatore heading towards the chief's office and stopped him.

"Excuse me, sir. Where are you going?"

"I need to see Raffaelle." Salvatore replied.

"I'm sorry sir, but the boss has given orders that unless you bring an order from Rome involving a case, he will not receive you."

Salvatore felt an indescribable anger.

"Well then, tell your little boss I will bring it to him, and he will have to make himself available to me whenever I ask him."

Salvatore turned to leave when he heard the sarcastic words of the watch officer.

"See you later, sir. Have a nice day."

Salvatore left the police station enraged and with more determination than ever. Now he felt the need to give everyone a lesson.

Franco receives a call from Guido at his office.

"Don Franco, the man who sells us the linen for the hotel, a certain Valentino is here, and he wants to talk to you. I told him you don't take care of that, but he insists."

"Yes, Guido let him in. I called him myself. I wanted to talk to him, because I don't see the same quality of linen as before."

"Excuse me Don Franco, that is my responsibility, and I did not realize that. I apologize. I will be more careful from now on."

"Don't worry Guido. You can't do everything." Franco replied.

The salesman was the representative of the hotel linen business Franco had founded with the purpose of making purchases from Maria's father's factory to avoid his bankruptcy. Only Luigi and Franco knew about the supposed salesman,

Valentino knocks on the door and Franco answers.

"Enter please."

Once Valentino is inside of the office, he closes the door and Franco stands worriedly from his desk.

"What happened Valentino? You should report to Luigi monthly. If you are here, it is because something has happened."

"Yes, sir, something intriguing has happened."

"But what? Talk once and for all." Franco tells him.

"This month I can't send you the linen order."

"I don't give a damn about the linen order." Franco yells at him.

"No, Don Franco, let me finish. Maria ran away from home. Her parents are going crazy trying to find out where she is. They went to the authorities and reported her missing. Since I am the only client they have, I developed a friendship with Don Pedro and Dona Angela. They told me Maria no longer went out on the streets, because people made fun of her, and she was in a state of depression. Don Pedro closed the factory for two weeks and dedicated himself to look for her."

Franco shakes his head and sighs.

"Oh God! That was the only thing I was missing now. You will give Don Pedro the money for two months."

"He won't accept it." Valentino responds.

"I know, but you will tell him you cannot lose him. That thanks to him, your business has prospered, and he must sign a paper where if in the future you are in trouble, he must give you two free orders even if the prices are higher."

"That's a good idea. I think he will accept it." Valentino responds.

"Thanks, Valentino, for coming and keep me up to date."

"I have tried to go to Don Pedro's house, but he has never let me in. He always gives me an excuse despite getting along fine with me.

"Do you think they relate this to me?" Franco asks.

"Not, however, they blame you for all their social and economic problems. I saw Maria burning a newspaper just because your picture appears in it."

"It's just that the police have already gotten used to coming here to look for the dead people and since they have found none, I will not be surprised if they come now looking for the living." Franco replied.

CHAPTER NINE

DON CRISTINO

After several months, Benito contacts Salvatore and gives him a list of nine names. As usual, Salvatore calls Umberto, but Umberto was not in the office. Salvatore leaves the list with the secretary. Salvatore, in his arrogant tone, tells her.

"Make sure you give him the list first thing in the morning and check for arrest warrants. I don't think that's too much to ask of you."

The secretary did not answer and hung up the phone. Salvatore could not believe the secretary had hung up the phone. He angrily threw the receiver and said. "Big mistake honey, you don't know who you are messing with. As soon as I return to Rome, you better start looking for another job."

Salvatore was in his tree taking photos of everyone who entered the compound and kept a detailed log of everything he observed from his post. One guest was Don Cristino. He was the leader of the Sicilian organization. Don Cristino was easy to identify, as he was 72 years old, was short, limped on his right leg and used a cane. Don Cristino greets Franco and tells him.

"Three days ago, the police raided my business. They were looking for me. I was not in the business, so I am sure I have an arrest warrant. Nobody knows I have come, but we must be alert."

Franco immediately asks for five employees. He meets them in his office and tells them.

"You are going to watch with binoculars from the room that overlooks the entrance to the hill. You will take a four-hours shift, but it will be 24 hours job for these four days. At night, you will look at the balcony of the apartment that is in the same corner of the entrance to the complex. If that light goes out, you must immediately notify us."

Franco puts his hand on Don Cristino's shoulder and tells him.

"If they come for you, we will take you to the shelter. There you will have a comfortable bed, water, and plenty of food. We still do not have electricity yet, but it will not be dark either. Don Augusto will visit you daily and he will bring you everything you need."

Don Cristino responds. "That is why we have you as a mediator and advisor, because you think about everything in advance, and you are always prepared."

Meanwhile, in Rome, Umberto did not show up at the office the next day and since the secretary disliked Salvatore, she decided not to inform Umberto of the list until Umberto showed up at the office. Umberto enters the office, and the secretary tells him.

"Don Humberto, Salvatore left a list for you. I have it on my desk." Umberto doesn't pay much attention and responds.

"Very well. I have a meeting now. It will take about three hours. Put the list on my desk and I will review it later."

Three hours later, Umberto walks into his office and sees the list, reluctantly takes it and begins to read it. Suddenly, he sees Don Cristino's name and screams.

"My God, Don Cristino is in Ischia!"

Umberto knows the capture of Don Cristino would be a triumph. He also knows on the island resources are limited and he cannot risk failing. He receives the approval of his superiors to leave immediately for Ischia with twenty heavily armed police officers dressed in civilian close, so as not to arouse suspicion.

Umberto arrives in Ischia at four in the afternoon the next day and from the port, he calls Raffaelle.

"Don Raffaelle, this is Umberto, the head of the organized crime investigation. I urgently need you to come to the port."

Raffaelle does not know what is happening, but goes out immediately with two police officers. When Raffaelle arrives at the port, he finds Umberto so excited it is difficult to understand what he is saying.

"We have a big fish on the island, and he can't escape. We need to surround the Monte Santo complex and close the island."

Raffaelle looks at Umberto in bewilderment and replies.

"Have you gone crazy? I do not have enough staff for what you are asking me."

"Don't worry, I brought enough people to lock down the entire island. I just need you to put them in key positions."

"Where are your men? Raffaelle asks.

"There they are." Umberto points to Raffaelle, who now understands it is a big operation.

"Do you want us to start now?" Raffaelle asks.

"Not now. In four hours, it will be dark. We will take them by surprise as soon as it gets dark. Let's start by securing the exits to the island and putting your marine patrol on alert. I also need you to bring Salvatore to me. I want to make sure he saw him getting inside the complex."

As soon as Umberto mentions Salvatore, Raffaelle's face changed immediately. His eyebrows closed, and he shook his head from side to side.

"What happened? Don't you like Salvatore?" Asked Umberto.

"It's not that I am superstitious, but that detective brings bad luck."

"I can't believe you are telling me that. Please change that face. We'll have a party shortly." Says Umberto excitedly.

Raffaelle places the men in strategic places and completely closed the island without raising suspicions. Salvatore arrives at the police station and is greeted with joy by Umberto, who gives him a strong handshake.

"Show me the photo of Don Cristino and please tell me he is inside the compound."

Salvatore felt important and his ego doubled instantly.

"Sure boss, that is the lame. He came in two days ago and he hasn't come out. I think I saw him in the garden this morning with his cane and a black cap."

Umberto screams. "Finally, the lame shows up. We raided his house and business, but we couldn't find him. Someone tips him off, but this time he can't get away."

Raffaele, surprised, asks Umberto. "How is that possible?"

"Yes, Don Raffaelle. Traitors are everywhere, even within the department. This time, he will not get away. I do not think a lame can outrun any of us." Umberto responds, laughing sarcastically.

Salvatore interrupts. "Chief, we should bring the press. This is a big blow, so it should be documented in history."

"You're right. Please, Raffaelle, could you call reporters at the station about fifteen minutes prior to the operation without telling them what is going on?" Umberto asks.

"Sure, leave that to me. I will tell them I need to talk to them at 8:00 PM."

"Perfect, we have the men in position. The island is closed, and we have an hour left. I invite you to have coffee because this will be a long night."

While they were having coffee at the police station, Umberto did not stop talking. He was happy, and Salvatore seemed like a peacock. Only Raffaelle maintained a certain distrust. Salvatore, arrogantly, asks Raffaelle.

"What is wrong with you, Raffaelle? Does it bother you we spoil Franco's party?"

"No, I just don't like to celebrate victory until I pass the finish line."

"So, you think the lame can get to the finish line before us? You do not have confidence in yourself?" Salvatore responds.

Raffaelle didn't reply. He just drank his coffee and kept quiet the rest of the time. Salvatore and Umberto continued talking about the party that awaited them with the capture of Don Cristino. They only stop talking when the reporters arrive at the police station.

Salvatore stood in front of the reporters and told them.

"It is time for you to prepare for the job of your life. I do not want you to lose any detail and hope that you repair the damage you did to us last time."

While Umberto, Salvatore, and Raffaelle prepared to go up the hill in a caravan, Franco held a meeting where they analyzed the steps to follow to repair the damage to Don Cristino's organization. Suddenly, the watchman comes in and yells.

"They are on their way. They are coming with the lights off."

Franco yells. "Everyone to their rooms."

Luigi runs and carries Don Cristino as if he was a doll and takes him in a hurry to the underground shelter. Don Cristino held his cane in his hand and shouted.

"Run Luigi, run! We still must move the barrel."

Franco had moved the barrel in case there was an emergency. Luigi hurriedly threw Don Cristino onto the bed and ran back to close the entrance with the gigantic barrel.

The police had the hill surrounded and two marine patrols kept watch on any boat leaving the island. Umberto, Salvatore, Raffaelle and three police officers enter the reception of the complex and Guido acts surprised. He comes out to greet them with a cup of chocolate in one hand and a large biscuit in the other.

"Oh, my god! What is going on?" Guido asks.

Salvatore, seeing Guido's astonished face, thinks they have been taken by surprise and Don Cristino could not escape. Salvatore yells at the officers.

"Run inside and find him."

Umberto looks at Salvatore with an unfriendly face and asks him.

"Since when have you become in charge of this operation?"

"Excuse me boss, we have a search warrant and every second count with these people."

Umberto did not want to answer and summed up that Salvatore was right.

"That is correct, but you are here to carry out my orders, not to give orders."

Franco shows up at the reception and asks.

"Gentlemen. What happened? How can I help you?"

Salvatore immediately stands in front of Franco, raises his tiptoes and, looking down on Franco, responds.

"You cannot help us. Better yet, you and the lame man are the ones who need help, but not even God will be able to help you this time."

That was the first photo. A defiant Salvatore standing in front of Franco pointing a finger at him and an immutable Franco looking at Salvatore with a cold, almost mocking smile. Raffaelle, seeing the scene, turned around and shook his head. Umberto saw Raffaelle's attitude and asks him.

"What is going on? Is there something you know I do not know?"

"No, we are repeating the same thing from last time and I don't like it at all."

Salvatore stands like a soldier in front of Guido. He stretches out his long arm, holding up the picture of Don Cristino.

"Are you going to tell me you don't know who he is?"

Guido with his mouth still full answers. "No, I do not know who it is"

"Don't be rude. Don't talk with your mouth full. Can you stop eating for a minute?"

Guido chokes the last piece of biscuit and swallows the hot chocolate in a hurry.

"Excuse me, sir, I was already finishing. I don't know him. I only saw him when he arrived, and that he was here for two days."

"Are you going to say that to my face? Do you think I am stupid?" Salvatore yells at him.

Guido, still chewing, looks at Franco and asks him.

"Don Franco, should I answer that question?"

"No Guido, I don't think we can find the correct adjectives to describe him."

Umberto intervenes, so things do not get out of control.

"Answer the question and I want no more comments. Is Don Cristino here?"

"Yes, I have seen him. He is the man with the cane." Franco responds.

"No, sir, he is not here." Guido responds.

Salvatore yells. "Of course he is. I saw him at 9 AM. this morning. He is here."

"Yes, it is true. He was here in the morning around nine, but someone called the reception asking for him and I passed the call to him. He spoke to that person and left in a hurry without even picking up his belongings."

Franco asks Guido. "Is his departure marked in the books?"

"No, Don Franco. He didn't say if he was coming back or not."

Franco goes to Humberto and tells him.

"I'm sorry, but I didn't know that. I thought he was here."

Salvatore laughs out loud. "Do you think I'm going to believe such a story? Listen, clown, you must be a little more imaginative."

"I am only saying what I saw and heard. If you want to believe it or not, that is your problem." Guido answers, angrily.

"And what did you hear?" Umberto asks.

"I only heard what Don Cristino said, not what the other person told him."

"That is understood. What did you hear?" Umberto says, annoying.

"I heard Don Cristino saying. Thanks Salvatore. I owe you my life, you will be well rewarded, then he hung up the phone and ran out to get a taxi."

There was a moment of silence. It was as if a bomb had exploded. Umberto and Salvatore's faces were completely confused and Raffaelle's mouth was open. All this went down in history with the fortunate picture taken by the reporter.

Salvatore reacts and grabs Guido by the neck and pushes him against the wall while screaming.

"How dare you slander me like that?"

Guido, almost out of breath, screams. "I didn't say it was you who called. I just said what I heard."

Raffaelle and Humberto must struggle with Salvatore to get him to release Guido.

"Control yourself Salvatore. Guido is right. He did not say it was you. Besides, that may be a provocation." Umberto says.

Franco tells Luigi.

"Luigi, please bring the taxi drivers to see who took Don Cristino."

Salvatore paced the lobby and punched his right hand into the palm of his left hand to hold back his anger. Umberto got restless, and Raffaelle was standing like a mummy. Umberto approaches Raffaelle and asks him.

"How many farms make up the hill?"

"The hill is composed of three farms which are very long, but not wide. At the top is the complex. There is a wooded area composed of ancient trees. There are only two entrances to the hill, one through the farms and the one from the complex. Everything is hermetically sealed since five in the afternoon."

"Very well. I want you to send a police officer immediately to get three search warrants for those farms. There will not be a stone unturned on this hill." Stated Umberto.

Luigi enters with three taxi drivers and says.

"Don Franco, here are the taxi drivers who are working today."

Salvatore, desperately, says. "Let's not waste time. We know he didn't go anywhere. He's here and they just want to divert our attention."

"Calm down Salvatore, I'm the one who decides what to do." Umberto tells him.

"Yes boss, excuse me, but I prefer to join the search rather than waste my time here."

Umberto looks at the taxi drivers and asks.

"Have any of you seen this man?"

"Yes sir, that's the lame. I took him this morning."

"Tell me everything. I want to know the where, when, and how." Umberto yells.

"I saw him coming out running off the complex, very fast, to be lame. He opened the door of my taxi and got in a hurry. He told me to take him to the port as fast as I could."

"Did you take him to the port?"

"No sir, when going down the hill, he told me to stop in front of the green building located to the left of the entrance of the hill. He got off, paid me, and told me to continue to the port."

"But if he got off, what did you go to the port for?"

"I don't know, sir. He paid me three times the fare's value. I went to the port because I thought someone was waiting for me there. Nobody contacted me, so after two hours, I came back. That is it, sir."

Umberto responds. "That makes little sense. A person who tries to escape does not stay near the place and sends you to another place for pleasure."

Franco calmly tells Umberto. "I understand."

"What do you understand?" Umberto asks.

"These are circumstantial evidence. I am not accusing anyone, but the person who tipped off Don Cristino is named Salvatore. That Salvatore had the information about the arrest warrant. Then he stays in front of the building where lives a certain Salvatore who is taking part in the search, I think it makes sense to hide in the person's home who is conducting the search until that Salvatore can move him from his home to a safe place. Also makes sense to send the taxi driver away, so he cannot see where he went after he left him."

When Salvatore heard what Franco said, he totally lost control and charged Franco. Luigi, Umberto, and Raffaelle held Salvatore, preventing Salvatore from hitting Franco.

The flashes of the reporter's camera look like fireworks. The situation was so tense that no one paid attention to it. One of the most famous photos was the one of Luigi, Raffaelle and Umberto trying to hold Salvatore while Franco stands with his arms crossed and Guido stands next to him with his eyes wide open while biting into a biscuit. After controlling Salvatore, Umberto sends Salvatore to the search party, to get him out of his sight.

Umberto, Raffaelle, Guido and Franco stay at the reception. Franco tells Umberto.

"I did not intend to provoke Salvatore. I only gave my opinion."

"I would appreciate it if you would save your opinions to yourself." Umberto answers.

"You know Salvatore accuses me constantly and I assure you he is not the person you believe he is. I will prove it to you since you so blindly believe in him."

After five hours of searching, Salvatore and two officers enter the reception, yelling,

"We have it!"

Franco felt an icy shiver in his back and almost fainted, but he kept his composure. Guido had his back to everyone. He closed his eyes and thought about how to escape. Umberto jumps out of his chair and yells,

"I knew it. That lame couldn't go far."

Salvatore stands in front of Franco and says.

"Franco, you under arrest for hiding a fugitive. Your vacation is over. Your new house will be a two square meter cell."

Franco was about to faint, but he was incredibly calm. Guido had sat down and made believe he was falling asleep with his eyes closed, waiting to be arrested.

Salvatore, in a sarcastic tone, asks Franco. "Do you have something to say to the press?"

Franco responds. "Yes. Where is Don Cristino?"

"Nobody better than you to show the press your ingenuity. Let's go to the winery." Salvatore responds.

Franco did the impossible to contain himself, but his nerves began to betray him. He looked noticeably worried. Thousands of misfortunes passed through his mind. He saw his cousin Augusto arrested and all because of him. He wondered how Salvatore had come up with the keg combination?

"I don't have to go anywhere. If you have him, bring him here."

Franco responds, trying to buy time, but Umberto lets himself be carried away by the taste of victory, tells Franco.

"You come with us, or we drag you there."

Franco understood he was finished. Salvatore had once again destroyed his life. He walked slowly, as if he was on his way to the gallows. Salvatore, Umberto, Raffaelle, the reporters and two police officers walked with Franco to the winery. They all left the reception and forgot about Guido, who had pretended to be asleep in a chair. As soon as they left, Guido got up from his chair and tried to escape, but was stopped by an officer who was guarding the entrance to the compound.

"Stop, stop." Orders the carabinero.

"I'm not going anywhere; I was just trying to catch some air. I've been sitting for hours. I need to stretch my legs." Guido answers, almost crying.

"Oh yeah, what a way to stretch your legs; it looks like you're running in an Olympic marathon."

"It's cold. I must warm up my body." Guido responds.

"Go inside and do all the exercise you want, but inside the complex."

Salvatore had led the group to the spacious wine aging cellar. Once inside, Salvatore stands in front of everyone and, as if he was giving a lecture, he says.

"Here we have the secret of Manino's disappearance. It is a marvelous engineering work. As you can see, we have three huge wine fermentation barrels, but one of those barrels has a double function."

Salvatore points at Franco and, making fun of him, says.

"Here our master of ceremony, the magician, the one and only Don Franco, will delight us with his magic of how to disappear a person."

Salvatore bows mockingly and asks Franco to take the lead. Franco was pale. He felt chills and cramps all over his body. His brain was only thinking of a plan to escape from the police station. Luigi looked at Franco, waiting for the order to attack, but Franco did not give it. Luigi, despite being prepared, would never take the initiative without Franco's approval.

"What are you waiting for? We are waiting." Yells Salvatore.

Umberto takes the initiative and stands in front of Franco.

"You look nervous. What are you afraid of?"

Franco knows this is the end, but he has never given up and this will be no exception.

"I only fear the unknown. I can't guess what is the new stupidity Salvatore will come with."

Salvatore stands in front of the barrel leading to the shelter and hits it three times and says.

"Here's the answer. This is your magic barrel. Teach your magic. I don't want to steal your credit."

Luigi looks at Franco, asking for the order to attack. Salvatore has found the barrel. There is nothing more to do, and he prefers to die before spending the rest of his life in jail. Franco understands Luigi will not respect his orders and at any moment there is going to be a great fight, which is a lost fight before starting. Franco tries to buy time and plays his last card.

"Please, Luigi, bring me the jug and a tray with five glasses."

Thanks to those words, a catastrophe was avoided, as Luigi was going to hit Raffaelle, who was the closest to him. Luigi stopped in time and looked for the jug with the glasses. Franco turned on the tap on the keg and filled the jug.

"Here is my magic. In our cellar, we have four barrels exported from France to add our wine. This wine is four years old, and it is our pride. Try it and you will see it has nothing to envy to any export wine."

Salvatore kicks the tray with the glasses from Franco, making it fly. Luigi is going to jump on Salvatore, but before he even moves, he has three weapons pointed at him. Salvatore pushes Franco, who falls to the ground and screams.

"It's over, enough of this theater. Since you don't want to reveal your trick, it's up to me to do it."

It was the first time Franco felt totally lost and at the mercy of fate. Salvatore taps the barrel three times and says.

"Listen to this sound." Then he hits the other three barrels and says. "Here is the answer. This barrel is empty enough to hide a person without drowning. We just have to move two boards from the top to open it and welcome our guest."

Franco took a deep breath and his soul returned to his body. Salvatore had not discovered the barrel combination. Luigi calmed down and stopped struggling.

"Don't be stupid. You don't see that those barrels are hermetically sealed." Franco said.

"That's what you want us to think, but you won't get away with it. You open it, or I will break it." Salvatore responds.

"You're going to ruin four years of work if you break that barrel."

"It's true that wine is more than stale. It has a 72-year-oldman inside. This is your last chance to open it."

Franco stood up and answered.

"I can't open it. It's hermetically sealed."

Salvatore took out his gun and started shooting at the rivets and the metal tape of the barrel. The wine spilled and when he broke the metal tape; it haloed the boards, causing almost a flood in the cellar. They all ran to the steps of the cellar entrance to avoid the spilled wine. Only Salvatore stood in front of the barrel, his white pants were stained past his ankles from the spilled red wine, but he was laughing and enjoying the moment. When the wine stopped spilling from the barrel, Salvatore screamed through the open space of the two missing boards.

"Come out Don Cristino. We are waiting for you to celebrate."

Receiving no reply, Salvatore put his head close to the barrel and yelled.

"Come out or I will come in to get you out."

Salvatore saw a great darkness inside the immense barrel. He stood next to the barrel, reloaded his pistol, and empty it out on the barrel.

Umberto screamed. "What are you doing? Didn't you say you were going to get him out?"

"Yes, but I can't see anything. That lame has nothing to lose. He can see me, but I cannot see him. If he's armed, I'll be an easy target for him."

"You are right. You must not risk it." Umberto answers.

Salvatore stands next to the barrel and yells again.

"This is your last chance to get out alive. I'll count to three."

Salvatore counted to three and shot the barrel, then screamed.

"Maybe I didn't hit you this time, but I have more bullets."

Salvatore fired again, and I waited for an answer. Having no answer, he shouted madly.

"If that is your wish, you will die happy."

Salvatore started shooting from every angle possible until he finished emptying his pistol again. The terrified reporters were taking photos one after another. Salvatore looked at Umberto and the reporters and told them.

"You are witnesses. He left me with no other option."
Umberto yelled at him. "Get him out once and for all."
Salvatore gives his gun to Umberto and tells him.
"Give me your gun."
"For what? That man must be dead?" Umberto answers.
"I will not take a risk. These bandits have more life than a cat."
Umberto gives him his pistol and Salvatore enters the barrel. As he enters the barrel, several shots are heard, everyone is horrified thinking Don Cristino and Salvatore have engaged in a duel to the death. There was an eternal minute of silence, Raffaelle asks Umberto. "What do we do now, sir?"

Umberto is unsure what to do. He scratches his head and responds.

"We can't shoot the barrel. Salvatore is inside, just like Salvatore said. He can see us, but we can't see him. We just have to break the barrel and pray that he doesn't shoot us."

Six police officers came running to the warehouse alerted by the shots. Umberto ordered the officers to handcuff Franco and Luigi, who offered no resistance. After a while, they saw a hand slowly coming out of the opening of the barrel. They all pointed their guns at the person coming out of the barrel.

Umberto realizes Salvatore is the one coming out of the barrel, but his white suit is stained red. It is not clear if it is blood or wine, but at least he is not dead. Umberto and Raffaelle run to help him get out of the barrel. They pull him by the arm until they get him out. Salvatore is lying face down on the ground and everyone thinks he is mortally wounded. Umberto, Raffaelle and all the officers fired at the barrel. After emptying their weapons, over 60 rounds were shot.

"Umberto, looking at the barrel, says."
"You paid with your life. You damn lame."
Salvatore turns onto his back and says.
"Sorry boss, the barrel was empty."
Umberto, putting his hands on his head, yells.
"What did you say, idiot?"
Umberto was walking in the cellar, maddened.
"Damn lame, damn Salvatore."

Franco, calmer but still worried, remained silent in a corner. Salvatore stands up and says.

"Boss, we have searched the entire complex, and we have surrounded the hill. This does not end here. We will search again in the daylight, and we will also search the adjacent farms. He could not have escaped."

Umberto looks at the reporters who, scared, make way for Umberto to leave. Raffaelle asks Salvatore.

"What do I do with the prisoners?"

Salvatore with an authoritative tone order.

"Bring them to the front desk immediately."

Umberto listens to Salvatore, turns around and yells.

"There are no prisoners here. Release them immediately. They are just detained while the investigation is being carried out, but if you do not find the lame man, you have nothing. Do you understand me? You have nothing."

The search resumes three hours later with sunrise, but this time all over the hill. Umberto went to the port to investigate with the port authorities, who recognized Don Cristino's picture. They confirmed they had seen him when he arrived, but had not seen him leaving the island. Umberto felt great relief. Not everything was lost. He did not plan to leave the island until he found Don Cristino.

The day ended with no result. There was no sign of Don Cristino. The next day, the photo of Don Cristino was everywhere on the island and appeared on the local television. They offer a reward to any information leading to the capture of him.

On the third day, Umberto was totally demoralized. The press asked him questions to which Umberto had no answers. To make it even worse, the newspaper published the story that a certain Salvatore was involved in the scape.

Umberto, offended, summoned the press, trying to repair the damage. Umberto, giving a live report, says.

"It is totally irresponsible to suggest that Salvatore has betrayed the department. That makes no sense and there is no evidence to support it. Salvatore's record is flawless and his dedication to this case has been crucial."

The reporter asks Umberto. "Have you read anything different in the article other than what Guido and the taxi driver said that night?"

"No, but your article damages the reputation of the people who dedicate and risk their lives to fight organized crime." Umberto answers.

"Is it true that you have closed Don Franco's complex for three days?"

"Yes, it's correct." Umberto answers.

"Is it true that Don Franco has collaborated with your investigation and that he has given free accommodation to three police officers in the complex so that they can search whenever and wherever they want?"

"Yes, it's correct."

"Have you searched Salvatore's house?"

"Your question is offensive." Umberto responds, flushed.

"Didn't you said there would not be a stone left unturned, or you don't want to check under that stone?"

Umberto realized his interview had been a failure, and he was doing more damage to the department. Umberto saw the opportunity to end the interview without giving suspicion.

"I have not searched Salvatore's house, because I know he is not a traitor, but to dismiss any suspicions, I invite you to accompany us to search his residence right now. I will get in touch with Salvatore, and I assure you he will give us consent to search his residence without a search warrant."

Franco was watching Umberto's live interview in his office. He immediately contacted Augusto and ordered that Don Cristino's cap be thrown on Salvatore's balcony. Augusto sent Donato in a hurry to throw Don Cristino's cap on Salvatore's balcony. Donato passed by Salvatore's apartment before the police and the press arrived. Since Salvatore had rented an apartment on the second floor of a building facing the entrance to the hill. Donato easily threw the cap onto Salvatore's balcony.

Umberto made a phone call to Salvatore from the press office and did not have to give any explanation, as Salvatore was also watching the interview. Salvatore replied.

"It will be a pleasure. I will show them I have nothing to hide."

An hour later, Umberto, Salvatore, two reporters, and three police officers enter Salvatore's apartment. Salvatore mockingly even opened the drawers for them to see and said.

"Look here, just in case Don Cristino hides in the drawers."

They were leaving, when Salvatore says.

"You are missing the balcony. Maybe he is there, sitting on a chair covered with a blanket."

"Enough, you made your point. We have no time to waste." Umberto answers him.

Salvatore, angrily, responds.

"No, my reputation has been questioned. I want them to search the balcony. Just as you said, there cannot be a stone left unturned."

Salvatore was enraged. He kicked open the balcony doors abruptly. They all turned when they heard the roar from Salvatore.

"Damn you, you're a son of a bitch." Everyone runs, thinking that Don Cristino is on the balcony.

Salvatore points to the cap and says.

"That is Don Cristino's cap. They are doing everything possible to get me involved."

Reporters run to the balcony and start taking photos. Umberto is speechless. He wants to strangle Salvatore. If this comes to light, the damage will be irreversible. Umberto takes the initiative and says.

"Please, I want to ask you a great favor. It is not an order or an imposition, it is a great favor. It is obvious that our enemies are following the news and are using the press to divert attention. They knew we would search Salvatore's apartment. It is very easy to throw that cap onto the balcony from the street. The only thing this shows is that Don Cristino is on the island and he is desperate because we are getting closer to him. If you publish this, you will do the criminals a great favor and a great harm to the investigation."

A reporter answers. "Our duty is to report what happened and the people must draw their own conclusions. We do not add or take anything away from the story."

"I'm not telling you not to publish it, just that it is not the time to publish it. I beg you, please."

The reporters decided not to publish what happened for the time being, and Umberto was relieved. Umberto was puzzled. He wondered how the cap could appear so quickly on Salvatore's balcony. For three days he had kept police officers in Franco's compound, one officer in each farm and the hill surrounded. Only the residents of the hill came in and out. He thought about the possibility Don Cristino was hiding in town. This would make the search much more difficult.

Umberto makes a call to Rome from Raffaelle's office reporting what happened and asks for more reinforcement, but his boss refuses and only gives him permission to keep the staff on the island for a week. Umberto finishes his call and Raffaelle tells him.

"Franco is on the line. He wants to talk to you."

"Tell him I have nothing to talk to him." Umberto answers.

"I think you better take the call, otherwise we will have problems."

"He is the one that has a big problem, not me." Umberto says, angrily.

"I'm sorry Don Franco, but Umberto can't talk to you now." Raffaelle responds.

"Very well. In this case, you are in charge of taking care of the problem."

"What problem?" Raffaelle asks.

"You are in charge of enforcing the law on our island. It is illegal to have an eternal search on my property, nor can my business be closed with no cause. I have collaborated and will collaborate with what is asked of me, but I demand I be allowed to open my business or be compensated for the time it remains closed. I agree to collaborate. You can have three police officers in the complex as long as they wear civilian clothes. If I don't have an answer in half an hour, I will file a lawsuit and go to the press to report this outrage."

Raffaelle closed her eyes, took a deep breath, and answered.

"Yes Don Franco, I will contact you within half an hour."

Umberto looks at Raffaelle and says. "So, now Franco orders you what to do."

"No, but what we are doing is illegal, and he knows it. He says he will sue us if we keep him closed."

"I don't give a damn if he sues us. Let him do it." Umberto answers.

"He says I must act to stop this injustice. I will be in trouble if you do nothing."

"But are you going to let yourself be blackmailed by that bully?" Umberto answers.

"It is not blackmailing. You know the law is on his side. I don't want my name to be dragged in the mid by the press."

"Did he tell you he would go to the press?" Umberto asks, a little worried.

"Yes, he says he would report us to the press and sue us."

Umberto gets up from the chair immediately.

"We're going to his complex. We will work out something with him, but we cannot afford any more negative publicity."

Raffaelle noticed Umberto's change in attitude when he mentioned the press.

"What happens? Are there problems with the press?"

"No, I just don't want this to turn into a circus."

Raffaelle and Umberto arrive at the compound, and Raffaelle thinks Umberto will stand firm in his position. Umberto sees Franco and tells him.

"I want to apologize for our delay and thank you for your cooperation in this case. I sincerely appreciate your offer to allow three officers to stay at the compound. Today I will replace them with others in civilian clothes. I would appreciate if you allowed free access to the complex."

Franco, with his characteristic coldness, answers him.

"I understand, and I regret not being able to help you with anything else. If I had imagined Don Cristino was such a character, I would have kept him for you. I want you to leave your staff here so that you can convince yourself I have nothing to hide. I assure you they will have full access to the complex. I could have never imagined a person so old who seems so harmless could be so dangerous."

Raffaelle turned around and separated himself from the group. He did not want to continue listening to that duel of lies. Umberto finishes talking to Franco and leaves the complex with Raffaelle, who asks him on the way.

"What is happening? I understand nothing."

Umberto shakes his head and answers.

"What is happening is that today we found Don Cristino's cap on Salvatore's balcony."

"What did you say? Oh, my God! It that can't be!" Raffaelle responds alarmed.

"Yes, I convinced the press not to publish it. They have a plan to divert attention and demoralize us. I think they have won that battle, but what worries me the most is that Franco is trying to make me believe Salvatore is involved. He said he will prove it to me. I know he is up to something, and I am afraid he will leak it to the press. He got me by the balls and each time he squeezes them tighter."

Franco saw a business opportunity and put out a commercial.

"Come to the safest tourist complex in the country, and if you find Don Cristino, not only your stay will be free, but you will receive a reward courtesy of the government plus an extra bonus from us. You can see Don Cristino's room with his belongings, which have been left intact as a museum."

The response to the commercial was instantaneous, reservations were almost impossible, and Franco began to charge for the tour of Don Cristino's room.

After two weeks, Umberto receives orders to return to Rome and his staff is cut to ten police officers on the island. Umberto says goodbye to Raffaelle, who remains in command of the operation, and the ten extra officers. Raffaelle shakes hands with Umberto tells him.

"I promise you I will do everything in my power to capture Don Cristino."

Raffaelle orders the police officers to withdraw from the complex and the farms, puts them in key points and maintains strict control of all ships leaving the island. Salvatore shows up at Raffaelle's office and, visibly offended, asks him.

"Under what authority have you withdrawn the police from the complex and the farms, since when you oversee this operation?"

"Since the moment Umberto ordered me to be in charge. You cannot be in charge. There are suspicions against you."

Salvatore flushed. "How dare you accuse me of something like that?"

"No, I am not accusing you. I just follow the procedures. I do not suspect you at all, but I have no alternative. I ask that if you have any information, please communicate by phone, but do not come back here until this is over."

Salvatore was about to explode. His jugular vein was clearly visible. He was adjusting his tie as if he was choking, but he understood Raffaelle was right. He turns to leave, then stops and punches three times on the wall and screams.

"Franco orchestrates this. He managed to get me off the case, but he won't get away with it, I swear."

After thirty days, Rafaelle received orders from Umberto to end the search. It didn't take long for the press to react. One of the most costly and lengthy operations in history had ended, to no avail. Luckily, the press never mentioned Don Cristino's cap found in Salvatore's apartment. Franco went every day to see Don Cristino, who was thrilled in his hiding place. Don Cristino asks Franco.

"When and how do I leave here?"

"We have to wait a month after they finish the search, we will use that month to find you a safe place in a place of your choice, then we will stab Salvatore one more time before you leave."

"What do you have in mind, bandit?" Asks the old man.

"When Salvatore is far from his apartment, we will take you to his apartment. You will stand on his balcony, and we will take photos and film from the street. Then we will take photos of you leaving his building and walking towards the corner."

Don Cristino could not stop laughing.

"You are worse than a bully, because they kill you with one shot and it's over, but you kill little by little."

"I have requested three special people for this operation, a locksmith, a big and ugly giant and a makeup and costumes artist."

Don Cristino laughs out loud. "My God! Don't tell me anything else. I want to enjoy the moment."

The expected day arrived. While Salvatore was far away from his house, one of Franco's employees drove an empty delivery truck with everything necessary to disguise Don Cristino. The locksmith and the big giant with the monster's face got out of the truck, went to Salvatore's apartment, and picked open the door without forcing it. Once inside, they gave the signal to Don Cristino to leave the truck and walk to Salvatore's apartment. Luigi filmed Don Cristino entering the building and having a drink on Salvatore's balcony. Don Cristino left his prints all over the apartment; he even used the toilet and did not flush it. When they were leaving, they made enough noise for the neighbor to come outside.

The neighbors were an elderly couple. They opened the door to investigate what was happening. At that time, the big giant pulled out a revolver and yelled at them.

"Inside, right now."

The terrified couple did not know what to do. They had recognized Don Cristino leaving Salvatore's house. The giant told the locksmith.

"You take Don Cristino. Salvatore's contact is waiting for you down the street."

Luigi filmed Don Cristino leaving the building and walking towards the corner. Once at the corner, he enters the back of the truck, where the make-up artist begins his transformation into an old lady.

Meanwhile, the old couple has been tied up, and their mouths covered. The giant tells them.

"If you say something about Salvatore we will return, but next time we will not be so friendly."

The locksmith went to the truck to get what they prepared for the elderly couple. It was a chair about a meter high with a funnel at the bottom. From the bottom of the funnel hung four rubber bands that held a large pot. The locksmith places a large block of ice on the chair and ties one end of the tie from the old man's hand with a rope, then ties the other end of the rope to the pot. Then they leave and close the door.

Franco calculated it would take three hours for the ice to melt, fall into the pot, which by gravity would lower and pull the old man's tie, freeing him. That would be long enough for Don Cristino to be in Naples. Don Cristino was disguised as a lovely old lady in a wheelchair. He would not raise suspicions at all, because the expert had entered the Island disguised as an old lady in a wheelchair and Don Cristino would use the same documents. Franco's plan worked perfectly. Two police officers who felt sorry for the old lady in the wheelchair helped Don Cristino. They helped her get on the ferry while the giant and the locksmith kept continuous surveillance at a safe distance.

Three hours later, the old man unties himself and calls the police station, denouncing what happened. Raffaelle cannot believe what is hearing, but he has no choice but to go to the scene.

The old couple is terrified. They have binding marks on their hands and feet. There is also the strange chair with the pot full of water in the elderly room. Raffaelle asks the elders.

"Have you talked to Salvatore?"

The old woman answers, almost crying and trembling with fear.

"No, they warned us clearly they would come back and kill us if we denounced Salvatore."

Raffaelle does not believe in the story of the elders, but he has evidence of a crime, so he must investigate. Raffaelle tells the elders they need not fear he will investigate Salvadore's apartment and return in a moment.

Raffaelle knocks at Salvatore's apartment, who had just returned to his apartment. Raffaelle's visit surprises Salvatore.

"Hello Don Raffaelle, what a surprise. Something must be happening."

Raffaelle doesn't even know where to start, but he needs to clarify the situation.

"Salvatore, I will begin by telling you I do not think you are involved in this and that this is another attempt to divert attention. I do not know what else to say."

"But speak. Nothing surprises me anymore." Salvatore responds.

"The neighbors across are saying Don Cristino left your apartment with two men and that they threatened to kill them if they reported you."

Salvatore laughs and says.

"Finally, something funny has happened to me today, because the day has been horrible. I just arrived and opened my door. Please check everything and take fingerprints. I do not want any doubt about my cooperation."

Raffaelle sends to take prints and while they take the prints, Salvatore tells Raffaelle.

"One thing I know for sure, these bandits are not stupid. They would not walk Don Cristino through the city, much less bring him to my house."

The police officer in charge of taking the prints comes over and says. "Boss, I'm done."

Salvatore could not bear his arrogance and tells him.

"No, you are not finished yet. You missed the toilet."

"I do not think that it's necessary." They laugh.

"No, I insist. It is the only thing you are missing."

Raffaelle and the officer refuse to go to Salvatore's bathroom. Salvatore goes to the bathroom. He is holding the door with his left hand while with his right hand he makes a mocking curtsy, inviting them to enter.

Raffaelle and the officer continue to leave Salvatore's apartment, when they hear a scream from inside Salvatore's apartment.

"Sons of bitches, damn Franco. He was here."

Salvatore had discovered Don Cristino used the toilet and did not flush it. Raffaelle walks in and sees the gift Don Cristino has left for Salvatore and he cannot help laughing.

"I do not find this funny. These bandits walk around your island with impunity and laugh at us that way."

"Take it easy Salvatore, this confirms you are not involved, but the question remains. Where is Don Cristino?"

Salvatore and Raffaelle went to see the elders to convince them it was all a plot by Don Cristino to implicate Salvatore. But from day on they slam shut the door if they saw Salvatore.

Three days later, Franco calls Raffaelle and tells him he has news of Don Cristino, but he will only give it to him in person. Raffaelle felt a cold on his back. He did not want to be entangled in this problem, but once again, he was forced to do his duty.

Raffaelle enters Franco's office, who was waiting for him with four envelopes on top of his desk. Franco tells him.

"I promised Umberto and you I would show if there was a relationship between Salvatore and Don Cristino."

Franco passes the envelopes to Raffaelle and tells him.

"Here are pictures and films of Don Cristino entering and leaving Salvatore's house. There are copies for you and Umberto. He is staying there. The rest is up to you."

Raffaelle takes the envelopes and tells him.

"Thanks Don Franco, I ask you not to give this information to the press."

"Why are you asking me that? Do you want to cover up for Salvatore? Franco asks.

"No, I just don't like to accuse anyone without being one hundred percent sure they are guilty. There is a possibility that Don Cristino has manipulated everything, so we would accuse Salvatore."

"You are absolutely right, and I admire you for your professionalism. It is a shame that Salvatore does not apply the same rules."

Raffaelle thanks Franco for his collaboration and leaves.

Upon arriving at the police station, Raffaelle calls Umberto and tells him he has photos and films taken by Franco of Don Cristino leaving and entering Salvatore's house and that Don Cristino's fingerprints were found in the apartment but that he has the feeling that Salvatore is not is involved.

CHAPTER TEN

MATEO

Salvatore returns to Rome and goes straight to Umberto's office. Salvatore sees Umberto's unfriendly face and realizes he is going to have a tough battle to ask for another opportunity.

"Well, Salvatore, this is your second consecutive failure. You already ruined Pablo's work in Naples, which means two years of work lost and now such a media fiasco."

"Boss, I spent three days analyzing what happened and searching for an explanation for this failure. I not only have the explanation, I also find out how to prevent them from getting away with it next time."

"Who said there is a next time? Are not enough three deaths, a burn detective and making me look like a clown in front of the media?"

"Excuse me, Umberto. We have lost some battles, but not the war. Please listen to me and you will understand why we will have no failure next time."

Umberto stares at Salvatore and responds.

"I do not recognize you. You are a different person. I told you that your obsession with Franco would bring you problems, but you are dragging me with you. I am not willing to fall with you because of your obsession with Franco."

"Sir, let me explain and in the end, I will respect your decision, but listen to me until the end, please." Salvatore answered him.

Umberto leaned back in his chair and answered. "Let's see Salvatore explain yourself."

Salvatore felt relief when Umberto gave him the opportunity to explain himself.

"Our plan was correct. Manino was murdered in the complex. Nothing more has been heard from him and no one else has ever seen him again. The photo was a trick. Everyone is being photographed twice on the same day with different clothes and with the day changed in the calendar. This way, they prove Manino left that day. All the taxi drivers work for Franco. It is obvious he testified he transported Manino to the port. We searched everywhere and there was no sign of violence, which means he was poisoned and buried in the garden, as it is the only place where the earth is constantly moved to plant new ornamental plants. That is why we do not find the body. There you have the answer to how they covered up the crime. Now the solution is simple. They think they beat us, and they will do the same, eventually. This time we will have dogs that detect corpses. As you can see, boss, a lost battle does not mean we lost the war. It is our decision to surrender or to regain the pride of our institution."

Umberto analyzed what Salvatore had said and saw logic in it. He wanted to give him the benefit of the doubt and he needed a victory, since lately things have not gone well at all.

"I will speak with my superiors, but I assure you, it will not be easy for me to convince them. Do not come back to my office. I will contact you when I have the answer. Now go home and take a week off. You look terrible. Go home and rest. I'm not suggesting it. I'm ordering you."

"I will do so, sir. Remember, if we have failed, it has been because of lack of resources and because if we had had the dogs...."

"Enough, Salvatore, enough, go home." Umberto answered, annoyed.

Salvatore left the office praying for a new opportunity. When walking through the corridors, he realized things had changed dramatically. It was not like before, when his colleagues greeted him with admiration and respect. Now they don't even look at him and try to avoid him.

Meanwhile, in Ischia, the organization pressured Franco to buy Vittorio's business. Franco had lengthened this moment because of the underground construction, which could house thirty people with all the comforts. Franco asked for more time. The electrical part and some plumbing details were missing. He explained that such construction done in secret takes time. They all agreed to give him one more year to finish the project.

Franco hoped that after such an embarrassment, Salvatore would not return to Ischia, but what was his surprise when, after four months, he heard the bird had returned to the nest. Umberto had convinced his bosses that with the help of dogs they would have found the body, since they have never heard from Manino again and next time they will send trained dogs with the undercover personnel as pets, so Franco would not find out about it.

Salvatore returns, but this time he comes with a letter from Rome and goes straight to the police station. He gives the letter to the on-duty officer and tells him.

"Give this to your boss and tell him I will contact him only if it is necessary."

Salvatore left without saying a word or saying goodbye to any of the c. The duty officer handed the letter to Raffaelle who, after reading it, punched the table and said.

"What a disgrace this man is. He is worse than scabies. This has become something personal for him and a circus for the press of which he is the clown and still does not realize it. What bothers me the most is that it involves us. We had always enjoyed peace until this stupid charlatan arrived."

Salvatore returned to his apartment and met with Benito again. Benito tells Salvatore.

"Franco is looking for the person who gives you the information. It is a matter of time before they discover me and if I am going to continue taking risks, you will have to give me double in case I have to disappear."

Salvatore was already putting money out of his pocket, but he needed the information and asking Rome for more money would be suicide for him, so he agreed to pay more. Luigi, through his contacts, found out Benito had contact with Salvatore and that Benito's economic standard had risen significantly. Luigi walks into Franco's office and tells him.

"Don Franco, I have information which I had not told you until I could verify it."

"Interesting. Let's see what you are bringing me." Franco responds.

"It is Benito who is giving information to Salvatore. He works in the port control office and we know they communicate. Also, Salvatore pays very well for the information, because Benito's standard of living does not match his salary."

"Very good job Luigi." Franco replies.

"I just wait for your approval to eliminate him. You know we cannot have a loose snitch. That means we are vulnerable, and we would lose respect."

"No Luigi, don't touch him. I have another idea. He might serve us in the future. We know Salvatore checks his tree once a week. One week before the next meeting, we will surprise him."

Luigi was confused.

"Don Franco, I do not understand, nor do I agree, but you are the boss, and you always see things far beyond. It will be done as you say. I am sure it will be a better result."

Franco tells Luigi.

"I need you to stop by Vittorio's business and tell him I need to speak to him. I would like his family to spend a weekend at the complex."

"Tomorrow I will pass by that location for sure because I have to buy cleaning supplies for the complex."

Luigi did not like the idea of going to see Vittorio. He still could not forget Vittorio had rejected Franco's offer. The next morning Luigi shows up at Vittorio's business, who recognized him instantly.

"Good morning, Don Vittorio."

"Good morning, ah ah ah!"

"Luigi, my name is Luigi."

"I'm sorry I didn't remember your name, but I remember you perfectly. How can I help you, Don Luigi?" Vittorio answers.

"Actually, I come on behalf of your friend Don Franco, who is eager to see you and wants to invite you and your family to spend a weekend at the complex when you can."

Vittorio looks at Luigi and answers.

"Don Luigi, Franco is not my friend, he is my brother. I haven't seen him for a long time. I would love to see him. I don't know Don Franco and I don't accept invitations from strangers. Anyway, I appreciate the invitation."

Luigi, annoyed, responds. "I want you to know Don Franco is your friend. Many people would like to have the privilege of having an honorable, faithful, and humble friend like Don Franco. It is a pity that you refuse to recognize his positive qualities and allow yourself to be carried away by the rumors and the injustice of Salvatore, who falsely accused him of murder."

Vittorio shakes his head and replies. "I know Franco and Don Franco have many qualities in common and I am glad, but my answer does not change. It is still "NO" and if you need nothing else, I must help my son fix an engine. Have a nice day."

Luigi felt the same anger again as the first time. Luigi thought when he left the business. "I must put this old man in his place."

Luigi entered Franco's office and Franco told him. "Vittorio told you no."

"How do you know?"

"Because I know him, and I was not expecting another answer from him. We will try another time. Now we have another little thing to do."

"But sir, we must put this Vittorio in his place. He treats us with no respect." Luigi answers, furiously.

"No Luigi! Don't you dare touch him. Vittorio is a man of honor, respectful, and brave. That must be respected."

Luigi felt furious. This Vittorio had rejected his boss for the second time, and his boss had defended him instead of giving him what he deserved. Franco changed the subject of the conversation so that Luigi would calm down a bit.

"Luigi, next month we have a meeting. Five days before the meeting, you need to go to Salvatore's nest and put on food, drinks, and a new blanket for him. You will also put the list of the names of people that will attend the meeting with a note that says Courtesy of Monte Santo Tourist Complex."

"But Don Franco, have you gone crazy?"

"Do as I tell you and you'll see what happens." Franco replied.

Luigi did not understand, but he trusted Franco blindly. Five days before the meeting, Luigi went to Salvatore's tree, brought groceries, drinks, a new blanket and put down the list of the names Franco gave him.

As usual, Salvatore went to check his tree on Monday morning. He could not believe what he saw. His hiding place had been discovered and even worse, he did not know since when. When he read the note, it was as if he had been stabbed. He realized his informer, to whom he had paid so much money, was discovered and Franco did not care at all. He kept the list to confirm if Franco's list would be the same as Benito's. Salvatore climbed down from his tree and left, totally demoralized.

That evening, Benito contacts Salvatore, and he tells him.

"I have good news. There is an important meeting. Thirteen people will arrive tomorrow. Something big is cooking. I will give you the list tonight. Do not forget the prices have changed."

"Of course, we already talked about that." Salvatore responds as if nothing had happened.

That night when they met, Salvatore pulls his list out of his pocket and tells Benito,

"Let me see your list to compare it with mine."

Benito, surprised, asked. "What did you say? How do you have a list?"

"I have a list and it cost me ten time cheaper, but I have to verify it with yours. It may not be correct." Salvatore replied.

Benito gives the list to Salvatore. Salvatore cannot believe it. They are identical. He was sure Franco was up to something, but he would think about it later. Now he had to negotiate with Benito. Salvatore gives Benito the two lists and tells him.

"As you can see, they are identical. You are not the only one who has this information. What can you tell me about it?"

"I do not know, sir. I thought I was the only one, but as you see, someone else can do it. I don't know how, but is true." Benito replied.

"However, I trusted you more than this other person, so we return to the initial price, or it is all over here." Salvatore said bluntly.

Benito understood that little is better than nothing. He agreed without thinking twice. Luigi had followed Benito since he left his job at the port. He witnessed Benito's meeting from a distance and watched the list exchange. Luigi went straight to see Franco. It was late at night, but that was Franco's order. Luigi entered the complex and Guido told him, Don Franco is waiting for you at the office. Luigi entered the office and Franco was waiting for him at his desk.

"Everything went as you predicted, Don Franco. But now what next?"

"Now we have him on the defensive and we will capitalize on his mistakes." Answers Franco.

Salvatore was scratching his head, trying to decipher Franco's plan. He concludes that Franco's plan was to discredit him. That after such a failure, no judge would give him a search warrant for the same reason without new evidence. Salvatore was happy. Now he had the dogs and that would reveal the exact place to search. Salvatore felt encouraged again. He would go to his tree and do the same things he had always done.

On Monday morning, Salvatore was in his tree and, as usual, took data and photos of everyone who arrived. He confirmed that the thirteen people mentioned in the list were in the complex. The meeting at the complex lasted four days, during which Franco announced that the underground shelter would be finished in two months and new contracts and alliances were made. Then Don Genaro asked to speak. Everyone thought they had finished, but Don Genaro, with a portfolio in his hands, addresses everyone.

"Unfortunately, within our group, we have a traitor."

Everyone was stunned by such an accusation.

"Don Mateo, not only he has robbed us, but he planned to sell us to the authorities."

Mateo stands up, enraged, and screams. "How dare you say such an infamy?

Genaro opens his portfolio, takes out various documents and photos.

"Not only do I say it, but I also prove it. Here is the proof of your thefts. The photos of you with the detective you have had meetings with."

Genaro passes the documents and pictures for everyone to see. The evidence clearly showed Mateo had diverted fifteen million lire to a secret account in Switzerland. Franco, who is chairing the meeting, asks for order and gives Mateo the opportunity to speak in his defense. Mateo knows he has no defense and responds.

"I can return the money plus the interest that you decide as a penalty."

Franco asks him. "And what do you say about the meeting with the detective?"

"The detective is a childhood friend. He gave me information and protection during operations. I never told him about you. No one should be scared, more than a detective, he is one of us."

Franco asks Don Genaro. "How long have Don Mateo and this detective been in contact?"

"As far as I know, it is over five months."

"Well, if you say five months, this means it has been much longer. If he was really working for the police, we would all be in prison by now." Franco responds.

"So, what are we going to do, Don Mateo?" Genaro asks, while everyone else shouts at Mateo "TRAITOR, THIEF!" Franco asks for calm and answers.

"Here the rules were set from the beginning, and all of us accepted it. Mateo, like Manino before, will serve as tomatoes fertilizer on Augusto's farm."

At that point, Luigi and two others immobilized Mateo and covered his mouth.

"What will happen to the detective?" Yells one in the group.

Don Genaro responds immediately. "You do not have to worry about him. He is already sleeping with the fishes. Maybe what Don

Mateo told us about the detective is true, but we could not take risks."

Franco moved a painting on the wall to the side. Behind the painting there was a series of different color switches. Franco pressed the red switch twice and put the painting back in its place. Franco asked for calm and thanked Don Genaro for his good work. In less than five minutes, Augusto showed up with his two sons.

"Here we are, Don Franco. What do you need?" Augusto asked.

"Just take this man and turn him into fertilizer for your tomatoes."

Without saying a word, Augusto and his two sons took Mateo away. Franco and the remaining twelve accompanied Augusto through the tunnel to Augusto's estate, where Mateo was eliminated. Then everyone returned to the complex, stayed one more day to take additional security measures and reaffirm that the end of Manino and Mateo would be the same for those who dared to steal or betray the organization. The next day, Franco's guests left. Salvatore photographed and wrote the departure time of each one. At 2:00 p.m., twelve people had left, and one was missing. Salvatore looked at his report and saw that Mateo was missing. He decided to wait for two more days before contacting Umberto.

Salvatore calls Umberto and explains to him what had happened. He asks for reinforcement and the dogs as soon as possible. Umberto goes to the island to oversee the operation. He was in debt to his superiors and needed a big win.

The very next day, Umberto, three police officers, and a police dog trainer arrived in Ischia. They went to the police station to see Raffaelle. Raffaelle immediately put himself at Umberto's orders. He took two more police officer with him. Umberto requested the press to join in. He needed to rebuild his image. The judge did not want to sign the search warrant, but he did when he learned there were high-ranking personnel who had come from Rome. Four police vehicles closed the entrance to the complex. Once again, Salvatore came forward to savor his victory, but he let Umberto be the one to speak. Raffaelle was with them, but he did not say a word. Guido calmly and said.

"Good afternoon, gentlemen. How can I help you?"

Umberto replied.

"We need to speak to Don Franco, please."

"Yes, sir, I'll call him right away."

Guido picks up the phone and asks Franco to come to the front desk. Franco shows up at the reception and says.

"Good afternoon, gentlemen. Welcome back. How can I help you?"

Franco understands that this time Salvatore is not in command.

"Don Franco, we have a search warrant for your complex."

Franco calmly responds.

"Sir, excuse me, I know we met before, but I don't remember your name." Franco responds.

"My name is Umberto. I am the chief of the organized crime investigation division."

It's a pleasure to see you again. As I said to Salvatore the last time he came with a search warrant. You can come as many times as you want. You don't need a warrant."

Franco, addressing Raffaelle, asks. "Isn't it true I told him that the last time, Don Raffaelle?"

"Yes, it is Don Franco." Raffaelle responds.

"Here, we do not hide or do anything illegal. You should know that by now. What I believe is illegal is Salvatore constantly spied on me, falsely accused me and that I lost my freedom because of circumstantial evidence he used to fabricate a case against me, knowing I was innocent of that crime."

Umberto was impressed. Franco expressed himself as if he was a lawyer.

"Why did you plead guilty then, if you were innocent?" Umberto replied.

Franco looks at Salvatore and asks him. "What did you come out with now, Salva?"

Salvatore responds.

"It is not what I invented but what I discovered." Defiantly Salvatore responds.

At that precise moment, the reporter shoots a photo almost identical to the previous one with a defiant Salvatore in front of a calm Franco, but this time Umberto is in the middle, as if he was the game referee. Salvatore shows a picture to Franco and asks him.

"Do you remember this man?"

"Not again with the same thing, Salva, please." Franco responds.

Umberto intervenes and tells Franco.

"Just answer. Your comments are unnecessary."

Franco responds. "Then I prefer you ask me. I am sure the questions will be more sensible."

Franco turns to Guido. "Guido, bring the records, please."

"You can save yourself the work. We already know your tricks on the photographs and the signatures. This time it will not work." Said Salvatore.

"No, we need the photos and the records. They are part of the evidence." Interrupts Umberto.

"But what am I accused of? Can someone tell me?"

"The murder of Mateo, from which you will not get away as you did with Manino."

"Oh my god, again with the same thing." Franco responds and asks Guido.

"At what time did Don Mateo leave?"

"I do not remember exactly, but it is in the log the officer confiscated."

Salvatore tells Umberto." If you look at the log, you can see the departure time. They also have photos of the reception and farewell, as I told you. They think we're stupid."

Franco goes to Guido and tells him. "Please call the taxi drivers."

The reporter's photo captured Salvatore's overconfident laugh in front of Franco.

"We already know your trick. The taxi driver will say he left him at the port or anywhere else where we can't track him."

Umberto says. "I want the information of the taxi drivers who transported him. They also will be charged with lying and covering up a crime."

"You are right, another one falls." Yells Salvatore.

Franco goes to Umberto and tells him.

"Sir, I feel Salvatore deceives you. He did not take that picture to create this whole circus, which is destroying my business and my reputation."

The taxi drivers enter, and Salvatore shows the photograph, yelling at them.

"Think carefully before answering, because whoever says he transported this person may get criminal charges for lying and covering up a crime."

A taxi driver says. "I remember him. I took him in my taxi."

Salvatore stands in front of the taxi driver. The taxi driver was a small man about five feet tall, known for his explosive temper. Salvatore looks down at him and hits the taxi driver on the head with his finger.

"Did you hear what I said, or do I have to repeat it again? Think before you answered."

The taxi driver got angry. He took a step back, took off his cap, and threw it at Salvatore, hitting him in his right eye. The taxi driver took a fighting stand while challenging Salvatore to fight. Umberto yelled at the taxi driver to stop, but the driver was out of control. Luigi grabbed the driver from behind and lifted him up while he kept trying to kick Salvatore. The picture of Luigi holding the taxi driver up in the air in front of Salvatore, rubbing his eye as if he was crying, became famous nationwide. The taxi driver would not stop until Franco asked him to stop. The taxi driver apologized to Franco and says.

"You don't need to repeat the question. I took him with me. I don't remember the exact time, but I remember where I took him."

"Sure, you left him in a place where we can't verify, like the port, on the corner, or a restaurant. Shall I continue?" Salvatore responds in a sarcastic way.

"If Mateo went somewhere else after I dropped him off, I don't know, and I don't care. The only thing I know is that I saw him entering the Roma Hotel. I think they must have logged his registration." The taxi driver replies.

Salvatore's and Umberto's faces suddenly changed to puzzled faces.

"Where did you take him?" Umberto asked.

"To the Roma Hotel." The taxi driver answered.

Umberto tells Raffaelle. "Please send a police officer urgently to confiscate the registration book of that hotel and bring it to me immediately."

"Yes sir," Raffaelle replies.

Salvatore mockingly says. "Too bad they don't have registration, or maybe Mateo changed his mind and went to another hotel. Right, sir?"

The taxi driver shrugs his shoulders and says, "Sir, if the hotel does not have registration or Don Mateo went somewhere else, I don't know, and I don't care. The only thing I know is that I saw him entering the Roma Hotel. I think they should have his registration."

"I knew it. That story is old. You could be a little more creative." Laughs Salvatore.

"Well, are you going to search, or are we going to talk and argue?" Franco asks.

Umberto looks at Franco and asks him. "Are you in a hurry, Don Franco?"

Franco laughs and responds. "No, on the contrary. I am not going, nor will I go anywhere for many years. I owe that to this man. The presence of Salvatore disgusts me and the day you find out who this man is, you will regret having him on your team."

"When he saw Franco's calm, he began to have doubts about the search. Umberto approaches Raffaelle and asks him in a low voice. "What do you think of this?"

"I don't know what to say, sir. I've already gone through an embarrassment, and I think we're going the same way. If it is true they eliminated this Mateo, I assure you that nothing worthwhile will be lost, but if we fail, the press will have a banquet and you will be the main dish."

Raffaelle's opinion put Umberto in more trouble, who had not given the order to start the search yet.

Salvatore asks Umberto. "What is the holdup, boss? We should start the search. Everything is happening as I told you it was going to happen."

Umberto was sweating and his only thought was what explanation he would give to his superiors for not having acted, because something was telling him not to do it. When Umberto called in the police dog. Franco was surprised.

"What about this dog, Salva? Is that your new plan?"

"Today you can call me Salva or whatever you want. You do not bother me. As you can see, the search won't last long." Salvatore replied.

"Oh, no Salva! You can't bring a whole zoo if you want. Your stupidity has stopped astonishing me." Franco replies.

At that moment, the phone rings and Guido answers it.

"It is for you, Don Umberto."

Salvatore says. "Let me guess. They have no registration available."

Umberto looks at Salvatore and tells him. "I don't want to hear another word from you. Is that clear?"

"Yes, sir." Salvatore replied, freezing.

Umberto picks up the phone and yells.

"What do you mean, he is registered? Bring me that book immediately!"

Umberto's face was red with rage and Salvatore looked confused. At that moment came the second photo from the reporters. Umberto did nothing, waiting for the Hotel Roma registration book. Salvatore began to despair, but he did not dare to speak a word. Franco tells Guido.

"Guido, please order something to drink for six people."

"Yes sir, right away."

About ten minutes later, Guido appears with the drinks and begins to distribute them. One for the police with the dog, two for the two reporters, one for Raffaelle, and one for Umberto. Salvatore extends his hand to take the last one, but Franco tells Guido.

"No Guido, that's for me. Salva is not on my guest list."

Guido turns around and Salvatore stands with his hand extended. Franco takes the drink, raises it as a toast and says.

"Enjoy it. It is the pride of our vineyard."

The police officer arrives in a hurry with the Hotel Roma registration book. Umberto takes it and checks the signatures, which appear to be authentic. Umberto punches the table. Salvatore approaches him and says.

"Sir, it is a well-thought-out plan. The signatures are authentic because they have connections with that hotel, but that man never left this place."

Umberto tells Salvatore. "Let me think in peace. I don't need your opinions."

Umberto passes by Raffaelle and asks him again. "What would you do?"

"A retreat is better than a defeat." Raffaelle replies.

Umberto looks at him and asks him. "Whose side are you on?"

"Neither side. I am on the side of common sense. If it smells very bad, it is because is very bad." Raffaelle replied.

Umberto began to distrust Raffaelle. Perhaps he was in Franco's payroll, so made his decision.

"Start the search. I want everything and I everything to be searched."

The police began to search with the help of the police dog. The more time they spent searching, the more Umberto became worried, and the more excited Salvatore became. Franco remained seated, reading a magazine. Raffaelle scratched his head and tried to find an angle in case the reporter took a photo, he wouldn't appear in it. After three hours, a police officer goes to Raffaelle and tells him.

"Chief, we have nothing." Raffaelle answers him.

"Don't tell me anything. Tell Umberto. He's in charge of the search."

Umberto felt like strangling Salvatore, but he held back. Umberto goes to the police dog trainer and asks him.

"Did you check everything, and the dog wasn't alerted?"

"Yes sir, there is no sign of violence, traces of blood or disturbed soil."

"Did you search the gardens?"

"Yes sir, I started in the gardens, but the dog didn't pick up an alert."

Umberto looks at Salvatore, wanting to kill him. Salvatore says furiously.

"It was to be expected."

Umberto yells at Salvatore. "What did you say, idiot? That was your great idea. Now you contradict yourself?"

At that moment, the flashes from the reporter's cameras seemed like fireworks, but that was the least of the matter to Umberto at that time. Salvatore tells Umberto.

"The dog is here in case they made the mistake."

"What mistake are you talking about, stupid?"

"Well, it is obvious they have spread some type of chemical or pepper so that the dog do not want to smell it and move away from the gardens."

Umberto, in despair, saw some logic in what Salvatore said and asked the police dog trainer.

"Is it true there are substances that can interfere with the dog's sense of smell?"

The officer takes a hesitates to answer. Umberto tells him." Just answer, yes or no?"

"Yes sir, it's true. The problem is, I think this is not the case."

Salvatore interrupts immediately.

"So, you have a better sense of smell than dogs. You can determine if there are substances or not."

"I only give my opinion based on the dog behavior and not my smell. The conversation is between my boss and I, so you stay out of it."

Franco could not hold back laughing and covered his face with the magazine so as not to disrespect Umberto. He knew the angrier Umberto got, the worse it would be for Salvatore. Franco gets up and tells the police officer.

"If you want, you can look in the garden again. Salva is very good at planting evidence. I wouldn't be surprised if he planted a skeleton in the garden."

Salvatore avalanches himself against Franco to hit him, but Raffaelle stops him. That led to another historical photo. Umberto analyzed what Salvatore, the police officer, and Franco said. Salvatore and the officer are right on what they said, but Franco was a mystery, because perhaps he said they should look in the garden, so they do not look in the garden. Umberto decides he is already involved, so he will go to the end.

"I want you to bring picks and shovels to check the gardens, even uproot the plants painted on the walls."

Salvatore felt relief when he heard that order from Umberto. Franco got up and said.

"No, you are going to destroy my complex. Who is going to pay for this?"

"So, first you wanted us to search and now you've changed your mind?" Umberto asks.

What Umberto did not realize was he was falling into Franco's trap. Raffaelle approaches Umberto and says in a low voice.

"Don't do it sir, you are letting yourself be carried away by your impulses and not by logic."

Umberto glares at Raffaelle.

"As you told your police officer, I am in charge here. It is my decision. You just make sure of getting the tools to check the gardens."

The flash of another historical photo, this time Umberto yelling at Raffaelle. After ten hours and the destruction of all the gardens in the complex, Umberto ended the search, to no avail.

Umberto left Ischia that night, but before leaving, he told Salvatore.

"Start thinking how you are going to get out of this mess you have gotten us into, because we will both have to testify before the bosses. I will wait for your call before 11:00 a.m. tomorrow. You better have the answer."

Salvatore was pale. He could hardly speak. "But boss, please understand."

"Nothing Salvatore, if you don't have an answer before 11:00 A.M.., forget that you ever worked in the investigations department."

CHAPTER ELEVEN

AUGUSTO

The next day, the photos of the failed search were on the front page with headlines of all kinds like: "Where are the Dead?" "Franco two Salvatore one". But the editorial that caused the most impact was: "Who Will Pay for This?" It showed photos of the destruction of all the grounds at the resort, plus multiple property damage. The article denounced all the damage done after the police dog trainer expert said the dog had not given an alert signal had been done with cruelty and revenge from Salvatore. Franco's popularity skyrocketed, but more importantly, even Umberto became suspicious of Salvatore after Franco's comments accusing Salvatore of fabricating evidence and false cases. Umberto decided not to investigate Salvatore. He knew Franco was not an angel either, and it would be a disaster if they discover Franco was innocent.

Franco took advantage of a reporter's interview to announce he would sue Salvatore for damages. When the reporter asked him.

"Why Salvatore and not Umberto? He was the head of the investigation or the investigation department?"

"Salvatore hates me. I don't know why. He has twice deceived Umberto into making false accusations which have brought not only material damage to my resort, but negative publicity. I am one step away from bankruptcy."

The reporter asks Franco.

"Why did you plead guilty if you say you are innocent? Also, the evidence was strong against you."

"That evidence you believe to be conclusive is circumstantial. The alleged witness who was going to testify against me was dead, but he made me believe he was alive and would testify against me to reduce his sentence. I had no choice. If I was going to trial, the witness would blame me for everything so he could get out free. That's why they offered me house arrest to accept the charges. If I had gone to trial, they would not have a case against me."

The reporter ends up telling Franco.

"Your defense sounds very interesting, but not convincing."

"I know, but I believe in a promise I made to Salvatore in which he was going to confess everything I have said is true, that I am innocent of that crime and that I was deceived and unjustly imprisoned."

The surprised reporter asks him.

"Did Salvatore promise that?"

"No, I promised that to Salvatore and now I promise you."

That interview was broadcast live nationwide.

After such publicity, Umberto was destroyed. Many things did not fit, but if he turned against Salvatore, it would be the end of his carrier, because he was the one who recommended Salvatore. Salvatore called Umberto at 10:30 a.m. and told him he had the answer to everything that happened, that he should not worry, but rejoice. He will show they not only acted correctly, but they discovered how the mafia worked in the complex. Umberto asked him to explain it, but Salvatore refused. He told Umberto that the meeting would be in a week, and he needed those days to gather more information. Umberto, not totally convinced, answered,

"It better be true because if I do not have an answer to convince the bosses and I lose my job because of you, you better disappear from the face of the earth."

Franco opens the tourist complex again to the public and closes it during the meetings. The business made a big profit since now everyone wanted to visit the famous tourist complex. Franco sent Luigi to contact all the members of the organization to explain to them the need to reduce the meetings to twice a year unless there was an emergency. Everyone agreed and they would continue to function as usual. Franco contacts the attorney who defended him at trial and asks him to represent him in a civil lawsuit against Salvatore for damages. The lawyer agrees immediately because not only would it be a renowned case, but he also wanted to retaliate for the arrogance with which Salvatore had treated him.

Umberto was in his office early that day since at 3:00 p.m. he had the meeting with his superiors. They have to explain why the operation failed. At 11:00 a.m. instead of calling Umberto, Salvatore shows up at Umberto's office. Salvatore's face was fresh and smiling, while Umberto was worried and tired. Umberto tells Salvatore.

"Come in and close the door."

Salvatore closes the door and sits across from Umberto.

"Boss, you have nothing to worry about. Not only I have discovered the reason for the failure, but we will show them we did the right thing within the law and that we also have the solution."

Umberto bluntly tells Salvatore.

"Well, I must answer for the failure, and you will add the way to remedy it, in a clear and convincing way, otherwise this is the last time you will enter this office."

"Pay attention, sir. Tell me if what I'm going to tell you doesn't make sense." Salvatore replies.

"Just say it, for God's sake!" Umberto yells at him.

"When I bought information from Benito, I stopped going to my observation point."

"And what the hell does that have to do with this?" Umberto yells at him.

"Listen to me to the end, please." Salvatore replies.

"I used all my free time to make friends and try to make new contacts. I hoped that someone would give me a clue, even if it was by mistake. One day, buying tomatoes in the plaza, I met Donato, who is Augusto's eldest son. Augusto is the owner of the farm that supplies the best tomatoes and vegetables to the markets."

Umberto interrupts him. "To the point, Salvatore, or I swear I'll kill you."

"Calm down and listen. One day when I was buying tomatoes from Donato. He nervously told me he had something valuable to me, but he wanted something in return. I ignored him because I knew Franco was spying on me. I thought it was a trap, and I did not know Augusto's farm adjoins the back of Franco's complex. Yesterday, after a lot of attempts, I could contact him. He told me that if I give him immunity and do not confiscate his money, he will give us what we are looking for."

Salvatore leans back in his chair. He is back to being the usual Salvatore.

"Now I understand why we found nothing, because the person who is going to be eliminated is first drugged, then they transfer him to Augusto's farm."

Umberto asks. "Did Donato tell you that?"

"No, but for a tomato seller to want immunity and not have his money confiscated, it must be he is involved with Franco."

Umberto feels his soul has returned to his body. Now he has a logical explanation for his bosses and the possibility of dismantling that criminal organization only by granting immunity to someone that nobody knows. Umberto felt more relaxed. Now everything made sense.

"What if we ask for a search warrant for Augusto's farm?" Umberto asks Salvatore.

"No, that would be crazy. We do not know if the bodies are there, or they are elsewhere. Remember, we are fighting against real professionals." Answer Salvatore.

"You are right. I must admit you know how to tie the dots to reach logical conclusions, but those bandits have always been one step ahead of us." Replies Umberto.

Umberto and Salvatore were silent, looking at each other as if they were trying to figure out what they were thinking. Umberto tells Salvatore.

"Franco has proven to be smarter than we thought."

"That's right, I agree with you."

"I also know that Franco is not a saint and if you cheated to force him to plead guilty, then he is paying for the things he has done and was not caught for. That does not mean I approve of such methods, but I would like to know the truth. I promise that this will remain between us. Did Franco kill Vicente, yes or no?"

Salvatore was surprised. He never expected such a question.

"You said it yourself. Franco is so smart he has planted doubts even in you, and it is totally understandable. Perhaps if I was in your place, I would have the same doubts, but for your peace of mind, as the newspaper said: Franco two Salvatore one. He has beaten me twice, but the one I beat him was totally clean and much more forceful than both of him. Salvatore answered with an offended face."

"Just curious. Please don't be offended." Umberto replies.

That afternoon during the meeting, Umberto and Salvatore convincingly explained to their superiors why the operation failed and how to remedy it. They clarified that there were no failures on their part and that the press only made a circus of what happened to sell their newspapers. The most surprising thing was they convinced them to give Donato immunity and respect his money. This document would be analyzed, approved, and drafted by the competent authorities, and it would take two weeks to be drafted. Umberto and Salvatore left the meeting very satisfied as what seemed like a failure had turned into a great victory. Before leaving, Salvatore tells Umberto.

"Boss, you must realize I have never failed you."

"Don't take it so hard, Salvatore, and let's get out of this once and for all." Replied Umberto.

"Tomorrow I'm going to Ischia to contact Donato and as soon as the pardon order arrives, we will act." Salvatore responds.

Salvatore returns to Ischia and starts going to the square to buy vegetables and tomatoes every day. The first two days, he only exchanged glances with Donato to make him understand he wanted to talk to him. After the last search of Franco's complex, Donato spoke with his father Augusto and his brother Carlos. He tried to convince them to take their money and go away before the police found out. Augusto instantly refused, telling him.

"This is a double betrayal. Franco is not only your employer, but he is family of blood. In our family, there are no traitors. He paid you lots of money and we are the only heirs since we are his only living family."

At the plaza, Carlos noticed his brother Donato making eye contact with Salvatore. Carlos told his father about Donato's betrayal as soon as he got home.

Augusto went to his room, where behind a mirror there were the communications switches to Franco's complex. Augusto pressed the red switch and went to the underground shelter with his son Carlos and his twelve-year-old grandson, Venancio, who was Donato's son. Franco rushes to the underground shelter. Such an urgent call surprises him.

"What is happening, Augusto? What is the emergency? What is Venancio doing here?"

Augusto was the only one who could call him Franco without having to use the Don Franco title, since he was not only older than him but also because he was family and they had known each other since childhood. Augusto says.

"Venancio is not a child. He is twelve years old, and he is of all my trust. I trust him more than one of my sons."

"What do you mean by that?" Franco asks.

Augusto shakes his head and responds.

"We have a serious problem with Donato."

Franco still does not understand and asks.

"What happened to Donato?"

Augusto tells him Donato had proposed to betray him after the last resort search, that Salvatore had returned to the island again and was going to the plaza every day to contact Donato. Franco lowers his head and says.

"Oh my God! I can't believe it, betrayed by my own blood."

"Are you telling me Franco? He is my son? Can you imagine how I feel?"

Franco looks at Carlos and asks him. "Have you seen them talk?"

"No, they have only exchanged glances, but those glances say much more than words. I am sure they have not spoken because I have been present."

Franco looks at the boy and asks him. "What do you think, Venancio?"

The child, firmly, as if he was an experienced adult, responds, "If my father is willing to sell us, then I have no father."

Augusto asks. "What do we do, Franco?"

"The first thing will be to know if he really wants to sell us."

"But how, Franco?" Augusto responds.

"Tomorrow you will tell Donato that Carlos will no longer go to the plaza with him. It is time for Venancio to get familiarized with the business. This way, he will not suspect we are watching him."

Franco looks at the boy and asks him.

"Would you dare to watch over your father?"

"He is no longer my father." Replies the boy.

"Listen to me carefully. I don't want you to feel forced to do something like this."

The child responds. "If my father sells you, he is selling my grandfather, my uncle, and the whole family. If he does not care about us, I don't see why we should care about him."

"You say that now, but what will you say tomorrow if something happens to your father, and you feel guilty about it." Franco replied.

"I would never regret saving the honor of my family. I prefer they say, there goes the orphan boy rather than there goes the traitor's son."

Everyone was stunned by such an answer. Franco himself did not know what to say. Franco says,

"Well, this remains between us. Venancio, welcome to your other family."

Franco stands in front of the child; he leans a little and tells him.

"It is your last chance. I want you to be clear the first family is your blood, and you can get married and go live far away, get divorced and come back as many times as you want. But in the second family, you enter married until death separates you, as the priests say."

"I will not change my mind. In our family, there are no traitors, and death does not scare me."

Franco says. "Nothing more to talk about. I must return to the complex."

Franco contacts his lawyer and tells him Salvatore has returned, that it is necessary to present him the lawsuit papers as soon as possible and to make it public so the press will keep Salvatore busy.

Salvatore goes to the marketplace early in the morning hoping to be one of the first and thus be able to talk to Donato. He was surprised to see Donato alone, not knowing his son was with him. Salvatore approaches him and says.

"I have what you asked for."

"Show it to me." Donato replies.

"It is approved. I will get it in nine days." Salvatore responds.

"Well, then come back when you have it and there is nothing else to talk about. How many tomatoes are you going to buy today, sir?" Donato says aloud.

"Four, sir." Salvatore replies.

When he returned home, Venancio told his grandfather what had happened at the marketplace. Augusto met with Franco and relayed the information to him. Franco thinks and tells Augusto.

"That document must be an immunity document. He has said nothing to save his skin. On the ninth day, don't send him to the marketplace."

Salvatore had breakfast in his favorite cafeteria. He enjoyed the beauty of the island, the sea breeze, the sun and all its charms. He had no worries. Soon it would all end. Perhaps, he would retire and stay on the island, but at that moment, someone pronounces his full name. "Salvatore Beato".

It sounded strange to him, because very few knew his last name. Salvatore turns around and sees a young man calling his full name again.

"I am an officer of the court. I come to give you the summons. You are being sued by Don. Franco Cano."

"What the hell are you saying, boy?" Salvatore answers him, angry and confused.

Salvatore's attitude did not intimidate the young man.

"Please sign here and take these documents. You or your lawyer have fifteen days to respond to the charges."

"But what the hell is this? What charges are those?" Angry and out of control, Salvatore asks the young man.

The young man just gives him the papers and leaves.

"I can't believe it. Now the gangsters are suing the authorities. When are we going to stop this nonsense? Not only do they use guns to steal, now they also use lawyers."

He had no alternative but to receive the documents. Salvatore signed the documents, threw them on the table, and preferred to finish his breakfast. When he returned to his apartment, he opened the court documents and read them. Franco was suing him for damages inflicted to the complex during the two failed searches. Salvatore laughs when he sees the sum of three million lire, but his face changes when he sees a detailed list that supported such a sum. What worries him the most was that he was the only defendant.

Salvatore called Umberto to tell him about the lawsuit and warn him Franco was surely going to sue him as well.

"I have received nothing so far. I do not think there is any legal complaint against the investigation department. They would already have communicated it to me. I will inquire about this, and I will give you an answer the day after tomorrow." Umberto responds.

"How many more days will the immunity document take for Donato?" Salvatore asks Umberto.

"One week." Umberto responds.

"Good, because I told Donato in nine days, I would give it to him."

"Don't pay too much attention to that the lawsuit, because with Franco in jail it will be discarded." Umberto tells Salvatore,

Salvatore laughs and responds. "The day I arrest him, I will put the lawsuit documents on his face and tell him that wanted to respond, but I cannot find the plaintiff."

They both laugh and hang up their phones.

Seven days later, Umberto calls Salvatore and informs him he already has the signed immunity documents in his possession.

"Great, tomorrow I'll go to the market to tell him he will have in two days."

"By the way, did you get any lawsuit?"

"No, neither any legal complaints against the Department of Investigations."

Salvatore asks Umberto to contact the Investigations Department attorney and do whatever is necessary to have this case dismissed.

"I already did, and they are studying the case. I will leave tomorrow for Ischia. I will take the documents and I will give you the lawyer's answer." Umberto answers.

"I'm glad you're coming back to the island. This time, everything will be different. Take care of yourself, boss." Salvatore responds.

Salvatore shows up early at the marketplace. As usual, he buys vegetables and passes by Donato. Venancio sees Salvatore approaching and stands behind some boxes. Salvatore looks around, sees nothing worrisome and says to Donato.

"Tomorrow at 9:00 a.m. I will bring you what you asked for."

"Then tomorrow, after you give it to me, you will have what you want." Donato replies.

"Buy tomatoes today. Don't leave it for tomorrow." Donato yells.

"You are absolutely right. Give me four big ones." Salvatore replies.

That afternoon when they got home, Venancio tells his grandfather his father Donato has an appointment in the market tomorrow at 9:00 a.m. with Salvatore and they will do some exchange. Augusto runs into his room, goes behind his mirror, and presses the red button. Fifteen minutes later, Augusto, Carlos, Venancio and Franco meet at the underground shelter. Augusto tells Franco,

"Franco, my son Donato plans to betray us tomorrow at nine."

Franco shakes his head and says.

"It's a shame. Tomorrow, you will tell him you need him at the farm. Tell him another employee will go to the market in his place. Let the neighbors know if Donato goes down the hill, they must stop him and bring him back home at any cost. Then the neighbors should go back to their posts and be prepared in case Salvatore wants to go up the hill. Tonight, check that the bell system is working, the tanker is full of water, and finally we must keep watch all night in case Donato tries to flee tonight."

"It will be done." Augusto responds.

Franco puts his hand on Venancio's shoulder and tells him.

"Let's hope Donato changes his mind tonight and doesn't go down the hill."

They all rush out of the shelter. Augusto, following Franco's orders, goes to inform the neighbors Donato should not be allowed to go down the hill and Salvatore should be prevented from going up the hill at all costs.

That night, taking the advantage that his father and brother had left, Donato went and packed all the money the family had hidden underground. He put the money in two sacks as if it was merchandise. He hid it on the side of the road and covered it with leaves and sticks. Donato returned to the house and felt relief when he saw his father and brother had not returned. Donato was confident no one had seen him, but Venancio had spied on him the entire time.

The next day, Augusto tells Donato he needed him at the farm and that other employees would go to the market for him. Donato was surprised. Such news did not please him at all. But in order not to raise suspicion, he said nothing.

"What do you need?" Donato asked.

"Son, you go to the market every day. That is why you are not aware of what is happening on the farm. One worker told me the irrigation system is failing. It may be the lines are clogging or there are breaks in the lines reducing the water pressure. I need for you and Carlos to fix those lines."

"I will fix them, father, that's easy. You must send Carlos to the market. I will stay and fix them. I prefer Carlos to be the one who handles the money. I am accusing the workers, but money is a temptation. We don't have to take that risk."

"You are absolutely right. If you can fix it alone, then I will send Carlos to the market later. I should have told you before. It is my fault for not telling you last night, but I came late, and you were sleeping."

Augusto looks at Donato and asks him. "Are you sure you can do it alone?"

"Sure, father, that will take me two or three hours the most."

"Perfect. Let's all have breakfast together first. We haven't done it in a long time."

"Okay father, that's a good idea. Is there something wrong with you? I see you a little down and sad." Asked Donato to his father.

"Don't worry son, it's old age. Maybe this family breakfast is what I need to lift my spirits. Family is the greatest medicine there is."

"Father, you are always so wise." Donato replies.

"Don't forget, son, family goes first. I think I've given you that example always."

"There is no doubt, father, no need to mention."

Augusto felt better knowing he had done everything possible to convince his son. Now everything was in the hands of Donato and God.

The family met for breakfast, Augusto, his eldest son Donato with his wife Marta, and his grandson Venancio on the right. On the left is his youngest son Carlos with his wife Laura and his six-year-old granddaughter Vera and in front of him is his life wife Berta.

"What a nice day, said Berta."

"And more beautiful when we are all together." Augusto replies.

"That bread smells delicious." Says Donato.

"Son, your mother baked that bread with love. No one in the world can make it like her. I remember when I met your mother. Your uncle Antonio invited me to his house one morning and your mother was a beautiful young woman. She had finished baking bread. When I felt that smell, she conquered me even without having seen her."

Berta interrupts him and speaks. "The rest is history. Forty-five years passed, two children and two grandchildren."

Everyone laughs except Augusto, who was running a tear.

"What's wrong Augusto? Are you crying? After forty-five years, now you regret it?". Says Berta and everyone laughs again except him.

Augusto wipes his tears and responds.

"It's that when you don't make me cry with rage, you make me cry with melancholy." This time, everyone laughs.

They spent almost two hours having breakfast and remembering the good times with the family. Augusto tried to make Donato feel some remorse, hoping he might change his mind.

Donato stands up and says.

"Father, excuse me, but I would like to fix the irrigation system before the sun gets hot."

"You are right son, go ahead if you want. We will enjoy a little more."

"Enjoy for me too." Says Donato and leaves.

Augusto had broken some irrigation lines, as the last hope for his son would change his mind. After Donato left, Augusto stood up and said. "Excuse me, I am not feeling very well. I must lie down for a while."

Augusto entered his room and pressed the yellow button, which gave the alert to the neighbors. He sat in his armchair, closed his eyes, praying for a miracle. He hopes Donato changes his mind and reports back to him, saying he had fixed the irrigation lines.

Salvatore and Umberto were in the market. They went to Donato's stall, looked at the tomatoes, and continued. Umberto asks.

"What's up Salvatore? Please do not tell me Donato isn't here?"

"I did not see him, but that does not mean that he is not here. Let's go around and come back." Salvatore answers.

"Okay, let's go for a walk. You are the one who knows him. Maybe he's here, but doing something else."

"Exactly, that's what I meant." Salvatore replies, but he couldn't hide the change on his face.

Donato did not even pass through the irrigation lines. He went straight to get the two bags of money he had hidden and went down the hill. He was sure no one had followed him. As soon as Donato entered the road, the yellow alarms went off and they would remain yellow until Donato had gone down the middle of the hill, then they would turn red, and Donato should be intercepted.

Salvatore returns to Donato's booth and asks.

"Excuse me, sir., Where is Donato?"

"He is fixing the irrigation lines. Can I help you?" Answered the farmer.

"It's that I always buy his tomatoes from him. Yesterday I bought some tomatoes, but I forgot the money at home. He gave me the tomatoes, and I promised him I would return the money today."

"Well, if you want, you can give me the money and I will give it to him." Replies the farm worker.

"I'm sorry, sir, but I don't know you."

"If I ever steal, I assure you it will not be some tomatoes. You look more like a thief than I. Get out of here before I break your face." The offended farmer yells at Salvatore.

Salvatore sees he has made a big mistake with the farmer. He tries to apologize, but the farmer, still mad with fire coming out of his eyes, responds,

"If you want to buy tomato, buy it. If not, get that hell out of my face."

Donato has come down the middle of the hill when he hears someone calling him. It was Ronaldo, the crazy old goat farmer, who was inviting him to enter his farm. The bells are already ringing; the alarms are flashing are red. Donato does not know the alarms are sounding. He stops for a moment and shouts at the old man.

"I must take this merchandise from my father to the marketplace immediately. I will just leave it there and I will pass by your house."

Ronaldo, in his peculiar way of walking, approaches him.

"It is just a moment. I need to give you something your father forgot last night when he was here in my house."

"As you can see, I'm loaded. I'll pick it up when I get back."

The old man, approaching him closer, says,

"It's that I gave him the money I owed him, and he forgot to take it. When you return, I won't be home."

Donato thinks a little more money is always welcome and goes inside the old man's house to get the money. Once inside the house, the old man looks for the money.

"Oh my gosh, where did I put it now?" Donato, after a few minutes, says.

"If you don't remember, don't worry. Give it to him later. I must deliver my father's order." Donato takes his two bags and prepares to leave, when he sees four neighbors entering the old man's property. Donato yells.

"Come out, sir, you have visitors."

The neighbors are standing in front of the old man's property gate. Donato walks at the entrance of the property and tells them. "Good morning."

"Good morning, Donato. Let's go to your house. Your father is waiting for you."

Donato tries to confuse them and tells them.

"You are wrong. I have to take this from my father to the farmer. I am sure my father meant to tell you about my brother Carlos."

Donato tries to take a step forward, but the four neighbors block him.

"It's not Carlos. It's you, Donato."

Old Ronaldo comes out of the house and mockingly tells him.

"No Donato, it is you who Augusto sent for."

Donato tries one more time and this time angrily tells them. "Why does my father want to see me if he sends me to deliver this urgently?"

The old man laughs. "Do you really want me to tell you?"

"Yes, tell me." Donato yells at him.

The old man approaches him and mockingly bows three times as if he were in front of a king, but with each bow, he tells him," For snitch. For thief. And for traitor."

The old man spits in Donato's face and orders the neighbors.

"Get this shit out of my face."

Donato knows it was all over, that they had discovered him and now he understands the messages from his father. He put up no resistance and was escorted by neighbors to his home. Augusto was waiting for him with Carlos, his son Venancio, Luigi, and two other workers from Franco's complex. Augusto had sent all the women in the house to visit a sick old lady, so they would not witness what was going to happen. The neighbors brought Donato to Augusto. Augusto thanked them and told them to go to their post and to follow the defense plan if necessary. Donato did not offer resistance when they took him to the underground shelter. While they waited for Franco, Donato was searched and wrapped in sheets like a mummy.

Franco entered, and everyone stood up except Augusto. Franco goes straight to Donato and tells him.

"So, you sold us."

"No, Don Franco, I have not said a word."

"Tell me, what did you tell them?" Franco repeats.

"Nothing Don Franco. Nothing."

Franco orders Luigi to put him standing on top of a chair.

"This is your last chance. Tell me what you told them."

"Nothing, Don Franco, nothing, believe me, I said nothing."

Franco tells Luigi. "Put the rope around his neck. That will refresh his memory."

Franco had promised Augusto he would not kill Donato. When Donato sees himself with the noose around his neck, he desperately begins to ask for forgiveness.

"Now I know you spied on me, but my son was there. He knows I didn't say anything."

Venancio stands in front of him and spits in his face.

"You are no longer my father."

Franco looks at Augusto and tells him.

"I'm sorry Augusto, I'm really sorry."

Augusto stands up and hugs Franco and, crying, he tells him.

"I know. We tried everything, but he sold us."

"What else do you know about Donato?" Franco asks Augusto.

"Only that he planned to steal all the money and sell us. He had in his pocket a map of our farm with the description of the secret underground shelter where we are now and the bell systems and the alarm lights."

Franco stands in front of Donato, who is standing in the chair with the rope around his neck ready to be hanged.

"Tell me, is the money I gave you not enough for you? You also had to steal from your father and brother. You would not only hand me over, but your father and brother. Your end has come, or you tell me what Salvatore knows or I will remove this chair and hang you."

Donato cries and asks for forgiveness.

"Father, you cannot allow this to your child."

An enraged Augusto pushes Franco to the side. Luigi holds Franco, so he does not fall to the ground, while Augusto, out of control, yells at Donato.

"You are a bastard, a traitor, a thief and now you call me father."

Totally out of control, Augusto kicked the chair and Donato fell by the neck. Everyone was speechless. No one expected what would happen. Franco yelled.

"Noooo! Augusto." But it was too late.

Franco, shaking Augusto by his shoulders, yells at him.

"What have you done? Did you go crazy?"

Augusto did not respond. It was as if he could not listen, then reacted.

"Oh, God! What have I done? I have killed my son. Franco, help me, please save him. He is my son."

Augusto puts his hands on his chest and falls to the ground, while his voice faded.

Salvatore begins to despair and tells Umberto.

"We are going through the back entrance of the hill. There is the path that leads to Donato's father's farm. But first I want to call the two reporters who made a fool out of us to come with us."

Umberto, astonished, answers him. "What do you say? Haven't you learned yet?"

Salvatore looks at Umberto and answers him.

"Boss, even the dogs know me here. If I get out of the car, I will raise suspicions, and Augusto may not let me talk to Donato. I stay in the car, you get off with the reporters and tell Augusto his tomatoes have become famous, that you want to interview him as the owner and Donato as the famous sales representative in the marketplace. This way, they will feel proud, and they will not put any objection to call Donato. When you are in front of Donato, you give him the papers and tell him to read it. Tell him it is a letter of appreciation for his good work in the agricultural development of the Island. After he reads the letter, he will feel safe and will cooperate with us. As you can see, boss, I have everything calculated, even unforeseen events like these."

Umberto shakes his head and tells him.

"I have to give you credit, very well thought out. However, I don't believe a journalist wants to go do a report on tomatoes."

"No boss, we tell journalists the truth. Because of the premise of such a story, they will surely agree to play the game." Salvatore responds.

Umberto raises and lowers his head and answers. "Now everything is clear. I don't know why things are going so bad for you lately."

"Not this time boss, you'll see." Salvatore replies.

Meanwhile, in the shelter, the situation is chaotic, Franco yells. "Silence!"

Franco never yelled. Franco sits down and thinks for three minutes. It was three eternal minutes. No one spoke a word. Franco got up and said.

"Listen carefully and do everything as I tell you. Our heads depend on that. Take Donato right now with that chair and two more chairs that are similar. Make sure that Donato's shoe prints are still on that chair. Find a suitable place where he can put the chair to hang himself. When he is already placed, then take off the sheets, clean the chair of any fingerprints it may have, except for Donato's shoes and hands. Clean the other two chairs and they must have prints of Augusto, Carlos, and Venancio."

Franco orders Luigi. "You will be in charge of this operation."

Franco looks at Venancio and Carlos and tells them.

"Pay attention to the story you are going to tell. You cannot change it."

Carlos and Venancio look at each other and respond. "Yes, Don Franco."

Franco sits in front of them and tells them everything they had to say to the authorities.

At that moment, Augusto makes a groan, and everyone screams. "He is alive!"

Franco orders them to take Augusto and find a doctor in a hurry. Before they leave, he tells them.

"Remember what you have to do and say does not change, nothing changes, nothing."

At that same time, the alarm sounds and the red light turns on.

"My God! The only thing I am missing now. Salvatore is trying to go up the hill. Run, run, run." Franco yelled at them.

At 1:00 p. m. exactly, Salvatore had the two reporters in the car and was going up the hill through the narrow dirt road that led to Augusto's farm. Salvatore was driving, Umberto was next to him and the two reporters behind. Salvatore turns around and tells.

"Prepare your cameras. Let's see if you take excellent pictures and make great comments as you did last time."

He has not finished speaking when he feels a pull on his arm and hears Umberto scream.

"Look ahead, stupid!"

Salvatore looks ahead and exclaims. "What the fuck is that?"

The tanker had dumped all its water onto the narrow dirt road, and a stream was coming down to meet them. As soon as the water hit Salvatore's car, it skidded and lost control. Umberto's screams were deafening.

"Do not speed up, we are going to overturn, stupid. Try to straighten the vehicle and do not speed up, you idiot."

The photos from behind the car captured the terrified face of Umberto yelling at Salvatore, who had his head almost out of the vehicle while screaming.

"Up, up, you can do it. I know you can make it."

Finally, Salvatore heard Umberto's screams and sped up no more. The water was running down the hill and Salvatore kept trying to go up the hill, but the car skidded again and slid backwards until it got to the starting point.

Salvatore and Umberto get out of the vehicle and Umberto yells.

"This shit will never go up that road under those conditions."

"Not the car, but we do. We have them, boss, we have them." Shouted Salvatore with joy.

The reporters looked at each other and one says. "This is where my report ends."

Salvatore was trying to run in the mud when he slipped and fell back two laps. Reporters snapped photos of the fall, the turns, and the stunning photo of Salvatore standing completely mired in mud, screaming. "Today is your day, Franco."

Umberto was holding on to the fences to climb the hill. He had mud almost to his knees, but he had not fallen. Salvatore went up the same way as Umberto. The reporters changed their minds instantly.

"I won't miss this for nothing in the world." Says one reporter.

"Here we did the month." Responds the other reporter.

Salvatore has tried so hard to climb that he has already passed Umberto, who, because of his age, tires. They are up about a third of the hill when Salvatore, who is leading the way, yells.

"No, no, no! You sons of bitches."

Umberto, who is climbing with his head down and almost stepping on his tongue, looks ahead and sees a herd of goats coming down the narrow path of the hill.

"Damn you, Salvatore." Umberto screams.

He turns to go down the hill when he sees the reporters. He thought the reporters had stayed down the hill.

"Are you running away, sir?" One reporter asks him.

Umberto made a face that made you want to cry.

"No, I just turned around to get a better grip."

Umberto and the reporters clung to the fence. Umberto was scared. He had always lived in Rome and only knew animals from books. Instead of holding on and waiting for the goats to pass, Salvatore tried to move forward. He gets rammed by the animals to the ground where he laid down flat while the goats were stepping on him going down the hill. The photo of Salvatore on the muddy road dragged by goats would make a front-page editorial. Salvatore drew his pistol and fired into the air to remove the animals from above, but he made it worse, because the goats got scared and ran everywhere trying to flee, colliding with Umberto repeatedly.

"Save me, my God! Get me out of here!" Umberto screams.

When the goats finished passing by, there was Salvatore, with three rags for clothes, with bruises all over his body and only his eyes were visible. The rest was pure mud. Umberto was on his knees, aching, out of breath, and sobbing. That's when they heard someone singing. "Oh sole mio."

It was Ronaldo, the crazy old shepherd from the goat's farm who was coming down the hill with his two dogs. Ronaldo looks at Umberto and asks him.

"Were you the idiot who scared my goats?"

When Umberto did not respond, the old man gives the dog's collar two wings and the dogs bark harshly, prepared to attack. Umberto screamed.

"No, God, please! It was that idiot."

Umberto's hand shaking with fear points back.

The old man yanks on the dog's collar and the dogs calm down. The old man looks at the journalist that was behind Umberto and says.

"So, it was you!"

Old Ronaldo pulls the dog's collar twice again and the dogs rage again. The reporter was begging for his life and pointing towards Salvatore, who was on his knees, still dazed in the middle of the road.

"It wasn't me. It was that idiot."

The second reporter pointing at Umberto tells the old man.

"Yes, sir, not this idiot. It was the other idiot."

Umberto, upon hearing what the reporter said, looked up at the sky and exclaimed.

"Why my God? Why?"

The old man gives a single wing to the dog's collar and the dogs calm down and with his mocking and crazed tone of voice, he looks at Salvatore and says.

"Too bad that shit isn't worth my dogs biting." He let his dogs lose while humming his song. One dog walks up to Salvatore, sniffs him, and then urinates on him. The old man yells.

"Hey, mud ball, my dog liked you. You can consider yourself my friend."

The reporter had the photo of the dog urinating on Salvatore. Salvatore stands up and says.

"If you think you're going to humiliate me, you'll see. You're going to kiss my ass when this is over today."

The four of them finally got to dry land, when they see a group of people screaming and running like crazy down the hill. Umberto knelt in the path, raised his arms in surrender mode, and said.

"No more, no more, I give up."

Salvatore stands in front of Umberto and says.

"Get up boss, we are thirty meters from the entrance. This is not the time to give up."

Another historical photo, Umberto on his knee and Salvatore in front of him yelling at him. The group consisted of about fifteen people, including men, women, and children. They yelled.

"A doctor! We need a doctor!"

Umberto looked back and told reporters.

"It should be for me. Even they see I am dying."

Umberto and the two reporters laughed.

"What are you laughing at?" Screams Salvatore.

"Let me laugh. This is the first time a defeat made me laugh. Let me enjoy it."

"There is not time for laughing." Salvatore yells.

The group stopped and kept yelling. "We need a doctor!"

One person from the group takes Salvatore by the arm and asks for help. Salvatore pushes him away and tells him.

"Well, look for somebody else. I'm not a doctor."

A woman in the group screams.

"I know that man. He is Salvatore, the detective. He has a car."

Umberto could not contain his laughter. "As you say, even the dogs know you and piss you, too."

When Salvatore refuses to give help, one person in the groups tells him.

"Don Augusto had a heart attack, and he is in serious condition."

"Well, if he's going to die anyway, let him die." Salvatore responds.

Those words exploded the anger in the group. One of them pulled out a machete and yells.

"Then you die before him."

Umberto stood up and ordered Salvatore to help.

"Boss, that car can't go up the hill, you know it," Salvatore answers him.

The neighbors kept yelling. We will bring them up on mules. You just help us find the doctor at the hospital.

Umberto stopped laughing and took command. Salvatore had no choice but to go down the hill again, slipping and falling a couple of times. The rest helped Umberto to go up the hill.

Umberto followed Salvatore's plan. Upon arriving at Augusto's house, he saw it wasn't a trick. Augusto was in a serious condition and his vital signs were almost none. Carlos offers Umberto and the reporters a seat and brings them something to drink. Carlos thanks them for helping to find a doctor.

"You don't have to thank me for anything. It's a duty to help each other in times of need. It's a shame, because these two reporters and I came to do a report on your tomatoes, which have gained fame throughout the island. I met Donato at the marketplace. He was the one who introduced me to your products." Umberto responds.

"Oh, you came with reporters!" Carlos exclaims.

Umberto is scared. He thinks they have discovered him. He answers, almost out of breath with a constipated voice.

"Yes, reporters."

With anger, Carlos answers. "Very well, in that case, do a good article on what happened here today. It is much more important than the tomatoes."

Umberto takes another deep breath. He realizes they don't know about his true identity.

"What happened here today?" Umberto asks, signaling the reporters to take notes.

Carlos calls Venancio and then tells Umberto. "It is better if my nephew Venancio tells you. He is the one who goes to the market with my brother, Donato."

Venancio comes and Umberto looks at him and says.

"But he is a child."

"What does it matter if he is a child? He is twelve years old, and he is Donato's son. He witnessed everything." Carlos responds.

Umberto looks at Venancio and asks him.

"What happened, son?"

Venancio tells him a famous detective named Salvatore had been trying to convince his father for a long time to say Don Franco had passed two corpses through the back of the farm, so he would disappear them.

"But what would your father gain by saying such a thing?" Umberto asked.

"The man promised him that if he did it, he would give him a document where he would not go to jail and then he would give him a lot of money."

"How much money?"

"I don't know, sir, a lot. This morning, my grandfather sent my father to fix some irrigation lines. My father told him he could not take this life anymore, that he was going to accept Salvatore's offer."

"But did your grandfather know about this?" Umberto asks.

"Yes, he had told us all, but my grandfather told him not to do it, that it was not honest. Time passed, and he never mentioned it again, but this morning he came back with the same subject saying that he would implicate no one in the family, that this would remain between Don Franco and him. My grandfather was furious. They argued for a long time. My grandfather took a stick and ran after him. My father fled, but he saw when my grandfather fell to the ground and instead of coming to help him, he hid. I don't know where."

The reporters took notes as if they had discovered a gold mine. The photos were coming one after another. Umberto looked smaller and smaller in the chair. His shoulders were hunched, and his mouth was open like a lizard. At that moment, the noise of the neighbors coming with the doctor on mules was heard. Umberto tells the reporters, Venancio and Carlos. "Not a word of this to anyone."

The doctor runs in and starts working in Augusto. Salvatore asks Umberto.

"Did you speak to Donato?"

"Not yet, but when we find him, we will talk to him."

Umberto stops and this time not as a reporter but as an authority, he says, "Listen up, look for Donato. Look for him even at the bottom of the well and bring him to me whatever it takes."

One neighbor asks. "Who are you to give orders?"

Umberto takes out his police identification and says.

"I am the authority, and you are going to do as I told you.

The neighbors were surprised, but Carlos said.

"You heard him. Start searching for him now."

They all scattered around the farm, trying to find Donato. Salvatore was going to join the search, but Umberto tells him.

"Where are you going?"

"Well, to look for Donato."

"No, you stay here, with me." Umberto ordered him.

Salvatore stopped short. He thought that something happened when he was gone, but he decided not to ask and wait.

Half an hour later, the doctor came out of Augusto's room and told Carlos.

"I'm sorry, Carlos, Augusto left us."

Carlos and Venancio hugged each other and started crying. Umberto looks at one neighbor and tells him.

"You go down and call the police. Tell them we need chief Raffaelle and a minimum of four officers here urgently. Tell them I, Umberto, want them here now. What are you waiting for?"

The farmer ran to carry out the orders. Salvatore felt annoyed, because Umberto was constantly ignoring him. Umberto asks the doctor.

"Can you confirm the cause of death by one hundred percent?"

The doctor answers. "Not, but ninety-five percent, yes."

"Well then, you will have to take him and do an autopsy."

Five hours had passed since Salvatore began to climb the hill and two hours since Umberto had entered Augusto's estate. It was a hot day with extraordinarily strong sunshine. The mud had dried on Salvatore's body. He looked like a doll out of the trash. Salvatore gets up and asks Carlos for water to wash his face.

"We have no water for you here." Carlos responds.

"What a way to thank! I brought you a doctor in a hurry and you refuse to give me water."

"As far as I know, you refused to help. It was only when this man ordered you to help you helped. My neighbors told me so, and they don't lie."

Salvatore could not answer back, it was true what Carlos said. He asked a reporter in a low voice.

"What is going on here?"

The reporter tells him in a low voice. "I don't understand either. Hopefully, when they find Donato, he can unravel this."

Salvatore was relieved. He thought Umberto was trying to become friendly with Carlos to have easier access to Donato, and this calmed him down.

Umberto looks at the reporter and Salvatore and tells them.

"Can you keep quiet?"

That annoyed Salvatore. Umberto was mistreating him. He would not allow Umberto to humiliate him in front of everybody.

"Excuse me, boss, but I think you are treating me like I'm a detainee."

"If I were one hundred percent sure that you should be arrested, I would have arrested you already and my treatment toward you was much more severe. I do not arrest anyone unless I am sure a crime has been committed, nor will I invent charges to arrest you, no matter how badly I feel about you."

Those words were like a stab directly to the heart of Salvatore. Now he was sure something had happened, and it was better to keep quiet and wait for Donato to appear.

The noise from the approaching vehicles was heard. Two police cars arrived at the scene. It was the chief of police, Raffaelle and three officers.

"What has happened to you?" Raffaelle asked.

"Better ask, what hasn't happened to us, that way the story will be shorter." Umberto replied.

"How did he get up the hill?"

"The road was already dry. If not, only the mules can climb them." Raffaelle replied.

"Yes, I believe it because I experienced it firsthand. But let us go to what are important issues. I need full collaboration in this."

"You will get it, sir. But will you listen to advice this time?"

Umberto, annoyed with those words, replies firmly.

"I listen to advice, but I take and assume responsibility for my own decisions and let no one doubt that."

"Perfect sir, I am at your command." Replies Raffaelle, who saw in Umberto an old man damaged by a couple of defeats, but with dignity and pride, who did not allow himself to be defeated and should be respected.

"I want Augusto's body taken away to perform a detailed autopsy of his body."

Then Umberto orders Salvatore to stand up. Salvatore stands up, as if he were a military man. He believes they are going to put him in command of something and they will give him an officer to help him. Umberto stands in front of Salvatore and says.

"Salvatore Beato."

Salvatore smiled. "Oh, this must be good! He is calling me by first and last name."

But before Umberto can say anything else, they hear screams from the neighbors who came in running and shouting." We found Donato, we found him."

Umberto turns around and says. "Thank goodness. We will finally have answers."

"But where is he? Who has him?" Umberto asks.

"He is dead, sir."

"What did you say? He cannot be dead. My God! What is this? Please give me a break."

"He has hanged himself, sir."

"Nobody touches him." Orders Umberto.

"No one has touched him, sir. We only found him. He will not leave; he is attached by a rope around his neck."

"Of course, he will go nowhere. What I meant to say is that no one touches him."

Umberto looks at Raffaelle and shakes his head from side to side saying.

"These people are stupid."

Raffaelle did not like Umberto's comment.

"Those people are not educated people, but they are humble and respectful people who do not deserve to be humiliated. As far as I can see, they were helping you to do your job."

Umberto realizes he has made a mistake, and the farmers did not really deserve such a comment.

"Yes, I am going to accept that advice. I believe you are absolutely right in what you have just said, is that I do not wish a day like today, not even to my worst enemy."

"I get it." Raffaelle replied softer.

"Please take us to Donato's body."

"Yes, sir."

The reporters ask. "Can we go with you, sir?"

Umberto looks at them, and with fire in his eyes, he responds.

"If you come, stay, or decide to hang yourself, I don't give a damn."

Raffaelle turns to hide his laughter.

"Laugh, Raffaelle, do not be ashamed to laugh. Today I had a lot of misfortunes, but I learned that laughter is the best remedy. It removes fear, pain, worries and brings enormous relief. Today I saw myself kneeling in the middle of the road, all covered in mud and I pissed in my pants, because I thought some crazy old man was going to throw some dogs at me to tear me to pieces. I was raising my arms like giving up. At that moment, I said something stupid that made the reporters laugh. It was such a simple and sincere stupidity that after I analyzed it I laughed and laughed with them at myself. I laughed so hard it restored strength to my body and peace to my soul, and I felt no more fear."

Raffaelle looked at Umberto in another way. He saw a human being totally different from Salvatore. That Umberto was not the old, grumpy, and arrogant he thought. That there was a person with noble qualities within Umberto.

"Thank you for that advice. I like it and I repeat, I am here to help you, not to judge or criticize you."

Umberto orders." Let a police officer to stay there and another officer should come with us."

They quickly leave after the farmers when suddenly Umberto sees Salvatore has joined the group. Umberto tells him.

"Salvatore, you stay there with the officer."

"Yes boss, I'll be there waiting for you." Salvatore proudly responds.

Salvatore returns to the group and tells them. "The boss has sent me back to supervise you until he returns. Do you understand?"

But nobody answers him.

"Didn't you listen to what I just said? Salvatore asks again, but no one answers him. Salvatore, to counter his lack of authority, tells them.

"I don't care if they don't respond as long as you do what I say."

Umberto arrives at the scene, and he asks Raffaelle.

"Is this Donato?"

"Yes sir, he's Donato."

Umberto carefully picks up the chair and places it next to Donato. Raffaelle looks at him in amazement.

"This is my job and my passion. This is the first thing to do. This will tell you if he hanged himself or if he was killed. If the chair does not reach his feet, then he was killed. But if the chair reaches his feet, it is possible he has hanged himself."

Umberto tells reporters. "It is better you come. Sorry for what I said earlier. I will need your photos."

Raffaelle was impressed with Umberto's power of observation and how he developed in his work. Umberto ordered to lower the body and gave the specifications of how to lower it, confiscated the chair and the rope as evidence.

Upon returning to the house with Donato's body and the evidence, Venancio began to cry, hugging his uncle and screaming. "Damn you, Salvatore. It's all your fault."

The women had returned to the house after hearing the terrible news. They were crying uncontrollably inside the house. Umberto tells Rafaelle.

"Apparently, he committed suicide, but you must do an autopsy to be totally sure, I also need the chair and rope to be checked, the chair must have prints, and on the rope, you never know what can be found under a microscope. I also need the fingerprints of all the residents of the house. I don't want them to rush. What I want is a job well done."

Finally, Umberto approaches Salvatore and says. "Salvatore Beato."

Salvatore stands firm in front of Umberto, showing off his military training.

"Yes sir, at your command."

"You are relieved from the case you were investigating and suspended from the Investigations Department until your case is reviewed."

"What did you say? What happens, boss? Please tell me?" Salvatore could not believe it.

"Didn't you hear me, or I have to repeat? Give me your weapon and the department's identification."

Salvatore looks around like a desperate beggar.

"I have put all my time, risked my life, put my own money in this case and this is the result."

"Well, so far, that is the result. Maybe in the end, the result is different."

"But what did I do wrong, boss?"

"Tomorrow you will receive a copy of my report. Now I have two dead people and a lot of work to do. I told you to give me the gun and the identifications. I will not repeat it."

Salvatore gives Umberto his pistol and his identification and asks him. "What do I do now, boss?"

"To begin with, I am no longer your boss. You can go home, but you cannot leave the island."

"But boss, if I go alone, these savages can kill me on the way. You already saw how one of them threatened to cut off my head."

"Well, I'll be left with the desire to kill you myself." Umberto replied.

Carlos intervenes and tells him. "We are not criminals here. I give you my word you can leave, and no one is going to touch you unless you provoke them."

"Bravo! Salvatore responds. You must be the new boss of the hill to give those assurances."

Carlos is offended and raises his hand to slap Salvatore, but is pushed in time by Raffaelle, who tells Salvatore.

"Look, you idiot. You are no longer an authority and Umberto does not have jurisdiction to arrest you, but I do. If you don't disappear from here right now, I'm going to arrest you for obstructing an investigation. You already know you can't leave the island. I order you to sign in at the police station twice a day, at 11:00 a.m. already 9:00 p.m., so you can prove you are here. If you cannot come, you must call, and an officer will visit you to sign. Any questions, stupid?"

Salvatore lowered his head and said. "No sir, understood."

Salvatore was leaving when he heard Umberto calling him. "What a tacky joke." Thought Salvatore, but he felt relieved. Things changed when Umberto tells him.

"With all these problems, I forgot to tell you the department's lawyer says he can't do anything for you, because neither the department nor the job is mentioned in the lawsuit, it is against you for using your power and the department to cause damages, so now you manage as you can."

Salvatore felt the world fall apart. He put his hands on his head and sat on the floor with his elbows on his knees.

"It can't be true. This is an injustice."

Raffaelle answers. "The court will decide whether it is injustice or not, but get up and leave, or I will take you to jail."

Salvatore gets up and starts walking, dragging his feet.

Salvatore walks past the front of the farm of the crazy old goat herder, who yells at him.

"Hey, my friend, come have some water and clean up your face at least. Remember who is a friend of my dogs, he is a friend of mine too."

Salvatore looks at him and thinks. Nothing could be worse. Maybe this madman gives me the information I need in these moments. Salvatore thanks him and enters Ronaldo's property. The old man brings a jug of water and is pouring water on Salvatore's hands while he washes his face.

"Thanks really, thanks!"

"You don't have to mention it." Replies the old man.

"By the way. Says Salvatore. What can you tell me about this, Carlos?"

"WHAT!! What did you just say?" Responds the offended old man.

"You have broken the most sacred rule on this hill. We never talk about our neighbors. Your friendship is over, and you have thirty seconds to leave my house. Hurry, I'm counting."

Salvatore stares at the old man to see if he can make him change his mind, but the old man whistle and he hears the dogs running madly. Salvatore let out a scream of horror and was sent running. The dogs were already catching up with him when Salvatore took an Olympic jump over the fence. Salvatore falls to the other side of the fence, stops and sees the angry dogs barking madly behind the gate. Salvatore yells at him.

"Damn crazy old man, damn dogs."

Salvatore sees the old man leave his house and hears him talking to the dogs. "Yes, I'm coming to open the gate so you can have fun with him."

Salvatore made another cry that was heard throughout the hill and ran away. Only a trail of dust was seen coming down the hill. The old man reached the gate and whistled again, and the dogs calmed down.

"Ah! He runs too fast. You will not catch him."

CHAPTER TWELVE

MARIA

Salvatore's dismissal from "The hill case" made the front pages of the most important newspapers in the country. The photos looked like something out of a comic series, with editorials like. "The third time is the charm", "When will this end?" but the editorial that caused the most damage to Salvatore and the department was "Salvatore did not find two of his dead bodies but caused two deaths." The big winner was Franco, his popularity increased, and his resort got international fame. It was almost impossible to get a booking at the complex. His earnings increased three hundred percent and were all clean. Umberto had his difficulties, but it came out very well in the end. Umberto was like the boxer who went down to the canvas but got the end of the fight getting a draw. The big loser was Salvatore, who was compared to a hot-air balloon that went up high but ran out of fuel and fell disastrously.

The prosecutor closed Augusto's case after the autopsies revealed no fault play on Augusto's and Donato's death. Salvatore's case went to the internal affairs of the department. They investigated whether Salvatore had lied or committed any inappropriate action. Salvatore's situation was critical and to that was added the civil lawsuit for damages in the amount of two million lire, for which he had not prepared. Salvatore fell into a state of depression and did not leave his apartment at all.

Finally, Franco got Salvatore out of his way and now his business was completely legitimate, so he could dedicate himself to fulfilling two new goals: buying Vittorio's business and finding Maria. Those, as easy as they seemed, were much more difficult than facing three Salvatore at the same time.

To accomplish his first goal, there was a big problem. Franco did not want to hurt his friend Vittorio, and he knew Vittorio would not give in.

To accomplish his second goal, it was even harder. Franco did not know where to start. Maria had been swallowed up by the earth. Valentino had formed a great friendship with Maria's parents since he was their only customer. Valentino had kept them afloat and kept them from going bankrupt.

After Maria's disappearance, Don Pedro and Angela received Valentino several times in their home. They had never allowed this before. There was a secret only Maria's parents knew. As a result of an intimate relationship between Franco and Maria the night before Franco's departure for Ischia, Maria had become pregnant. Maria did not know she was pregnant with Franco's baby. She found out about it, two months after that tragic night when Franco was arrested. That was the reason Maria went to father's factory during the first two months and after that, her parents locked her up in the house. Maria's parents, unable to convince her to end her pregnancy, asked her to give her child up for adoption. They did not allow her to leave the house, so no one would know she was pregnant. Maria agreed to the adoption, but in reality, she was saving money to run away from home. She would never kill or give her baby away.

One night, while her parents were sleeping, Maria ran away from home and went to the train station. She went to Rome and from Rome to a small town called Fermo, which is on the east coast further north of Rome. Maria put almost half a country between her and her parents. She went to a place where no one knew her. Maria was six months pregnant when she arrived in Fermo, with little money and no one to support her.

Upon arriving in Fermo, Maria went directly to the church. After kneeling and asking God for help, she took the strength to talk to the priest.

"Father, I need your help."

The priest looked at her. "I have never seen you before. Who are you?"

"My name is Maria. I am not from here. I am from far away and have run away from home."

"You ran away from home?"

"Yes," Maria replied.

"Where is the father of that child? Why he does not help?"

"The father of this baby does not know, nor will he know, he exists. Just his name would harm him, and I will allow no one to harm my baby."

"And why didn't your parents help you?"

"My parents wanted me not to have him, but I refused. They told me I should give him up for adoption. I would never kill a child, nor would I give him away as if he were a puppy."

"Did your parents force or accept that you had relations with someone before you got married?"

"No, they never did or would do something like that."

"Interesting." Answers the priest.

Maria looks at him. With mixed emotions between offended and confused. She asks the priest.

"What do you see interesting about this?"

"Well, you disobey God and your parents. You have relations with a man who, according to you, just the name can damage someone's life. You ran away from home. Now you remember God and come to his house for him to solve your problems."

Maria was stunned after hearing what the priest said, and she did not know how to answer. The priest saw Maria did not know what to say or what to do, so gave the last thrust. He sarcastically asks his last question.

"Do you have something else to ask God?"

After this, the priest waited for Maria to turn around and leave; however, Maria responded without fear and looking straight into his eyes.

"You saw me on my knees in that corner. What I had to ask God I already asked, what I had to say to God, I already told him and what I have to say to God in the future, I will tell him in my prayer."

The roles were changed. The priest was the one who did not know what to say, because he never expected such an answer, but he tried to compose himself and return to the attack.

"Out of curiosity, what did you ask God for?"

"I asked for him to help my son, but I am going to kneel again to ask him for something else."

Now the priest was curious. What this young woman would come out with?

Maria went back to the same corner and knelt. After a while, she got up and walked toward the church exit. The priest could not stand his curiosity. He knew if she left the church, possibly he would never see her again and would not know the answer.

"Young lady." Exclaimed the priest.

Maria stopped. "Yes, father."

"Can I ask you what you asked God for? I want you to know you are not obligated to tell me."

"I know, father, but yes, I will tell you." Answered Maria.

"Very good, then tell me."

Maria looked at him and asked him.

"Let's see, father. What is my name?"

"Sorry, but if you told me, I don't remember."

"That's why I knew I had to talk to God again."

"Sorry, I really don't understand what you mean."

Maria looks at him and says.

"Well, I asked him that the next time he sent an innocent baby to this world, he should not send him with a woman named Maria, because here men prefer for him to be born among the animals in a manger before helping him. That, instead of listening, they ignore. That instead of helping, they judge. Instead of forgiving, they condemn. Look at you, father. You do not even remember my name, but you remember all the negative points. You, without knowing the full story, convicted me and supposedly you were the person God sends me to get help. But what am I going to do? It seems that, according to you, God also makes mistakes."

The priest was stunned. Where did this young woman come from who dares to give such an answer? Answer that can be classified as disrespectful, but true. The priest was used to being the most intelligent, the most cultured, that when he spoke, people listened and did not respond. No one had ever dared to contradict him, or worse, put him against the ropes.

Since the priest did not speak and his face was completely confused, Maria told him.

"Well, father, you know what I came for and what I'm going to do. I hope God has prepared a good day for you, and you have prepared a good answer for God."

Maria turned around and left the church. She had walked about thirty meters, when she heard the priest calling her with an authority as if he was her carnal father.

"Maria, Maria, where do you think you are going?"

"Well, to do what I couldn't do here, father." Maria saw the priest was furious and told him.

"Father, if you're going to lecture me, do it, but quickly. I don't have time to waste."

The priest, in the form of a scolding, told her.

"Who told you to go away? Return immediately to the church. I have an empty room where you will spend the night. Tomorrow we will go to the house of a parishioner who needs company more than help. We will talk with her and see what God decides."

It was obvious Maria had made the priest feel guilty and since the priest was a true believer; he had no choice but to help her.

Early the next day, the priest and Maria went to see Patricia, who was a sixty-year-old woman who lived in a beautiful village on the outskirts of Fermo. Patricia saw the priest and Maria coming and went out to greet them.

"Good morning, father. Who is this beautiful young girl who accompanies you?"

Maria responded instantly. "Good morning, Patricia, my name is Maria. It is a pleasure to meet you."

"Oh, Maria, like the Virgin Mary."

"That is just another coincidence." Answers Maria.

"Ha, ha, ha. Do you mean that the father's name is Jose?"

"His name is not Jose and I believe the baby will not be named Jesus either, but the coincidence is that I am going through a difficult time just as the Virgin Mary was going through."

The priest interrupts and says. "Maria ran away from home."

Patricia kept silent for a moment, shook her head and says.

"She must have had a very good reason to do something like that."

"You are absolutely right." Maria replied.

The priest intervened again.

"She needs help. I didn't let her leave church yesterday, and I thought of you, since you told me that the girl who helped you for so many years got married and went to live with her husband."

Patricia interrupts him and tells him.

"No! She doesn't need help, but the baby does. I don't care who you are or what you did. I care about that baby. I know this baby has committed no sin. If you brought her to me, then she was sent by God, and it is enough for me. Didn't you teach us to do good and not to judge, father?"

The priest flushed, for those words were like a scolding from God directed at him. Patricia goes to Maria and tells her.

"There are priests who say one thing and do another, but I can assure you something, our father here has never let us down."

The priest lowered his head and avoided looking at Maria. She took Patricia's hand, and the priest closed his eyes, because knowing Maria, he did not know what to expect. Maria took the priest's hand with her other hand and said.

"Patricia, I have always been a believer and now more than ever, because this priest has made me feel closer to God and has proven God never abandons us."

"Amen!!!" Patricia answered.

The priest was left with his mouth open. He hugged and kissed Maria, saying, "God bless you, my child, and thank you for strengthening our faith. At least I speak for myself."

Patricia took both of Maria's hands and said to her.

"Welcome home. The rules are as follows. First, I am your employer. If you behave, I will stop being your employer to be your friend. Finally, if you earn it, I will stop being your friend to be your mother and grandmother of that child."

Maria's tears ran down her cheeks. She hugged Patricia tightly and said.

"You can't be real. You are an angel, and you don't even know it."

"Oh, my child, I also have my fleas. You'll see."

The priest also wiped his tears and said.

"I must leave you. I must go to see a sick person."

"No father, you cannot leave without breakfast. "Said Patricia.

"Girl, do you like to cook?"

Maria answered sharply. "No!"

Patricia looks at the priest, who had closed his eyes and had a constipated face.

"I love it." Maria replied.

The priest took a deep breath and said to Maria in a tone as if they had known each other for many years.

"Why are you abusing me, Maria? Why?"

The three of them laughed and Patricia took Maria by the arm and said to her.

"Come on, daughter, I'll show you your room. But tell me. Is that all you got?"

Maria carried only a small suitcase with her.

"No, I have many things, but this is all I need."

That morning, Maria took pleasure in preparing a breakfast that won over Patricia, and especially the priest.

Franco calls Luigi to his office. Luigi walks in and Franco tells him.

"I need you to go see Vittorio and tell him please I need to see him. That it is very important and that I will thank him forever."

"But Don Franco, how many times do I have to go to see this Vittorio, so he can tell me no? If you will only allow me."

Franco interrupts and tells him.

"No! Luigi no! Do only what I tell you."

"Yes, sir, that is how it will be. Anything else, sir?"

"No Luigi. thanks."

"I'll go see him this afternoon. He's always alone with his son in the afternoons."

Umberto had remained in Ischia by order of his superiors. He joined the prosecutor in the criminal investigation into the deaths of Augusto and Donato. After a week, Umberto had all the results that he needed to reach a conclusion together with the prosecutor. Umberto asked the prosecutor not to make the results public until he spoke personally with Salvatore.

Umberto and Raffaelle went together to see Salvatore. They had formed a strong friendship, and apart from age; they had many things in common. When they saw Salvatore, they were shocked. Salvatore had lost over twenty pounds in just one week, sounded incoherent many times and had totally neglected his physical appearance, which he bragged about a lot. They both felt sorry for him, but they came to give him the result of the investigation and they had to do it without delay. Umberto said.

"Salvatore, I have supervised the investigation from start to finish with the prosecutor and the results are that there was no criminal act in the deaths of Augusto and Donato."

Salvatore closes his eyes, leans back in his chair and says.

"You failed Umberto, you failed."

"What failed?" Umberto asks calmly.

Salvatore. "Defensive trauma."

Umberto. "There is none in either of the two victims."

Salvatore. "Drugs."

Umberto. "There is no presence of drugs in either of the two bodies."

Salvatore. "Prints on the chair."

Umberto. "Only Donato's footprints and fingerprints. I went further because the chair seemed very beautiful for a farmer, but they have two more identical chairs. Augusto had bought one for himself and one for each son. I processed them and they only had the fingerprints of the relatives of the house. Analyzed the rope and nothing either."

Salvatore. "Evidence of violence in the house."

Umberto. "There is not."

Salvatore stands up screaming like crazy.

"Can't you see Umberto? They are professionals. Did you forget everything we went through that day? So many coincidences cannot be coincidences. Are you going to take their side?"

Umberto, about to lose control, responds.

"No, but criminal cases are based on factual evidence, not circumstantial evidence. You know that better than anyone, and I do not have real evidence. I also think like you, and I agree with you, but I have nothing. However, not everything is bad. This evidence exonerate you from any criminal charges and in a civil case, it is your word against theirs and the one that has the answer is dead, so I don't see that those charges can be sustained. I also spoke to the judge handling your case in the civil lawsuit against you. I explained to him about your emotional stage and that the negative bombardment of the press in the case of the hill had a detrimental influence against you and favors Franco, so it would be fair to postpone the hearing for at least fourteen days. The judge agreed with me, and you will have your first hearing in twelve days."

Umberto realized he was speaking, but Salvatore was not listening. He went round and round with his right hand on his chin, as if still thinking about the case.

Luigi approaches Vittorio's business, who was fixing an engine with his son next to him, trying to convince him of something which caught Luigi's attention. The boy was talking about welding underwater. Luigi thought it must be a science fiction book. It is impossible to weld underwater because the flames would go out. The conversation was so pleasant Luigi did not bother them and kept listening for a long time while Vittorio and his son did not realize they had company. Vittorio drops a tool and, when he picks it up, he realizes Luigi is next to them.

"Luigi, how long have you been there?"

"Excuse me, Vittorio, the book the child is reading is very interesting. I've always liked science fiction."

The child responds. "It is not fiction; it was invented in Russia many years ago."

Luigi looks shocked. "Seriously?

"Sure sir, that's the future and I try to convince my father to let me study it."

"He doesn't quite understand it is very dangerous, and he does not need to take those risks." Vittorio answers.

"I know nothing about the matter, so I better not say anything. All I know is that if the man had not taken risks, we would still" be in the Stone Age." Luigi said.

Exactly sir, see father, he thinks like me. Sir, I am sure that you are not afraid to take risks."

"I have never been afraid. I am only afraid to be afraid."

Vittorio did not like Luigi's comment, and Luigi realized just by seeing Vittorio's face.

"But just remember, boy, most of us who take risks do it because we have nothing to lose. I think this is not your case. Your father is also right. It is best to talk with him and agree in the middle in which you both are satisfied."

Vittorio looked at him and smiled. "It's the only sensible thing I've heard from you since I've known you."

"Perhaps because Don Vittorio has never paid attention to my words."

Vittorio tells his son. "Alberto, it's late, go home. I'll arrive a little later. I must discuss a matter with Luigi."

"Father, I will wait for you."

"No, son, go home." Vittorio insisted.

Once the two were alone, Vittorio says.

"What does Franco want? If it's the same thing, let's not waste our time."

Luigi responds. "Excuse me, but I'm just following orders."

"That is the difference between you and me. I do not answer to anyone, nor do I take orders from anyone."

Luigi realized nothing would change the outcome.

"Look Vittorio, Don Franco asks you. He begs you to come visit him. If you don't want to take your family with you, then go alone, but go please. It's very important."

"For whom it is important? For him or for me?" Vittorio asks.

"I am not authorized to speak, but I know it is good for both of you."

"Pleaer Don Luigi. This is the first time I have spoken to you without getting angry. Why we don't stop here, and we will both have a more pleasant dinner."

"You are absolutely right. Have a good night." Answered Luigi.

After the internal affairs commission decided on Salvatore's case, Captain Mancini goes to Umberto's office to give him the verdict. Mancini asks Umberto to call Salvatore. Umberto tells Mancini he will do it immediately. Mancini sits while Umberto calls Salvatore. When Salvatore answers the phone, Umberto informs him the internal affairs office had determined there was not enough evidence to find him guilty of committing a crime or having acted inappropriately during the handling of the case, so he would not be expelled from the department. That he would be offered the opportunity to return to his job, but not assigned to the Franco case, which would go to another detective. Salvatore, angry, yells at Umberto.

"I have been on this case for a long time. How could it be if they themselves admit I have not committed a crime and I have not acted incorrectly, then they will take me off the case and give it to someone who does not have a fucking idea of what these gangsters are capable of."

Umberto answers him. "I have taken a decisive role in your favor. I have stated that all the actions you took, however disastrous they turned out to be, made sense and that there were many points where I agreed with you. But your obsession with this case is kind of sick. That you have not committed a crime or acted improperly does not mean that your many failures do not merit being removed from the case. So, you report to work in fifteen days, or you quit work."

Umberto thought this would make Salvatore react, but he responded.

"Well, I resign. I will never give that victory to Franco. I will not return, and I will stay here. Remember what you could not do in three years, I did in three days. I will show everyone who is Salvatore. I will bring this mobster to justice by myself and with no one's help."

"I wish you luck," Umberto replied and hung up the phone. Captain Mancini, upon seeing Umberto's puzzled face, asks him.

"What happened?"

"I think a miracle has happened; the best thing can happen to all of us."

"And what is it?" Mancini asks.

"Salvatore resigned. He is not coming back," Umberto replied.

CHAPTER THIRTEEN

GOING BROKE

Salvatore's father created a fortune in communications. He was among the first to have radio stations, reaching twenty across the country. Salvatore was the only child and his parents tried to bring him into the family business, but he never showed interest in it. His love for power and his narcissism found more reward in law enforcement. His parents sold the business to enjoy the fruits of their labor during their old age. They had also passed the entire fortune in the name of their only son, Salvatore.

Salvatore represented himself, since he believed he knew more about the law than any lawyer on that small island. Salvatore was in an unstable emotional state, but his arrogant attitude had not changed. When asked by a reporter, Salvatore replied.

"I take this demand as a battle between Franco and me. I would not give up or accept that someone would fight this battle for me."

On the preliminary day of the trial, Salvatore appeared dressed impeccably. He was the most elegant, one of the tallest. He still felt in control and had not assimilated the seriousness of the situation he was facing. Salvatore asked the court for a trial without a jury that he would abide by the judge's decision, since it would be impossible to find people who were not contaminated by the press or biased in favor of Franco. The judge listened to Salvatore's arguments and asked Franco's lawyer if he had any objection to Salvatore's request.

"No, your Honor, there is no objection."

The judge granted the motion to Salvatore, so there will be a trial without a jury.

Luigi breaks the news to Franco that the judge has accepted a motion filed by Salvatore for a trial without a jury. Franco laughs and says.

This Salvatore is more stupid than I thought."

"Why do you say that, sir? Luigi asks.

"Because if you hold a jury trial and lose it, you can use those same arguments to ask for a new trial. That way, he would gain time."

"Time for what, Don Franco? "Luigi asks.

"To transfer the fortune back to his parents, who are the true owners, and that way if you win the second trial nothing happens, but if you lose, you lose nothing."

"Don Franco, you also know about laws?" Luigi asks.

"Luigi, what you can learn through reading is incalculable. I read everything that comes into my hand. That creates a wealth of wisdom that is stored as if it was money in the bank to be used when needed."

"Reading makes me sleepy, Don Franco. That's not my thing."

"Each one to his own. There are things I only entrust to you, because I know you do them better than anybody. But let us change the subject. I need you to see Vittorio again."

"Oh my God, but how many more times? You know that if you don't change the approach, he will not give in." Luigi responds.

"You are right, but this time you will tell him I ask, I beg, I implore him, so when he says no, then you tell him. I shouldn't tell you this, Don Vittorio, but if you don't meet with Don Franco, you and Don Franco both are going to get into trouble, and Don Franco doesn't want you to get hurt."

On the day of the trial, Salvatore dressed in his best suit. He had a beautiful watch that almost forced everyone to look at it when he moved his arm. He carried a briefcase that made him look like a high-profile lawyer. There were many reporters in the courtroom. They knew where Salvatore went, there would be news for sure. Salvatore was three minutes late. His purpose was for everyone to see him arrive and be the focus of attention. The reporters ran toward him with microphone and camera in hand. Salvatore raised his head and kept walking. After a few meters, the reporters stopped following him, and Salvatore kept walking. He thought they would follow him to the end like paparazzi, but when he saw they had lost interest in him, he turned around and told them.

"Do not worry, I will give you the opportunity when I finish with these clowns."

The judge orders Franco's lawyer to present his arguments. The lawyer stands and looks at everyone.

"Good morning, your Honor. Today we will show that here the defendant has used the position of authority vested in him and the department to which he belongs, to rage against my client. As you will see, your Honor."

The lawyer opens his leather portfolio, somewhat old and deteriorated from continuous use, and takes out several documents. The court officer takes the documents and passes them to the judge.

"You will see, your Honor, a detailed list of canceled events and the number of losses for each event throughout these past three years. You will also see physical damage caused to the property during the last search, after the K-9 police officer told him that the dogs did not pick up any alert. Nevertheless, he insisted and convinced his supervisor to destroy the gardens of the property in a malicious and vindicated manner."

Salvatore gets up and screams.

"Your Honor. Are you going to allow this guy to continue offending our intellect?"

The surprised judge responds.

"Mr. Salvatore do not interrupt. At this time, the plaintiff is presenting his case. Even if it seems to you, it is irrelevant. Sit down and do not interrupt."

Salvatore sits down and comments to a reporter.

"You, clearly, can see which side the judge is taking."

The judge heard the comment and turned red, making believe he hadn't heard. When Salvatore's turn came, he got up, looked around and pointed his finger at Franco's lawyer, and said.

"In front of you is the misfortune of this country. People who, instead of respecting the law, sell themselves to the gangsters. Yes, mobsters! Because he is representing a mobster who is in prison for murder."

Franco's lawyer interrupts.

"Objection, your Honor. My client's condition is irrelevant to the case."

The judge says." Objection granted."

The judge looks at Salvatore and tells him.

"Please, be specific to the defense of this case. Franco is not on trial."

Salvatore turns around and, looking at the audience, he opens his arms with the palms of his hand facing the audience, making a gesture as if to say, "Here you see". Salvatore turns around again and says.

"It's a very simple case, since your client cannot rob at gunpoint any longer, now your client uses you."

Salvatore points to Franco's lawyer. "Yes, you, that does not mean he is tired of robbing at gunpoint. It just means it is a lot easier and safer to do it through a disgraceful lawyer. It was me!! who put him in jail. He is the one who harasses me. As I told you, now through a lawyer he wants to steal my parents' fortune."

The judge yells, "Salvatore". But he ignores and continues.

"I also have my evidence."

The judge angrily says, "Show me your evidence."

Salvatore opens the portfolio and takes out a large, sealed envelope which was about to explode from the number of newspapers inside of it. The court officer takes it and brings it to the judge. The judge opens it, and many newspaper clippings fall on the judge's desk.

The judge says. "But these are newspapers!"

"And it means nothing to you?" Replies Salvatore.

"There is the proof." Salvatore yells.

"But proof of what?" About to explode, the judge asks.

"I'm sorry, your Honor, but if you do not consider that as evidence, then believe me when I say that I feel forced to do it."

The judge, visibly angry, stands up and yells. "To do what?"

The judge realizes he lost control. It is the first time he got emotional during a trial, but Salvatore is like an unstoppable train. The judge sits down, takes a deep breath, and says,

"Continue please."

Salvatore knows he got on the judge's nerves, so he turns his back to the judge, faces the public, and says,

"Today I will let everybody know the real issues are we are we are facing here."

The judge was about to ask the court officer to remove Salvatore from the court, but for some inexplicable reason, he gave him one last chance. Salvatore points to the judge's table and says,

"You have in your hands my evidence. Franco has not only bought the court through this lawyer who lends himself to such infamy. But he also bought the press and orders them to only criticize the work of those who fight crime, glorify the criminals, and portray them as victims. This could not be easier. A lawyer without principle gets paid well, and a percentage of the settlement goes to the judge."

Salvatore scratched his head while saying.

"That would be around 100,000 lire, and the verdict is bought. There, you have it. A perfect, totally legal scam."

Everyone in the room talks. No one thought Salvatore could make such a fuss. The judge punches the table, screaming.

"Order! Order!"

Finaly, the judge established order and Salvatore is still standing in the center with one hand on his waist and the other raised and waving as if he was conducting an orchestra.

"See how easy I have exposed how these crooks are stealing the country from us?" Salvatore exclaims.

"Are you accusing me of being corrupt? The judge, enraged, tells Salvatore.

Salvatore looks at the judge and responds.

"You answer that question with your verdict. Sorry if I unmasked the plan and spoiled the party."

The judge stands, and everyone thinks he is going to give the verdict, but he says.

"I will take a few minutes to analyze the evidence and give my verdict."

Franco's lawyer was surprised because Salvatore, with a lot of inconsistencies and stupidities, had inadvertently put the judge against the ropes. Reporters write hastily and comment with each other. Salvatore sat cross-legged and enjoyed the moment. The judge was sweating. He wanted to kill Salvatore for his lack of respect and false accusations. It was a simple case in favor of Franco since Salvatore had presented no defense, but it would create rumors if the ruling was in favor of Franco and if he gave a verdict in favor of Salvatore, it would bring more rumors, since Salvatore had not put up a defense, except the accusations to the judge.

The judge has high blood pressure. He felt on the verge of fainting. The more time passed, the more Franco's lawyer became concerned, and the more speculation was heard in the room. The judge knows people will talk about him anyway and that his career of so many years will be tainted. He decides to make Salvatore pay for it. The judge returns to the courtroom, and everybody becomes silent. The judge orders Franco's lawyer and Salvatore to stand up.

"After analyzing the evidence in this case, the defense has presented nothing conclusive to counteract the claim and its evidence has been void, so I have no alternative but to give a verdict in favor of Franco Cano."

The room exploded as everybody was talking. A reporter yelled at Salvatore.

"What do you say Salvatore?"

This was like an order of silence. Everyone was silent, because Salvatore's responses were always like opening a box of surprises. The retreating judge stopped to hear what Salvatore would say. Salvatore was still enjoying the moment without realizing he was ruined. He replied.

"Just analyze the last words of the judge. He has given himself away. He first says I have presented no defenses, that my evidence is irrelevant. So why did he leave for so long to deliberate? When he comes back, he comes sweating as if someone had poured a bucket of water over him and then he talks with a broken voice. I will explain what he went to deliberate. He went to put his principles on one side and the money to receive on the other side and the decision was clear."

The judge, who was already on the verge of fainting, collapsed, but the court official grabbed in time, preventing him from falling to the floor. The judge was rushed to the hospital to receive medical attention since his pressure rose to a critical point.

Salvatore made headlines again. It was the first time such a high judgement had been granted and the first time a defendant had sent a judge to the hospital. Salvatore realized he was ruined about three days later. He had spent the whole time talking about the comments in the newspaper where the judge had been hospitalized because of him.

Salvatore starts facing reality. He sits on a chair in his kitchen, puts his left hand on his forehead and says.

"My God! What do I do now? I have no job and no money."

Salvatore fell into a deeper depression. He did not leave the apartment for a week and he would not open the door to anyone.

Luigi returned to Vittorio's business, arriving at closing time so he could talk to Vittorio alone.

"Good afternoon, Don Vittorio."

Vittorio looked at him and replied.

"Good afternoon, Don Luigi. I must admit you are persistent and before you tell me what you came for, I will tell you it is a pity that I cannot please you."

"Look, Don Vittorio, I confess it is not a pleasure for me to come here for the same thing always. Also, I assure you Don Franco respects you and for him to insist there must be a reason. Don Franco asks you, begs you, implores you to come to see him. You know he can't come here, otherwise he would be here."

"As you said, it's a shame." Vittorio replies.

Luigi approaches him and whispers.

"I shouldn't tell you this, but if you will not talk to Don Franco, the two of you are going to have big problems. Don Franco doesn't care about him, but he doesn't want you to have a problem."

Those words caught Vittorio's attention, and he changed his attitude. Luigi thought Vittorio was finally going to come to his senses. Vittorio was silent for about three minutes. It was clear he was thinking about Luigi's words. Finally, Vittorio answers in the same low voice Luigi spoke to him.

"Tell Franco thanks, but no thanks. If he needs help to solve his problem, he can count on me as long as it is legal. I will face my problem when it arrives, just as I have faced many other problems before. Have a good night, Don Luigi."

Luigi smiles and shakes his head. "You too Don Vittorio."

Maria had given birth to a beautiful baby. Patricia was crazy with happiness and at last there would be a child in the house who would give color to the life with his laughter and crying. Maria found in Patricia an unconditional mother and Patricia in Maria, the daughter she never had, and she always dreamed of. Maria was educated, smart, entrepreneurial, with responses that were on the verge of being disrespectful, but correct. She said things the way she saw them, but she was always open to dialogue and to change her mind if she was shown otherwise. The priest passed by twice a week. Maria had won him over with the food she prepared.

One morning, Patricia was carrying the baby while Maria was cooking; Patricia looks at Maria and asks her.

"Do you miss your parents?"

"Of course. What more would I want than to have them by my side. They did everything for me and tried to do the best for me, in their way of thinking. I do not hold any grudges against them. The good and the bad that they did, they did it, thinking it was the best for me. That is why I do the same for my son. God gave him to me to protect him, educate him. Unfortunately, he could not be at their side."

"You are an extraordinary human being." Patricia told her.

"As you told me once before, I also have my fleas." Answers Maria.

Patricia hears that someone has arrived.

"Who would that be? I'm not waiting for anyone."

It was Romulo, Patricia's younger brother.

"Oh my gosh, I didn't know you had a nephew."

"As you see, I already have an heir to the house." Patricia responds.

Patricia's joke was not funny to her brother. He only cared about inheriting the house. He had never cared about his sister, but the house where she lived. Patricia introduces her brother to Maria.

"This is Romulo, my younger brother and only living relative."

"I didn't know you had a brother." Says Maria.

"Yes, I have one brother, even though sometimes I wonder if I have one or not."

"How can you say that, sister?"

"I say it because you pass by once every two years and then you disappear. I call you, and you don't answer. I write to you, and you don't answer."

"You are wrong, sister. I care about you so much that I spoke to a friend to buy all that empty land that you have which is neglected and full of bushes."

"It is neglected because it is too big for me to clean it. It takes at least three men to clean it and I have to pay them."

"That is the reason I want to take that headache away from you."

Maria understands Romulo is not interested in his sister at all and is only looking for money. Maria interrupts and says.

"But excuse me, Patricia and I have already talked about that area."

Patricia was surprised, because she had never told Maria about those lots. She knew Maria did not know about what lots they were talking about.

"Really!" Romulo asked, surprised.

"Yes sir, that was two days ago." Answers Maria.

"So, you mean the two of you are going to clean it up?"

"No, we will buy three goats. Those animals are like land-cleaning machines. There are places that rent them to clean inaccessible land. Not only will they clean the land, but we will have milk from which we will make cheese and sell meat. When the land is clean, we will buy laying hens. We will have eggs and not even have to fence the land because those animals will not leave if we provide the conditions. We have many more plans, but we will start with that."

"Romulo was stunned by what Maria said.

Where did you get this little girl from?" Romulo asked.

"I didn't get her. She was sent to me."

"By whom?"

"By God," Patricia replied.

Romulo was upset. Maria had spoiled his plans.

"God sent you a husband and after three years, he took him back and he did not even give a child. Only left you this villa, which is already falling apart."

Patricia couldn't stop her eyes from watering. She got up and asked her brother.

"Are you going to stay?"

"Yes, sister, I will stay for two days."

"Great! I am going to prepare your room."

Patricia left the room and leaned against the wall, because her brother's words were so hurtful she needed to recover. Maria also noticed Romulo had hurt Patricia and had upset her a lot. Romulo thought Patricia was not near, so told Maria.

"Listen girl, I don't know where you come from, but I know where you are going to. If you think you're going to stay in this villa, you're wrong. You and your son do not have the right."

Maria, offended, tells him.

"The one who has no right is you. How you dare speak to me in that way? For me, the material things are of low priority, unlike you, who are like a comet that passes every four years, dragging a long tail of ambitions and problems. You should know the only thing of worth in this villa is your sister, who is priceless. You prefer to go see someone else to propose the sale of a piece of land rather than coming to see your sister. You cannot wait for her to die and to take over her possessions. You are trying to sell her properties, even while she is alive."

Romulo raises his hand to slap Maria, but he stops and tells her.

"I should break your face to teach you to respect."

"You do not teach by hitting. You teach by example. So, learn to respect others, so that you inspire respect." Maria responds.

Patricia reacted and came out to prevent things from getting worse.

"Your room is ready."

"If this disrespectful young woman stays here, I have nothing to do in this house. I will not set foot in this house as long as you have her here."

"But brother, let's not lose control, not that bad."

"This is quite simple, this intruder or me."

"I cannot throw her out onto the street with a baby." Patricia responds.

"Then I'm leaving and when she leaves, then I will visit you."

Romulo turned around and left. Patricia burst into disconsolate tears. Maria, very ashamed and feeling guilty, approaches her and says.

"Please forgive me, your brother is right. I have said thing I shouldn't and have taken attributions that do not belong to me. I am deeply sorry to cause you this displeasure. I think it would be better for me to find another place."

Patricia, still crying, answers.

"No Maria, you have only told the truth that I never dared to say."

Maria hugs her and calls her "Mother." When she called her "Mother" she did it without realizing it. It had come from her heart.

"It might be true, but I don't have the right to say it. I have caused you pain, and you do not deserve it."

Patricia dried her tears and hugged Maria tightly. It was the first time in her life someone called her mother.

"Thank you, daughter. When you called me, mother, gave me the strength to carry on. We have many things to do, and it was all your idea."

"What ideas are you talking about?"

Patricia looks at her and asks her. "What happened to the word mother? If you don't use it from now on, we will have to start over again."

"What do you mean?" Asked Maria.

"It means, I will become your employer, and it will not be so easy for me to become your mother."

Maria hugged her. "NO, NO, MOTHER, MOTHER!"

CHAPTER FOURTEEN

A CLINIC AND A FARM

The months passed, and Salvatore recovered little by little. He had some money kept in a secret account he had opened many years ago, hidden from his parents. That money kept him from falling into misery for a few years. He dedicated his body and soul to put Franco once and for all behind bars. This way, he would recover his fortune, his honor, his job, and the newspapers would be obligated to talk about him and recognize his merits. He went back to the tree to see if it was in place or if it had been cut down. It was a great surprise to see the tree and his hiding place were intact. It was like an invitation to continue watching over the complex. Salvatore hugged the tree and said.

"I know you missed me. I'll be back soon. I'll take a week off. We will start the battle again."

Patricia and Maria went to a neighboring farm to buy three goats, just as Maria had told Romulo. Maria never thought Patricia was going to take her words literally, but Patricia insisted on carrying out the plan. Once at the farm, Maria stayed with her baby to feed him while Patricia bought the goats. About forty minutes later, Patricia returns with three goats.

"Look Maria, these are the animals we are taking home. I told them I wanted to show them to you first."

Maria angrily asks. "Is that what he gave you, or what you ask for?"

"That is what he gave me."

Maria tells Patricia. "Please mother, you stay here. I am going to have a talk with that man."

Patricia, kind of worried, asked. "What do you mean? Don't you like them?"

"Nothing mother, I just have to talk to him."

"No, Maria, I know you. I'm going with you. Please, I don't want any problems before we even start."

"Don't worry mother, there will be no problem."

Maria asks Patricia. "Show me the man that sold you the goats?"

Patricia points at the man. "That man, he was very kind and helpful."

Maria calls the man, who comes immediately.

"Can I help you with something else, madam? Asks the farmer to Patricia.

Maria immediately responds.

"Sir, take back your goats and give me back my money."

"But what happened? Asked the farmer.

"You know very well what happened, so either we started over or there is no business."

"Explain it to me. I don't understand you."

"Fine, since you want me to explain, then listen. We are women, not idiots. How come you are going to give us three male goats? By the way, one of them is quite old. Let us both do business, not only you."

"I have given you the best I have." Replied the farmer."

"In that case, give me something other than the best you have, so you will earn more."

Patricia did not know what to do. She knew Maria was a time bomb. She was swinging the baby in her arms faster and faster. Patricia tries to intervene.

"But Maria!"

"Not now, mother! No!" Maria responds, looking at the farmer.

"Listen, it is your choice. You can give me two females and a male, two males and a female, or a male, a female and two puppies. In this way, you keep your best. I assure you, most likely we will continue doing business in the future."

The farmer looks at Patricia and says.

"Very smart, your daughter!"

Patricia realizes the farmer was cheating on her.

"My daughter knows a lot about farms, and I know nothing about it." Answers Patricia.

"Look, young lady, of the three options you gave me, choose the one you want. But next time, it will be better if your father or your husband comes to do business."

"Thank you very much. You are truly kind, so in this case, I will take a male, a female, and two puppies."

"You are ripping me off." The farmer, annoyed, says.

"You told me to choose. Didn't you?"

"Okay, but remember, next time, it must be your father or your husband."

"That will be very difficult. They have to stay at home cooking for when we return."

The farmer could not help laughing when he heard such an answer. "Yes, I believe it. Of course, I believe it."

On the way back home, Patricia tells Maria.

"I did not know you knew about those animals."

"You are right. I know nothing."

"So, how did you know he was cheating on us?"

"Simple. None of the three had teats, and three males will not give us a herd." Answers Maria.

"But how did you know one of them was old?"

"I didn't know. I just thought if he wanted to give us three males, he also wanted to give us the oldest one."

That same afternoon, the farmer took the animals to Patricia's villa. When he realized they were two women alone, he apologized to Patricia. He told her he did not want to deceive them. He was angry the men in the house would send women to do such work.

Salvatore kept spying on the tree, but not daily. He did it spontaneously, so they would not know when he was going to be watching them. It was more difficult to detect a suspicious activity because the complex was always full of tourists constantly coming in and out. One day Salvatore climbs the tree and finds a cup of hot chocolate, a package of cookies and a list with the names of the guests. Salvatore was furious. He understood Franco knew in advance when he was going to the tree. That was because he did not have a vehicle and had to walk up the hill to get to the tree. Salvatore drank his cup of chocolate and ate his cookies.

One day, Salvatore observed that the complex was empty. That puzzled him a lot, and he remained in the tree until he saw some people in the garden. He could not recognize them because they were far away. The complex was empty for another three days and then he saw about eight people leave. He could not recognize them because it was raining extremely hard. The next day, the complex was filled with tourists again. Salvatore analyzed what happened and concluded that when Franco had a mob meeting, he kept the complex closed.

Salvatore gave Umberto a call. Umberto answered the phone and recognized Salvatore's voice. He thought about hanging up, but out of pity, he talked to him to see what state he was in. Salvatore did not tell him about Franco immediately, only almost when he finished, he told him.

"I spend hours reading on my balcony and you know, my balcony faces the entrance to the hill. It is unavoidable not to see the number of taxis going up and down the hill, but last week there was no activity. I recognized the face of one of those gangsters. I am sure he left because traffic has returned to normal."

Umberto responds. "Interesting. The department plans to assign a detective to Franco's case because there are many things that are not clear."

Salvatore smiles and says. "I know that deep down you know I am right."

"I have never said you are right or wrong. I said your actions make sense, but your results are catastrophic, so let's end this conversation. I am glad to know that you are better."

Umberto hung up the phone as the conversation was taking a course he did not want to touch. Once again, he had to admit that inside his madness, Salvatore had some logic, and this was not an exception.

Franco makes a call to the police station and asks to speak to Raffaelle. This call surprised the officer on duty, but he had no alternative other than to transfer the call.

"Boss, I have Don Franco on the line. He wants to talk to you."

"With me? What can that man want from me? Tell him I have nothing to talk to him about."

The officer goes to Raffaelle's office.

"Don Franco says he is one of the biggest contributors to the island's government through his taxes, so it is totally unfair you ignore him when he needs something."

Raffaelle leans back in his chair and crosses his arms. He realizes Franco is right, and he does not want any kind of confrontation with Franco.

Raffaelle takes the phone and says.

"Good morning, Don Franco. How can I help you?"

"Good morning, Don Raffaelle, everything is fine, but I have a problem only you can solve."

"I don't think so. If you can't, I can't either."

"Yes, you can. I'm a little sick and I need to see a doctor. I can't leave this place. Only you can bring him here or transport me to the hospital."

Raffaelle was surprised. He did not expect this, and Franco was right.

"Oh, I am sorry to hear that, Don Franco. I never imagined such a thing. When do you want to go to the hospital?"

"Whenever you can take me."

"How about this afternoon at two?"

"Perfect." Answers Franco.

Raffaelle tells the officer on duty.

"I need two police cars and two undercover cars. Today we are taking Don Franco to the hospital. I want one undercover car in front and another behind, just in case Don Franco is planning to escape. I also want the marine patrol to be on alert."

"Yes, chief." The officer answered.

That afternoon, Salvatore sees two police cars going up the hill and says.

"Damn, Umberto, you stole the information I gave you to take credit for arresting Franco, but you will not get away with it."

Salvatore goes to the entrance of the hill to wait for the vehicles to come down. The undercover officer saw Salvatore but did nothing. They knew him and only made fun of him. Salvatore sees the two police cars coming down the hill and stands in the middle of the road. Raffaelle has to brake to avoid hitting Salvatore, who screams wildly.

"You have used the information I gave Umberto to arrest him and steal my credit, but you will not get away with it. I will report you."

Raffaelle pops his head out of the vehicle and yells at him.

"Get out of the way or I'll arrest you. I am tired of your stupidity."

Salvatore moves out of the way and sees a taxi coming down the hill. The taxi brakes to avoid running over Salvatore, who gets into the taxi and tells the driver, follow those police cars quickly.

The taxi driver follows the police vehicle and Salvatore asks him.

"Can't you pass the vehicle behind them?"

"No sir, I've tried three times, but the vehicle won't let me."

Salvatore says.

"Now I understand. They must be undercover officers. It doesn't matter. Follow them and don't lose them."

After about twenty minutes, the police vehicles enter the hospital and Salvatore tells the taxi driver to keep going.

"But sir, you told me to follow them."

Salvatore, crying out, says.

"Keep going, make a "U" turn and go back to where you picked me up."

The taxi driver stops the taxi and yells.

"Get out of my taxi."

"Why? Just take me back."

"I told you to get out." The taxi driver yells, furiously.

"If you don't take me back, I won't pay you." Salvatore responds, firmly.

"I don't care if you don't pay. I am about to kill you and I don't want to end up in prison."

After the doctor's visit, Raffaelle returns to the hill with Franco.

"You should rest and eat better." Raffaelle advises Franco.

"That doctor is wrong. I do not have anemia, and these tests will not show my diagnosis."

"Don't be pessimistic. Let's wait for the result. What is clearly visible is that you should rest." Raffaelle replies.

Franco looks at Raffaelle and says.

"One block south of the hill, there is a building in poor condition for sale. Please talk to the governor and tell him if they buy it, I promise to fix it and build an emergency clinic for the residents on this side of the island. Even you will be closer to it than to the hospital in case of an emergency."

"You are right, but I don't think the governor wants to do business with you."

"He will not be in business with me. The clinic would belong to the island and not bear my name. No one will know I was involved."

"I will relate your proposal."

"Tell him he has until Thursday to respond."

"Why until Thursday? Why?"

"Because today is Monday and if in two days, he can't recognize the citizens need that clinic, then there is nothing more to talk about and I will build it myself."

"I give you my word. I will convey your message today."

Going down the hill, Raffaelle sees Salvatore walking back to his apartment. He had walked for about two hours. He was sweaty and tired. Raffaelle gets out of the vehicle and approaches him and tells him.

"If you get in my way again, I swear you will have to leave the island. If I don't arrest you now, it is because I do not even want to see your face in prison."

Salvatore didn't answer. He was tired and sweaty. He looked confused, as if he had just arrived from another planet.

In the last meeting, the members of the group demanded Franco to put pressure on Vittorio to sell his business. The geographical position made it a vital point for the organization. Franco promised he would convince Vittorio, but it would not be a simple task, and any method other than peaceful would jeopardize everything obtained so far.

Raffaelle walks into the governor's office and tells him.

"Good morning, I bring you a message from Don Franco."

The governor looks at him, surprised, and responds.

"Don't tell me, you are not only his taxi driver, but you are also his messenger."

Raffaelle and the governor had been friends since childhood. They used to tease each other when they were in private.

"The hell with you. I'm not up for your jokes. I am telling you because he set a deadline for your response."

"Look Raffaelle, that crook will use you as a taxi driver, a messenger and will put ultimatums on you, but not on me, so I can tell you he can go to hell."

"I don't know how the people would vote for you. If they only knew what kind of person you are, you are out of the office. Anyway, Don Franco says there is a building near the hill that is for sale. If the government buys it, he promises to fix it and turn it into an emergency clinic for the residents of the area."

"Are you crazy, Raffaelle? I can't go into business with Franco."

"He will not appear in anything. No one will know he was involved. That would serve you more than everybody else."

"I know it's a good deal, especially with elections coming up soon, but I will not let that crook put an ultimatum on me. It would send him the wrong message. I accept, of course, but I will not get with him after Thursday."

"If you don't tell him before Thursday, he's going to build it on his own. If you're going to say yes, do it now. Do not mess with this guy. That could backfire on you."

"Please do not tell me Franco intimidates you. Are you carrying a water pistol?"

Raffaelle responds. "I must go. I have no time to waste with politicians. So, Mr. Governor, with all the respect you deserve, you go to hell."

On Monday morning, Raffaelle to go see which building Franco was talking about and sees a construction crew working on the building. When Raffaelle arrives at the office, he calls the Governor and sarcastically tells him.

"Hello, Mr. Governor. You told me you were going to call Don Franco after Thursday, but I see you are not stupid. You would not miss an opportunity like that, especially when you will soon be in the re-election campaign."

"Why are you talking about? I did not call him."

"I thought you called him because I saw they are already working on the building."

The governor laughs and answers.

"I am sure he started the project, thinking I was going to call him immediately. I will make him wait a few days to show him he is not in control, and I do not give up on his ultimatum."

Raffaelle laughs and tells him.

"You know what to do. If you have been able to convince the people to vote for you, I do not doubt you can convince Don Franco."

"Bravo! Even you call him Don Franco."

"I don't know why I can't talk to you without sending you to hell." Raffaelle replied and hung up the phone.

The Governor thought Raffaelle was playing a prank on him, so he decided to check if they were working on the building. Submerged in his arrogance, the Governor thought Franco only wanted to ingratiate himself with him, as gangsters do to buy politicians.

On Wednesday, Franco receives a call at his office.

"Good morning, Franco, this is the Governor of Ischia."

"Good morning, Mr. Governor. How can I help you?"

Raffaelle was telling me of a project about an emergency clinic you wanted to do and needed the help of the government."

"Oh, it's a pity Raffaelle misinterpreted me, or you misinterpreted Raffaelle."

"Actually, I do not think it is a problem. I see you have begun to repair the building. Today I will speak with the lawyers, so they buy the building and give priority to the project."

"Thank you, but it will not be necessary. I bought the building when I did not receive a response from you. It is an excellent location, and I did not want to risk someone else buying it."

The Governor still felt in control.

"You have done the right thing, Franco. This way, you have ensured this project cannot be interrupted by anyone. I congratulate you. Please have the documents ready. Our lawyers will pick them up to transfer the property to the government and reimburse you. Everything will continue as you told Raffaelle."

Franco takes his time and responds.

"I was very clear to Raffaelle. Now the building and all the contracts are in my name. I don't think it would be convenient for you to enter into a partnership with me."

"Nobody will find out what happened. Everything will be as you asked at the beginning."

"I'm sorry, Governor." Franco responds.

"But Don Franco, everything has a solution in this life."

The Governor understood his arrogance had betrayed him and changed his attitude completely, even calling him Don Franco.

"I agree with you, so when you did not call me, I found the solution. I will do the clinic myself and I will not take more time from you, because you are a very busy man. Have a good day Governor."

The Governor went to see Raffaelle at the police station right away.

"Raffaelle, I need your help."

"What's going on?" Raffaelle responds.

"This Franco. He wants me to beg him for the clinic project."

"But you didn't call him before Thursday as he requested?"

"I told you I will call him after Thursday and the truth is he does not want to reason with me. Maybe you can convince him."

"He is not my friend. I don't want to ask that guy a favor. I don't want to owe him no favor."

"Well, if he thinks he's the boss, I will show him who is in charge of this island. I'm going to sabotage the construction and there will never be an inauguration."

"I do not advise you to do that. He will return your own torpedo and sink your ship."

"Whose side are you on?"

"On yours, of course. That's why I warn you not to do things that could affect your re-election. Franco is a rich and intelligent man. Do not turn against him without reason or you will regret it."

"I am leaving. I knew it was a waste of my time coming to see you." The governor says angrily.

"Well then, as always, go to hell, Mr. Governor." Raphaelle replied.

Patricia's villa was prospering. The vast land was completely clean, the goats had multiplied, and it became necessary to fence the property. Patricia tells Maria.

"Maria, I think we should get rid of the goats. The fence would cost us what we don't have."

"Mother, today is a special day. It is the first day the child goes to school. When we return from school, we will talk about that."

"Yes, daughter, I just wanted to let you know."

Patricia's brother had never visited her again, but he kept in touch with a friend who informed him about his sister's property. Before leaving the house, Maria says,

"After leaving the child at school, we will take the train and go to Ancona."

"For what, Maria?"

"We will walk through the markets to look for eggs."

"For what?"

"We need to get eggs, not from farmers, but from those that come packed from a large company. The packing must say the name of the distributor, and then we will call them."

"But Maria, how are we going to buy from a distributor? We don't have a lot of money or stores to sell them in?"

"Mother, leave that to me." Answered Maria.

Upon returning home, Maria makes a call to the company egg supplier.

"Good afternoon. I need to talk to the company's purchasing manager."

"Good afternoon. From what company are you calling, please?" A girl replies.

"On behalf of the Fermo distributor."

"I had not heard of that company."

"Yes, and if you do not pass me to the manager, he will never hear about it either."

"One moment, please."

Maria had taken information from three companies which were wholesaling.

"This is the manager speaking. How can I help you?"

Maria spoke clearly and firm, as if she was in total command.

"Good afternoon, sir. I have a business proposition for you. Note that the distributor "Uno" and the distributor "Fresco" will come to a meeting at my business in three days. If you are interested, you can come."

"I don't think it would be a good idea to go when two other companies are present. That's not the way we do business."

"Well, in that case, come first and beat the others."

"You just told me you had made an appointment with them in three days and now you're going to waste their time. That's not professional and we are a serious company."

"Excuse me, but don't put words in my mouth that I haven't said. That's not professional either. They chose that day. I do business with the first one that suits me."

"You are right. What do you think about the day after tomorrow we meet?"

"Now I see you do not waste an opportunity and you are strict. I like that a lot."

Maria gave him the address of the villa and they made an appointment at two in the afternoon. The owner of the distributor saw the face of the purchasing manager was a little strange and asks him.

"What happened on that call?"

"A lady tells me that the Uno company and the Fresco company are interested in doing business with her, but we can go earlier."

The owner thinks and responds.

"If Fresco and Uno will meet, it must be worth it. I will take your place and go myself."

A middle-aged man shows up at Patricia's villa and knocks on the door. Maria opens the door wearing an apron.

"Good afternoon. May I speak to the lady of the house?"

"Yes, of course." Maria gives out a yell. "Mom, there is a man looking for you."

"Patricia appears with a plate of food saying.

"If I don't force him, he won't eat. This child is very strong. Tell me, sir, what do you want?"

The man flushed. "If this is a joke, then it is of a very bad taste. Yesterday, a lady called me on the phone to talk business and gave me this address."

Maria says. "Yes, of course, it was me."

Maria takes off her apron and hands it to Patricia, whose face turns red.

"Please, come with me."

The man, not in a very good mood, follows her. Maria exits the house and shows him all the land and she says.

"All this is ours. I want to propose something to you."

The man interrupts her and says.

"I am the owner of the company. The only reason I'm here is because you said that Uno and Fresco were interested. I'm a very busy person and I can't waste my time this way."

Maria looks at him and says.

"If you leave without hearing what I am going to tell you, and already say you are wasting your time, then we have nothing to talk about. Remember, you were the one who let pass the opportunity. Perhaps others do not think like you, but it will be too late for you."

The man looks at Patricia, who, totally embarrassed, tries to avoid her gaze.

"Tell me, young lady, what do you propose?"

"Very simple. You build a farm here. The first three years you will earn ninety percent of the earnings, the next three years you will earn eighty-five percent of the earnings, the following three you will earn seventy-five percent of the earnings and from then on you will earn forty percent. You are located much further, and this will allow you to expand south without having extra expenses. These terms will assure you that you will triple your investment in ten years. You will have forty percent income for life just by taking care of the maintenance, which is minimal."

The man, as a business executive, changes his attitude and responds.

"I'm interested. I'll tell my lawyer to write the contract."

"But remember, you must fence the land." Says Maria.

"This is immense, it will cost a lot." Replies the man.

"I know, but it's for protecting your own investment. If you don't want to, let me know."

"Okay, I'll fence it."

When the man left, Patricia, crying out of joy, tells Maria.

"I can't believe it. I was terrified that when my old age came, I would have no money. The money my husband left me would run out in the next three years. You, without spending a penny, have fenced off the land and put it to produce."

Maria answers.

"This is just the beginning. In a few years, you are going to be the owner of Fermo."

After a year, two new businesses were inaugurated almost simultaneously. Franco and Luigi's lawyer inaugurated The Hill Emergency Clinic, where poor people were treated totally free and those who paid did so at a reasonable price. Half a country to the north, in the City of Fermo, the mayor, Patricia and the priest celebrated the inauguration of Patricia's Farm.

In Ischia, the inauguration was even sweeter, since the governor had tried to sabotage the project, but Franco called reporters and told them.

"Did you know a project to build a clinic that will serve the poor for free is apparently being delayed on purpose by the governor?"

That exploded like a bomb. The governor was interviewed about it, but as a good politician, he answered.

"Franco has been a controversial member of our community, but anyone who does work for the benefit of our community has my unconditional support. I regret not having been aware of what happened, but I will make my priority that this project becomes a reality in the shortest possible time." Those who heard the mayor's statement clapped like seals.

The priest blessed the new farm built on Patricia's property. At the ceremony, Patricia was the sensation of the moment. She would employ ten residents of the area. It was a beautiful afternoon. Life was finally smiling at Patricia. When everyone had left, Patricia asks Maria.

"Maria, my child, why do you want nothing to bear your name? You are not even in the opening pictures when you have done everything here."

"For me, it is enough that you are happy. You have given me much more than I can give you. There is no money in the world that can pay the debt I have with you. I also do not want my name to be made public. Remember, I don't want to be found."

Patricia hugged Maria and tells her.

"My dear Maria, with me you will always be safe."

CHAPTER FIFTEEN

ENRICO

Umberto meets with Detective Enrico to assign him to Franco's case. He puts a rather large file on the table and tells him.

"Enrico, you have six years of experience in the department. We choose you, because you don't take work personally. You are methodical and highly professional."

Umberto picks up the heavy file and drops it on the table.

"As you can see, after a lot of years behind this individual, the results are four deaths, an undercover detective who miraculously saved his life, and another who was not only dishonorably removed from the department but ended up broke. There are many things that do not fit in this story, but I do not want you to take any action unless you are two hundred percent sure. One hundred percent is not enough. You need to keep a low profile. It will be as if you were on vacation. Only the chief of police will know of your existence. Franco has accumulated a substantial fortune and has invested in the community creating an emergency clinic for the community and recently built a naval mechanics school where he gives scholarships to low-income students. As you will understand, this is a Franco strategy, since politicians do not dare to touch him for fear he will put his own candidate. The residents adore him, so it is very difficult to find someone to betray him.

"For real, that man has that much power?"

"That's right, I'm not exaggerating at all."

"You don't have to worry. I do not intend to fall into temptation or do crazy things. I will keep you informed of any incident."

Enrico took the voluminous file, stood up, and shook Umberto's hand.

Two days later, Enrico arrives in Ischia, and for a week, he traveled the island to familiarize himself with all the key points. Enrico calls Raffaelle and tells him he has a message from Umberto. He asks him to stop by his apartment but dressed in civilian clothes. That afternoon, Raffaelle shows up at Enrico's apartment.

Raffaelle introduces himself. "Good afternoon."

"Good afternoon, please come in." Enrico responds.

"Umberto told me a lot about you. I can tell you; he admires you."

"Likewise, we had our ups and downs, but in the end, we have many things in common. We developed a beautiful friendship."

Enrico opens a drawer, takes out Franco's file and puts it on the table.

"What is that?"

"This is Franco's file."

"Oh my! All that?"

"Yes, everything is here since the investigation began in Naples, years before he settled in Ischia."

Raffaelle scratches his head and says.

"I don't even know what to tell you. This is a lot more complicated than you can imagine."

"Believe me, I know. I did not come here to do crazy things or start a war. I will be honest with you. I only accepted this case because I cannot refuse it, so I need your help."

"I will help you just as I helped Salvatore and Umberto, but it has not been useful."

"Not that kind of help. I just need you to get me a job as a health inspector. I need you to introduce me as your cousin, whom you are helping. After getting the job, we will hardly keep contact. Please tell me. What should I know about this man?"

"What you should know is that every time we thought we had him, everything had gone the other way around. He always comes out stronger, to where the island's residents think of him as a saint."

"What is he like?"

"He is a kind, educated, apparently doesn't mess with anyone, and he has health problems."

"What about Salvatore?"

"He knows about Franco more than anyone. He has devoted his soul to persecute him for many years. Needless to say, he has not done well at all, despite being methodical, acting with logic and using all available resources."

"I wish you good luck and I will contact you when I find the job for you."

" Thank you very much." Enrico replied.

Franco calls Luigi to his office and tells him.

"On Monday next week, the complex will be closed to the public. You must go to see Vittorio."

Luigi shakes his head and responds. "You know what the answer is. He will not accept."

"It does not matter Luigi. This time you will not go alone, and you will take two men with you. You will wait for him before he opens his business. You will try to convince him once more. If he refuses, just tell him I sent him his belongings."

"What belongings are you talking about?" Luigi asked.

"Please listen to the end." Franco responds.

"You, with the help of two other men, will unload a wooden box out of the truck and carry it to his business. Act as if the box was heavy. That way, the three of you can enter Vittorio's business. Then immobilize him and do not forget to cover his eyes. Bring him to the underground shelter where I will wait for you all."

"Now you will talk to him. I promise you." Luigi responds.

Franco looks at Luigi and says. "Make sure you don't hurt him."

"We will try, but we might have to use force."

Franco interrupts him and tells him. "NO!! It is an order. You cannot hurt him."

"Yes, Don Franco, we won't hurt him."

On Sunday afternoon, Salvatore, as usual, was reading a book on his balcony and notices there was no traffic to Franco's compound.

That caught his attention. He kept surveillance from his balcony all afternoon, but he did not see any vehicle going up the hill. Salvatore could not contain his curiosity and walked up to the tree to see if everything was in order. Then he returned to his apartment and decided he would go to his observation point early in the morning. At dawn, Salvatore left armed with his camera, binoculars, and a notebook. He climbed the tree and felt excited again, waiting for a miracle.

Luigi was anxiously waiting for Vittorio to appear. He would love to force Vittorio to see Franco. He would like to have permission to give him a good shake. Luigi sees Vittorio approaching and gets out of the truck to greet him.

"Good morning, Don Vittorio."

A surprised Vittorio answers him. "Good morning, Don Luigi. How come you come so early and not when I am about to close as usual?"

"It is an emergency. Don Franco needs you. Please understand."

"Luigi, how many times will it take for you to understand I'M NOT INTERESTED!"

"It will be only once. Do it for an old friend." Says Luigi.

"My God, but how can I make him understand? I am not a friend of Don Franco. Franco and Don Franco are totally different people. There is no friendship between us."

"Don Vittorio, I respect your decision. I will transmit it to Don Franco, but first I must leave you something Don Franco sends you."

Vittorio is surprised. "What can Franco send me? I need nothing from him."

Luigi turns around and answers. "That is a between you and him."

"But what is it?"

"I don't know, nor do I care. I will just give it to you. You use it, throw it into the sea, you sell it, you give it away, I don't care. But I assure you, I am not coming back here never again."

Vittorio said nothing. He saw Luigi going back to his truck, and he thought, finally, Franco wouldn't bother him anymore.

Luigi orders the two men. "Bring the box, but be careful."

Vittorio sees the two men are carrying a box, which seems very heavy.

"What is that, Luigi?"

"This is what he sent you. Don't worry, it's not a dead body."

At that moment, one man asks for help.

"Don Luigi please. Can you help us?"

Luigi responds. "You are useless. You might drop it and break it."

Luigi runs towards the two men carrying the box and takes a position in the center as if they were carrying it between the three of them.

"Please, Vittorio, open the door. This is heavy."

"I will not open any door if you don't tell me what it is."

Luigi says with a choppy voice, like the one who speaks when he lifting a heavy load.

"A shitty piece of a ship and if you don't open the door, you're going to have to bring it in by yourself from here."

Vittorio believes the men are carrying something very heavy, and they might fall and hurt themselves. He quickly opens the doors.

"Put it in that corner." Vittorio says.

The three of them go to the corner, but they put the box on top of a table. Luigi tells him.

"Can you help us lower it down? Between the four of us, it will be much easier."

When Vittorio approaches the box, Luigi catches him off guard, holds his two arms and takes him to the ground. One man quickly covers Victorio's mouth, while the other ties his feet. The three of them tied his hands and put him inside the box. Luigi puts a portable sign on the sides of the box which says, "HANDLE WITH CARE." They transported Victorio to Franco's complex immediately.

Salvatore is up in his tree when he sees the truck approaching. He recognizes the truck and does not pay much attention to it. Salvatore takes his binoculars to observe the truck. He sees they are getting a big box out of the truck and placing it on the ground. Salvatore almost falls from the tree, when he saw them getting a man out of the box. Even though the man has his hand and feet tied up and the mouth cover, he recognizes the face.

"Oh, my God! It is Victorio. Franco kidnapped Victorio!"

Salvatore lets go of his binoculars in a rush to get his camera, but the camera slips from his hand and falls to the ground.

"My God! Give me a break, not now."

Yells Salvatore. He comes down the tree as fast as he can, but when he gets up to his observation point, Victorio was not where to be found. Salvatore hurries down from the tree, takes a taxi, and heads for the police station. He enters the police station and runs to the officer on duty.

"Please, I need to speak to Raffaelle. It is urgent."

The officer looks at him and responds. "Hey man, you don't get tired?"

"Please, do me a favor and call Raffaelle. Tell him it's urgent."

"The boss is busy in his office."

"I will not repeat myself. You call Raffaelle right now." Salvatore replies, raising his voice.

He looks at Salvatore and tells him. "Listen, you idiot, the boss is busy, but if it is so important, tell me and I'll tell him."

Salvatore distrusts him. He believes Franco has bought everyone on the island.

"No, I will talk only to him, so call him right now."

The officer knows Salvatore will not rest until he calls the chief, so he picks up the phone and calls Raffaelle.

"Boss, Salvatore is here like a madman and says he has to talk to you, that it is urgent."

"Ask him what he wants." Raffaelle replies.

"I already asked him, but he says he will only talk to you."

"Tell him I'm busy, that he will have to wait."

"I'm sorry, Salvatore, but the boss says he is very busy, so you will have to wait."

Salvatore screams. "Damn!! How long is it going to be?"

"That, I do not know, but feel free to sit and wait."

Salvatore walked around the lobby of the police station. He went in and out of the building. After an hour, he sat and waited for Raffaelle.

Luigi blindfolded Vittorio and took him to the shelter, where Franco was waiting for him. Luigi removes the blindfold and unties his hands. Vittorio, enraged, asks Franco.

"Where am I?"

"In a safe place and forgive me, but you gave me no other option." Franco answers.

"You have kidnapped me. I would never think that of you. How low can you go, Franco?"

"After you listen to me, you will understand why I have done it."

"Well, I'm here, so just tell me and finish it once and for all."

Franco tells him. "You need to sell me your business. I'll pay you more than it's worth."

"You know that's impossible. Money doesn't matter to me. My grandfather found it and my son will soon take over it."

"Understand please, it's not me. I'm not interested in it. Unfortunately, it is a strategic point, recognized by many people who are prepared to get hold of it by other means if you don't accept."

Vittorio is speechless. "Would you allow such a thing?"

"How many times have I sent for you so you would know what is happening? You could be the instructor of the naval school. You don't have to leave; it will be as if it was yours. I pay you whatever you want."

'No Franco, let them kill me if they want to kill me, but no, I am not selling.'

Franco looks at him and presents a signed check to him.

"Write the amount. Write enough, so you never think you made a mistake."

Vittorio stands in front of Franco. "What the fuck don't you understand? No! is no! and it is over."

Franco looks at him sadly and says. "You don't know how much I admire you. I wish I could continue helping you."

"And what the fuck have you helped me with? Tell me, Franco?"

"I have delayed this moment for many years, but it is already out of my hands. Unfortunately, the day you saved Marcelo, it was the beginning of all this problem."

"My God, I did them a favor, and that's how they pay me." Vittorio responds.

"Please understand for once that it is not me. I have fought for years, so this does not happen."

"You represent those men. There is no difference between you and them and the answer is still NO!"

"Tell me, Vittorio, what do you want this business for?" Franco asks angrily.

"You would never understand. It belongs to the family and will remain in the family."

"What family, stupid?"

"It will pass to my son."

"Open your eyes. If you don't accept, there will be no son to pass it on to." Franco yelled at him.

Vittorio froze, sat down, and put his hands on his head.

Franco tells him. "Help me save your son. I will do what you ask, but don't stain me with your son's innocent blood, I beg you."

Vittorio cries.

"I promise I will pay you enough so you can be happy with your family for the rest of your life."

Vittorio, enraged, tells Franco. "How can you be so cynical to tell me I can be happy with my family? When you shattered our pride and tradition?"

Vittorio pushes Franco, who falls to the ground. Vittorio was surprised because he had not pushed him hard. He realizes Franco is physically weak. Luigi instantly grabs Vittorio, but Franco yells at him.

"Leave him alone. He did not hurt me, and he has every right to be enraged."

Vittorio tells Franco. "Forgive me. I did not want to hurt you. This is too much to assimilate at once. Give me a week and I will give you my answer."

Franco extends his hand to Victorio and says. "Thank you, Vittorio," Vittorio leaves Franco with his hand extended and avoids looking at Franco. He feels betrayed by Franco.

"Take me back. I want to get out of here."

"Do you understand I should cover your eyes?"

"Yes, I know, do it fast. Get me out of here now."

Raffaelle called the duty officer every thirty minutes to ask if Salvatore had left, but three and a half hours had passed, and Salvatore was still waiting. Raffaelle understands Salvatore will not leave and goes out to see him.

"What happened now, Salvatore?"

"I will not speak in front of anyone."

Raffaelle takes him to his office to get him out of the way. Salvatore, with startled eyes, tells him.

"Franco has kidnapped Vittorio."

"My God, the only thing missing! Where do you get such idiocy now?"

"I have seen it with my own eyes."

Salvatore tells Raffaelle everything he saw from the tree. Raffaelle stays quiet for a moment. He sees no logic in Salvatore's story.

"Why would Franco kidnap Vittorio? They have been friends since youth and there is nothing to tide Vittorio with the organized crime."

Salvatore tells him.

"I've also asked myself the same question and the only thing that comes to mind is that Franco started a naval mechanics school and is forcing Vittorio to sell him his business to put the school hands on training there."

"But you don't tire of talking bullshit. Franco is going to kidnap someone to build a school. Why don't you go back to your house and stop fucking with the people who are really working?"

Raffaelle yells at Salvatore, who puts his hands on his head and walks in a circle about four times while screaming.

"I can't believe how stupid you all are. It is time for you to learn something from me. It is not the school. It is the exit to the sea. Marcelo escaped us by sea. It is the most strategic point of all the shipyards on the island."

Raffaelle looks at Salvatore and acknowledges that as crazy as he might look, he always made sense in what he says, despite his appearance of a patient that has just escaped from a mental hospital.

"You, as always, are sticking your nose everywhere. I'll go to investigate."

"I'm going with you." Salvatore begs.

"No! I will go alone. I will not make a fool of myself going to see Franco. I'll go see Vittorio at his business."

"He will not be there. I told you. I saw when they kidnapped him. You have to believe me."

Raffaelle and two police officers get in a patrol car and head to Vittorio's business. Salvatore runs to find a taxi to go to Vittorio's business.

Raffaelle walks into Vittorio's business and sees Vittorio working on an engine. He thinks that once again he is going to make a full of himself just by listening to Salvatore, but he decides to check anyway since he is already there.

"Good morning, Vittorio."

Vittorio turns around, scared. There have been too many frightening experiences for a single day, and the chief of police did not make him feel better.

"What's wrong Vittorio, did I scare you?"

"No, nothing. I was not expecting anyone."

Raffaelle notices Vittorio is not well. Something strange has happened to him, but he is not kidnapped.

"How can I help you, Don Raffaelle?"

"Well, the truth is Salvatore went to my office saying you had been kidnapped."

"Do you listen to that crazy man? Didn't you all get enough from him?"

"I know, but it's my duty to make sure it's not true."

"You are absolutely right. I thank you, but I'm fine, as you can see."

Raffaelle looks at Vittorio's arms and sees they have marks and that Vittorio is trying to conceal them.

"Tell me, Vittorio, what happened to you in your arms?"

Vittorio responds, a little nervous.

"Oh, that's nothing. I was pulling some ropes and entangled them in my arms so they would not slip when I pull them."

Raffaelle looks around and sees no rope anywhere.

"Vittorio, you can trust me. If you have problems, I'll help you."

"Do you really believe that man? If I was kidnapped, I wouldn't be here."

"You are right. But once again, I am here to help in any way possible."

Raffaelle sees Vittorio is very nervous, but refuses to collaborate. He keeps looking at Vittorio straight in his eyes and Vittorio turns around, trying to avoid looking at Raffaelle.

"Sorry Vittorio, have a good day."

Raffaelle gets out of Vittorio's business and is about to get into his patrol car when he sees Salvatore getting out of a taxi and running toward him.

Raffaelle looks at Salvatore and feels sorry for him. Salvatore sees Raffaelle is about to leave and he thinks Raffaelle is going to Franco's complex.

"I told you he was kidnaped. Do you believe me now? Let's get him." Screams Salvatore.

Raffaelle shakes his head and answers.

"He is not kidnapped. I just talked to him. He is working in his shop."

Salvatore froze for about thirty seconds. His mouth was open and there was no expression on his face.

"It can't be. I saw it. I swear, I saw it."

Tears roll down Salvatore's cheeks. He was emotionally destroyed.

"I believe you, Salvatore. I know you saw him, but he is not kidnapped and please do not go inside to disturb him." Raffaelle asks Salvatore.

Salvatore says nothing. He just turns around and leaves.

Raffaelle tells him.

"Come on, I'll take you home and forgive me I couldn't see you earlier."

Raffaelle understood Salvatore was right. Something really happened, but as always, he had nothing.

Raffaelle visits Enrico and tells him what happened early today.

"What do you think?" Enrico asks him.

"I know something is going on, but if nobody comes forward and we have no evidence, then we have nothing. It is as if we are against a ghost."

"Do you think if I talk to Salvatore it will bring me problems?"

"I don't think so, as long as you don't get carried away by him."

Franco calls Raffaelle and tells him.

"You don't imagine how sorry I am to bother you, but I can't stand the pain. I need to go to the doctor."

"When do you want to go?" Raffaelle asks him.

"As soon as possible, please."

"Is that okay today at three?"

"Yes, that's fine with me."

"If it's an emergency, I'll go right now, but I need to pick up my cousin at the port and then I'll pick you up."

"Perfect thanks." Franco replies.

Raffaelle calls Enrico and tells him.

"How about if you accompany me to take Franco to the hospital? I told him you are my cousin, and I had to pick you up at the port."

"Very good idea, cousin."

That afternoon, Raffaelle shows up with Enrico at the complex. Enrico was carrying two suitcases in the back of the car. Luigi comes out to meet them and stares at Enrico, somewhat confused, but Raffaelle says.

"He is my cousin. I just picked him up at the port."

Luigi gives a handshake to Enrico and says.

"Welcome, my name is Luigi."

"It's a pleasure. My name is Enrico."

An employee approaches with Franco in a wheelchair. Franco had aged a lot, he was very thin and haggard, his hair was almost completely white.

"Don Franco. Why didn't you tell me you were like this? I would have come at once and pick up and my cousin later."

"Thanks, Raffaelle, but it is only pain. I need a prescription."

"Is this young man your cousin?"

"Yes, he is my cousin."

Enrico says. "Good afternoon, Don Franco. I have read so much about you. I am happy to meet you."

"Does that mean you like danger?" Franco responds.

"No, not at all. I prefer the tranquility, the sea, the wine and the girls."

"Then you are in the perfect place."

Franco asks Raffaelle.

"Where are the other officers, or do you have them undercover?"

"I don't think you want to escape from here, and if you do, you would do me a great favor."

Franco cannot help but laugh. "I did not think that with so much pain, someone would make me laugh. You are right, I am an involuntary prisoner, but at the same time, very happy, I would never escape."

Raffaelle tells Enrico. "Leave your bags here. We need more space."

Luigi lowers the suitcases and hands them to Guido.

"Come with us. If you are going to kill us, I'd rather be killed by a professional thug." Raffaelle tells Luigi.

Franco laughs again, but neither Luigi nor Enrico laughed, and their faces were very serious.

"Come on Luigi, don't make that face." Franco tells him.

Raffaelle looks at Enrico and says.

"Enrico, don't be such a jerk. It looks like you haven't changed at all. No one here is going to kill anyone."

Enrico understands Raffaelle's game and plays nervously and says.

"I can wait for you here, so you have more space."

This time everyone laughs except Enrico, who plays scared.

"Do not be a coward and get in. Remember, I am your cousin, I am older than you and on this island I am the authority."

Enrico gets in the car but keeps his scared face.

Upon arriving at the hospital, they transferred Franco to a wheelchair. This time, Raffaelle does not put handcuffs on him. He seems more his company than his custodian. Luigi pushes the wheelchair all the time and takes care of Franco as if he was his father. Franco was in great pain and could not walk.

"You go in, I will stay outside. Doctors make me nervous." Enrico says.

"Don't tell me you're still afraid of needles. When are you going to get over that? You're not a kid anymore." Raffaelle tells him.

"I do not see the humor and remember, I can also talk about you, so you better stop it." Enrico seriously responds.

Franco and Luigi exchange glances, but don't say a word.

Enrico follows the game and, with an annoyed face, says.

"Enough of this. I will wait outside."

Raffaelle, Franco and Luigi enter the doctor's room and Franco tells Raffaelle. "I think your cousin is upset."

"I thought he had changed, but he is still the same jerk. His father died when he was five years old and he slept with his mother until he was twelve, because he was afraid of sleeping alone."

The doctor comes in and brings some X-rays.

"Tell me, Don Franco, how long have you endured this pain saying nothing?"

"I don't want people to feel sorry for me." Franco responds.

'The pain serves a purpose. If you ignore it, you are only cheating yourself and delaying the treatment. You have come several times and said you were weak and tired. You were even misdiagnosed the first time, based on the information you gave the doctor."

The doctor gives the X-rays to Franco and tells him. "Look at this."

Franco doesn't look at them and puts them on the doctor's table. The doctor asks him.

"What is it? You don't care?"

"I do care, but neither you nor I can do anything about it. What I need from you is to give me some pain prescriptions."

The doctor stares at him and says. "You are not a doctor. We give prescriptions according to the diagnosis."

"Then give me something to ease my pain, because my condition of Pelvic Solitary Plasmacytoma is already advanced. It has no cure, and it is killing me."

The doctor, Raffaelle and Luigi, were stunned. From where Franco got such a diagnosis?.

"What doctor gave you the diagnosis?" Asked the doctor.

"None, I am a person who reads and nobody better than me knows my symptoms, because I am living it. Or I am wrong?"

"You are not wrong, you are a hundred percent correct." The doctor replies.

Luigi and Raffaelle, surprised, look at each other.

"You are a walking encyclopedia, Don Franco, and now also a doctor," Raffaelle tells him.

"I only know I still have a lot to learn. We do not use even a third of our brain potential."

Raffaelle says. "And some people refuse to use it at all. Isn't that right, Luigi?"

Luigi does not like the joke. "What happened to you today? Do you think you are funny, or are you looking for trouble?"

"Don't worry Luigi. It is not such a big deal." Franco tells him.

"We are not that close for him to make such a comment about me."

Raffaelle apologizes to Luigi. The doctor was so nervous he could hardly speak. He was impressed with Luigi's size and the fury in his eyes. Raffaelle's uniform and gun added to the problem. Franco sees the situation is getting out of control and takes command.

"It seems the prisoner is going to have to take control, so you both shut up and no more jokes."

Franco points at Luigi and says. "Luigi, calm down. It is not so bad. Do you understand me?"

Luigi responds. "Excuse me, Don Franco."

Luigi looks at Raffaelle and tells him. "I apologize Don Raffaelle."

Raffaelle has been left with his mouth open. The prisoner has taken control and has given him orders, but deep down he knows Franco is right, and it is better to turn the page.

Raffaelle answers. "Yes boss."

Those words went straight to Luigi's heart, who turned red and said.

"My God! You are looking for trouble and you are going to find it."

The doctor was shaking while writing a prescription in a hurry. He hands it to Luigi, who looks at him and makes him tremble even more. The terror on the doctor's face is so obvious the three of them must hold back laughter in order not to disrespect him. When they left the office, the three of them were laughing, because after all, the doctor's face put out the fire between them. Enrico sees them laughing, and he asks them.

"Do you come from the doctor or from a comic show?"

Raffaelle answers him. "You don't know what you've missed."

"Was it that good?"

"More than good." Luigi responds.

"Too bad I missed it." Enrico says.

"Yes, for being such a coward." Says Luigi.

"What did you say?" Enrico replies angrily.

"No, I did not say that. Your cousin said it."

People looked at them as celebrities, because Franco was famous, but they only knew him through pictures. Upon returning to the complex, Franco thanks Raffaelle and Luigi. He gives Raffaelle a handshake, and tells him,

"You know, you are not so bad after all. I think you are a good person."

"Does that mean you are going to spare my life?" Raffaelle answers.

Luigi intervenes. "Don't push it, He only means that we will make suffering less."

When Raffaelle and Enrico leave, Franco asks Guido.

"Did you check his suitcases?"

"Yes sir, just clothes."

"Very good, but we cannot lower our guard."

Meanwhile, in the car, Raffaelle comments to Enrico.

"It is a pity this man is not on our side. I congratulate you. You did very well."

"I stayed outside in case someone came to do something."

"Very well, thought, but the truth is you have missed a show better than those of Hollywood."

"Yes, I could tell you had a good time."

"Franco will not run away, he is very ill and there is no cure for his illness, at least it is one less concern."

"How did he take the diagnosis when the doctor told him?"

"No, you're wrong. He told the doctor the diagnostic and asked for the prescriptions. He knows as much as the doctor. I tell you, that man is a genius. No wonder he drove Salvatore crazy. Be very careful with him."

"That's the way it will be cousin. He looks so simple and kind that anybody can fall for it."

"That's right, and you'll convince when you know what's left of Salvatore."

Vittorio is having dinner at home. He has been quiet and avoids making eye contact with his family at the table. He knows he has no choice but to sell his business. He takes a deep breath and tells his wife and son.

"I have something to tell you, which I have been thinking about for a long time, and finally I decided. I think after thinking about it and having analyzed it for a long time."

Aurora interrupts him. "Speak once and for all. You've been around and around for an hour and you have said nothing."

Alberto says. "Yes father, speak up. You say you have been thinking for a long time and that must be hard for you since you haven't even talk to us for a week already. Just say it, whatever it is."

Vittorio's eyes are watery, and he finds the courage to say.

"I decided to sell the business."

Alberto and Aurora are in shock. They look at each other in disbelief.

"Can you come up with something more real? Please tell us what happened to you? Do you feel sick? Are there problems that we do not know about?"

"Yes, father says it. We are a united family and whatever it is, we will face it together."

"Didn't you hear me? I want to sell the business."

Aurora and her son were silent for at least three minutes.

"Are you going to say anything, or do I have to repeat it?"

"No, father we have heard you, but we do not believe you."

"Why son?"

"Because it is heritage, it is our history, and those are not my words. They are yours."

"No son, on the contrary, we are going to buy another one with more possibilities of expansion where you are the one who will set the limits, not like here, where we have already reached the limit."

"Wait a minute father. Are we leaving?"

Aurora tells him. "Have you gone crazy?"

"Look son. You were one of the first to do underwater welding, which was your dream as a child. We have spent a lot of money on equipment, and you have only done four welds. It's not your fault there is no work here."

"But where do you plan to go?"

Vittorio answers. "We'd better not talk about it anymore, because if they don't give me what I ask, nothing will change."

"And how much would you ask?"

"Not less than 450 thousand lire."

"Then we have nothing to talk about, because nobody is going to give you that amount of money."

"Then even better, you have nothing to worry about."

Enrico shows up at Salvatore's apartment.

"Good afternoon, sir. Are you Mr. Salvatore?"

"Yes, I am. Who are you?"

"I am Enrico."

"That does not tell me anything, nor does it interest me. What do you want?" Salvatore immediately responds.

"Easy sir, calm down. I come from Umberto."

"If Umberto wants something from me, he calls me. He doesn't send anyone, so either you prove it to me or leave. If you are a reporter, I want you to know I will give no more interviews."

Enrico sees Salvatore is totally out of control. He takes out his identification and tells him. "Do you believe me now?"

Salvatore recognizes the identification immediately.

"If you would have started by showing your identification, we wouldn't have wasted our time. Please come in. It's not good for them to see you with me. Everyone knows who I am, but you should stay undercover."

Enrico walks into the apartment and Salvatore asks him.

"What does Umberto want? Now he wants me to do the job for him for free. First, he kicks me out and now he sends emissaries."

"No, Mr. Salvatore. I mentioned Umberto as a reference. I am in charge of the case. Umberto and Raffaelle say that no one knows more than you about this case."

Salvatore was flattered. He had not felt important in a long time.

"Not only am I the one who knows the most, I am also the only one who has put him behind bars."

"You are right about that. I want to leave you my phone number where you can pass me any information you think is important. I promise if that information leads to Franco's arrest, you will be the one with the merit, not me. Also, remember, no one should know our link."

"You don't need to say that to me. I was undercover when you were running in the streets in shorts."

Enrico shakes Salvatore's hand and says. "I will not take any more of your time. It has been a pleasure to meet you."

Luigi shows up at Vittorio's business.

"Good afternoon, Don Vittorio."

"Good afternoon, Don Luigi."

"I come for your answer to Don Franco."

"I do have an answer, but I have to talk to him, face to face."

"Whatever you have to say, you can tell me. I transmit it without removing or putting anything."

"I will speak with the owner of the circus, not with the clowns."

Luigi clenches his fists and steps forward, but stops.

"You take advantage because Don Franco spoils and protects you. If that was not the case, I would make you swallow your words." Luigi angrily tells him.

"Just think it is not the case that and make me swallow my words. You may be in for a big surprise. Remember, the bigger they are, the more noise they make when they fall."

Luigi bit his lip to hold back his anger. "Okay, I'll inform Don Franco. Luigi goes to Vittorio's desk and picks up the phone to call Franco."

"Who gave you permission to use my phone? Hang it up immediately."

Luigi looked Vittorio in the eyes. Vittorio saw Luigi had reached his boiling point. Luigi said quietly and slowly says.

"Come and take it from me, so I can teach you to respect a clown."

Vittorio thought about it, but realized that he was playing with fire and Luigi was not to blame for his situation.

"Don Franco, it is me, Luigi. Your friend says he will only talk to you."

"Well, bring him in."

"Very well, Don Franco. Be careful when leaving the complex. I will take him to where I took him the last time."

This way, they made sure that Vittorio did not know where the underground shelter was located and Victtorio would think it was somewhere else outside the compound.

Luigi tells Vittorio.

"I'll take you to see Don Franco. Close the business and sit in the car. I need to blindfold you."

Vittorio didn't say a word. He knew Luigi had reached his limit. Once in the shelter, Luigi takes off Vittorio's blindfold. Franco is sitting in a wheelchair in front of him. Vittorio asks him.

"What happened to you? If I hurt you last time when I pushed, I apologize. It was not my intention."

"Don't worry, it's not your fault. I've been ill for many years. I just can't hide it anymore."

"Is there anything I can do for you?"

"Nothing, this is my true sentence, but there is a lot you can do for yourself and others, and you don't even know it."

"Explain yourself, please."

"I'll explain, but first tell me your answer."

"If you cannot assure me of this, then there is no deal. You will get my son a shipyard in America. I want him out of here. You must promise me none of you will ever bother him. He must never know what had happened here. That is all I want. I want my son to live thinking the family legacy has moved to America. If you agree to my terms, my business is yours."

Franco looks at him and answers.

"Thank you, my friend. I promise your son will not go through what we have been through, but I want to ask you for something else. I want your shipyard to become part of the naval school where you will be the dean to teach the boys the practical part."

"Didn't you tell me you wanted it for your organization?"

"Yes, the organization wants it in case of an emergency. I don't think it's fair to have it empty when it can be used by boys who are struggling to get ahead in life. I don't want any young person to get into trouble for lack of opportunities. That is the reason I built a clinic, a school, and I want to continue spending in the future of our country."

"You sound like a politician." Vittorio tells him.

"You offend me. A politician is a bandit like me, but he doesn't do the things that I do for the people, things I have done with my money. They say the same things, but they steal the money, the hope and future of our youth."

"I don't know whether to hate you or admire you, but I have to admit you do more for the people than all those politicians who claim to be the good guys. I promise to work in that school if my role would be just a simple teacher."

Franco and Vittorio shake hands, and Vittorio sees Franco cannot stand up. He gives him a big hug.

"It hurts me to see you like this."

"It hurts me more not being able to go to a restaurant and walk on the beach," Franco responds.

Vittorio looks at Luigi and says.

"I have been unfair to you. I have provoked you and disrespected you. I want to apologize."

"I will only excuse you when you show me you are sincere. Believe me, I wanted to teach you a little respect, but Don Franco protects you, which is enough for me."

"Time will tell you I am sincere when I speak." Vittorio replied.

"Take Vittorio home, please, and do not forget to blindfold him." Franco tells Luigi.

"You don't trust me, Franco?" Ask Vittorio.

"He trusts you. He does it to protect you, which he has been doing for many years, but you have not wanted to realize it." Luigi answers.

"I already apologized, but I will not kneel before you." Vittorio says.

Franco intervenes. "Luigi enough. This is a very special day for me. Vittorio is as important as you are. Both of you are the only people I trust with my eyes closed."

"Excuse me, Don Franco, it will not happen again. A clown like me talks a lot of stupidity. Isn't that right, Vittorio?"

"No Luigi, I think I was the clown."

CHAPTER SIXTEEN

FALLING IN LOVE

Franco calls Guido on the phone from his office and tells him.

"I need you to get in touch with the heads of the families. Tell them in three months we will have a meeting. This one might be the last because of my health. Tell them this will be a meeting of grandparents and grandchildren. Whoever doesn't have a child must borrow one, but no one will be admitted without a child."

Franco hangs up the phone and asks Luigi. "How is your relationship with Vittorio?"

"That depends on him."

"I need you to tell him I want him present at the next meeting. First, to thank him for agreeing to sell and second, so each member of the organization makes a promise in front of him and me they will never bother his son. Also, tell him he must bring me the amount he wants for the business."

"I will do it today, Don Franco." Luigi responds.

Luigi is at the entrance of the compound when he hears a loud noise, as if a tank firing its cannon is coming up the hill. Luigi looks back and sees Franco and Guido disturbed by the noise.

"What the hell is that? Are the Russians or the Germans invading us now?"

A minute later, an old, rickety vehicle parks in front of the complex. Enrico gets out of it and Luigi tells him.

"Where the hell did you get that from?"

"This car had been parked for over ten years and they gave it to me to work."

"I totally disagree with Raffaelle. I think you have really big balls, because I would not go up the hill on that shit for nothing in the world. It's a miracle it didn't explode."

"What am I going to do? I have to make a living. This is the only job my cousin could get me here. Now I am the assistant health inspector, and I must go wherever food is cooked for the public to examine the hygienic conditions."

"But you don't look very hygienic to me." Luigi responds.

"I know. It's this damn car. The smoke is killing me. The restaurant owners don't want me to park close to the restaurant, because the smoke pollutes their premises."

Luigi takes him to Franco's office. Enrico sees Franco reading a newspaper.

"Don Franco here is Enrico, our new health inspector."

"Hello, welcome boy. Are you the one who was driving the tank?"

"Are you guys going to make fun of me, too?"

"No, Enrico. It is just a question. Go ahead and do your job."

Enrico takes a citation book out of his briefcase and asks them.

"Can you take me to the kitchen?"

"Yes, of course."

Franco looks at Luigi and tells him. "Luigi, would you take him to the kitchen, please?"

Luigi walks into the complex's kitchen and hears Marina arguing with her daughter. Luigi stops and holds Enrico.

"Oh, this is going to be good. I love when these two argue."

"Why are you bringing the food back?" Asks Marina to her daughter.

"What can I do? Don Franco does not want to eat." Answers Adriana.

"How many times have I told you to tell him, if he does not eat it, I am going to feed him myself?"

"Mother, you can tell him that, but I can't." Answers Adriana.

"What is wrong with you? I ask you to do something and you tell me you can't. Now I'm going to have to make him eat. As if I don't have things to do." Marina tells her daughter, kind of mad.

Luigi sees Marina is angry and enters. Enrico gets behind Luigi, and Luigi covers him completely.

"And you, dinosaur, get out of the way. Don't you see I have to get out?"

"I brought Enrico; he is the new health inspector." Luigi answers.

"Did you bring him into your pocket? Because I do not see him. I hope this one eats less than the previous one. I think that to check if something is clean you don't have to eat it. Where is he? I do not have time."

Luigi moves and Enrico is exposed.

"Where did you get him from? He is going to mess up my kitchen." Marina tells Luigi.

Marina looks at Enrico, puts her hands on her waist and tells him.

"Listen boy, it will be a good idea if you take a good shower and put on a clean uniform if you are going to inspect the food."

Enrico was sweaty and had oil stains all over his pants. All this time Adriana, Marina's daughter, was washing the dishes at the end of the kitchen. Enrico takes out his citation book and begins to inspect. When he approaches Adriana, he remains standing waiting for her to move, but she continues singing, not paying attention.

"Move girl." Yells Marina.

But Adriana kept singing like she always did, paying no attention to what was happening around her.

"Excuse me please." Enrico tells her.

That is when she hears a strange voice and turns around. Enrico was paralyzed by the beauty of that young woman. He opened his mouth, and his eyes almost came out of his face. Luigi looked at Marina and she asked him in a low voice.

"What happened to this boy?"

Adriana looks at Enrico and turns red. She could not hide she had also felt a crush. Marina immediately realized what was going on, and with the instinct of a protective mother, says.

"Move girl. Don't you see you are in the middle?"

Adriana moves, but she keeps her gaze fixed on Enrico, who continues to look at her. Marina intervenes again.

"Hey boy, the sink is here, not there."

"Yes, I am very sorry. Please forgive me."

He turns quickly and awkwardly, but unintentionally, he drops his citation book into the sink.

"My God, I have ruined today's work!"

Luigi turns around and laughs out loud. Marina is not happy about it.

"And now what, boy?" Marina asks.

"Nothing, madam, this kitchen is the cleanest I've seen since I've been working." Enrico replies, with the citation book in hand dripping water on the floor.

Marina shakes her head from side to side and says. "My God, the only thing we need now."

"I'll finish in just a moment. I just need to inspect the grains and we finish."

Before Marina answered, Adriana says. "We keep them on the other side of the kitchen. I'll show you."

Marina responds. "It's not that far. I am sure he can go alone."

Enrico, with a choppy voice, answers. "Yes, of course. I can go alone."

Luigi walks into the office, grabs Franco's wheelchair and tells him.

"Don Franco, sit down. You are missing the show."

"What is going on?" Franco asks.

"Don't ask, we're wasting time." Luigi hurries Franco off to the kitchen.

Marina sees Luigi is bringing Franco in a hurry and yells at him.

"So big and so gossipy. You should work here with the women in the kitchen."

Luigi enters Franco's wheelchair in the kitchen and tells Marina.

"Marina, please, tell Don Franco what happened here."

"Nothing has occurred here."

"What's up, Luigi, what is this?" Asks Franco.

"This smells like a wedding." Luigi responds.

"What!!!!" Franco says mischievously.

Marina, a little annoyed, replied. "But you too Franco. Are going to get stupid too?"

Franco looks at Adriana and sees she did not know where to hide and changed color as if it were a traffic light.

"No! Enrico and Adriana?" Says Franco.

'Yes, Don Franco." Luigi responds.

"I was not expecting that."

Enrico returned with his wet citation book and when he saw Luigi and Franco with smiles on their faces, he understood he was the dish of the day.

"You know, Don Franco, the best defense is a good offense."

"What do you mean by that?" Franco asks.

"This lady commented you had not eaten, and she was going to feed you."

Marina looks at Enrico and shakes her head. She understands if she does not join Enrico on the attack, she will end up on the defensive side.

"Yes, I said that. So, Luigi takes Franco to one of those tables."

Franco counterattacks." Of course, Luigi, take me to the table. Adriana is going to bring food to Enrico and me."

"Yes, Don Franco. By the way, they say love enters through the kitchen. I assure you, when Enrico tastes Adriana's food, we will have inspections twice a week instead of once a month."

Marina sees she cannot do anything to stop Luigi, and she just says.

"Listen, you bastards, I'm going to cut off your balls if you keep messing with my daughter."

Franco is already seated at the table, and Enrico is paralyzed next to a chair. Luigi puts his hands on Enrico's shoulders and, with his enormous strength, makes him sit down next to Franco. Marina looks at Enrico, who was embarrassed and was asking for help with his eyes. She says.

"Franco, if you want to show off, you will regret it."

She looks at her daughter and says.

"Adriana, bring two well-loaded plates, one for the spoiled kid that does not want to eat and another for the one who is shivering and is not from cold weather."

Adriana brings two well-loaded plates and Franco says.

"You know that's too much for me."

"You wanted war, then eat or Enrico will see how I feed you."

Adriana puts the dishes on the table and Enrico thanks her.

"You are welcome." Adriana responds, but she does not look at him.

Franco tells her. "Don't be sorry, girl, you can look at him. We will protect you from your mother."

Marina sits next to Franco and says in a grumpy voice. "You eat that plate until the last bite."

Enrico and Luigi laugh. This time, it was Franco's turn. Adriana had the drinks on a tray, but she was noticeably nervous. Her mother asked her, "What is happening to you, girl?"

That made the young woman even more nervous, and she could not prevent the drinks from spilling. Franco and Luigi cry of joy, as if they were partying. Marina, out-of-control, yells.

"But what the hell is wrong with the two of you? This one drops the citation book in the sink, and now you drop the drinks."

"Mother, forgive me, I slipped."

"And how the hell did you slip if the floor is dry?"

This time, except Adriana and Enrico, they all laughed. Adriana returns with the drinks and totally embarrassed by the teasing, tells them.

"Excuse me, I have things to do."

Enrico stands up. "You do not have to leave. I'm the one who is leaving. I'm running late."

Marina slaps the table.

"Listen boy, maybe you haven't realized yet that the owner of the complex is Franco, but I'm the one in charge here. I haven't said you can go yet."

Enrico did not know what to do. He was not prepared for that. His face gave him away. Franco tells him.

"If you don't want problems, do as I say. Sit down and eat."

The three of them say in chorus Marina's famous phrase "Until the last bite."

The next day, Raffaelle went to see Enrico. He was curious to know how his first visit to the compound had gone.

"How was it?" Raffaelle asks.

"A disaster. I am more confused than a blind Italian in the middle of Beijing."

"Why? Don't tell me you're going to end up like Salvatore."

"That is not what I meant."

"Then explain yourself."

Enrico tells him. "Sit down, so you won't pass out."

"Really!" Raffaelle responds.

"Have you ever been in the complex or interacted with the employees?"

"No, I have only been in the front and never passed the reception area, also I have only dealt with Franco, Luigi and Guido. You and Pablo are the only ones who have been able to enter."

"Well, let me tell you. There is an old lady who is the one who really commands, and she is the cook."

"You are kidding me." Raffaelle replies.

"The few times I have dealt with Franco and Luigi, they have seemed like two normal and simple people."

"I agree with you." Raffaelle replies.

"But there is a big problem in this case. The old lady has a daughter who is a real beauty. I can't get her out of my head. To make things worse, I think she likes me too. I cannot think clearly and if I fall in love with her, it will be a conflict of interest. If I cannot overcome it, I must leave the case."

Raffaelle laughs and tells him. "Well, you already have a job and a car. You don't have to worry."

"Are you going to make fun of me, too?"

"What do you mean?" Raffaelle asks.

Luigi and Franco made fun of me all afternoon. Nobody had ever made fun of me like that before."

"Did they disrespect you?"

"No, it was healthy, and it was a feeling of friendship, as if we had known each other for many years."

"Be careful Enrico, with these people you never know where they are coming from."

"Next week I will go again. I will bring them the inspection's receipt and see Adriana."

"If you play with fire, you are going to get burned. It is unfair to use her in your investigation. Even I would reproach you, and her family will not forgive you. You don't play that way here. You can end up hurt if you come out alive, that all."

Meanwhile, in Fermo, the profits from the poultry farm had allowed Maria and Patricia to accumulate enough money to live comfortably, to give Maria's son Pedro an excellent education, and to participate in charities. One morning, an employee approaches Maria and tells her.

"Doña Maria, I need to speak with Romulo, Patricia's brother."

"That man has not been around here for many years."

"I know he's in town. My sister saw him, but he slipped away."

"I didn't know he was in town, and I doubt Patricia knows it, either."

"He stole money from my father a few years ago. We know he comes at least twice a year to visit his friend. Once we went to his friend's house and he was there, but he hid, and his friend blatantly said he had left."

"Why did your father loan Romulo money for?" Maria asks.

"Romulo told my father this farm belonged to him and his sister. He wanted to sell his part because he was not interested in the farm. He brought him a contract and the title to his part of the farm. My father paid him half of the money and agreed to pay the second half after they transfer it to my father's name. The next day, he showed up early in the morning and told my father to show him the second part of the money. Upon arriving at the attorney's office, he told the secretary he had an appointment at eleven. The secretary told him his appointment was at eleven-thirty. Then he told my father they must wait thirty minutes. He took out the money my father had given him previously and told him it was dangerous to carry so much money. He asked for the second part of the money to deposit everything in the bank in front of the lawyer's office. My father gave him the money and saw him entering the bank. He thought everything was fine, since he gave him the contract and had the appointment with the lawyer. Romulo had invited him to lunch after the signing to celebrate. When Romulo did not return, my father talked to the lawyer and showed him the contract and all the documents where Romulo appeared as the owner of half the farm. The lawyer told him those documents were false, and that Romulo had made an appointment to start a divorce lawsuit."

Maria could not believe what she was hearing, but she knew Romulo was a dishonest person.

"I am sure Patricia knows nothing about this. I assure you that, if we know anything, we will inform you so you can go to the authorities."

"The authorities will do nothing. My father reported him to the police. When they arrested Romulo, he said he did not know what they were talking about, that it was not his signature in the document, and he would never sell something that is not his. At the bank, they did not find any deposit since he had no account on that bank. He said he made an appointment with the lawyer, but he went half an hour early by mistake. He went out of the office for a moment to kill time, but had a personal emergency and could not return. He added, he ran into my father at the attorney's office by coincidence and it was obvious my father had a plan to scam him. Everything ended there. It was my father's word against his."

Maria hugged the employee and said.

"You don't know how sorry I am, but remember whoever does wrong on earth will pay for it on earth and in heaven, too. Divine justice is implacable with them. I only ask you not to tell this to Patricia. It will only hurt her, and she cannot do anything, anyway."

Franco tells Luigi.

"I want you to contact Salvatore. Tell him that at the next meeting, he will be my guest of honor."

"Have you gone crazy?" Luigi responds.

"No, Luigi. Just remember to keep your friends close and your enemies closer."

"I will do it, sir. You know what you're doing." Luigi answers.

Luigi and Franco hear the roars of Enrico's car approaching and Luigi says.

"It seems we have a visitor. That visit should be once a month."

Franco looks at Luigi and asks him. "What have you found out about, Enrico?"

"Nothing, we have nothing."

"He seems like a good boy, but let's not lower our guard."

"No need to say that, Don Franco."

One morning, Salvatore was having breakfast at his favorite cafeteria when Luigi came up to him.

"Good morning, Salvatore. May I accompany you?"

Salvatore was surprised. Luigi, Franco's right-hand man, had contacted him. Thousands of ideas were flying in his brain. The one he liked the most was Luigi was tired of Franco and wanted to negotiate to save his skin.

"Good morning, Luigi." Salvatore replied with a big smile. His eyes were shining, and his heart was pumping at full speed.

"It was about time you tired of following Franco's orders and thought of yourself. You have come to the right person. I promise not to have your assets confiscated and I will use all my influences to get you a light sentence or, better yet, to get you in a witness protection plan where you can start all over again."

Luigi tried to avoid laughing. He sat down at the table and said.

"I have a message to you from Don Franco."

Salvatore changed his expression instantly and his brain was still working at full speed, but this time he could not find any answer.

"What did your master orders you to tell me?" Salvatore asks him, dismissively.

"First, he is not my master. He is my friend and my family. Second, I am here to tell you in about three months, he is going to celebrate what may be his last meeting. He would like you to be the guest of honor. If you decide to attend, he will give you the list of participants, so you do not have to climb the tree. We are getting old and a fall from that tree could be fatal."

Salvatore glares at him and responds.

"Knowing the type of bandits you are, I don't know what to tell you."

"Well, you have two days to decide. If you don't answer in two days, it means you will not attend because you are not interested.

Therefore, the tree does not have a purpose to exist and we will cut it down."

"Are you pressuring me to attend? Does Franco want to eliminate me that bad?"

Luigi puts money on the table and says. "Breakfast is on me."

Salvatore looks at the money and his eyes widen. He had been counting the pennies for a long time. Luigi stands up and tells him.

"Don Franco said nothing about eliminating you, but that would not be a bad idea. I will communicate it to him."

Salvatore yells. "Listen you cheap thug, I am not for sale or afraid of you at all."

Luigi does not answer and keeps walking away. A man sitting next to Salvatore's table tells him.

"That's how men talk, tear his money to pieces and throw it in his face."

Salvatore stands up, grabs the money, and sees Luigi is already quite far. He responds to the man.

"I don't mess around. That big man owed me money, and he came to pay it back."

Salvatore kept calling Enrico all morning. He did not know Enrico worked normal hours. Enrico answers Salvatore's call at 1:30 P.M.. during the lunch break. Salvatore angrily tells him.

"What kind of detective are you? I've been calling you all morning and you haven't answered."

"I was busy." Enrico replies.

"Didn't they teach you it is part of your job to respond to your superiors and informants immediately?"

"I'm already answering you. Tell me what you want to inform me."

"Not over the phone. I don't trust anyone. It must be in person."

"Very good. See you tonight at 8:30 P.M."

"What do you mean at 8:30? What are you going to do all afternoon?"

"That is not your problem. You are not my boss, neither do I owe you explanations." Enrico answers, a little angry.

Salvatore with an attitude as if he was in command answers back.

"Remember at 8:30 not a minute later, and he hangs up the phone."

Enrico goes to see Raffaelle after work and tells him what happened to Salvatore. Raffaelle answers him.

"I have not had contact with Salvatore since he told me Franco had kidnapped Vittorio. I'm sure something happened, but like always, he struck out. Be careful because the last two detectives related to Salvatore. One came out dead and the other came out miraculously alive."

"I'll keep that in mind, thank you."

Salvatore had to leave his apartment near the hill. His financial situation was precarious, and he rented a room with a bathroom in a very marginalized area where many undesirables lived. Salvatore had been waiting for Enrico since 8:00 p.m. on the street. He walked the block up and down, thinking what Franco's plan would be to invite him to the gangster's meeting. Enrico finds Salvatore on the street and almost does not recognize him. Salvatore looks like a homeless person. He is wearing old dirty clothes, has long hair, and has a grown beard. Enrico tells him.

"I knew you had moved, but not to this area. It is not good they see us together. Let's go to your house."

"Follow me." Salvatore tells him,

They walk to the end of the block and enter an old house in terrible condition, which had several rented rooms. Enrico looks at Salvatore and feels sorry to see him in the almost subhuman way he was living in.

"You told me that your parents live in a mansion on the outskirts of Rome."

"That's right." Salvatore responds.

"Why don't you go to live with your parents? You will keep them company and that will do you good, too. Forget Franco. He is not worth the sacrifice."

"This is my place. I won't leave here until I clean up my honor and finish that damn mobster."

Salvatore informs Enrico of Franco's invitation. Enrico asks him.

"What would be the purpose of inviting you to such a meeting?"

"It is very obvious; I am a stone in the shoe for him. It is true I could not prove the things I have said about him, but that does not mean they have not happened, and Franco knows it. If Raffaelle had listened to me last time, immediately, he would have found Vittorio at Franco's compound. Maybe Franco did not kill Vittorio because he knew I had discovered him. He is afraid one day he will not run with the same luck, and I will catch him off guard. He does not know you are investigating him. If I disappear, no one will notice and those who find out would be happy. He can't accept that I put him behind bars."

Enrico analyzes what Salvatore said and understands what Salvatore says makes sense.

"What do you want me to do?"

"I want to go."

"How many days will that meeting take?"

"They always last several days. This will be only one night, which means it is called specifically to eliminate me, giving the assurance to the rest of the group no one investigates them and taking revenge on me for having put him behind bars."

"What do you want me to do?"

"I want you to not let Franco get away with it. That if I die, it won't be in vain. You can watch from the tree and I will give a sign of life from the garden. If I am not seen in four hours, it is because they killed me or they are torturing me. Then you can arrest him."

"Perfect. Give me all the information you gather before the meeting, and I will discuss it with my superiors."

The next day, Enrico tells Raffaelle what happened during the meeting with Salvatore. Raffaelle stays quiet for a while, like if he does not want to answer. Enrico read in Raffaelle's face he was not happy with what was going on.

"Talk to me, please. Tell me what you think?"

"I told you to be careful and you are already falling into the same thing that Salvatore fell for."

"It just makes sense what Salvatore says." Enrico replies.

"It always makes sense, but the results are catastrophic."

Enrico looks at Raffaelle and asks him. "Will you help me?"

"Of course I will help you. But what do you want me to do?"

"I'll tell you when the time comes, I must think it over."

The only thing Enrico had in mind was whether he would give up his job. It was a great conflict of interest to have a girlfriend with the intention of marrying her, while investigating Franco, who was almost like a father to her. It was a catch 22. If he does not arrest Franco and marries her, there will be always a doubt of whether Franco bought him out, or he was incompetent. If he arrests Franco for sure, he will lose the love of his life.

Enrico and Adriana's relation became stronger as time passed. Enrico had lunch every Wednesday with Franco, Luigi, Marina, and Adriana in the complex's kitchen. Saturdays he spent his time with Adriana in the complex, helping in the kitchen, as he liked to cook as well. Sundays, they went to church and then rode in the old rickety car he had fixed.

Enrico had never felt so happy in his life. The life of Raffaelle's supposed cousin was much more pleasant and welcoming than of the undercover detective. He had to report to Umberto weekly, and that was the only time he remembered he was on a mission. His happiness ended when he received the call from Salvatore.

"Mr. Enrico, I have called you all morning and you have not answered me."

"Sorry, but I was busy."

"We must talk. The time has come."

"Perfect. See you tonight at 8:30 P.M."

"Not again with the same thing. This is important. What the hell are you going to do this afternoon? Is more important than meeting with me?"

"Many other things. That's why I told you at 8:30 P.M."

Enrico got upset and hung up the phone. He has to make the decision, which he had tried to avoid and postpone as much as possible. That afternoon, the hours seemed endless to him. He prayed to heaven Salvatore would tell him something stupid so he would not have to act.

Enrico met Salvatore again on the street. This time he was more agitated than ever, constantly adjusting his tie and repeating the same phrases two and three times.

"Calm down, Salvatore, so we can understand each other. Let us go to your house, please."

"Yes, yes, yes, yes, let's go." Salvatore said.

Once inside Salvatore's room, Enrico tells him.

"Take a deep breath, calm down and begin again."

Salvatore took some time to calm down.

"As I had told you, this time is serious. He wants to eliminate me. Luigi told me the meeting is next Saturday. They will arrive in the morning and the meeting will begin at 9:00 p.m. I must be there at 8:00 p.m. I ask Luigi why I should go at night if they arrive in the morning."

Enrico interrupts him and tells him.

"Please, Salvatore, not that fast. Let me at least ask a question."

Salvatore, exasperated, responds.

"Don't you understand me when I speak?"

"Yes, I understand."

"Then what do you want to ask?"

"I need to know. Who is coming?"

"Ah, ah, yes, yes, I forgot."

Salvatore takes a list out of his pocket and hands it to Enrico.

"This is the list of the gangsters who are coming."

Enrico takes the list and reads it. He sees that there are several names of people of interest.

"I need to keep this list. I must inquire if there is a warrant on any of these individuals."

"Yes, you can keep it. It's for you. Franco is disguising this meeting as a party for grandparents and grandchildren. Because I do not have a grandson, I will only take part in the adult's party. As you can see, they call my elimination a party. Now tell me. What is your plan?"

"I will contact the office; they will review the names on the list, then I will meet you the day after tomorrow at 8:30 p.m. right here."

"This is unbelievable! It seems you don't give a damn about what happens to me. You take two days to give me an answer. You are so incompetent you have no clue of what to do."

Enrico felt like grabbing Salvatore by the neck and strangling him. Salvatore not only kept yelling, but he would not shut up for a minute. Enrico realized his peaceful stay on the island had ended.

"Yes, I take my time." Yells Enrico at Salvatore.

"I will take whatever time is necessary, so I don't make the shit you did. I will not rush because you are scared like shit."

Salvatore went out of his mind. He yelled and pushed Enrico by the chest with his two hands.

"Get out of my house before I break your face. I have balls to give you and your whole family. Make no mistake of that. I was imprisoning gangsters while you were playing in shorts on the streets. You little punk."

"Yes, you are right. It is better I leave. If you want to know my plan, call me in two days, before 7:00 a.m. or 1:00 p.m. to 1:45 p.m. If I don't receive a call from you, I won't even show up around here."

"Go away. I don't need your help."

"Fine, screw you then." Enrico said and left.

Enrico was angry. He wanted to get out of this nightmare as soon as possible. When he got home, he called Umberto, who, worried, answers.

"What happened Enrico? You are calling me so late?"

"Sorry, Umberto, I have a list of names to give you and I need all possible information for tomorrow at 1:00 p.m."

Enrico tells Umberto everything that is happening to Salvatore.

"Oh my God Salvatore again, be very careful, Enrico, please."

"Yes boss, I know, but if I do nothing and something happens to him, I will never forgive myself. I have achieved what no one else has. Not even I thought I could have achieved, and now this madman is going to ruin everything."

"What do you mean?" Umberto asks.

"I have lunch with Franco and Luigi at the complex every Wednesday. On Saturdays I spend all day at the complex. I am like an intimate friend."

Umberto was speechless. "I cannot believe what you are saying. How did you do it?"

"That's not what matters. What matters is that everything will go down the drain because of this Salvatore."

"Do not expose yourself. We cannot afford to lose what you have achieved."

"I'm sorry boss, I'll try to do my best, but I couldn't live with my conscience if Salvatore gets killed."

"I understand and admire you. Good luck and keep me posted."

The next day, Enrico called Raffaelle and asked him to come see him at his house at night. Raffaelle went to see Enrico that night. He was worried because he knew Enrico had gotten into the wolf's den.

"Good evening, Enrico. What is going on? You worry me."

"Thank you for worrying. I need you for this Saturday. I really need your help."

"What is happening this Saturday?"

Enrico told Raffaelle what was going on with Salvatore.

"Oh my God, but you also fell into the same thing. I warned you several times. You have achieved what no one has been able to and now you will ruin everything for that idiot."

"I won't ruin it if you help me."

"How can I help you?"

"You can put an officer observing in Salvatore's tree. Salvatore will give a life signal in the garden. If, after twelve o'clock, there is no sign of life, you will go to the complex and tell Franco Salvatore told you about the invitation. Tell him that Salvatore asked you if at twelve AM, he has not communicated with you, check on him because he fears this invitation is to kill him. I am sure Franco will not be stupid to kill Salvatore, but anything is possible. That way, I don't expose myself and it remains between you and Salvatore."

"I understand. You want me to make a fool out of me."

"No, that will not happen. You will only do your job. If Franco has done nothing to him, he will show Salvatore to you. He does not want problems and that will show once again Salvatore is seeing ghosts where there are none."

"What if he does not show me Salvatore?"

"Then there is a problem, but not for you. Franco does. We are going to infiltrate two police officers into Augusto's farm at night to make sure nobody passes through the back of the farm."

"I see you have thought it through. You sound like Salvatore."

"What do you mean by that?"

"When Salvatore exposed his theories, he convinced us all. He even convinced his bosses in Rome and when push came to shove, Franco always laughed in our faces."

"I understand, Raffaelle, but this time it is simpler. Salvatore is there or not. They cannot remove him from behind. Salvatore will arrive at eight and we will look for him at twelve. In four hours, a body cannot disappear without leaving traces."

"Now you sound totally like Salvatore. He assures us it is impossible for them to do something, and, in the end, we all look like clowns."

"But do you really think they are so smart and we are so stupid?"

Raffaelle looks at him and kept silent for a while. Then he tells him.

"Listen to me, Salvatore."

"What did you call me? Make no mistake, I am Enrico."

"You are not Enrico. Perhaps without knowing it, you have used Salvatore's phrases. They are so smart, and we are so stupid. Listen, boy."

Enrico felt uncomfortable when Raffaelle called him "Boy". He felt he had called him inexperienced, foolish, and how many other adjectives came to his mind, but he held back so as not to endanger Raffaelle's help.

"I am going to give you the help you ask for, but only if you promise me, that if I make a fool of myself, you will never again involve me in your affairs, you will seek help from Rome if you need it. That is the deal. You take it or leave it."

Raffaelle was very upset.

"I give you my word. If you make a fool of yourself, I will never ask you for help. But if Franco shows Salvatore or you find a crime has been committed, does not count."

"Of course, it doesn't count. It's only if because of you I make me a fool of myself." Raffaelle replies.

"Then you have nothing to worry about. I don't see how you can make a fool of yourself. First, you are not accusing him of murder as Salvatore did. You are only asking for a person who asked you to check on his welfare in case he did not report to you. You just are doing your job."

Raffaelle stood up and said.

"With that assurance of yours, I am totally convinced everything will be fine. Have a good night, Mr. Salvatore."

The encounter with Raffaelle had left Enrico with a bitter taste. Raffaelle had compared him to Salvatore, but Enrico was sure this time it was totally different. That night Enrico could not sleep. The trust he had in his case crumbled without knowing why. He analyzed Salvatore's cases and put himself in Salvatore's place and those cases also seemed closed cases to him as well, but he also knew the results had been a disaster.

He wondered what could go wrong and, despite finding no faults, his mistrust grew by the minute. It was too late to back out. What worried him the most was his relationship with Adriana. If she found out he had lied to her, it would be the end. Enrico did not think about it anymore. At the end of the day, he will do what his instinct tells him.

Enrico finishes work and asks himself a question to end his dilemma. Where will I be happier for the rest of my life? Is it in the investigation department or with Adriana? He kept thinking and driving, as if he was on automatic pilot. Suddenly, he realizes he is in front of the hill. Enrico thought it was the sign he needs, and without thinking twice, he goes up the hill. He enters the complex. He meets Guido at the reception.

"Hello Guido, please, I need to speak with Don Franco."

"He is busy with a sales agent in his office."

"Will it take long?"

"I don't know. He just came in and he always takes his time. If you want to give me the message, I'll pass it on to him."

"Thank you, Guido, but I must speak to him in person."

"I understand, but you will have to wait or come back tomorrow."

"I will wait as long as it takes. Just tell him please I am waiting."

"I'm sorry Enrico, but when he's with someone, unless it's an emergency, we don't bother him."

"It is important for me, but it is not an emergency."

Every month, Valentino meets with Franco to inform him about Maria and her parents.

"Don Franco, we do not know where Maria is. Her father has practically left the factory to search for her. After six years without results, he has fallen into depression. The factory is still operating because of us, but he does not care anymore. He told me he will close it at the end of the year, for he has no more strength to keep going. He is aware nobody is going to buy a factory that is almost bankrupt with only one customer."

Franco answers. "If he closes the factory, we will lose contact with him."

"You are correct, Don Franco. I have tried to convince him, but he is determined."

"Then tell him you will buy the factory. Offer him double the value, but with only one condition."

"What condition, Don Franco?"

"That he remains in the factory and handles the administrative part. Tell him the administration is not your strong point and you need someone trustworthy and knowledgeable in the business. I know Don Pedro will feel good if he sees you trust him. Make him believe you need him. He will feel useful and grateful. Only then he will accept without problem."

Franco, Valentino, and Luigi were talking for over three hours when Valentino says.

"It's late, I'm going to sleep. I must leave early tomorrow."

"It's true, it's almost twelve o'clock, and we didn't notice the time." Franco says.

Franco and Valentino exit the office and find Enrico still waiting. Franco, surprised, tells Enrico.

"What are you doing here so late? What is going on?"

Guido intervenes. "He wants to talk to you. I told him you were busy, but he insisted on waiting."

Enrico tells him. "It's important to me, and I know it's late. If you prefer, I'll be back tomorrow."

"It must be very important if you waited until midnight."

"Yes, it is, Don Franco."

"In that case, come inside with me." Franco heads to his office and Enrico follows. Upon entering the office, Enrico sees Luigi is in the office. Franco says, take a seat and tell me. What is going on?"

Enrico responds. "Can you and I talk alone?"

Franco looks at him and responds. "You are wrong Enrico, there are no secrets between Luigi and I. If you distrust Luigi, you also distrust me. You don't know what is to have a friend like Luigi. That's why you can't understand it."

"What do you mean?"

"Well, your expression has given you away. But go on. What did you come here for?"

Enrico understood that with his reaction to a simple phrase, Franco had discovered him and there was no way back.

"Don Franco, I come to tell you the truth. I cannot continue lying and please understand my decision has not been easy, but lying to you is lying to Adriana and I cannot make a solid relationship based on lies."

Luigi, confused, asks him. "What the fuck are you talking about? Can you get to the point?"

Franco answers him. "What Enrico means is he is not Raffaelle's cousin. He is an undercover detective who infiltrated us but fell in love with Adriana and now prefers to betray his department rather than betray Adriana. Isn't that so, Enrico?"

Enrico was left with his mouth open. He had practically said nothing and Franco discovered everything. Enrico looked at Luigi and answered.

"Yes, it is true."

Luigi lost control, he grabbed Enrico by the neck and lifted him up.

"Damn bastard, this is how you pay back those who take you in as a friend and feed you."

Luigi smashed Enrico against the wall and Enrico did not put up any resistance. Franco yells at him.

"Luigi enough, leave him."

"But Don Franco. How is it possible?"

"Don't forget, Luigi, Enrico or whatever his name is ....."

"No, Don Franco. That's my name." Enrico replies.

"He has proven to be cunning, charismatic, have big balls, but above all, honest. However, Samson has fallen into Delilah's traps again."

"I come to tell you tomorrow I am resigning from my job, and I will continue working in the health department. I want to marry Adriana and if you don't want to see me anymore, I understand. We will leave. It is the first time I have been happy, and I will not give it up for anything in the world."

"Do you love her that much?"

"Much more than I thought myself."

"Then boy, in that case you should not give up anything, because I have nothing to hide. Tell me, have you seen something illegal here?"

"No, Don Franco."

"You've been here longer than any other detective, and you've practically been one of us. Have you seen something illegal?"

"No, Don Franco."

"Then do your job and convince yourself once and for all."

"Understand me. I don't want to get involved in anything. I just want to change my life completely."

"Are you asking me for permission to quit your job?"

"Yes." Enrico responds.

"Well, you don't have it."

"But why?"

"Because if you do, they will send someone else who may be an unscrupulous person, like Salvatore, who fabricates evidence and imprisons innocent people. At least you have shown principles and honesty."

Enrico puts his hands on his head and says.

"Oh God! I can't believe this is happening to me."

Franco puts his hand on Enrico's shoulder and says.

"You know that for your own good. This conversation never happened because you will lose Adriana, you will lose your job and they will accuse you of treason."

"You are going to force me to get involved." Enrico says.

"Why do you say that?"

"Salvatore told me you want to kill him."

"It's true. He didn't lie to you. I want to do it with my own hands."

"Salvatore told me you invited him to the compound on Saturday and that you want to kill him that night."

Franco, undeterred, replies. "It is true."

"No! No! No! You cannot do that. Have you gone crazy? I cannot look the other way if you commit a crime in front of my. I beg you, please do not do it."

"What's wrong Enrico? You can be honest with me and I can't be honest with you?"

Enrico yells, "Shit!"

He turns to leave, but he is Luigi in front of him like a wall, blocking his exit.

"Move out of the way." Enrico yells angrily.

Luigi does not move, and Enrico gives him a push that almost makes him fly. Luigi falls on his butt. Enrico exits the office and slams the door. Guido hears the screams in the office and comes running. Guido asks Enrico, who is visibly upset.

"What happened, Enrico?"

"Nothing Guido, nothing happened."

Guido walks into the office and sees Luigi sitting on the floor and Franco laughing.

"What happened here?"

Franco responds. "A midget put the giant on his ass."

"I do not see it funny. I was unprepared."

"How can you be unprepared? He told you to get out of the way."

"I never expected that midget to have the strength of a bull."

Luigi, still sitting on the floor, asks.

"What are we going to do now, Don Franco?"

"Nothing Luigi. Remember, this is the last meeting. We have a totally legal business. There is no need to worry. Regarding Enrico, it is better the one we know than another Salvatore."

"I agree with you on that."

On Saturday morning, seven members of the organization arrived at the complex. Each one came with a child. A group of children received at the entrance of the hill them from the village to celebrate together. They climbed the hill on seven ponies and then were received by clowns with balloons and music.

Marina enters Franco's office while Franco is talking on the phone. She tells him.

"Hurry, I need the phone."

"Do you have an emergency?" Franco answers her.

"Yes, I do; hang up, now."

Franco hangs up the phone and hands Marina the receiver.

"Who are you calling?"

"I am calling Enrico."

"For what?"

"A girl in the kitchen was sick yesterday, and I told her not to come today since Enrico comes every Saturday. Now I need him, and he has not come."

Marina calls Enrico, who was surprised to receive a call from Marina.

"Hello Enrico. What are you doing?"

"Hello. Who is this?" Enrico, in a broken voice, responds.

"This is Marina. What are you doing?"

"Nothing, I just woke up."

"Are you coming today?"

"I don't know. I thought you wanted to rest from me this weekend."

"You are wrong. Come as soon as possible. I need you today. Aren't you the one who says you love cooking?"

"Yes, Marina, I will get ready right away."

Franco would have preferred Enrico not to come that day, but he said nothing. Half an hour later, Enrico arrives and sees the children's party. He enters the reception and Guido looks at him, surprised. Enrico has no idea who knows what. He even thinks he may be in danger, but he acts as if nothing happened.

"Good morning, Guido. Marina asked me to come."

"She is in the office with Franco."

"Thank you, Guido."

Enrico knocks at the door and Franco answers. "Enter."

Enrico enters the office and Marina tells him.

"Today I need you, not as an assistant. Today you are really going to work."

Enrico looks at Franco and Marina tells him.

"Don't look at Franco. It's with me you're going to work with."

Marina takes a hat and an apron out of a bag and tells him.

"Put it on and let's go."

Enrico takes the apron and the hat but keeps his gaze on Franco as if he wants to figure out what Franco's plans are. Franco notices Enrico is scared and distrusts him.

Franco says.

"Marina, I need to talk to Enrico for a moment."

"Just for a moment. We are late."

Marina leaves, and only Franco, Enrico and Luigi are in the office. Enrico asks.

"Don Franco, who knows about last night?"

"Only us." Franco replied.

"Promise me it remains between us."

"You don't have to worry. Now give me your gun."

Enrico was speechless." What did you say?"

"You heard me. Give me your gun."

"How do you know I am armed?"

The fact you did not come today as you always do, tells me something bothers you. I can see distrust in your eyes."

"I got to give it to you. You are a master, Don Franco."

Enrico takes out his weapon zand gives it to Luigi.

"Now go, Marina needs you. After you finish working, we will kill you."

Enrico closed his eyes. He felt more confused than ever. How could it be possible that they will use him and then get rid of him as a disposable object? Enrico lowered his head and walked away as if he had ten pounds of lead on each foot.

Enrico worked without saying a word. He was expecting at any moment they would come for him. He always kept a knife near him and any other object he could use as a weapon to defend himself. Adriana asked him several times what was wrong with him, why he was so serious.

Enrico was visibly nervous and sweating. He answered.

"I am nervous because today I cannot fail to your mother."

Enrico had the background check results from all of Franco's guests. Even though none of them had arrest warrants, they all had ties to organized crime. He looked at Adriana and thought. "How can I be so stupid to let myself get killed for this woman?" But he did nothing. It was as if his hands were tied. The minutes seemed an eternity.

At lunchtime, Marina tells her daughter.

"Adriana, get a table ready for the four of us."

Adriana answers. "Don Franco has many guests today. Most likely, he is not coming."

"He told me he is having lunch with us, as usual."

Enrico thought. "How far could the cruelty of these people go? They cannot be human beings. It is unconscionable to have lunch with a person as if nothing happened, knowing you are going to kill him."

Adriana was finishing setting the table when Franco and Luigi enter the kitchen. Enrico sees them coming and does not know what to do. He concealed a knife behind his back. "Maybe I should kill them both before they kill me, but I don't have a reason to back me up. How could I explain I did it in self-defense if nobody knows they were going to kill me?"

"Enrico, we are waiting for you. What is wrong with you today?" Marina yells at him.

"I'm washing these dishes."

"I'll help you later. You don't want to eat with us?"

Enrico does not answer. He goes to the table and sits down. Franco looks at him and laughs.

"Change that face; it looks like you're at your last lunch."

Enrico stares at him. "If you say it, it is because you know it and enjoy it."

Franco, Luigi and Enrico are sitting at the table, Marina and Adriana are not at the table, but their food is at the table. Marina just went to turn off the oven and Adriana went to get the refreshments. Enrico and Franco are staring at each other like in a western cowboy duel. Enrico takes his plate and switches it with Franco's plate. Franco does nothing. He keeps staring at Enrico and then smiled. He slowly switches his plate with Adriana's plate. Enrico in disbelieve tells Franco.

"I understand you want to kill me, but to kill an innocent person who has been like a daughter to you shows you have no heart."

Enrico takes Adriana's plate and switches with his plate.

"I rather die than see her die."

Franco smiles and answers.

"The poison was in your plate, not hers. You are the one who switched plates around."

Marina comes back and sees Enrico has not even tasted the food.

"Look Enrico, since you arrived you put on a donkey face, and I don't have to put up with it. If you did not like it, I asked you for help. Just say it. You don't have to stay. You can leave."

Enrico understands Marina is not aware of anything and she is misinterpreting what is happening.

"Forgive me, it is that I ate something yesterday and since then my stomach is killing me. You know I really enjoy being with you all."

"Why didn't you say it before? I'll bring you a purgative right now. You should only drink liquid."

Enrico takes a deep breath, closes his eyes, and thinks. "Oh, my God! This is the only thing I am missing now. I am starving, there is poison in my food, Marina is saving me from eating it, but she is going to give me a purgative and then Franco is going to kill me, anyway."

Marina gets up from the table to get her recipe and Enrico says.

"Please don't bother, you don't have to."

Franco and Luigi laughed out loud.

"Of course it is necessary. Now you are going to find out what a Marina breast purgative is. She forced me to take one two years ago, and it is still working on me."

Everyone was laughing except Enrico, who was about to explode. Adriana gets up from the table and says.

"I'm going to bring you some pills to counteract my mother's purgative, otherwise you'll be running for three days."

Franco, Luigi and Enrico are alone. Enrico tells them.

"You are monsters. You enjoy torturing me psychologically before killing me."

"What's wrong Enrico? Monsters have no right to have fun?"

"Today you die shitting." Luigi said, laughing.

Enrico punches the table and Marina, who was approaching, says.

"What was that? What happened?"

"Nothing. It's that Enrico says he will not take the purgative." Luigi responds.

"Stop fucking around with the boy. I know you. Take this, open your mouth."

"I don't think it's necessary." Enrico pleads.

Luigi and Franco chanted and clapped their hands on the table. "Take it" "Take it."

Marina yells. "Open your mouth. It is only three tablespoons."

Marina gives him the first spoonful and Enrico wrinkles his face. "These tastes horrible."

Franco and Luigi chanted with each spoonful. "One" "Two" "Three" and on the third they applauded "Bravo" "Bravo."

Enrico did not say a word during the whole time they were having lunch.

Luigi devours his plate and asks Marina.

"Who prepared the food today? It is delicious."

"Enrico has all the credit. He was the cook today." Marina responds.

"Bravo Enrico, you have a great future ahead of you as a cook."

Luigi takes Enrico's plate and says.

"What a shame you cannot eat it, but I will not allow this to go to waste."

Enrico sees Luigi is eating his plate. He realizes there was not any poison in his food. Enrico stood up angrily.

"Go laugh at your mother. I'm out of here."

Enrico started walking towards the exit and heard how Marina reprimanded Franco and Luigi for their behavior. Enrico heard Franco calling him.

"Enrico, where are you going? Wait, come to my office."

Enrico was so angry he kept going without looking back. Suddenly, he thought they might think he was running away as a coward. He returns and enters Franco's office without knocking and closes the door.

"I came back so you don't think I'm scared of you. Let's see who is going to kill me. You, who can hardly walk, or you, who with a push fall on your ass. Let's see I'm waiting."

At that moment, four men enter the office. Enrico was in a corner and the men entered without seeing Enrico. Enrico takes out the knife has hidden in his back, thinking they were the men who were coming for him. His heart and breathing increased one hundred percent. It was a decisive moment for Enrico. He knew he would die there, but he would take a few of them with him.

Franco could not see Enrico as the men blocked his view. Enrico entrusts himself to God. He had killed no one, but he was not afraid to do so in self-defense. He looked at which one was the biggest man to stab him first and, using the surprise factor, he was sure that he could stab at least three before Luigi could shoot him.

He firmly gripped the knife, raised his hand, stepped forward and when he was about to stab the man, one man says.

"Don Franco, all the ponies are secure in the stable, the yard is clean, and the children are out of the pool. Do you need anything else?"

"No, that's all, thanks guys. I'll see you tomorrow."

Miraculously, Enrico stopped and did not stab the man. He felt a chill all over his body and he imagined three innocent men bleeding on the floor because of him. Enrico quickly put the knife away. The men turn to leave and see Enrico pale with a face as if he had seen a ghost. One man greets him.

"Hi Enrico, we didn't see you. What's wrong with you? Are you okay?"

"Yes, I'm fine, just a little tired. Today was a very hard day."

The men leave and Enrico drops the knife to the ground and says.

"You are sons of bitches. I almost killed a person thinking they were going to kill me."

Luigi with a profoundly serious face says.

"If you think we need four men to kill you, you are wrong, boy. That is a job I do not delegate to anyone."

Enrico looks at Franco and Luigi and says.

"How disappointing. I had another concept of you."

Enrico throws the knife to the ground and walks towards the door to leave when he hears Luigi.

Luigi takes out a gun and calls him.

"Wait Enrico, this is not over yet."

Enrico runs towards the knife, but stumbles, rolling on the floor. He grabs the knife. He gets up from the floor and says.

"Shoot me, because if you take one step toward me, you are a dead man."

Enrico understands the only thing that could save him was throwing the knife at Luigi. Enrico takes the knife by the tip and raises his arm to throw it when Franco yells.

"Enough, enough."

Enrico stays with his arm up and Luigi changes his face and starts laughing. Luigi tells him.

"Enrico, you forgot your gun."

"He takes it by the barrel and gives it to him."

Enrico takes it with his left hand, still holding the knife. Luigi turns his back on him and walks away, laughing. Enrico cannot take it anymore. He almost killed an innocent man and almost threw the knife at Luigi and could have killed him. He gets on his knees and crying yells at them. "Son of bitches, you are sons of bitches."

Franco approaches him, puts his right hand on Enrico's shoulder and says.

"No Enrico, we only made you feel what you thought we were going to do to you. You were the one who came and accused us of murder. You are the one who investigates us as murderers. Now you better run home, before that purgative does the effects, I doubt you will make it on time."

That night, Salvatore arrives at the agreed time. Franco and the members of the organization welcome him. They enter the meeting room, which is prepared for a great party. Vittorio is also in the room, but keeps separated from the group. Salvatore sees the large amount of food prepared for the party and could not resist it. He goes straight to the food table and serves himself a large plate. Franco approaches him and says. "Wait, we have not started yet."

"If I'm going to die, I don't want to die hungry." Salvatore replies.

"You're absolutely right. Take advantage of your last dinner."

Everyone waits for Salvatore to finish eating, then Franco speaks.

"Friends, it is a great honor for me to have you all here together. All of you have been close to me for many years. Loyalty and honesty have been the key to getting where we are. Today, will be sixteen years since we held our first meeting. Throughout these years, for some reason or another, you have missed a meeting here and there, but within this group, there is a person who has never missed a meeting. He has always made it despite not being physically among us. I want to introduce you to Salvatore. He has always been aware of our meetings. His perseverance is admirable, and I can't imagine how boring this would have been without him. Let's give a hand to the one and only Salvatore."

They all stand up and applaud him. Salvatore could not believe it. He had not received applause since he incarcerated Franco and now he is applauded by the group he tried so hard to imprison. Franco goes to Salvatore and tells him.

"Please come and address the group."

""I don't think you want to hear what I have to say."

"No please, come on and say what you want. Remember that you are our guest of honor."

"Very well. If you want to listen, then don't regret it later."

Salvatore walked to the front and speaks.

"It is difficult to find words to express what I feel. I know very well that more than honoring me, you are making fun of me, but the last laugh is most enjoyable. I have fought your criminal activities a lifetime and after death, I will continue to do so. I sleep peacefully at night, but I doubt you can. I have no wealth because even that has been stolen from me. However, you will never be able to steal my dignity and take away my principles. Yes, let's toast. You toast for your unpunished crimes, and I toast for the justice coming to you. But just in case, I will take Franco's cup and let him take mine."

Everyone laughs. Salvatore takes Franco's cup and Franco takes Salvatore's. They raise their cups, and the group claps, raises their cups and toast, while chanting "Salvatore" "Salvatore".

Salvatore had several cups of champagne. The old gangster friends sang O Bella Ciao and started eating while the music played. Salvatore refilled his plate again and did not even notice when they put a narcotic in his drink. Salvatore fell fast asleep, and Franco rang a bell, and everyone fell silent.

"Our guest of honor has fallen asleep. Please take him to his room."

Two workers from the complex took Salvatore away. Franco rings the bell once more and says.

"Since our friend has retired, let us begin our meeting. As you all know, I am retiring. My health does not allow me to give you the attention you all deserve, but the doors of this house will always be open to you. Our business is over, but our friendship is eternal. I want to introduce my friend Vittorio."

Vittorio stands up. Franco continues. "He was also a partisan."

Everyone gets up and claps. They approach Vittorio, shake his hand, and hug him as if he was part of the group. Vittorio had kept himself separated from them all the time. Some of them had greeted him, but coldly. It was obvious the mere fact of having been a partisan united them. Vittorio was flattered, and despite their differences, he sincerely hugged them. Franco rings the bell again.

"The main purpose of our meeting, besides being our farewell, is to introduce you to my friend Vittorio, a faithful and courageous partisan. He has finally decided to sell us his business, where we will build the workshops of the naval mechanics school. He will be the dean of the school based on his vast experience. But before signing the documents."

Franco pulls out the sales contract and holds it up in front of everyone.

"All of you must promise no one will disturb his son, who will travel to America to settle permanently. If someone does not agree, say it now."

The room is silent. No one objects to Franco's request.

"In this case, each of you must stand up, shake Vittorio's hand, and swear that his son will not be touched, or will know what has happened here."

They all got up one by one and made their promises to Vittorio. Franco rings the bell again and asks.

"Vittorio, give us your price."

Vittorio, with tears in his eyes, gives a piece of paper to Franco. Franco opens it up and sees that Vittorio had asked for fair market value for his business. Franco lifts the paper and says.

"Our friend Vittorio is asking 450 thousand lire for his business. Our lawyer found out what is the true value and gave me the same amount for which I will add another sixty thousand lire on my behalf."

An old man from the group stands up and says.

"Me too, from partisan to partisan."

Everybody from the group stood up and one by one added more money, raising the total sum to 950 thousand lire. Vittorio could not believe it, he had tears running down. Franco rings the bell again and says.

"I want you to know thanks to Vittorio, Marcelo escaped."

That was the final touch. Vittorio turned into the hero of the moment. The music continues until late at night.

The police officer in Salvatore's tree informs Raffaelle that Salvatore has given no sign of life. The officers infiltrated in Augusto's estate reported there has been no activity at the rear of the complex. Raffaelle reluctantly shows up at the complex and tells Guido.

"I need to speak to Franco."

The party is in full swing. Franco tells Raffaelle.

"Welcome, please coming and enjoy a little with us."

"Thanks Don Franco, but actually I come to make sure Salvatore is okay."

"So, you don't want to take part in the party?"

"No, I just want to verify Salvatore is okay."

"Don't worry. He's in good shape."

"I need to see him, please."

"Then I'm sorry. You will need to wait until he comes out or to get a court order to get in."

"Please, Don Franco, call Salvatore. I need to see him."

"Did Salvatore tell you I want to kill him?"

"Yes, that is what he told me."

"Well, he didn't lie to you, and you know it doesn't matter to me, because I have little left. If you are going to come back with a court order, please tell me so I can get drunk."

Raffaelle angrily replies. "Who do you think you are?"

Franco answers him.

"I know very well who I am. I am the one who is living his last days and does not care much what comes."

"Well, you are going to care. So, get drunk because I'll be back."

Franco called the reporters who had covered all the previous encounters. "Hi there".

"Who's calling at this time of night?" Answers the reporter.

"This is Don Franco. Raffaelle is on his way here with a search warrant."

Franco did not have to say anything else. Right away, the reporter called his friend and in fifteen minutes, they were in front of the complex with all their equipment. About forty minutes later, Raffaelle appears with three officers. He does not have time to speak. He sees the flashes from all angles. Raffaelle looks at the reporters and he understood the mere presence of the reporters tells him he is bound to a big failure.

"Here is the search warrant. Read it."

"It is unnecessary. I know you are an honorable person. Please tell me again what you want?"

"You know what I want."

"If you want to know about Salvatore, I will tell you everything and then you take what is left of him."

Raffaelle felt a chill.

"What do you mean? Did you kill him?"

"No, Raffaelle, how I am going to kill him. He still hasn't confessed he lied to put me in jail. Salvatore has been asking me for a job for a long time. He is living in precarious conditions. He says no one helps him and it is my moral obligation to give him a job since I took his fortune from him. I hired him to take care of the barn because the ponies have escaped several times. The workers complained he came to work drunk and instead of taking care of the barn, he went to sleep. Please take him with you and tell him I will not pay him a penny. I understand now why no one gives him a job."

Raffaelle orders two police officers to bring Salvatore. The reporters did not miss the opportunity and ask Franco.

"Can we go too, Don Franco?"

"Of course, you verify I am not lying."

Fifteen minutes later, the two officers return, dragging Salvatore and tell Raffaelle.

"Chief, we found him in the barn. He was lying asleep with a bottle of wine next to him. We try to wake him up, but he is too drunk and doesn't wake up."

Raffaelle tells Franco.

"I have treated you with respect. Why do you ridicule me this way?"

"I have not ridiculed you. It is you who ridicule yourself by playing Salvatore's games. I never thought you would fall in Salvatore's game, but just like you, I was wrong. The difference is that my mistake goes unnoticed, but yours shows up in the newspapers."

The next day, the newspapers had a photo of Salvatore sleeping in the barn with a bottle of wine and another of the police taking him out of the compound. The headlines were: "Salvatore is in the news again." "This time it's Raffaelle's turn." "Hired and fired the same day."

Raffaelle calls Enrico's boss at the Public Health Department.

"Hello, good morning. This is Raffaelle. Could you tell me where I can find my cousin, Enrico?"

"Good morning Raffaelle, he has not come to work today, he called in sick. Before I forget, you came out very well in the newspaper photo."

Raffaelle angrily tells him. "Fuck off."

All his friends called him to make fun of him. Raffaelle took the three newspapers and said. "This Enrico is going to hear me out."

Raffaelle knocks on the door of Enrico's apartment. Enrico takes a long time to open the door. Raffaelle continues knocking harder and harder. Enrico opens the door and Raffaelle sees Enrico is pale and weak.

"What happened to you?"

"Nothing, I took a purgative yesterday. I am spending more time in the bathroom than outside of it."

Raffaelle throws the three newspapers on the table and says.

"Here results from your investigation."

Enrico knew nothing about what happened. He thinks Raffaelle is coming to give him another kind of news.

"I told you, I was going to make a fool of myself, and I was not mistaken."

Enrico read the headlines and scratched his head.

"My God! This can't be possible."

"I told you Enrico, I told you a thousand times, but you did not believe me. You're alone in this from now on."

"I'm sorry, Raffaelle, forgive me. Please understand me."

"No, it is my fault. You don't know how many people have called me to laugh at me, thanks to you."

"I promised you I won't bother you anymore."

"I hope so, and you better stay away from me for a long time."
Raffaelle turned and left, slamming the door angrily.

CHAPTER SEVENTEEN

STROKE OF LUCK

Vittorio returned to his house at six in the morning. He had spent an incredible night. He had cried and laughed. He had felt alone and among friends. His admiration for Franco remained the same. He remembered how Franco made fun of the Nazis in their faces, and he enjoyed how Franco once again made fun of the authorities that night.

Vittorio opens the door and sees his wife and his son waiting for him. It was the first time Vittorio had gone out without them.

"What happened, dad?" His son asks.

"You told us you'll be back in about two or three hours. You stayed out the whole night and didn't even call home."

"Dad, rest today. I'll open to the business."

"No, son, we will not open the business today."

"What did you say? What happened?"

"I have sold it." Responds Vittorio.

"What? Are you crazy? I know you wouldn't do something like that."

"Son, we had already talked about it and last night. You will follow our tradition in America. It is the land of opportunities where you can achieve your dreams."

"In America! It will cost twice as much as ours is worth. Our business is not worth over four hundred fifty thousand lire. How much did you sell ours for?"

"You won't believe it, son."

"Of course, they took advantage of you and gave you three hundred thousand."

Vittorio laughs.

"What are you laughing at? Because I feel like crying." Answers his son.

Vittorio takes out the check and puts it on the table. Alberto does not want to look at the check.

"I'm sorry, father, I am not going to America. I only speak a little English. That money is not enough, and I will not leave you alone here without resources."

"Well, you will have to do it with half of that amount. If it is not enough, it is because you do not know how to manage your finances."

Aurora takes the check from the table, unfolds it and reads it silently.

"Oh, my God! What did you do?"

Alberto thinks the amount is much less than three hundred thousand lire.

"What has dad done? You have wiped out the sacrifice of three generations."

Aurora gives the check to her son. Alberto reads it and he opens his mouth and eyes.

"Dad, is this correct?"

"Yes, son, it is correct."

"Oh, my! And you did not want to sell? With half of this, I will find a small place in America and there is enough left for us to live comfortably."

"No, son, the boatyard in America is already bought. They will inform us of the address later. I want you to use half the money to establish yourself. Don't worry about us. I have a new job."

"What did you say? What will you do now?"

"Something I have always liked. I will be a naval mechanics professor. Our yard will become the practical workshop of the naval school and I will the decan."

Aurora asks him. "Are you happy now?"

"I think so, Alberto will continue our legacy in better conditions. I will do something I like and we are better than ever financially."

"Father, why don't we buy another business here and we stay all together?"

Vittorio said sharply,

"No! Do not even think about it. They already bought a boatyard in America, and that is an opportunity you cannot miss."

What Vittorio wanted was to remove his son from any possibility of being involved with organized crime.

"Congratulation, dad. You are a great businessman. I cannot imagine how you twisted those people's arms to get so much money from them."

Vittorio said proudly. "Your father has talent, son." However, inside, he thought. If you only knew, I agreed to save your life.

Vittorio puts his hand on Alberto's shoulder and says.

"From tomorrow on, you will start studying English. You know a lot, but related to your work, but that is not enough."

Patricia and Maria celebrate that Pedro, Maria's son, in a month will represent the city in the national championship of physics and mathematics. It is the first time her son will be away from her. He was a sixteen-year-old young man, bright with a high IQ. He liked to read, his friends respected and admired him as a born leader. Pedro did not know who his father was. Maria always dodged the issue. Once he pressed her on the issue and she told him his father only loved himself and hurt everyone around him, that for his own good he should forget about him. After those words, Pedro never again asks about his father.

Patricia tells Maria.

"You must accompany Pedro to Rome; he is only sixteen years old."

"No mother, I don't want to expose myself, but if you go with him, I will feel better."

"Of course, I'm going. My grandson can't go alone as if he had no family."

"Thank you, mother. I'll take care of everything here, but before you leave, you must sign some papers for me."

"What papers?"

"I got a contract for the export of goat cheese and the sale of cattle and goat leather."

"But when did you do that?"

"I've been negotiating for two months and finally reached an agreement. I can't sign it because everything is in your name."

"Daughter, I have told you this is a big mistake if something happens to me. You have nothing."

"Mother, I have told you I do not want to expose myself. When the child reaches the age of nineteen, we will put something in his name."

"Sure daughter, you did everything. Everything is yours."

"Mother, everything I did is thanks to you. Please do not talk about it anymore."

Maria had a gift for business. The poultry farm was three times bigger than the original one. She had bought three lots of land near the village and had cattle and goats. She employed one-fifth of the city's population. Everyone thought Patricia was an entrepreneur in business because Maria kept her name totally hidden.

Young Pedro, despite his age, managed all the business accounts. His talent with numbers was extraordinary. Romulo, Patricia's brother, had not seen his sister in years. He only kept in touch with a friend who informed him of what was happening in the Villa. They had planned to take over the house and the business after Patricia's death. Romulo had sold part of the business to his friend in advance at half the price.

Two months after the sale of Vittorio's business, Luigi and Vittorio inaugurated the practice workshop at the naval school, founded by Franco. That day, it was like a holiday on the island. All the politicians attended.

The mayor asks Vittorio. "May I say a few words?"

"Yes, of course Mr. Mayor." Answered Vittorio.

The mayor stands in front of the opening ribbon and says.

"Dear citizens, members of the governing council and journalists present. I am proud to be part of this community and to have been chosen by you to represent and guide you through the path of prosperity. Only a small account of the achievements of my mandate shows a clinic was built where members of the low-income community are cared for, a naval school where students pay minimal tuition and those who show talent study totally free. What was a dream yesterday, today is a reality with the inauguration of the naval mechanic's workshop. Now, our students can complement theory with practice. We accomplished all this without raising a penny in taxes and this is just the beginning. I ask you all to move forward together and not be fooled by those who ask for a change."

The mayor pulls out a pair of scissors he hid in his pocket, cuts the tape, and screams.

"Let's begin the party!"

Reporters videotaped the mayor and took the pictures. Luigi and Vittorio were pushed aside and ignored. Luigi held Vittorio to avoid a fight.

"Take it easy Vittorio, I'll fix this."

Luigi said went to see the reporters who had always reported Franco's incidents. The construction of the workshop had been so fast that very few knew Franco was the founder.

Luigi approaches the reporters and tells them.

"Do you want a juicy story?"

"Sure Luigi. Tell us where?" They instantly respond.

"It is right here. Just interview Vittorio. He was the owner of this place."

"No Luigi, that doesn't make news."

"You will not regret it." Luigi responds.

"We will do it because you have always called us and we are indebted to you, but we do not promise we will publish."

"Okay, you decide."

Reporters approached Vittorio.

"Don Vittorio, were you the owner of this place?"

"Yes, it has been in our family for three generations."

"And how do you feel today?"

"I feel like killing the mayor." Vittorio yells at the reporter. They did not expect such a response.

"Does that mean you are happy?"

"No, that means if Luigi didn't hold me, I would have punched the mayor."

This time, the reporter changed their attitude and filmed the interview.

"That shameless made a political campaign out of the inauguration. He spoke as if he had built the workshop, but the only thing he did was to charge us for the construction permits. Don Franco did all this."

Luigi could not believe it. It was the first time he heard Vittorio call Franco" Don Franco".

The reporters realized they had a great story.

"Would you tell that to the mayor in his face?"

Vittorio, out of control, yells.

"I tell the mayor and the president if necessary."

"We'll be right back. Please don't leave Don Vittorio."

A reporter rushed out to find the mayor, but the mayor had left in a hurry to avoid being discovered. The reporters said nothing to the other reporters to make sure their newspaper was the only one carrying the story.

The next day, three newspapers had pictures of the mayor's inauguration of the workshop and praised him for his good work, and one newspaper had the picture of Vittorio accusing the mayor of being a liar. This produced a tremendous scandal that further increased Franco's popularity.

The mayor defended himself, saying he had never said he had built the workshop, but that no one can deny it was built during his term. The news was echoed in the national press. A famous reporter wrote an article about Franco entitled "You'll be the judge". The report recounted Franco's life, his good deeds, nasty rumors, and the case where he pleaded guilty to murder. The opinions of the island residents about Franco were all favorable and only one unfavorable, which was a brief interview with Salvatore.

Pedro comes home from school and tells his mother.

"Today the teacher read us a very interesting article entitled, "You'll be the judge." I brought the article with me. I want you to read it and give me your opinion. In the class, we all had different opinions about the article. Maria takes the newspaper and sees Franco's photo. She gets nervous and says.

"I don't have time for that now. That man is a murderer."

"How do you know if you have not read the article?"

"Son, this is not the first time that man makes the news."

"But he says he didn't kill anybody. He was forced to plead guilty, and that detective ruined his life."

"Son, all criminals say they are innocent. I assure you, he is not the exception. If you want my opinion, "Guilty" and let's not talk about it anymore."

The young man takes the newspaper from her and tells her.

"My God, you talk as if this man did something to you."

Maria was impressed with the physical resemblance between Franco and Pedro. It was as if Franco was chasing her.

Enrico went to visit Salvatore, hoping to find something that would give him a clue. He found a different Salvatore, who was totally disoriented and resigned to defeat.

"Are you coming to laugh at me, too?" Salvatore tells him.

"No Salvatore, I believe in you, but I need something to work with."

"Unfortunately, I have nothing to give you. I failed once again. I would prefer they killed me that night because I no longer want to live."

"Don't say that, Salvatore. Franco is also paying for it with his life. Didn't you see how sick he was? He doesn't have much left to live."

Salvatore recovers immediately. "What did you say?"

"Yes, he does not have too long to live."

"I saw him in a sad shape, but I did not know he was that bad."

"That is why I am telling you to forget about him. It's not worth it."

Enrico's words brought Salvatore back to life.

"You are right Enrico. I must hurry and solve this case before Franco dies.

Enrico realized he had awakened the sleeping monster within Salvatore. He left before things got worse.

Enrico continued with his double life, but it was not at ease. His relationship with Adriana was getting stronger. Marina had asked him when they were getting married.

On Wednesday, Enrico goes to have lunch at the complex as usual. This time, he arrives earlier, goes to Franco's office, and knocks on the door.

"Come in," says Franco.

"Good morning, Don Franco. Do you have a few minutes?"

"Of course, Enrico, come on in."

Enrico enters and says. "I'll be brief."

"Good, because I'm starving." Answers Franco.

"Marina asked me when I am thinking of getting married."

"And what did you answer?"

"I told her I needed to raise more money to get married."

"How much do you need? I will be the godfather and cover whatever is needed."

"The problem is, I cannot get married and live a double life. I decided to leave the Investigation Department. I will do so next week."

"Can I ask you a favor?" Franco tells him.

"Yes, Don Franco. Just tell me what you need."

"Do not quit. Get married. If something happens, I will answer and explain everything. It terrifies me to think they could send someone else. You are honest, but I have had unpleasant experiences with your department. I am paying for one of those bad experiences. If you really love her and have consideration for me, please don't quit."

"Please understand, Don Franco, it is a conflict of interest. I am marrying one of your employees and you are the best man at the wedding. Anyone can accuse me of treason."

"I understand you a hundred percent. I would love to have the answer, but I don't have it. It is your life, and you have the right to be happy. Do what you think is right."

"I will try to find a solution, but on Saturday we will decide on the wedding date."

"Very well, I congratulate you, and I think you are doing the right thing. Now let's go to lunch because I'm hungry."

"Where is Luigi?" Enrico asks.

"He will not be with us. He went to kill a client."

"That little game has to stop. I have not forgotten what you put me through last month."

Patricia had tried to communicate with her brother to invite him to the party, but Romulo would not respond to her message. Patricia kept insisting, and one day, by mistake, Romulo answered the phone.

"Hi there!" Romulo responds.

"Hi little brother, finally you answer me."

Romulo sees it was not the person he expected and has no choice but to respond.

"Hello, sister. This phone doesn't always work. I'm going to throw it away."

"I am calling you to invite you to a party. We are celebrating my grandson's departure to Rome."

"How can you call that bastard your grandson? They are intruders who only want your money. I told you that, as long as they're around, I'm not going to your house. You have chosen them, so enjoy your party." Romulo hangs up the phone.

On the day of the party, of the party, all Patricia's employees and teachers from Pedro's school were present. The priest speaks. "You cannot imagine how proud I am to have been in the lives of these people."

The priest points at Patricia, Maria, and Pedro. "They have taught me more than I have been able to teach them."

The priest approaches Pedro and tells him. "I ask God to enlighten you, so just as your mother and grandmother have put our town on the map of prosperity, you represent us in science. I want you to know that no matter the result, we are proud of you."

Everyone clapped and toasted. Patricia was happy. It was obvious Pedro was her great pride.

Maria went with Patricia and Pedro to the train station. Maria was crying as if it was a last goodbye.

"Mother, take care of my baby. He is the only thing I have in this world. Do not forget to call me every day and make sure the child eats well."

"Mom, when will you realize I am not a child anymore?"

Patricia slaps him on the back of the head and Pedro screams.

"But grandma what happened? Why are you hitting me for?"

"For being disrespectful. You are and always will be a child to us."

"Okay, if that is what it takes for you not to hit me in front of everybody, then I will."

Young Pedro was delighted in Rome. Pedro spent the three days he had before the tournament visiting historical places. He felt like a child in a toy store. His passion for history was so great, he even corrected the tour guides on more than one occasion. They were surprised to see a young man with so such history knowledge.

Pedro arrives about five minutes late to the tournament because the taxi in which they were traveling was involved in an accident. The event organizers were explaining the tournament rules to the participants when Pedro arrived. Pedro enters the building, and an event representative stops him.

"Young man, where are you going?"

"Sorry I am late, but our taxi was involved in an accident."

The man looks at him, sees Pedro dressed like a man from the ninety thirties, and laughs.

"Are you sure you are not traveling in time?"

"What do you mean?" Pedro responds.

"My grandfather had a suit like yours." The man says and laughs with two other even organizers.

Pedro, keeping the calm inherited from his father, answers him.

"That means your grandfather had good taste and those two gentlemen are laughing at your grandfather."

The man changed his face. He did not expect such an answer. The other two men laughed again, but this time not at Pedro. Patricia enters the building in a hurry. She was paying the taxi driver. The man looks at Patricia.

"Madam, are you with this young man?"

"Yes, he is my grandson."

"I think you have wasted your time. The tournament is about to start. You are late."

It was obvious; it was the way to get revenge on Pedro. The event's chief organizer was the faculty dean of physics and mathematics at the University of Rome. He said nothing, but he did not think it was fair.

"Sir, we have traveled from far away. You can't do that to us." Responds Patricia.

"Did you just arrive?"

"No, we arrive three days ago."

"And how come you never stopped by to register at the event?"

"The problem is that the child." Pedro closed his eyes when she called him a child. "He spent all his time from museum to museum."

"From which city do you come from?"

"We are from Fermo."

"From where?" He asks her sarcastically.

"From Fermo." Patricia responds.

"Where is that, boy?" Sarcastically, the man asks Pedro.

Patricia felt offended and standing in front of the man she tells him.

"That, is located in the ass of a mule. It is the same ass you are going to kiss when you see that a farmer, without resources, can beat all your gifted pretty boys."

"Well, he cannot come in. I'm sorry." Responded the man furiously.

Young Pedro, with tears in his eyes, said. "It is not fair! It is not fair!"

Patricia's words offended the dean. He approached Patricia and told her.

"So, according to you, this young farmer can win a contest where students from the most prestigious specialized science schools in the country take part?"

"I don't think so, I assure you so," Patricia answered.

"Very well. The rules say that anyone who is late cannot take part. But I will make an exception since you were involved in an accident."

"Thank you very much, sir," Pedro said.

"Not so fast, young man, only if you and your grandmother agree to give a public apology if you don't win the tournament."

Pedro doesn't answer, but Patricia says.

"Okay sir, but I assure you I will not apologize because he is going to win."

"Remember, you gave me your word, A PUBLIC APOLOGY," the dean repeats.

Usually, the contestants took six hours to finish, and Patricia had been waiting in the hallway. The dean approaches her and tells her.

"You can go, eat something and then come back."

"Thank you, but I am waiting for my boy. I don't know why he is taking so long."

The man laughs. "Lady, it has only been two hours. It will take at least three more hours for the students to finish the contest."

Patricia points at Pedro, who was approaching them. "No, look sir, my boy is coming!"

The man turns around and sees Pedro.

"You did well boy, if you don't know the answers, why suffer then? Are you ready to apologize?"

"No sir. How am I going to apologize if I did not rate me yet?" Answers Pedro.

"The boy is right." Replies Patricia.

The dean could not believe such charlatanism.

"In that case, go to eat and come back in half an hour. I should have your contest results."

The dean knew it would take an average of four more hours for the tournament to finish and the results were usually announced the next day, but in this case the dean would review Pedro's answers during the time they waited for the rest of the students to finish.

"I'll wait for you here when you come back." Said the dean, waving a red from side to side, implying he was going to correct many mistakes.

The dean enters the office with Pedro's papers. The other two tournament organizers were inside having a pleasant conversation.

"Gentlemen, our genius has finished, and his grandmother took him for lunch."

All three laugh. If he finished, it is because he did not answer more than ten questions and who knows how many of those ten are right."

"Just like he said, it's not fair. We didn't ask him questions about cows and tomatoes."

Everyone laughs. The dean takes the papers out of the envelope and sits down at his desk. There were a hundred math problems and a hundred physics problems. One professor tells the dean.

"Don't have all the fun yourself. Give me the physics and have fun with the math."

"Okay, here you go. Make sure you have plenty of red ink."

Both teachers are reviewing the answers while the third reads a newspaper. About twenty minutes had passed and none of the teachers had said a word. The third teacher puts the newspaper aside and asks.

"Why are you so quiet? It can't be so difficult for our genius. Let's see! Let's see! How many tomatoes should a goat eat to get fat like a cow?"

The dean looks at him in amazement and says. "Shit! I am in question forty and he has not failed one yet."

The teacher gets up, as if his chair was on fire.

"What did you say? It can't be. Are you kidding me?"

"I'm not kidding."

The dean asks the teacher checking the physics questionnaire. "How are you doing?"

"I'm taking my time to review it. I'm checking question thirty."

"How many wrong do you have?"

"None, I still don't have one."

"That is impossible. Someone has stolen the answers and gave it to him to embarrass us. We have to investigate who is behind this."

The dean responds.

"Watch your mouth. You are questioning the reputation of our institution."

"Please understand. I don't see any other alternative."

"Let's keep checking. Maybe at the end we find mistakes."

The teachers rigorously reviewed all the answers, and after an hour, they found no errors. Then they swapped papers and rechecked them again, to see if one of them had missed a detail but could find none. After two hours, Patricia and Pedro returned. Patricia talks to a teacher who was standing at the entrance.

"Good afternoon, sir. We come to get the results of the child."

The teacher looks at her and laughs. "Madam, I think you have made a mistake. I don't know what you are talking about."

"The contest's result."

"Do you mean the physics and math contest that is being held here?"

"Of course, that is what I just said."

The teacher laughs and replies.

"Well madam, to get a result, first you must take part and you have just arrived."

"No sir, the child finished two hours ago."

The teacher can't help laughing. "Look madam, with all due respect, the tournament started four hours ago, and no one has finished yet. Usually, participants finish between five to six hours."

"Well, sir, that is not my problem. My boy finished two hours ago."

"I told you no one has finished yet. I think you should leave. We do not play that kind of joke."

Pedro did not say a word. Patricia protected him like a lion protects her cub.

"Look sir, I am too old to make those kinds of jokes. Find me the director now, because he knows the child participated. We have made many sacrifices so he could be in this tournament."

"Madam, what I'm going to do is to call security, so they can kick you out of here if you don't leave on your own."

"Then, you will have to kill me, because I am not leaving."

The teachers had checked Pedro's papers twice and found no mistakes. The dean hears an argument at the entrance and asks.

"What is going on out there? I am going out to check what is happening."

The dean comes out and sees Patricia arguing with the professor.

"Silence please, you are affecting the participants' concentration."

"I'm sorry sir, but this lady insists on asking for this young man's tournament results, who has not even participated in the tournament."

Patricia sees the dean and speaks.

"Ask this man if my child did not participate. He saw my child this morning. He has his papers."

"Madam, I repeat, that this young man has come in the morning does not make him a participant. No one has finished yet."

The dean walks over and says.

"Didn't you hear me? I said shut up. You are affecting the participants' concentration."

The teacher says. "The lady insists."

The dean interrupts him. "I know what the lady wants. I will handle this."

The dean tells Patricia. "Lady, no one has finished yet."

"What do you mean nobody has finished? My child finished two hours ago. Do you have the results?"

"Yes, but I cannot give it to you yet. I will give the results tomorrow. If there is a winner, he will get the trophy. If there is a tie in first place, then they will take a six questions test and only one hour to answer to break the tie."

"Okay, in that case, we are leaving." Patricia says.

"Please give us the address of your hotel."

"What for?" Patricia asks.

"Because you never came to register and arrived late, there is no record of your participation."

Patricia gives him the address and says. "Let's go boy, we have time to see the Colosseum again."

The professor tells the dean. "Thank God you got rid of them."

The dean responds. "They came late. That's why you didn't see him."

"But how did he finish in two hours?"

"It is also true."

"Well, if he did not know the answers, I think he took a lot longer than necessary."

The dean looks at him and responds.

"You're right. Something is not right with this boy's head."

The dean asked the other two professors not to divulge Pedro's results. After reviewing all the results, the highest scores out of a hundred questions were ninety-six in physics and ninety-eight in mathematics. Those results belonged to the student who won the two previous tournaments and was the favorite to win again.

The next day, the auditorium was full, and Pedro had not arrived. The dean was worried. He delayed the start for about fifteen minutes, but Pedro did not appear. The dean told one organizer to start and try to lengthen the ceremony while he went to Pedro's hotel, which was not far away. The dean was angry. He felt Pedro and Patricia were playing tricks on him. He remembered about a possible leak of the answers to demoralize the institution. That was the only logic explanation for what was happening, because winning such an award and not attending the award ceremony makes no sense whatsoever. The dean arrived at the hotel and asked at the reception.

"Good morning. Can you tell me if a lady named Patricia and a young man named Pedro are your guests?"

"Yes, sir, they are."

"Can you please call their room and tell them they have a visitor?"

"I am sorry, but the lady was taken in an ambulance to the hospital this morning and the young man left with her."

"What happened to her?"

"I do not know, but it is serious. The boy cried inconsolably."

"Oh, my God! Do you know which hospital?"

The receptionist passes him a note with the hospital address.

"Thank you very much." Said the dean and left in a hurry.

The dean goes to the hospital and finds Pedro heartbroken.

"What happened, son?"

"My grandmother had a cerebrovascular accident."

"A what?" Asks the dean.

"A cerebrovascular accident." Pedro repeats.

"Oh! Yesterday's accident in the taxi."

"No, sir."

The dean understands nothing.

"Can you explain a little better?"

Pedro answers.

"It is a blood clot formed in the body that later enters the bloodstream and allocates in the brain. It causes paralysis according to the part of the hemisphere where it is allocated. A person can have a blood clot from trauma and not know it until a tragedy like this happens. My grandmother is used to living a quiet life. She has been under a lot of stress since we arrived in this metropolis, especially yesterday when they told her I could not take part in the tournament. Perhaps that stress from yesterday busted a blood vessel in her brain and caused this. The fault is mine. I kept her from museum to museum. I was reading until late and I didn't see what was happening to her. I would have been able to recognize her symptoms and act to prevent this tragedy. I could make incisions under her nails so that she would bleed, lowering her blood pressure. But this is possible only if you do it immediately. She would not end up like this. But this is possible only if it is done immediately.

The dean, still confused, asked him.

"Can you tell me in simple Italian what happen to her?"

"She had a stroke." Answers the boy.

The dean was impressed with the boy. "How can we help?"

"I want to take her home, but the doctors will not let me."

"But of course. you should not take her out of the hospital, you are not a doctor."

Pedro answers him. "What difference does it make? They cannot do anything either. An operation to remove the clot from the brain is more than a risk, it is a death sentence. Recovery will be very slow, if she ever recovers. Actually, the best therapy is to be in a carefree environment, and I doubt they can give it to her here."

The dean does not even know what to say. The general knowledge of the young boy is way above his age.

"What is it called your grandmother had?"

"A cerebrovascular accident, which is called an embolism or stroke."

"Ah stroke! You should start there without having to give me a medical dissertation."

"I am sorry if I confuse you, but you asked me."

"Yes, son, it is really my fault for asking you. I just want to congratulate you on winning the tournament. I would like to take you for a moment to the awards ceremony and then I will bring you to the hospital."

"Thank you very much, sir, but I will not leave my grandmother for anything in the world."

The dean was shocked by the simplicity of the young man.

"Allow me to apologize for what happened yesterday. We are the ones who must give you a public apology. Now, I must leave, but if it does not bother you, I will return to see you and pray for the recovery of your grandmother."

"Thank you very much. I will be here." Pedro responds.

The dean could not stop his eyes from watering. He hugged Pedro tightly and told him.

"Everything will be fine, son. You can count on me for whatever you might need."

The award ceremony had been delayed by an hour. The young man who had taken second place was a brilliant young man from a wealthy family. He had won the two previous tournaments, and his parents were present, waiting to receive the award and take pictures together. That photo would surely appear on the social pages as it had previously. The dean goes up to the pulpit and everyone sees him excited with the tears in his eyes. He grabs the microphone and says.

"First, I want to congratulate all the contestants. The mere fact of participating is a glorious victory, regardless of the achieved results. Congratulations to your parents, who have supported you to excel in the branches of science. This is our third tournament, and here we have our brilliant winner from the previous two tournaments."

The young man stands up, and everyone applauds him. The dean continued.

"This year has not been the exception, as he got the excellent scores of 96 and 98 out of the hundred, so I ask for a round of applause for him and his parents."

Everyone applauds, and the reporters take several photos of them. One teacher brings the second-place trophy, and the dean says excitedly.

"Unfortunately, our first-place winner is not among us to receive the trophy."

Those words were as if a bomb had exploded. The dean had to ask for silence several times. The young man, who believed to be the winner again, was walking with his parents to receive the trophy. The young man's father yells.

"I hope it's a joke, and it is a very bad one."

"No! It is not a joke and I beg you to listen to me until the end."

The father, clearly angry, took his wife and his son and left without receiving the second-place trophy. The dean addresses the audience again.

"None of you have seen the winner, as he never took part in the three days of preparation for the tournament. He used that time to visit all the museums and historical places in Rome. He comes from a humble family in a small town I had never heard of. The day of the tournament, he was late because the taxi in which they were traveling had an accident. His grandmother accompanied the young man. One of our professors made fun of them. I will not deny I also make fun of them. Then we denied him participation for being late. They refused to accept the decision. I allowed him to take part, since they had a legitimate excuse for being late. But I made a deal with them. It was that they would have to make a public apology when he fails the test. I was sure he was going to fail. That young man not only started later but finished in a record time of two hours."

Again, there was an uproar, and the dean had to ask for silence several times.

"When he turned in his paper, we made fun of him again, saying he did well. Why suffer if he does not know the answers? To our surprise, this young man did not fail a single question, scoring one hundred on each exam. I regret they are not present, because I would like to apologize to him and his grandmother in public."

One parent gets up and yells suspiciously.

"Where is that, genius? Why didn't he come?"

"He is currently in the hospital taking care of his grandmother, who suffered." The dean takes out a paper from his pocket and reads it. "A cerebrovascular accident. For those who do not know what this means, it is a stroke. I tried to convince him to come, but he refused to leave his grandmother alone."

The tournament went from being a social event to national news. Reporters ran to verify and report the story. Pedro sees three men running towards him carrying cameras in a hurry.

"Are you Pedro?"

"Yes. What has happened?"

"You won the science tournament held yesterday."

"That's what a man told me this morning."

"What happened to your grandmother?"

The journalists did a long interview with Pedro, who had inadvertently exposed his mother.

"Why did you come with your grandmother and not your parents?"

"I live in a small town called Fermo. I live alone with my mother and my grandmother."

"Did your father die?"

"Yes."

"Do you miss your mother?"

"No, I always have her with me." He proudly takes a picture of Maria and shows it to the reporter.

Reporters take a picture of Pedro holding Maria's photo.

"What is your mother's name?"

"Her name is Maria."

Pedro became a celebrity and received visits from many celebrities. Even the young winner of the previous tournaments went with his parents to visit him. Young Pedro thanked all the help they offered him, but he did not accept any. He used the money won in the tournament to rent an ambulance and transport his grandmother home.

When Patricia and Pedro arrived home, the people greeted them with joy and sadness. Everyone in town came to see her and offer their help. Maria was heartbroken. The relationship between Maria and Patricia was much greater than Maria and her carnal mother. Maria did not know about Pedro's interviews and that her picture was published in the newspapers and shown on national television. She had many things to do while she was alone.

Franco is in his office reading a newspaper when he sees Pedro's photo showing Maria's picture. Pedro's resemblance to Franco was clear, and Franco recognized Maria's face instantly. He could not believe after so many years of searching for Maria, he found her in a newspaper. Franco read the entire article and there were things that did not fit. Perhaps Maria had married and had a son who was an orphan and the resemblance to him was pure coincidence. What he was sure of was that the person in the photo was Maria.

Franco calls Valentino immediately.

"Hello Valentino, I found Maria."

"How did you do it? Where is she?" Valentino responds, surprised.

"Reading a newspaper."

"Do you know if Don Pedro knows anything about this?"

"I don't think so, he would have told me. He doesn't read newspapers. He hates it. He says they only give bad news and high society propaganda."

"It is better this way." Franco answers.

"I need you to tell him you are going on a trip for a month. Ask him to send the order to your warehouses. You must go check the story and let me know what is happening."

Franco gives him all the newspaper and Valentino promises to leave as soon as he talks to Maria's father.

Luigi enters the office and Franco tells him with great joy.

"I have found Maria."

"Your Maria?" Luigi asks.

Franco shows him the newspaper. "We should not talk to anyone about this until the story is verified. Valentino will leave as soon as possible. You get ready just in case he needs you."

"You can count on me, Don Franco."

"You will be the last resort, because Maria knows you very well. That's why Valentino will go first. She does not know him, and Valentino is talented handling situations like."

"I am sure she's in good hands. That old fox is capable of selling the Colosseum to anyone."

Valentino shows up at Maria's parents' house early in the morning. Maria's father opens the door.

"Good morning, Don Pedro."

"Good morning, Don Valentino. What a surprise to see you around here so early."

"I just need a big favor from you. I am sorry to bother you."

"Oh no! Just say. How can I help you?"

"I am contemplating expanding our business and will go on a trip for a month. I want to observe the actual movement of the business and not just believe what the sales agents tell me."

"I think it is a good idea. But what do I have to do with this?"

"I need you to send the usual order to the warehouses."

"Count on me for that. Leave without worries."

"Thank you very much, Don Pedro."

Valentino realized Pedro knew nothing about the newspaper article, and he could leave in peace. Valentino calls Franco on the phone.

"Hello Don Franco, just as we thought. Don Pedro knows nothing. I am leaving this afternoon."

"Thank you very much, Valentino. Make sure you take a good sum of money. You do not know what you will find there, or how long you will be there."

"I am prepared, Don Franco. I have never failed you."

"I know you are an expert on the matter, but I am curious about how you will approach them."

"I do not know, Don Franco, that comes spontaneously. I have always preferred to improvise, so that I don't need a Plan B."

"I know you are the best. Good luck to you and keep me informed, no matter what time it is."

"Will do, Don Franco."

Franco hangs up the phone and Enrico knocks on the door.

"Come in Enrico, please."

"Enrico comes in and says.

"Do not tell me you can see through walls now?"

"No, it is that you knock different. Maybe you have not realized yet."

"I have always said that you are a box of surprises. But tell me what is it I am missing, that you are so happy?"

"Today, by chance, I found something I had lost a long time ago."

"You are right. There are things we find after we thought we lost them forever, and that makes you happy."

"That is how it is. Life gives us surprises." Answers Franco.

"I come today with my decision."

Enrico, please. "I am happy today. Do not spoil my day."

"No, only you can spoil it."

"Explain it, I do not know what you mean." Franco responds.

"I will not resign only if you handwrite a letter explaining to Adriana that when I fell in love with her, I confessed to you my identity and purpose on the island. That I was going to give up everything to marry her and you asked me not to do it. Explain to her you asked me to live this double life."

"Consider it done. Let's shake hands and go to lunch."

"But it is early. I am not hungry." Enrico replies.

"Don't spoil the day. We have to talk about your wedding."

During lunch, Franco says.

"Attention, I have an announcement to make."

They all look at him curiously. Franco raises his cup of wine and says.

"We will have a wedding soon."

Enrico turns red. Luigi yells, finally. Marina's face does not look happy, and Adriana dodged her sight in distress. Franco continues.

"Tomorrow, I will write a letter where I explain why Enrico has been so serious lately. He wanted to marry, but I stopped him. Today, we reached an agreement and settle our differences."

Marina, with fire in her eyes, asks Enrico. "Is that true?"

"Yes, it is, and excuse me if I have been a little upset lately.

Marina gets up from the table and tells her daughter.

"I think you should reevaluate who you are marrying to, because if this asshole needs someone's permission to marry you, he's not showing any pants."

Marina goes to Franco and tells him.

"And who the hell are you, to decide in my daughter's future?"

Marina leaves the table, annoyed. Her daughter goes after her, trying to calm her down. Franco, Luigi, and Enrico remained at the table.

"I think I screwed up." Franco says.

Enrico tells Franco.

"You better find the way to fix this mess. Because if I lose Adriana, somebody will die here and it will not be me."

Enrico got up and left without saying goodbye.

Luigi asks Franco. "What are you going to do now?"

"I will tell Marina I wanted to pay for the entire wedding, give him a house and money to start a small business, but he flatly refused. He only will accept it if I write a letter specifying I was lending him the money and he will pay everything back."

Valentino shows up at the villa and knocks on the door. Maria opens the door and thinks he is a salesman and tells him.

"Good morning and sorry. I am not interested in buying any products; nor have the time to listen to you now. So goodbye."

She closes the door on Valentino's face, but Valentino knocks at the door again and Maria angrily opens the door.

"I was very clear to you. Please go away."

Valentino, with his persuasive way that characterized him, tells her.

"At least, let me wish you good morning."

Maria understands she has been rude to the old man.

"Ok sir, tell me what you want?"

"My name is Valentino. I am a representative of the Switzerland Sciences Faculty University. My job is to search for talents and offer them a scholarship totally free. I understand one talented boy lives here. A diamond in the rough that after polishing its potentials are incalculable."

"My son is not going anywhere. Thank you, but no thank you." Replies Maria.

"And he does not have to leave anywhere. We pay for his tuitions and after his graduation, we simply guarantee him a job with a competitive salary."

Pedro hears his mother talking and comes to see who she is talking to.

"Are you saying there is no need to travel or a commitment to work for you?"

"I said it, and you repeated it." Valentino responds.

"See, madam, 90 percent of our students end up working for our companies, because our salaries are extremely competitive. That assures us our employees are the most qualified in the market."

Maria changes her attitude and kindly responds.

"That makes sense. Please come in."

"Thank you very much."

Valentino enters and takes data to prepare the registration. Romulo enters without knocking the door and interrupts them. Romulo had found out his sister Patricia had had a stroke, could not speak or write. He saw the opportunity to take over the Village.

Maria, totally annoyed, tells him.

"Don't you know how to knock before entering?"

"I don't have to knock or ask permission to enter my house." Romulo responds.

"Since when is this your house? This is Patricia's house. She has not died, like you would love her to in order to take everything she has."

"I only do what a concerned brother will do. I am her only living relative."

"Since when do you care about your sister? You never came to see her. You just live your life as a cheap mobster with your underground clubs in Ancona. Those people are your real family. You haven't come to see your sister in over ten years and as soon as she gets sick, you show up."

"I do not care what you say or think. If my sister cannot speak or write, then she can't take care of herself. I must take care of her and all her assets. The lawyer is preparing the document that gives me legal custody of my sister. That process lasts four days since a judge must approve it. That is the time you have to get out of here. Next time I come, you better not be here or I will bring the authorities to kick you out."

Maria understood she was in a difficult situation. Only a miracle could save her, but she did not show fear. Her face was red, and her eyes were on fire.

"Listen Romulo, you know I have done everything here and never asked for anything. All this belongs to Patricia, and you want to steal it from her."

"I do not care. You got three days to get out."

Romulo turned around and left. He did not even see his sister. Valentino did not say a word. He only listened to gather as much information as he could. Valentino sees Romulo is leaving and tells Maria.

"Excuse me, but I think this is not a good time. I will be back another day."

Maria starts to cry. She believes Valentino left because of Romulo's scandal and that most likely she will be thrown out on the street.

Valentino leaves in a hurry and approaches Romulo. He calls him by his name. Romulo looks at him, surprised because Valentino had called him in a way as if he knew him.

"Who are you? What are you looking for?"

"My name is Valentino, and I am looking for you."

"Well, I do not know you and I am not interested in anything from you."

"Of course, you do not know me, but I know you and yes, you will be interested." Valentino tells him in a convincing manner.

Romulo looks at him up and down.

"I told you I don't know you and I'm not interested. Now go away and leave me alone."

Valentino reaches into his pocket and takes out a roll of bills. Romulo's eyes were fixed on the money. Valentino breaks the wad of money in two and puts one half in Romulo's pocket.

"This is half. I will give you the other half tonight, after we talk at my hotel. If after we talk, you are not interested, you just keep the money, but if you are not interested in talking tonight, give it back to me and nothing had happened here."

Romulo was speechless. That amount of money for just listening.

"Excuse me, sir. I didn't mean to be rude. I am just upset with those people. Of course, we'll talk tonight."

Valentino already had all the information he needed. He knew Romulo's weaknesses, what he dedicated himself to, his plans to take over Patricia's possessions, and throw Maria with her son to the streets. Valentino went straight to the hotel and updated Franco on the situation.

Franco tells him.

"Do whatever is necessary. Keep me posted and don't worry about the money."

"I am going to need a lot of money, a lot more than usual, but in the end, we will get it all back."

"I trust your abilities. I repeat, do whatever it takes. Money shall not be an issue."

That night, Romulo shows up in the hotel lobby at the agreed time.

"Good evening, Romulo."

"Good evening, sir. I am sorry, but you never told me your name."

"It is not true, I told you, but you did not pay attention. My name is Valentino."

"It is a pleasure, Don Valentino. Please tell me. How do you know my name?"

"I know more about you than you think."

"I do not think so. You know my name because that woman mentioned it in front of you."

Valentino was a master. His ability to tell convincing lies was incredible. He read body and facial expressions with accuracy, which allowed him to speak with authority. Even though he rarely knew what he was talking about, he easily convinced the most distrustful people. Valentino smiles and tells him.

"Let me invite you to a drink at the hotel bar."

Once seated at the bar, Romulo breaks the silence.

"You told me you wanted to talk to me, and you have not said a word. I have done my part. If you are not going to talk, give me the second part of the money. I am leaving."

Valentino takes out the second part of the money, gives it to him, and tells him.

"I am a bandit, but I am a man of my word. The only reason I have said nothing is because for this operation I need someone I can trust, know how to read between the lines and not do stupid comments."

Romulo, offended, replies. "Did you call me stupid?"

"No, I did not call you stupid. I am educating you. I just said your comment is idiotic."

"Tell me Romulo. How many times has somebody given such an amount of money just to attend a meeting with no commitment? Who would you give you that amount of money without investigating if you have the right person? Don't you think that if I give you that amount of money, it's because that sum is insignificant compared to the earning if we reach an agreement?"

Romulo is stunned by such a barrage of questions. They are all logical and he takes the bait.

"Excuse me, Don Valentino. I didn't analyze it that way. Now I understand. I only have one question for you."

"Ask me and perhaps I will answer it."

"Why perhaps? If you know the answer."

"Because there are questions that shall not be answered for your own good or of those who collaborate with you."

Romulo asks. "I just want to know what you know about me and who gave you the information?"

"The answer to the first question is everything. I cannot tell you the answer to the second question. I just told you a moment ago I must educate you if you are going to work with me. You are about to enter the big leagues. For that reason, you must understand the rules. The first rule is to give the minimum information and to get as much information as possible."

Romulo is impressed with Valentino, Valentino's impeccable wardrobe, his logical and authoritative way of speaking inspired trust and respect. It was obvious the money with Valentino would be much more abundant than what he was making.

"What you just said is wise. I am willing to learn. I am happy you are selecting me. Now tell me, what this operation is about?"

"I told you this is not a game. This is serious business. You are not inside yet. You must convince yourself you want to enter, because there is an entrance door, but no an exit one."

Those words finally convinced Romulo. He felt important, and his dreams of belonging to a family of powerful gangsters seemed real. Valentino knew he had Romulo eating from his hands.

"I will tell you the rules and you tell me if you accept them.

A - Total loyalty to the family.

B - Absolute honesty to the family.

C - Your problems are our problems, and you cannot solve them alone unless authorized.

D - Disclosure of secrecy is treason, and treason means death.

E - Total obedience to your superiors and you will demand the same from your subordinates.

F - The interests of the family go above your own.

G - Your subordinates are your responsibility, and their welfare goes above your own.

Do you think you can live with this?"

Romulo's eyes shone with happiness. "Of course, Don Valentino. I have lived by those codes without realizing it. That is my way of being and thinking. I don't see any problem."

"Very good. See you tomorrow at the same time."

"How come? This is it? Are we supposed to talk about something?"

"Don't worry, Romulo, you have twenty-four hours to think about it and make a decision. Meanwhile, I must pass on the report to my superior."

"And who is your superior?" Romulo asks.

Valentino looks at him seriously.

"I just read you the rules and one of them says. Disclosure of secrecy is treason, and treason is death. I also told you. Give as little information as possible and get as much information as possible. Are you not paying attention to me or are you stupid? How can I recommend you, if I try to teach you and you don't pay attention? This is the last time I correct you. One more and forget that you ever saw me."

With this, Valentino achieved Romulo's total submission.

"Excuse me Don Valentino, I am so excited that I could not control myself. I promise it will not happen again."

"You can leave now. Have a good night. If you change your mind tonight, just don't come tomorrow."

"I understand. I assure you; I will not change my mind." Romulo responds.

Valentino pulls out the other half of the money and Romulo's eyes almost pop out of his face. Valentino tells the waiter.

"I am paying. How much do I owe you?"

Valentino pays for the drinks and puts down a huge tip.

The waiter takes the money and says.

"Sir, I think you made a mistake."

"No, I did not. The rest is for you, a good job should be well rewarded."

"Thank you! Thank you! Thank you very much!"

"It's nothing son, don't mention it."

Romulo was convinced that if he worked for Valentino, he would never have to worry about money.

Valentino calls Franco and tells him.

"Everything is fine, and the first phase is over. Tomorrow, we begin the second phase. I need you to have ready four huge men with terrifying faces. When I call for them, they must be here the next day."

"Don't worry, I have four individuals who actually don't kill a fly, but they have faces even dogs don't dare to bark at them." Franco replied.

Romulo shows up in the hotel lobby the next day. He had been waiting all day to meet Valentino.

"Good evening, Romulo."

"Good evening, Don Valentino. Let's go to the bar. Today is my treat." Says Romulo, trying to gain some points with Valentino.

"I appreciate the invitation, but it will be at another time. Today we will go to the hotel restaurant. That way, we can make sure no one sits next to us when we speak."

Romulo says. "You are right. Anyway, I invite you."

Valentino fixes his tie and asks Romulo.

"Before going to the restaurant, tell me if you decided?"

Romulo looks like the little boy waiting to receive a birthday present.

"Don Valentino, I think I have a lot to learn. I will learn, but most of all, I am sure together we can do substantial business."

"Are you sure of what you are saying?"

"One hundred percent, sir."

"Very well. Let's go to the restaurant."

"But this time I pay." Insisted Romulo.

"From this moment on, you will be on probation. You and your problems belong to me. Do you understand?"

"Yes, sir."

"You can make three mistakes if they are small, but if you make more than three, then you are no use to us."

"Okay, Don Valentino."

Romulo and Valentino went to the restaurant and Valentino tells him.

"You select the table.

Romulo chooses a table in the center of the room. Valentino tells the waiter.

"We change our mind. We prefer that one in the corner."

Valentino tells Romulo.

"This is not a mistake. It is only for you to learn. If you sit in the center, everyone will pass by your side. You will not know who is casual and who is spying on you. If you are in a secluded corner, you eliminate that problem. Now, if you do it again, it will count as a mistake."

"I promise you, it will not happen again. I am a good learner."

"I hope so. Now let's order dinner."

Romulo, trying to impress Valentino, says. "Remember that I am paying today."

Valentino maintains a cold and dominant attitude.

"You are wrong. I am your provider. I am your superior and a superior must take care of and provide for his subordinates. I told you that yesterday when I read the rules."

"Yes, it's true, I remember." Romulo responds.

"Also, remember that a subordinate never doubts or challenges his superior."

Romulo does not respond.

Valentino asks him. "Did you hear that part, or you don't agree?"

"Are you asking me to do what you say blindly?"

Valentino responds. "Yes, just as I do what they ask me, and as many times as they ask me. If you cannot do it or you think you will change your mind, it is better you tell me now before you start."

Romulo has never had a boss. He was used to giving orders, but it was too much money to miss the opportunity.

"Yes, I'm willing, boss."

"You don't need to call me boss. Just respect my orders. Now we will get to the point. Before starting, you realize, if you comment with someone who is not superior to you, you are revealing a secret and that will be fatal for you."

"Yes, I understand, sir." Replies Romulo.

Valentino tells him. "I like your friend. It's a shame she's married."

Romulo looks at him, confused. He has no idea what Valentino is talking about. The waiter puts the menu on the table and says.

"When you are ready, give me a signal and I will be with you."

"Of course. Just give us five minutes." Valentino responds.

When they are alone again, Valentino says.

"You must be alert. That man approached you and you did not see him. When something like this happens, you change the conversation to something totally irrelevant. This way, if the one who comes is a spy, he will get nothing, at the same time alert your partner someone is approaching."

Romulo felt like he was attending a bandit university. He felt important and was learning little details he had always overlooked. The waiter returns and Romulo says.

"You order first."

"No Romulo, if someone does not eat today, it will be me. You will eat before me."

Romulo was speechless. Not only was the money insured, but his well-being was above his supposed boss, and with this, Romulo swallowed the bait completely.

"I will do the same one day." Romulo replied.

"I hope it will be soon." Valentino replied.

Valentino rubs his hands, leans back in the chair and says.

"Let's get to the point. Our family had to move our underground casinos out of Rome. For twenty years, we never had a problem, but someone inadvertently filtered information. I say inadvertently, because he was a high-ranking person and that would go against his own interests. His lover was actually a police informant. We moved all our casinos out of Rome and placed them in small towns all around the country. For some reason, small towns are safer, and their owners have the perfect mindset for the business."

"How can a person of high rank make a mistake like that?" Romulo asks.

"That shows you cannot talk about your business with anyone unless he is superior to you. He swore to us it would not happen again."

"He sure learned from that mistake." Says Romulo.

"We made sure it didn't happen again, because dead people don't make mistakes."

Romulo's face changed expression, and he gulped.

"Yes, Romulo, the rules are not for the low-ranking. They are the same for everyone. You will take me to see your bars, and I will choose which one we will prepare."

"What do you mean by we will prepare?"

Valentino says. "What kind of question is that? We have to make sure our clients win and lose, but in the end, everyone must lose."

"I understand, Don Valentino. I can see where you are coming from. But if you know everything about me. Why should I show the bars?"

"Simple, because if you try to hide one, I will know you are not to be trusted. You are on trial, but inside now. You know things about us and if we cannot trust you, then you are of no use to us. The one who is useless ceases to exist to avoid worries."

Romulo became more and more convinced he was in the big leagues. He felt like an important person.

"I agree. The one who is useless should not be in the way." Romulo responds.

"What would be my earnings on this?"

"We distribute the profits at the end of the month. Yours is fifteen percent, so the more they lose, the more you earn. Fifteen percent is more money than what you could have earned in a year. Your employees are your responsibility. If you have the slightest doubt, then they cannot work in the casino. If one of your employees fails, the failure is yours. Setting up a casino costs a lot of money, but it is an investment that pays off quickly. That's all. Welcome to the family. Tomorrow we will choose the best place."

"I'm free after 11:00 A.M." Romulo responds.

Valentino stares at him and asks. "What did you say?"

"I said that after 11:00 a.m. I am free."

"And what do you have to do before?"

"I have an appointment with the lawyer who is preparing my sister's incapacitation papers so I could take legal custody of her. You know the rest. You were present that morning when I told those people I was going to throw them out."

"Yes, I remember, but that is not your problem now. It is our problem. Tonight, I will communicate it to the superior so they can tell what to do."

Romulo says. "Understand that as soon as they give me those papers, I will put my sister in a sanatorium and sell everything. I will get good money from it."

Valentino tells him. "We have a problem, then."

"What is the problem?"

"If you think that is good money, then you don't know what good money is. I understand you probably never seen money counted by weight."

"What does money count by weight mean?" Romulo asks.

"In order not to waste time counting the bills, we separate the money by its value, weighed, and that gives you the amount. A thousand more or less does not make a difference, nor do we care. Forget crumbs. You are not here for that. Anyway, I'll tell you tomorrow at eight the boss's decision."

Marco was Valentino's assistant. He was part of the operation and was waiting for him outside the hotel. Romulo and Valentino are saying goodbye when Valentino tells Marco.

"Hey, come here."

Marco comes right away. "Yes, sir."

"From this moment, you are under Don Romulo's orders. If he gives me a complaint about you, then your ass is mine. If he tells you to shit in the square fountain, you lower your pants and do it. But, Romulo, better have an explanation about why it was necessary for him to shit at the square fountain, otherwise you are the one who will have problems. He is your responsibility from now on. You can discuss the business with him, as I allow you to do so. You have the same rank in the family, but he is below you. The purpose of this is to see if you have what it takes to be the leader we need, because I don't intend to be here all my life."

Valentino tells Marco. "Go up to your room and pick up your things. You are going with Don Romulo."

"Yes Don Valentino." Marco responds.

"Don Valentino, I am not prepared to take anyone." Romulo says.

"That is not the attitude of a leader. A leader improvises, he shares what he has, he takes good care of his people, and they will give their life for him."

Valentino takes out a bundle of money and gives it to Romulo.

"Learn once and for all. I solve your problem, and you solve your subordinate's problems. That makes us strong and gives us confidence."

Romulo had been under the spell of Valentino. Not only did he feel important, but he already had someone under his command. Valentino had achieved the second part of his plan, which was to avoid the eviction of Maria and Pedro from the Villa, to have total control over Romulo, and to plant Marco to monitor him constantly.

Valentino calls Franco.

"Hello Don Franco, we finished the second phase. The day after tomorrow we begin the third. I need a crew of men to prepare a casino that has all the tricks available."

"You will have it. I will talk to Don Martino and he will send them to you. Do you need more money?"

"Not for now, but I will need a lot for the fourth phase."

Franco answers him. "Leave it to me. Just keep me informed, please.

CHAPTER EIGHTEEN

EXONERATED

Romulo shows up early in the hotel lobby, accompanied by Marco.

"Good morning, Don Valentino."

"Good morning, Romulo. How was your night?"

"Very well, thanks."

Valentino tells Romulo. "I have the answer for you."

Romulo turns around and tells Marco authoritatively.

"Marco, wait outside; Don Valentino and I have to talk."

"Yes, Don Romulo." Marco responds submissively and leaves.

Valentino tells Romulo. "The bosses don't want distractions, so they ordered me to solve that problem as soon as possible. We will go see your lawyer first thing in the morning, and then the bars."

Romulo felt happy because he wanted to throw Maria out on the street.

"Tell me, Romulo. What is your ultimate goal with this?"

"I want to have the pleasure of throwing those people out onto the street and then sell everything."

Valentino says, smiling. "You are not the only one who wants to make those people suffer. My sources told me you were going to see your sister that day, so I went to the villa. I tried to make time waiting for you, so I pretended to be a representative of the University who was offering a scholarship to her son. They treated me like trash. I really enjoyed the way you treated them."

"I will make it a priority to make them pay for what they did to you." Says Romulo.

"You are wrong about that." Valentino replies.

"Why?" Asks Romulo.

"Your priority now is to get the casino up and running. Then you and I will have fun evicting them."

"It would be my pleasure." Says Romulo.

After an hour, Romulo and Valentino enter the lawyer's office. The lawyer's office was small, not very clean, with folders thrown everywhere. A large ceiling fan was the only ventilation in the office, which constantly blew the documents, and the lawyer had to hold them. The lawyer was an old man with a shady reputation. He would do anything for money. He wore a shirt that probably a few years ago was white, a tie stained with tomato sauce and immense thick glasses.

The lawyer says. "Don Romulo, here are the documents that officially make you the legal custodian of your sister. You can take control of everything in that villa."

"Thank you very much. I will pay you right now."

"Wait a minute." Says Valentino.

"Who are you?" Asks the lawyer.

"I am Romulo's boss. He works for my company, and he is a very busy man. He doesn't have time to constantly come here."

"What do you mean by that?" The lawyer asks.

"What I mean is I need you to go to the city hall, search the records for all the businesses registered in Patricia's name. I want you to make sales contracts for each one of them. Prepared those contracts as soon as possible. Check if Maria and her son Pedro appear on the payroll of those businesses. If they do not, then all the assets belong to Patricia. Finally, prepare an eviction order for Maria and her son Pedro from the Villa."

The surprised lawyer asks Romulo. "Is that correct, Don Romulo?"

"Yes, that is correct. Do what my boss told you."

"How long does it take and how much is the total fee?" Valentino asks.

"Something like that will take three weeks, and cost a lot more."

"That is understandable." Valentino responds.

The lawyer looks at some books, writes an amount and passes it to Romulo, who looks at it and opens his eyes.

"This is a lot of money!"

Valentino asks Romulo for the note. He reads it and pays the lawyer.

"Are we okay now?" Valentino asks.

"Yes, sir."

Valentino gives the lawyer ten percent extra.

"What is this for, sir?"

"So, you can do it in three days and call me at this number. I'll pick up those documents myself."

"I will call you as soon as I have them ready, sir."

Romulo and Valentino leave the lawyer's office and Romulo tells him. "You want to throw them out more than I."

"Not only am I going to throw them out, but they cannot take anything with them. We will give them two sheets to cover themselves and that is how they will leave the villa. I am implacable with those who treat me the way they did. I told you I was going to take care of your problem."

"Yes, Don Valentino, I could not be more grateful."

At the end of the day, Valentino had selected the bar with the best conditions to turn it into an underground casino. Valentino asks Romulo.

"How many employees do you have at this bar?"

"I have four."

"Can you trust them?"

"I have never had a problem with them."

"That is not my question. Would you put your hands on the fire for them?"

Romulo doesn't know what to say and Valentino tells him.

"Your silence is the answer. I will tell you how this works one more time and then you choose. If some of your men make a mistake, the mistake is yours. If you cannot guarantee them a hundred percent, then it is better they send us men. That way, we are not responsible if something happens."

Romulo did not think twice. "I do not recommend them."

Valentino laughs and says, "You are learning fast. I recommend no one either."

"How come you recommended me?" Asks Romulo.

Valentino laughs again. "No, you are wrong. They sent me to recruit you. The recommendation is not mine. It comes higher up. If you mess it up, you and someone else would have to flee Italy, not me."

Romulo made a scared face, and Valentino put his hand on Romulo's shoulder. "This is how this business works. By the way, you can send those men to the other clubs. Tell them you are retiring from the business and rent the other clubs at fifty percent commission."

Valentino's plan worked like a Swiss watch. Since Romulo did not use his men, he was totally isolated and knew if he made a mistake, he would have to leave the country and never return in order to save his life.

On the second day, a group of men arrived with the sole purpose of converting the underground club into an underground casino. Valentino and Romulo are showing the club to the construction crew sent by Franco. Valentino asks the crew chief.

"How long will it take to turn this place into a casino?"

"Approximately twenty days, Don Valentino."

"Let me introduce you to your boss." Valentino points to Romulo.

"He will take carer of all your needs."

Romulo feels more important than ever. He turns to them and asks them. "Is that clear?"

"Yes Don Romulo." The workers respond.

"If by any chance I am not present, you can go to Marco. He will let me know."

Valentino tells Romulo. "Make sure you get them accommodation and food. They will not leave the premises until they are finished. Marco, and you are responsible for their security twenty-four seven."

"Yes sir, considered done."

Valentino calls Franco and Luigi answers the phone. "Good morning. This is Valentino. I need to talk to Franco.

"I am sorry, Valentino, Don Franco was admitted to the hospital. I am in charge of the project."

"Tell me what you need?" Luigi responds.

"First, I need you to pray a lot for Don Franco's health. Second, the team that will work in the casino. Third, the team who will be the players and, finally, a very large sum of cash."

"The casino's workers are ready, and the money will go out with the players." Luigi answers.

"Perfect. Please tell Don Franco Maria and her son Pedro are out of danger, but I could not find out if Maria was married."

Franco was admitted to the hospital and guarded by the police. Rafaelle had given orders that no one could visit Franco in retaliation for what Franco put him through in the complex.

Enrico goes to see Raffaelle.

"Hello Raffaelle, how are you?"

Raffaelle responds coldly. "Hi there."

"Do you think I could go with you to the hospital to see Franco?"

"No! Franco cannot have visitors."

"It will not be a visit. I will be with you. Remember, he thinks I am your cousin."

"No! Franco cannot have visitors."

Enrico tells him in a higher tone.

"Do you understand you are obstructing an investigation?"

Raffaelle looks at him and says.

"Did you forget you gave me your word you would not involve me in your investigations?"

Enrico realized Raffaelle was right. After the humiliation, Franco gave Raffaelle because of him, he had promised never to ask for help again. Enrico understood this was the precise moment to tell Raffaelle he was going to marry Adriana.

"Yes, you are right Don Raffaelle, that is why I have done things I do not know how it could end."

Raffaelle changes his attitude. He was angry with Enrico, but he did not wish him bad.

"What did you do, boy?"

"I will marry Adriana, Marina's daughter. She is one of the people with the most influence on Franco. I have penetrated them completely."

Raffaelle looks at him and says.

"Congratulation you have achieved what no one has ever been able to, but you are hurting an innocent young woman. I am sure that she really loves you."

"Yes, Don Raffaelle, her love for me is real."

"I do not approve of these tactics. They are as low as theirs. You have let me down, Enrico. You have exceptional talent. It is a pity your moral standards are not at the same level. Do not count on me to go to that wedding. After today, your cousin ceases to exist. I do not approve of hurting innocent people and please, I am busy."

Enrico felt ashamed. He saw great human qualities in Raffaelle. He would have liked to give him a hug and tell him the whole truth, but he could not. He just lowered his head and left with the hope of one day being able to show him Franco's letter, exonerating him of such infamy.

Franco had formed a great friendship with his doctor. They had many things in common. The doctor was a knowledgeable person and could speak about any subject. That was the best medicine he could provide to Franco because his illness had no cure. Franco asks the doctor.

"Can I ask you a favor?"

"Of course, Don Franco, as long as it is not something illegal."

"No, sir. I would not ask you to do anything illegal. Just when Salvatore contacts you, inquiring about my health. Tell him my days are counted. Tell him most likely I will not exceed a week."

"That is all?" The doctor asks him.

"Yes, that is it."

"Ok, I can do that for you."

Franco told him the story of Salvatore and him. The doctor was the only person who believed Salvatore had framed Franco, so he agreed to help him. A week later, Franco improved his health, and the doctor discharged him. The police were transporting Franco out of the hospital when someone screamed.

"There goes Don Franco!"

People began to gather and surround the police. Everyone wanted to see and greet Franco. His stay in the hospital had been kept secret, since Franco had become the key figure on the island. They immediately informed Raffaelle of the situation. He rushed to the hospital with four police reinforcements. Raffaelle realizes it was not an escape plan, but the people wanted to thank Franco for everything he did for them. Raffaelle addresses the crowd.

"Ladies and gentlemen, please understand, Don Franco appreciates what you are doing, but he is in poor health and must rest. We must transfer him to his house."

"We will accompany you, the crowd shouted."

Raffaelle had no choice but to go slowly surrounded by the ever-growing crowd and drive from the hospital to the hill complex at a very low speed, which represented an hour and a half trip. It was the noblest way to thank the man who had built them clinics, schools, built roads to communicate almost inaccessible communities and had always listened to whoever had asked for help.

Upon arriving at the complex, Franco greeted the people again from his wheelchair and asked them to return home. Rafaelle tells Franco.

"I want to congratulate you for achieving a politician's dream without saying a word."

"You don't win the people with words and false promises. They are grateful, intelligent and understand actions of good will. I do not care about politics, but I do care about my people."

"I did not allow you to have visitors in revenge for what you did to me, but after seeing this, I am glad I did so. The crowd would have overrun the hospital, and you would not have had any rest."

"You are correct about that. It was better that way. I apologize for what happened between us. Salvatore and I continue at war and innocent victims always during war."

Franco had made national news again. His picture appeared in the newspapers, a prisoner escorted by the police and the people from the hospital to his house. Young Pedro comes home with the newspaper and says.

"Mom, you will not believe this."

Pedro gives the newspaper to Maria, who reads it and throws it aside.

"Are you fascinated with bandits?"

"If he is a bandit, then he is not just any bandit. He has done more for the people than all the honorable politicians."

"Look, son, I have a lot of problems in my head and need to dedicate myself to those things. At any moment, Romulo knocks on the door and throws us into the street. Your grandmother does not improve, and now you are worried about a bandit."

"I understand. This is not the time to talk about this, but it seems to me that every time I mention this man you get angry like if it was personal."

"That is what you think." Maria replies.

The day before the casino opens, Valentino meets with the five employees who will work in the casino, the five construction workers who built it, Romulo, and Marco. Valentino tells the construction workers.

"Gentlemen, I congratulate you on the good job you have done. The casino is perfect, and you can go home now."

The construction workers leave, and Valentino tells the remaining five.

"Gentleman, everything is like the previous casinos, so there is nothing to explain except that Romulo oversees the money collection. He will take it to the office where Marco will count it and putting it in the safe."

Valentino looks at Romulo and says.

"Romulo, if by any chance we need help, you will operate the roulette."

Valentino gets behind the roulette and calls Romulo.

"Come here, Romulo."

Romulo approaches and Valentino tells him. "Touch here."

Romulo touches the edge of the table and says. "It is not wood!"

"Exactly, it is plastic."

"There is a button under the plastic on the right corner of the table. The roulette ball has an almost undetectable positive charge. When we press the button, the roulette's bottom will create a negative field to stop the ball. For example. If we do not want the roulette to stop at twenty-five, we just wait until the ball slows down. When it passes twenty-five, then press it. That way, the ball will stop at another number but twenty -five. Always try to stop at the lowest bet. If we have a sound bet, you must make sure it does not win."

"Any questions?"

"No, sir." Romulo answers.

Valentino calls Romulo at the office and shows him the safe that had just arrived.

"Look what beauty they sent us."

Romulo is impressed. "Yes, it is a beauty."

"Write down the combination."

Romulo looks for a piece of paper to write the combination and Valentino tells him.

"No! You memorize it. If you lose the paper and someone finds it, we could have problems."

"You are right, as usual."

Romulo opens the safe and almost collapses when he sees the amount of money.

"Oh, my God! I have never seen so much money."

"Then get used to it. That is the money to start. Now look on this side, there is a loaded gun, in case someone tries something stupid. Do not hesitate to use it, otherwise the dead person will be you."

Valentino points to the bottom of the safe and says.

"Those papers below are the contracts that the lawyer prepared. I picked them up four days ago, but we were busy."

Romulo is happy. He is living a fairy dream.

"When are we going to evict those people?"

"Do not rush. First, we must start the business. In a month, we will report the earning to see if we have covered the investment. The next day, we will drop by there. Anyway, each day that passes is another day of torture for them, waiting for us to kick them out on the street."

"I agree. Let those bastards suffer a little more, ha, ha, ha."

The casino finally opened its doors. It was a great night. Many locals showed up. Valentino's order was not to abuse the locals to maintain the flow of customers. Every night, one of Franco's men lost a considerable sum of money. Romulo was in the office salivating every time they brought a briefcase with money. Valentino walks into the office and asks Romulo.

"How is business going?"

"Much better than I imagined. At this rate, in three days, we are going to need a bigger safe." Romulo answers.

"Thanks for letting me know. I must tell the boys to let the clients win a little, otherwise they won't come back."

"Don Valentino, we are doing great."

"No Romulo, to catch a fish you must bait it."

A week after the casino was running, Romulo overhears the conversation between two casino workers.

"You did very well last night. Yes, that fool even lost his shoes and since he was not a local customer, we can peel him mercilessly."

"What percentage do you receive?"

"My contract is ten percent plus salary."

"Mine is six percent plus salary."

"Yes, but I have been working longer than you."

Romulo went directly to see Valentino.

"Don Valentino, is it true these men earn salary plus commissions?"

"Yes, it's true. The commission is an incentive for them to earn more."

Romulo says. "One of them says that he earns a ten percent commission, and that is a lot of money."

"When they earn ten percent, we earn ninety percent. Who do you think earns the most?" Valentino responds.

Romulo had tasted Valentino's bait. Now he only had to wait for Romulo to swallow the hook. Three days later, just as they had planned, the old man operating the roulette wheel tells Romulo.

"I am terribly ill. I cannot continue working like this."

Romulo asks him.

"How many years have you been working?"

"Twenty-six, Don Romulo."

"It is a long time. What percentage do you receive?"

"I receive eight percent because my job is the least complicated. It is just pressing a button."

"Very good money for the push of a button." Romulo tells him.

"I am not complaining, Don Romulo. I am very happy, but my health is telling me it is time to retire."

"Romulo goes to the office and sees Valentino and Marco packing money.

"Don Valentino, Tony, the old man, told me he is very ill, and he cannot continue working."

Valentino, angrily, says.

"I knew that would happen. Tony has been working ill for many years. I asked them to send someone else, but they did not have one."

Marco says. "I will take his place. There is no need to worry."

Romulo yells at him.

"You shut up. Nobody is talking to you. Get out of the office right now."

"Excuse me, Don Romulo. I just wanted to help."

Once alone in the office, Romulo says.

"We are three who can operate the roulette. You cannot because you oversee casino. Marco is very young and does not inspire trust or respect to the customers, so I will be the one to operate it."

"Are you sure of that?"

"Yes, totally sure. I think Marco can do it too. It is quite easy to operate."

"No, Marco is very young and easy to distract. We should not take risks."

Valentino laughs and tells him.

"Romulo, you are not fooling me. There is no wrong in trying to take Tony's job. I would do the same if I could. The truth lies in the extra percentage. Is that you are looking for?"

Romulo smiles and answers. "That percentage is not bad at all."

Valentino laughs and says.

"Ok, but don't even think you are going to be there permanently. It will be until we get the replacement. Don't let me down, please."

"I will never let you down, Don Valentino. Your business is my business." Responds Romulo.

Romulo had swallowed the hook completely. He asked to operate the roulette.

Luigi shows up at Salvatore's house. Salvatore thinks he comes to kill him. He grabs a knife and gets ready to fight. Luigi raises his hand to show he came in peace.

"I did not come to hurt you. I have a message from Don Franco."

"I won't fall into your trap again. I don't need invitations."

"Don Franco is very ill. He wants to be at peace with you before he dies."

"Not even in the next life will I make peace with him."

"That is up to you. He wants to confess everything and make up for the damage he has done to you. This is your last chance. Then, do not regret it. The doctor has given him very few days to live."

"I don't care. Get out of here."

Luigi left, but he noticed Salvatore had been paying close attention when he heard that Franco's days were counted.

Salvatore inquired about Franco's doctor until finally he contacted the doctor.

"Good morning, Doctor."

"Good morning, sir. How are you feeling?"

"I am ok, I am not sick."

"Why do you want to see me, then?"

"I want to ask you a question."

The doctor looks at him, takes his time to respond.

"What do you want from me?"

"You have been Franco's doctor for a long time."

"I am everyone's doctor and that includes Don Franco."

"How true is it he has only a few days to live?"

"The medical history of a patient is secret. It is unethical to reveal it."

"I heard he is in his final days."

The doctor moves his head up and down slowly.

"Yes, it is an open secret. I think he will not last a week. His body cannot resist any longer."

"Thank you doctor, you have a great day."

"Don't go repeating what I told you, please."

"Don't worry, doctor, I won't tell anybody."

Salvatore left the doctor's office with a great dilemma. This could be another Franco trap, but everyone knew Franco was very weak. If Franco dies, the chances of reclaiming his honor would also die.

Meanwhile, the underground casino was in full swing. The news had spread like wildfire in the town and Valentino had to advance the plan for fear they would be discovered. Valentino approaches the office and hears Romulo yelling at Marco.

"Do you have the commissions up to date?"

"Yes, Don Romulo."

"Make sure you put my percentage correct."

"It is correct, Don Romulo. You can check if you want to."

"Yes, but the fact I review it does not mean you write it down."

"You, Valentino, and I have access to the books. You can check it as many times as you want."

Valentino comes in and says.

"Good morning. Today is a special day. Today comes a big fish from Naples. He owns a cargo shipping company and the ferries from Naples to Capri and Ischia. This tycoon usually plays hard and is always guarded by four thugs. It is very important he wins and loses. He cannot lose all at once."

Marco says. "I remember two years ago, old Tony killed him at roulette. He loves roulette and wants to get revenge."

"Yes, I remember. I was told Tony bought a villa with the commission he earned that day."

Valentino says,

Romulo was sharpening his teeth. He had done very well in the roulette. He had earned more than he earned in three months, only on commission. He hadn't received a penny yet, since he was supposed to get paid monthly.

That night, Luigi enters accompanied by four men dressed in black capes. Luigi's bodyguards were very impressive. The casino had been running for about three hours. Valentino was with Romulo at the roulette table when Luigi with his bodyguard entered the casino.

Valentino taps Romulo with his elbow.

"There they are. I bet you they are going to come straight here. "Good evening, gentlemen. What a pleasant surprise to have you here."

Luigi approaches Valentino.

"Good evening, Don Valentino. I heard the police ruined your business in Rome."

"Some doors close and others open." Valentino responds.

"I like this place., You have good taste. I congratulate you, Don Valentino."

"Thank you very much, Don Felipe."

Luigi tells Valentino.

"I need you to vacate the premises. I don't want any distractions."

"Very well, Don Felipe. You will have the casino for yourself." Valentino responds.

Valentino and two casino employees dismiss all the visitors and only Luigi stays, who was posing as Don Felipe. Luig's bodyguards remain in the casino. Luigi sits at the poker table and says.

"Tonight, it will be me against the casino."

One bodyguard stands behind Luigi, the second stands next to the front door, the third stands by the exit door, and the fourth constantly walks around the room as if watching for any strange movements. It was a scene worthy of an Oscar. Luigi smoked a huge cigar and acted arrogantly. The card dealer was sweating and acting nervous. There was complete silence in the casino. Only Luigi spoke from time to time. As agreed, Luigi won and lost, yelling with joy and cursing when he lost. The bodyguard who was walking through the casino approaches Romulo and tells him.

"I've never seen you before."

"I'm new to the casino." Romulo responds.

"What is your specialty?"

"I'm at the roulette."

The bodyguard looks around and asks him.

"Is that roulette fixed?"

"No, sir, the casino is illegal, but roulette is not."

"I offer you four percent of the profits."

Romulo separates from the bodyguard and goes to a corner.

An employee approaches Romulo and tells him.

"Don Romulo, Valentino needs you at the office."

When Romulo enters the office, Valentino and Marco are waiting for him. Valentino asks him.

"What were you talking to Felipe's bodyguard?"

"Nothing, Don Valentino."

"I repeat one more time. What did you talk to him about?"

"He just told me he had never seen me before, and I told him I was new to the business."

"For the last time. What did you talk to him about?"

"That is it, Don Valentino."

"So, they didn't offer you a percentage for betraying us?"

"Don Valentino, I will never betray you. This is my business, too."

Marco yells. "I was behind you. He offered you a percentage. I don't know how much of the percentage, but he offered it to you."

Valentino stands in front of Romulo and asks him.

"Are you going to deny it?"

"Yes, that is true, but I never accept it. He offered me four percent. It would not make sense to betray you. I get eight percent."

"So, you mean if the percentage is higher, you betray us?"

"No, sir, I didn't mean that."

"Why didn't you tell me they were trying to bribe you?"

"I don't know. The situation is very tense. I've never been in a situation like this. I also think you should trust me."

"Let it be clear to you, Romulo, no one is trusted here. Something like this should be reported immediately, especially when millions are being played over the table."

Romulo was sweating and his hands were trembling, his face was terrified.

"Yes, Don Valentino. It will never happen again."

"I'm sure of that." Valentino replies and leaves the office.

Romulo tells Marco." You're a fucking snitch."

"And you are a damn traitor. Get out of the office. This is not your place." Marco replies.

It was 3 a.m. and everyone was around the poker table. Valentino makes the sign that he will let Luigi win this game. Valentino makes sure Romulo sees the sign. Luigi puts in a large amount of money. Luigi gives shouts of joy and says.

"Enough for today. I already hurt you bad."

Valentino acts nervously, like if they were facing a significant loss if he walks away.

"What's up Felipe? It's early. You never leave this early."

"Yes, but I am leaving."

Valentino gives the signal, which meant: "We cannot let him go." They offered him wine, other types of games, but Luigi refused. Romulo was paralyzed. The earnings for the month had vanished. Valentino had instructed everyone in a situation like this, everyone had to try not to let the player go. Romulo had not said a word. He was worried about the previous incident, but also if he did nothing, it could be worse. Some workers looked at Romulo seriously and made a hand signal for him to join the group. Romulo felt he had no choice but to say something.

"Don Felipe, I heard rumors you like roulette, and today is your lucky day."

Luigi looks at him and asks. "Who are you?"

"I am new to the family, but I hope you visit us more often."

Luigi walks towards Romulo, who is next to the roulette wheel. Luigi stands and looks at the roulette wheel for a long time, then he looks at Romulo directly in the eyes, as if he is giving him a message.

"You're right. Today is my lucky day. All or nothing."

Luigi tells his bodyguard. "Go to the car and bring the titles."

"Right away, Don Felipe."

Luigi puts all the money earned on the table.

Romulo says. "Place your bet, sir."

"Not so fast. Wait a minute."

My bodyguard is bringing me some documents. When the bodyguard brings the documents, Luigi passes them to Valentino and tells him.

"All this is also part of the bet."

Valentino says. "Wait, I cannot approve that bet. I don't have enough money."

"Then call your boss for approval."

Valentino acting nervous tells him.

"I think you are taking an enormous risk."

"Not tonight. You have always beaten me, and today is my day." He takes out his revolver and put it on the table.

Valentino says. "I will make a call and give you the answer."

Five minutes later, Valentino comes back and says.

"They only guarantee four million on top of what we have here."

"Very well. Bring everything you have."

"I don't have a lot of money." Valentino responds.

Luigi punches the table. "You don't fool me."

Luigi points at one bodyguard and orders him.

"You go with him to the office and bring everything you see there."

"Yes, Don Felipe."

After a while, the bodyguard comes out of the office with Marco.

"Don Felipe, they have little cash, but there were these documents."

Romulo opens his eyes and says.

"Those documents are mine."

"A few minutes ago, you told me you belong to the family. Didn't you?"

"It is true, I am part owner of the casino."

"Then you must bet too. Those are the rules."

"Whose rules?" Romulo says.

Luigi stands imposingly in front of Romulo and two of the bodyguards join him.

"Mine. Any problem?"

"No Don Felipe, none."

Valentino gives the signal to Romulo to win, and Romulo answers it. Valentino brings out bottles of wine to celebrate. Luigi raises his glass and says, let's go, all or nothing.

Luigi asks one bodyguard to place all the money and the documents on top of a poker table. It was an impressive amount of cash, plus Romulo's contracts.

Romulo is super happy. Not only will he recover everything he lost, but his commission would be enormous. Luigi stands up and says.

"I want to propose a toast before I triple my fortune."

Luigi looks at Valentino and tells him.

"Valentino, bring the champagne. I am inviting, let us celebrate."

Valentino smiles and answers.

"As you wish, Don Felipe."

Valentino orders to bring champagne, and everybody is holding a cup. Valentino gives the signal again to Romulo, who answers with a smile.

Luigi tells Romulo.

"You told me that tonight was my lucky night, so give me the winning chip and tell me the lucky number."

"That will be my pleasure, Don Felipe."

Romulo gives him a chip and tells him.

"Place your bet in number 15. That is your lucky number."

Luigi stands up, grabs the chip, kisses it, and places in number fifteen.

"Are you ready, Don Felipe?" Asks Romulo, thinking he became super rich.

Luigi did not answer, he just kept looking at Romulo straight in his eyes. Everybody kept staring at them, moving their heads from Romulo to Luigi.

Valentino asks.

"Is everything ok between the two of you? Is there something I should know, Don Felipe?"

"No, Don Valentino, let's get it on." Answers Luigi.

Romulo starts the roulette and presses the button to activate the magnetic field under the roulette.

Luigi screams. "Go baby go."

Romulo did not know that right in front of Luigi there was the main button that when pressed it takes over the roulette magnetic field. Romulo's heart was pounding with happiness without knowing Luigi had pressed his button.

The ball slowed down, and Luigi was screaming like a madman. Romulo had a big smile on his face, his eyes were wide open, and he kept biting his tongue. The ball was going slowly and then it stopped at fifteen because of the magnetic attraction. Luigi picks up the chip and yells.

"I will frame this one and put it in my office."

Romulo was sweating. He looked at Valentino, who was staring at him with fire in his eyes. Valentino dropped his cup of champagne as if he was in shock. Romulo was pale, speechless, and trembling. The casino workers put their hands on their heads, yelling.

"My God, this can't be!"

Marco leaves the office with the revolver, but Valentino yells at him.

"What are you doing, stupid?"

Luigi's bodyguards had all drawn their weapons, and they were aiming at anyone who moved.

Valentino says. "Don Felipe, you have won. My men have reacted incorrectly. I apologize. Take your prize and we will send you your two million in a week."

Luigi puts a wad of money in Romulo's pocket and tells him.

"You've earned it. You were right. Today is my lucky day."

Romulo with a broken speech and is about to faint answers.

"There is no need for that, Don Felipe."

Luigi leaves and everyone is looking at Romulo. Marco says.

"I told you he was selling us out, and you didn't want to believe me."

Valentino takes the revolver from Marco's hand and points it at Romulo.

"You betrayed us."

"I did not. I swear to you. It must have been a button failure."

"Very well, let's see." Valentino looked at the workers and says.

"You all will be witnesses. Let's see if it's true."

One worker looks at Valentino and says.

"I cannot be a witness. I don't know how it works."

Valentino yells. "Are you trying to cover for him?"

"No, Don Valentino. I just want to be fair. How can I judge on something I don't know. Remember, his life depends on it. I don't want blood in my hands or any guilty feelings."

When Romulo heard that, he started shivering, his face turned pale, his mouth felt open, and he almost fainted.

"Very well, gather around and I will explain how it works. Let me be clear: Romulo has been working on it and has made very good money. There has been no failure until now."

Valentino throws a bottle against the wall and yells.

"Yes, until now. On the highest bet since I have been dealing in this business."

Valentino gets behind the roulette table and says.

"There is a hidden button right here. I want you all to touch it."

All the workers pass by and touched the button.

"Any question about the button?"

"No, sir."

"When I press the button, it creates a low positive magnetic field. The ball is charged with a low negative field. When the ball slows down and I press the button, the ball will slow down even more because of the attraction on the magnetic field. It will stop six numbers after I press the button. It means if I do not want it to stop at number fifteen, I will press it after the ball passes fifteen and it will stop at twenty-one. Now, if I want it to stop at fifteen, then I will press the button when it gets to nine. Questions?"

"No, sir." They all responded.

"That is the reason, Romulo has made more money on commission than all of you together, because he damn sure learned how to operate it, but his greed took the best of him."

Romulo, almost crying, answers. "No, Don Valentino. I could never do such a thing."

All the casino workers get behind Romulo. Valentino presses the button to activate the magnetic field under the roulette and says.

"Remember that I must lose. I bet fifteen."

Romulo spins the roulette wheel and when it slows down and passes the fifteen, Valentino tells Romulo to press the button so it will not stop at fifteen. Romulo presses the button and prays the roulette would stop at fifteen, but it stops at twenty-one.

"Very well, now I bet the forty-five."

Romulo has no choice but to press the button again, as he had five witnesses behind him. The roulette stops at fifty-one.

Romulo was screaming like crazy.

"It can't be, I swear!"

Valentino says. "It is obvious you pressed the button at nine, so it will stop at fifteen. That way, you made sure Don Felipe won and you get whatever percentage you have negotiated with his bodyguard. If it was not because you were part of the business, I would have already killed you, but I must make sure the bosses know about this and respect their decision. We must repeat the test three more times."

Valentino makes three bets, and the five witnesses are behind Romulo. Romulo was only thinking about how to escape alive from there.

Valentino says. "It is proven it was not a failure of the roulette. You betrayed us."

Valentino points at one worker and tells him.

"I will check the books to see how much money we lost. You inform one of the bosses of the situation."

"Shall I call Giovanni, Don Valentino?

"No, anyone but Giovanni. He is the one who recommended Romulo, so he will pay for Romulo's betrayal. Most likely, both will die tomorrow."

Romulo fainted to the floor. If they were going to kill one of the big shots, then nothing was going to save him.

Valentino punches the wall three times and yells.

"Damn you, Romulo, better yet watch him. I am going to report to the boss."

Marco says.

"Don Valentino, you need to ask for money. We don't have any to operate the casino."

"I told you to keep money out of the safe."

"Yes sir, I put one hundred thousand lire inside the lining of the office chair, but it is not enough."

"Damn traitor. If they give me the green light, I'll kill him tonight. Valentino says.

"Marco, you stay inside the office with Romulo and make sure he does not escape through the back window."

Valentino orders workers. "Two of you, stay by the office door and make sure Romulo does not escape. The other two come with me as witnesses to the report of what happened here tonight."

Marco tells Romulo. "Get inside, traitor, rather yet corpse."

Romulo enters, followed by Marco, who closes the door. Romulo thinks he will only get out alive if he escapes immediately. Marco opens the safe and says.

"Look, thanks to you, it's empty, and we owed two million."

Marco turns his back on Romulo to close the safe and Romulo hits him on the head with the telephone receiver. Marco falls to the ground and plays to be unconscious. Romulo takes a letter opener from the desk and breaks the lining of the chair, takes the money that was wrapped in an envelope and hurries out through the window. He was convinced if he did not disappear from the country; he was a dead man.

As soon as Marco realized Romulo had escaped, he got up and opened the door.

"Mission accomplished."

Everyone was waiting for him with champagne to celebrate. Valentino had put a man hiding in the back of the casino to follow Romulo's escaped through the window that night. The report came the next day that Romulo had escaped to Greece.

Valentino shows up at Franco's office with Luigi, and Franco was waiting for them with a big party.

"Everything is under control, Don Franco. We did not spend a penny. Romulo invested everything he had, and the money he took with him was part of his own money."

"How did you do all that, you old fox?"

"It's a long story to tell. I'll just say I gave him two things: a good scare and a little of his own money. The money will run out, but the scare will last forever."

Everyone laughs and toasts.

Franco says. "Stay here today. It is a day to celebrate."

Valentino says. "Don Franco, I want your permission to take Don Pedro and his wife to see Maria. That way, we will know for sure if you are the father of that child. They don't know I am related to you."

Franco shakes his head and says.

"Maria is much smarter than you think. She will unmask you."

"I don't think so, but if she does, you have done nothing wrong but take care of her parents the best you could and save them from Romulo."

"You are right, but they are very stubborn people." Franco replies with a smile.

"The truth will come out eventually, and for you, it is better if it comes out sooner."

"You are right, Valentino. My illness progresses fast. I don't know how much more I have left. You have my permission. Do what you think is right."

Valentino shows up at Maria's parents' house early in the morning.

"Good morning, Don Pedro. How are you doing?"

"Good morning, Don Valentino. How was that trip?" Pedro replies.

"I am undecided. I have spent a month following the business movements and I can't decide. I need your help. You have much more experience than I in these matters."

"Of course, you can count on me, but come inside. We will not talk at the front door."

"Thank you very much." Valentino responds.

Angela, Maria's mother, says.

"You have come at the right time. Please have breakfast with us."

"Who can resist the smell of that bread?" Valentino responds.

After talking for a while at the table, Valentino says.

"I need a favor from the two of you."

"Just say. What you need." Replies Pedro.

"I just want you to come with me to the city of Fermo. I know you can tip the balance in my decision."

"Don Valentino, you know as much as I."

"Exactly. Two heads are better than one."

Don Pedro shakes his head and answers.

"If in a month you could not decide, I advise you not to do it."

"I agree with Pedro." Says Angela.

Valentino lowers his head and says. "I have to confess something."

"What have you done?" Pedro asks.

"I took the liberty of reserve the train ticket and hotel for the two of you."

"How do you do something like that without consulting us first?"

"You are right, Don Pedro, but my impulses carried me away. When I reacted, it was too late."

Angela say. "What do I have to do there? That's a men's business."

"The problem is, I would not know what to do in case Don Pedro needs help with his medical condition. Besides, you also will enjoy a change of air. The hotel is on the oceanfront. Take it as a very well-deserved vacation. When was the last time you left Naples?"

Angela keeps quiet. She remembers the last time she traveled outside Naples she had a bad experience.

"That was many years ago, and we had such an unpleasant experience we have never left again."

Valentino puts his hands in a plea and tells them.

"We are basically the same age, and we are related in business. I consider you family. I only can trust you in a decision like this.

Pedro and Angela kept silent.

"Are you going to abandon me now? I am sure we will have a great time. It will be a vacation trip for business purposes. You will not regret it.

Pedro feels sorry for Valentino. Thanks to him, he has avoided an economic disaster. He feels morally in debt to him. Pedro answers.

"If you ask me that way, I can't refuse, but I don't think Angela wants to be part of it."

Valentino looks at Angela and says.

"Don't let him go alone. This old fox wants to go alone to find a girl."

Angela and Pedro laugh.

"Pedro is right. I have nothing to do there."

Valentino takes a moment, thinking about what to say and suddenly says. "You have forced me to reveal the surprise."

"What surprise?" Angela asks.

"The truth is, I loved the business. I made a contract and the only thing missing is your signatures."

"Have you gone crazy?" Pedro tells him.

Valentino responds. "Thanks to you, I have remained active when I had no more desire to live. I have no family other than the two of you. I want both of you to be in the title in case something happens to me."

"Sorry Valentino. We can't accept something like that." Replies Pedro.

"The contract is in our names. If we do not sign it, not only we will lose a great business, but I will lose all the money I gave for the down payment."

"Have you really lost your mind?" Pedro tells him.

"Yes, but I am a happy madman who wants to enjoy life and share what he has with his friends. If you do not want to accept, only the money will be lost. Don't think I am going to be angry with you. I should have told you this before doing it."

Once again, Valentino had achieved his goal, Pedro and Angela could not refuse. They felt morally obliged to accept.

"Okay, but promise me you will never do something like that again."

"I promise you, Don Pedro, I give you my word."

Salvatore contacts Enrico and tells him Luigi went to see him to give him a message from Franco. Enrico is surprised.

"Salvatore, you do not learn. Didn't you get enough?"

"I don't know what to think. I heard Franco's health is very poor. He can die at any moment."

"That is true, he is in wheelchairs and in a terrible shape, but his mind is still perfectly clear."

"He says he wants to die with a clean conscience, and he wants to confess everything to me."

"Do you believe him?"

"No, but what I do know is if he dies, I can never clean my honor. One more embarrassment will change nothing, so I have nothing to lose."

"What do you want from me?" Enrico asks.

"Only your opinion. You are inside, and you may see things differently. Please give me your opinion."

Enrico looks at Salvatore and feels sorry for him.

"Give me three days. I will see you right here and give you my answer. I don't want you to take it as the correct one. It is just a suggestion."

"Okay, thank you very much." Salvatore responds.

Enrico walks into Franco's office and asks him.

"Is it true that you sent a message to Salvatore with Luigi?"

"Yes, it's correct."

"Is it true you told him you are going to confess everything to him because you want to die with a clean conscience?"

"Yes, it is true."

"Have you gone crazy, or do you want to drive me crazy? You know my wedding is scheduled in two weeks. I cannot marry this going on. If you confess to a crime, I will have to arrest you."

"I know, and I hope you do your job with no interference. You came to do a job, and it is your duty."

Enrico puts his hands on his head.

"Oh my God! What kinds of game is this?"

"It is not a game. My time is running out and I want to put everything in order."

"Well then, have your meeting with Salvatore after the wedding."

"I do not want to pose in the picture in a wheelchair. I need two more weeks to recover. By that time, I hope Salvatore has agreed to come."

"How are we going to celebrate a wedding if you go to jail?"

"Life will continue, with me in jail or dead. Let's stop talking about this and go to lunch."

"I'm sorry, Don Franco. I understand you less every day. It is becoming more difficult for me to help you and be your friend." Enrico replied and left.

Enrico meets with Salvatore and tells him.

"I have analyzed Franco's behavior. He presents certain characteristics of the person who awaits death and wants to put everything in order before dying. Perhaps he is saying the truth."

Salvatore makes a beaming face of joy and Enrico tells him.

"I want you to know I said "Maybe". Don't take it as an assurance."

"That is enough for me." Salvatore replied happily and left.

Valentino traveled with his assistant Marco and Maria's parents to Ancona, a city facing the sea near Fermo. Angela says to Valentino.

"Thank you for bringing us. It has been a long time since I had a vacation in front of the ocean. This place is beautiful."

"It is my pleasure. Today you enjoy Ancona. Marco and I will go to Fermo to prepare for the appointment with the lawyers."

In reality, Marco was going to Fermo to make sure Maria's son was not present during the meeting in case something went wrong. Marco was Valentino's right hand. He had a special talent and Valentino knew he could delegate to him difficult tasks.

Marco shows up at Maria's house and knocks on the door. Maria opens the door and says.

"What do you want, young man?"

"Good morning, mam, I'm Valentino's assistant."

"And who the hell is Valentino?"

"He is the person who was here a month ago. He is the Dean of the Faculty of science at the University of Switzerland in charge of searching and recruiting talents."

"Oh yes! I remember, now."

"He asked me to stop by again to see if the young man was still interested."

"Yes, I remember what happened that day. I think what you are here is to verify if that man had not thrown us out of the house."

"Excuse me mam, I don't understand what you mean."

"Don't worry, Valentino knows what I'm talking about." Maria replies.

The young Pedro was arriving at that moment from the farm, and Maria asked him.

"Do you remember the man who came to recommend to you a scholarship?"

"Yes, of course, I remember."

"Well, this young man wants to know you are still interested."

"Yes, of course I am!"

Marco takes out a paper with an address and tells him.

"Please, you need to be at this address this afternoon, with the following documents to fill out your application."

Pedro takes the paper, reads it and says.

"But this is in Ancona!"

"Yes, we have two more students applying. If you do not have transportation, we will pick you up."

Maria says, "Don't bother, the child knows Ancona very well. He knows how to get there."

"Perfect, please don't be late. If you can be twenty minutes earlier, we would appreciate it."

"Don't worry, he'll be there early. "Answers Maria.

With young Pedro out of the way, everything was ready for the meeting. Valentino arrives at the villa and Pedro says.

"This place is very nice. Angela adds, I love the flowers in the garden."

"Yes, the owner loves flowers."

Valentino knocks on the door, and Maria opens the door with a jug of water in her hand. Maria turns pale and drops the jug to the ground. Angela screams.

"My daughter! She hugged Maria tightly while she kissed her and cried."

Pedro didn't say a word. He didn't even move. Pedro didn't know what to do. His pride kept him from expressing his true feelings. He had been looking for his daughter for years. Now she was in front of him; and he did not dare to hug her.

Maria and her mother wept inconsolably. Patricia had improved thanks to the care and attention Maria had given her. Patricia hears Maria's cry and tries to scream, making a sound between moans and words.

Maria hears the sound coming from Patricia's room and yells.

"Mother!" Pulling Angela by her arm. She takes her into Patricia's room. Maria sees Patricia is very nervous. Patricia's tears flowed, and she made sounds desperately trying to communicate. Maria hugs her and kisses her.

"Do not worry mother, this crying is of joy. Look mother, this is my other mother. I am the happiest woman in the world. I can hug two mothers at the same time."

Patricia calmed down instantly and squeezed Maria's hand. Maria says.

"Oh my gosh, she almost spoke and got movement in her hand. This is a miracle!"

Maria takes Patricia's right hand and tells her.

"You took care of us when we needed it most. You will always be my mother."

Angela takes Patricia's left hand and tells her.

"I am indebted to you for life for having taken care of my daughter all these years."

Angela looks at her daughter and tells her.

"I am sorry for not having enough courage to face your father. For I am also guilty. Forgive me, daughter."

Pedro and Valentino had remained in front of the house. Pedro was terribly upset and looking furious at Valentino he says.

"You lied to me. How do you dare to do something like this? We considered you family, and this is the way you pay us back."

"You have suffered for many years looking for your daughter. Now you have her in front of you and not even give her a hug. Your wife is enjoying the moment. She doesn't let her resentment and pride spoil the occasion."

"How dare you talk to me like that? I should break your face."

Maria and Angela hear the argument between Valentino and Pedro and run to the front of the house. Angela screams.

"Pedro, what happened?"

"What do you mean, what happened? Does it seem ok to you this man has lied to us so miserably to bring us here?"

"What I see here is that this man has given me my daughter back, and with that, the desire to continue living."

Maria tells him.

"Father, I am glad to see you again. I want to hug you as when I was a child, with no resentment."

Maria approached to hug her father, but Pedro raised his hand as a sign of stop and tells her.

"Wait a minute, first we must talk. You will have to explain a lot of things."

Maria felt as if a bucket of cold water had been poured over her. Her father was still the spiteful person who cared more about what people thought than his own feelings. Maria was an independent woman and unafraid of her father. She had suffered a lot, and she was not willing to be humiliated by anyone.

"Very well, let's talk. What do you want to talk about? Do you want to talk about how you kept me captive in your house, as if I was a curse to you? About how you wanted to kill your own grandson? Maybe you want to talk about how you wanted to give your grandson away. Yes, your grandson! Your own blood, as if you were the owner, and he was an animal or your property? If you want to talk about it, go ahead, get it off your chest."

Maria's words had reached the deepest part of his heart, but instead of acknowledging his mistake, he raised his hand to slap her. Valentino grabbed his hand in time.

"What are you doing? Years of crying for your daughter, and now you want to hit her?"

Pablo pushes Valentino and squeezes his chest. Everybody went silent and scared. Pedro sits on the ground and is almost on the verge of fainting. They all ran towards Pedro. Maria grabs him by the right arm, Angela by the left arm, Valentino by the feet. They pick him up, take him inside the house and sit him in an armchair.

Maria was crying. She passes a wet cloth over his father's forehead while saying,

"Forgive me, dad, I lost control."

Angela and Valentino were fanning him with some magazines. After five minutes, Pedro recovered. Pedro squeezed Maria's hand and said.

"For a moment I thought I was dying and understood how stupid I am. Forgive me, daughter, for all the damage I have done to you."

"Father, the past is past. We only have control over the present. Let's try to make it more pleasant."

"You are right. Please forgive me."

Maria and her father hugged each other tightly. When everything is returning to normal, Maria looks at Valentino and says.

"So, Dean of the University of Switzerland, now tell me. Who the hell are you? Where is my son?"

That was like pouring gasoline on a fire that was almost out. This time, it was Valentino who was in trouble. Even Patricia almost screams from her room. It was obvious she heard everything, and she was aware of what was happening.

"Nothing happens to your son. I just didn't want him to be present during this dramatic meeting and he should arrive soon."

Maria asks him. "How did you know I was here?

Valentino takes the newspaper out of his portfolio the newspaper with her son's interview with the picture of Maria.

"I found out from the newspaper. I remember seeing you when I went to your father's factory."

"Do you think I am going to believe you remembered me? That was sixteen years ago."

"I don't know what you mean by that." Valentino responds.

"You appeared at the factory a month after I broke up with Franco and he sent here. It was Franco who saw the newspaper and sent you here."

"You are wrong. I have been your father's client for many years."

Pedro and Angela were just watching, trying to assimilate what was happening. Maria asks.

"Father, do you know this man?"

"Yes, he has been with me since before you ran away from home. When all the clients left us, he was the only one who stayed with us. When we went bankrupt, he bought half the business, and we were able to survive thanks to him. I am very upset with him, but if it hadn't been for him, we would have lost everything, including you."

"Don't you realize Franco put this man to put spy on you and find my whereabouts?"

Angela asks Maria.

"Do you think Franco is going to put a man for so many years just to find out where you are?"

"Yes, Franco's ego is very big, and he can never accept I left him standing on the wedding day."

Maria yells at Valentino.

"Get out of this house. Tell your damn boss I will accept nothing from a murderer. No matter how much fame and money he has created, I will never forgive him for his deceptions."

Pedro looks at Valentino and asks him.

"Please tell me the truth. Are you related to Franco?"

Valentino responds. "Yes, I am."

Pedro puts his hand on his head, Angela covers her mouth and Maria looked at him with fire in her eyes.

"Get out of here. We don't need any help from Franco. Mother Patricia and I have raised the child without his help. Today, he is an educated young man with great moral convictions. He lives without the shadow of organized crime over him. I never want him to know his father is a murderer."

"Franco is not a murderer. He is innocent. He only cared about you, despite knowing you hate him. He understands you, sees things differently, and he does not judge you."

Pedro interrupts. "So, Franco is the one who has supported us all these years?"

"No, he provided the conditions for you to continue working. He did not turn his back on you when everyone else did. When everyone pointed their finger at you, he defended you."

Maria yells at Valentino.

"Perhaps my father can indirectly be grateful, but I don't have to thank him for anything. Absolutely nothing. Do you understand? NOTHING! And get out. I never want to see your face again!"

Valentino replies. "I am very sorry your resentment is ripping you apart and you think Franco has never helped you."

"I do not owe that man a penny. I have never received or will accept help from him."

Valentino responds.

"I am leaving in peace, because I have done everything possible to reunify you. That at least gratifies me. Who knows where you could be today if Franco had not intervened for you? Where would you be today?"

"What do you mean, where? I am here. Don't you see me here?"

"No mam, you and your son would be on the street. Did you forget Romulo was going to kick them out?"

Angela, worried, asks Maria.

"What does Valentino mean? What is he talking about?"

"Nothing, mother, it is something unimportant."

Valentino opens his portfolio and takes out a thick envelope.

"What is that?" Maria asks.

"Your peace of mind."

"I am fine. The only one who bothers me is you."

Valentino points at her and tells her.

"If it wasn't for Don Franco, the one you hate and for me, who is the only one who bothers you. Patricia would be abandoned in a nursing home. You and your son would be penniless on the street. Don Franco didn't let that happen. Although he knows, and it has been proven, you hate him. You must know he loves you and your family. Here are the documents which will not allow Romulo or anyone else to evict you or take your property."

Valentino gives the thick envelope to Maria and tells her.

"That Franco has done all this, knowing you would not appreciate it. I wish you all a good afternoon and take advantage of the time you have left together."

Valentino was leaving, but he stops turns around.

"I forgot to tell you Franco opened an account in the Bank of Switzerland in the name of your son Pedro, where he will have enough to cover his studies. Your son does not know about it, neither he must find out. I hope you do not spill poison against his father."

Maria yells at him. "That child is not Franco's son."

Valentino responds. "Don Franco doesn't care about that, he's your son and for him that's enough."

Valentino left, and everyone was speechless for a long time. Only the sounds of Patricia, who was getting closer to talking, could be heard. Maria read the documents and tears came out. She could not believe they were free from Romulo. But she was stubborn as her father and at no time she gave a sign of gratitude.

Angela asked.

"Who is Romulo? How is it he was going to throw you out of here?"

"Romulo, Patricia's brother, is a bandit who has never cared for her. He has even sold Patricia's properties illegally. He had incapacitated Patricia to declare himself her legal custodian and take possession of all the assets."

"Why didn't he do it?"

"I don't know, mom. The papers were prepared a month ago. Everything is signed by Romulo as if he had sold it."

"What do you mean by that?"

"It means if I sign this document, then all of this is mine, but I will not sign it, because this belongs to Patricia."

Pedro says. "How can Valentino and Franco do something like this?"

"I don't know, father, or better yet I do, surely at gunpoint, the same way they solve everything."

Pedro gets up from his chair. "I find it hard to believe Valentino is a mobster. He has been our only friend all these years. If not for him, I don't know what would have happened to us. All our so-called friends abandoned us, and that old man always stood by our side. Oh, my gosh, this is a nightmare. I would have never received help from him if I had known he came from Franco."

Angela answers. "That's why Franco did it through Valentino. He knew how stubborn you are and whether you like it or not, if we did not lose everything it is thanks to him, if we found our daughter it is thanks to him and if the girl is not on the street, it is thanks to him. But the two of you are spiteful and stubborn. Franco is not perfect, but then again. Who is?"

Maria hears her son is opening the door.

"My God, the child arrived!"

The young Pedro enters and sees his mother with two strangers. The grandparents looked at him, amazed.

"Good afternoon. I didn't know we had visitors."

"They are not visitors. They are my parents, your grandparents."

"What did you say?" Pedro, confused, asks his mother.

Angela tells him." This is not a joke. We are your grandparents. Can I hug you?"

The young man hugs her and tells her. "Today is the happiest day of my life. I have recovered my grandparents, and I have received a scholarship from the University of Switzerland to pay for my studies."

Salvatore calls Enrico and tells him.

"Today in the morning, I will go see Franco."

"Does he know you will see him?"

"No, that way I don't give him time to prepare anything. Besides, if he wants to confess, he doesn't need to prepare for that. I just want to ask you to wait for my call this morning. If I don't call you, then you know something is wrong."

Enrico tells him." I'll wait for your call. If you don't call, I will go to check on you. I give you my word."

Salvatore shakes hands with Enrico. "Thank you very much, comrade."

Salvatore shows up at the complex and Guido greets him and asks him. "What is the reason for this visit, sir?"

"I come to see Franco."

"Does he know you are coming?"

"No, he does not know."

"I don't know if he could see you now."

Salvatore hits Guido in the chest with his index three times, while saying.

"Just call him and let him decide that."

Guido wanted to hit Salvatore over the head with the phone but calms down and calls Franco.

"Don Franco, Salvatore is here. He says he wants to talk to you."

Guido hangs up the phone.

"Wait here, he is coming."

Salvatore asks Guido defiantly.

"Why are you looking at me? Do you have a problem? Just keep swallowing cookies. That is the only thing you can do well."

Franco comes out in his wheelchair, pushed by Luigi.

"I thought you changed your mind and were not coming." Franco tells Salvatore.

"I don't trust you. I know you are sick. At last, we will be free from you."

"Thank you very much, Salva, for your compliments, but I have no time for fights and much more with you."

"You have been behind me like a shadow. You have kept me entertained and I thank you for that."

Franco asks Luigi. "Please take us to the garden."

Luigi pushes Franco's chair and tells Salvatore.

"Follow us please."

Salvatore hesitates a moment, but he follows them.

The garden had a beautiful view of almost the entire island and a breathtaking view of the sea with a constant sea breeze.

"If I will miss something from this world, it will be this garden." Says Franco.

"Yes, it is quite beautiful. It is a shame your presence damages the landscape." Salvatore responds.

Franco asks Luigi to bring something refreshing to drink.

"You will drink it alone. I do not trust you."

"You do not have to drink if you do not want to. Lower your guard. I have asked you to come so you can ask whatever you want and forget nothing."

Luigi returns with the drinks and puts them on the table. Franco takes the jug and pours himself. Salvatore looks at him.

"I will not fall into your trap."

"I will not argue with you today. Let's get to the point. Did you bring a tape recorder?"

Salvatore responds. "No, I didn't know I had to."

"How are you going to present your evidence? That will not work in court."

Franco tells Luigi.

"Please bring a camera and a tape recorder."

"Are you sure what you are doing, Don Franco?"

"Yes, I am. Do what I told you."

Salvatore felt uncomfortable. He did not trust Franco. He was thirsty, but he did not want to risk it. Luigi returns with a tripod, a movie camera, and a sound recorder. Franco tells him, make sure the recorder is working. I don't want surprises. Luigi does a sound check and everything is in order.

Franco asks Salvatore. "Ask me what you want to know before I change my mind."

Salvatore wasted no time and asked him.

"Did you kill Manino?"

"Yes, I killed him."

"What did you do with the corpse?"

"I buried it in the garden. You checked everything except the garden."

"Were the pictures of Manino from the day of his alleged departure from the complex fake?"

"No, they were real. They were just taken the day he entered. All the participants took two pictures the same day, with the calendar behind. That was our agreement."

"Did you kill Mateo?"

"Yes, I killed him."

"What did you do with the corpse?"

"I knew that the next time you would be prepared, so I dug up Manino's corpse, got rid of all the dirt in the garden so as not to alert the dogs and paid Augusto a good sum of money to disappear the two corpses."

Salvatore could not believe it. Everything had been just as he had said it, but he had always been one step behind Franco.

"So, the pictures of Mateo's departure and his registration in the downtown hotel were fake?"

"Of course, I knew I could not repeat the same thing. You were telling me what you knew. Perhaps if you had kept quiet, things would have been different."

Salvatore responds. "I was very frustrated. I just wanted to show that you had not fooled me, that I had discovered you, and that you were not as smart as you thought you were."

"Yes, I know, and I thank you very much. Thanks to your outbursts, I realized what changes I had to make for the next one."

"Did you kill Augusto and his son?"

"Augusto's son paid for the betrayal of his family and me. Are you going to deny you offered him money?"

Salvatore doesn't answer and Franco tells him.

"It is not fair. I confess the whole truth of my actions, but you will not confess yours. You do not have to fear. It is not illegal to pay for information."

"It's true. I offered him money." Salvatore responds.

"What happened to Augusto?"

"Augusto died of a heart attack caused by the betrayal of his son."

"Did you obstruct the road to Augusto's farm so that we could not rescue Donato?"

"Yes, it was a plan I had prepared in case you wanted to attack me from behind."

"Did you kill Donato?"

"I am partially responsible for his death."

"I ask you again, did you kill Donato, the son of Augusto?"

"Yes, I killed him. The penalty for treason is death."

"Did you kidnap Vittorio?"

"Yes, I had to."

"Why?"

"He did not want to sell me his business, I kidnaped him and told him this was just a warning that the next time I would burn down his business and kill his son."

"What types of meetings did you hold here?"

"All the representatives of the different organized crime families met here to conclude agreements or eliminate traitors. I made sure they complied with the agreements. Also, I personally eliminated those who steal, like Manino and Mateo."

"Who alerted Don Cristino?"

"I don't know. It must be one of your guys. He has many connections, and he is very resourceful."

"How did he escape?"

"I have no idea, but I enjoyed it. He even sent me pictures of him in your apartment, and I sent them to Umberto."

Salvatore stays silent and Franco asks him.

"Do you want to know anything else?"

"Yes, I want to know if you have recorded everything."

Franco tells Luigi. "Please let us listen to the recording."

Luigi rewinds the magnetic tape and replays the sound. Salvatore cannot believe it. After sixteen years following Franco with no results, he now has all the evidence provided by Franco himself and voluntarily. Franco exhales and says.

"Thanks, Salvatore, for helping me to take off this weight from my chest."

Salvatore answers him. "You never stop surprising me. I have another question, but it has nothing to do with your criminal life."

"If it is from my private life, perhaps I will answer it."

Adriana interrupts them, bringing two huge plates of food.

"Don Franco, it is time for your lunch and medication."

Adriana puts the tray down and takes the tablecloth she had on her arm.

"Excuse me sir, can you help me with the tablecloth? Salvatore was captivated by Adriana's beauty. It seemed Cupid, instead of throwing him an arrow, had thrown a missile at him. Immediately, he stood up like a knight to help her. While Salvatore helped Adriana to set the table, Adriana flirted with him, and Salvatore felt young again. His eyes were fixed on Adriana's body. He did not realize the magnetic tape and film tape were exchanged for new blank ones.

When Salvatore and Adriana finished setting the table, Adriana tells Franco.

"You have to take your pills before eating."

"Yes, I'm not a little boy."

Franco takes his pills and tells Salvatore. "If you don't want to eat, I understand, but I always remember what you said at the last meeting."

"What did I say?"

You said. "If I'm going to die, I want to die with a full belly. I have taken that motto for myself."

Salvatore laughed. It was the first time he felt relaxed. Salvatore suspiciously tells Franco.

"That evidence means nothing, as long as it is in your possession."

"You're right, Salva.

Franco orders Luigi to give the tapes to Salvatore.

"Why Don Franco? Why?" Asks Luigi.

"Don't argue, Luigi, and bring the tapes."

Luigi takes the tapes and gives them to Salvatore. Salvatore takes the tapes, smiles and sarcastically tells Luigi.

"So many muscles and so little brain, I am sure you were a watch dog in your previous life."

All this time, Luigi stands in front of Franco and Salvatore, blocking the view of the tape recorder and the camera. An employee places new tapes on the video and sound recorder and presses the record bottom.

Luigi angrily yells. "Are you crazy Don Franco? Don't you care what will happen when this comes out?"

"I explained it to you clearly. You decided to stay. You still have time, you can go."

Salvatore interrupts. "Don't worry Luigi, I'll ask the judge to lower your sentence. I promise I'll cut a sweet deal for you."

"The food looks and smells wonderful, but I still don't trust you."

"That is easy to fix," Franco said and sent for extra cutlery.

"You can mix the food. That way, we poison each other."

Salvatore served the food, and Franco began to eat. They changed the subject and talked as friends about the beauty of the island from when they were young. Salvatore could not overcome his hunger and gluttony. He began to eat and savor the food. Franco says. "What did you want to ask me?"

"Yes, I almost forgot. If you left me penniless and the court gave you my parents' mansion, that was in my name. Why have you never evicted my parents from the mansion and never let them know the mansion does not belong to them?"

"They are not responsible for your actions. I could never send an old couple to the street."

"What happened to that young woman who was going to marry you the day I took you to prison?"

"I don't know about her. That is the hardest blow you have ever given me. You know well it was a low blow. You better than anybody know I did not kill Detective Vicente. You know our capes were exchanged by mistake before Marcelo met Vicente. You saw me go out and follow me home. You know I was home when Marcelo killed Vicente. You won that one. You imprisoned me, even though it was an illegal arrest, but you did it."

Salvatore is silent and Franco tells him.

"What happens Salvatore? You don't have the balls to admit your thing? You already have what you want in your hands. By the way, you are holding it tight."

Salvatore tells him.

"I did not come here to make confessions. It is you who wanted to confess."

"You are right, but I also remember I plead guilty thanks to your lies and blackmail."

"I did not force you to do anything. You did it alone. The judge asked you if someone had forced you to plead guilty and you said no."

Franco laughs and responds.

"But Salva, stop it, you're talking to me. You know, I was in solitary confinement in jail. I couldn't give the order to kill the witness. Then you told me the witness was going to testify against me if I didn't accept the plea bargain deal. You made me believe I had no alternative when, in reality, your witness was dead. As you can see, you won again. You are not a poor, innocent victim."

Salvatore tells him.

"Yes, I lied to imprison you. I know you did not kill Vicente. I also lied about the witness and forced you to plead guilty, but as you well know, "The end justifies the means." I do not regret it. That is nothing next to what you have done to me."

Franco tells him. "I congratulate you. You achieved what no one has achieved. You have kept me in captivity all these years."

Salvatore felt empowered and went back to being sarcastic as he was before.

"Remember Franco, The End Justifies the Means."

"I will not be angry with you. I have invited you to make peace before I die. We chatted as friends. We have had lunch together and I do not want any bad blood between us from now on. I forgive you for the damage you did to me. It is up to you to forgive."

Salvatore again uses his trademark sarcasm. "Don't worry, I forgave myself a long time ago."

"Well, if you forgave yourself and I have forgiven you, that is a reason to celebrate."

Franco calls Luigi. "Luigi, bring the best wine you have in the cellar."

"Don Franco, the doctor has forbidden you the alcohol." Luigi responds.

Franco laughs. "Yes, you're right. If I don't drink alcohol, I could live for one more day. Do not contradict me, and do what I ask you."

Luigi goes to get the wine, takes a bottle, and injects a narcotic with a syringe. When Adriana returns to clear the table, she asks Salvatore. "Did you like the food, sir?"

"I loved it. Did you cook it yourself?"

"Yes, sir."

"Then the man who marries you will never leave you."

"I hope so," Adriana responds.

Luigi brings a bottle and two glasses. Adriana tells him.

"What are you doing, Luigi? You know he can't drink alcohol?"

"I know, but he insists."

Adriana tells Franco with a strong character.

"You can't drink alcohol."

"It is a very special occasion. Do not spoil it, please. I promise you I will not do it again."

"Do you promise me?"

"I give you my word."

"Fine, but take your pills."

"Not now, please." Franco says.

"If there are no pills, there is no wine." Adriana responds.

Franco takes the pills and asks her. "Satisfied?"

"Yes, but don't tell anyone I let you drink wine."

Adriana leaves, and Franco tells Salvatore.

"She is a beauty. What a pity she is in love with that asshole."

"Who are you talking about?"

"Enrico, Raffaelle's cousin."

Salvatore feels triumphant. He has the evidence in his hand. Why not to stick the dagger in Franco to humiliate him?

"That whom you call an asshole is a secret agent who has infiltrated you."

Franco looks astonished and responds. "No! That's impossible!"

Salvatore laughs and tells him.

"You are not only sick, you are also in decline."

Franco changes his attitude and says. "Well, now even more, I want to toast in honor of such a surprise. I hope this Enrico does his job fast."

"He will do it. I will make sure that he does it." Salvatore says.

"Then call him to come over at once. Let's get this over with."

Franco asks Luigi. "Does the telephone cable reach this far?"

"Yes Don Franco."

"Then bring the phone, please."

Luigi brings the phone and puts it on the table. Franco tells Luigi.

"Leave us alone, please."

Franco gives the phone to Salvatore and tells him.

"Enjoy the moment. You deserve it."

Salvatore calls Enrico. "Do you hear me, Enrico?"

"Yes Salvatore, what happened?"

"I need you to come. I have the proof in my hand of all Franco's crimes. He decided to confess before he dies. I think it is the only honorable thing he has done in his life. I must thank him. I cannot believe it, so hurry before something strange happens here."

Enrico tells him. "I do not believe you. Where are you?"

"I am here with Franco."

"Let me talk to him, please." Enrico says in disbelief.

Salvatore gives the phone to Franco and Franco says.

"Enrico, it is true. The truth must come to light. The confession is in Salvatore's hands. He has an audiotape and a film of the confession. If you really came to do a job, do it without fear of consequences. How long does it take you to come?"

"It will take me thirty minutes."

"We are waiting for you." Franco hangs up the phone and tells Salvatore.

"You should invite those reporters who have done so much damage to you to take pictures and have them swallow their words."

"I would love to, but I do not know their numbers."

Franco picks up the phone and dials the number. Salvatore talks to the reporters and tells them in fifteen minutes they must be present for the report of their life.

Franco asks Salvatore if he wants to open the bottle.

"Yes, of course. I must make sure there is no trick." Salvatore examines the bottle and opens it, picks up his glass, rinses it with water and turns it upside down to drain the water, then wipes it dry with his napkin. He serves Franco first and tells him. "You drink first."

Franco laughs, raises his glass and says, "For the truth and the mistrust."

Salvatore answers him.

"I will only trust you when I see you dead. Franco takes the cup from him and replies. That is a cruel comment."

"Yes, but today I have been honest with you. I have hidden nothing from you. Wasn't that what you asked of me?"

"Yes, I prefer the truth, even if it hurts." Franco takes another cup and another one. Salvatore realizes that if he does not drink, Franco will drink the entire bottle. It is an expensive a wine, so he doesn't want to pass the occasion.

"Wait, don't drink it all. I'll join you in the toast."

Salvatore lifts the sound and film tapes in one hand and raises his glass in the other and says. "For the hidden truth."

Franco also raises his glass and says. "For the truth!"

At the third glass, Salvatore felt dizzy and had no control of his movements even though he could hear what was happening around him and holds the tapes firmly in his hands. He tries to stand up and falls to the ground. Franco kneels in front of him and says.

"Salva, Salva, Salva. Your stupidity has no limits. The pills I took were the antidote to the drug you took. Don't worry, it's not lethal and you'll be fine soon. I told you I was going to see you on the floor in front of me and I was going to spit in your face."

Franco spits in Salvatore's face. Salvatore tells him.

"You are finished. I have the evidence."

Luigi lifts Salvatore off the floor, sits him on the chair. Salvatore was still holding the tape firmly in his hands. Luigi removes the wine bottle and glasses from the table, brings a bottle of cheap wine with real poison and two cups, puts the bottle in Salvatore's hands to plant his prints, does the same with a cup, then opens the bottle and pours a little wine in the glass. Finally, Luigi throws the cup to the floor. Luigi ties Salvatore tightly to the chair. Salvatore comes to his senses and tells Franco.

"I don't know what you're planning, but you won't get away with it."

"I just wanted to spit in your face. I doubt you would have agreed to let me do it voluntarily. Now I can go to prison in peace. We are at peace. You have my confession and I spat in your face."

"Why do you have me tied up?"

Because you were acting crazy. I didn't want you to hurt yourself. If you want, I'll let you go."

"Yes. Let me lose."

Luigi untied him and Salvatore says. "I can wash my face, but you are finished."

"You are not telling me anything I don't know, or I'm not prepared to face."

Salvatore hears the siren of the police cars arriving at the complex. He could not hide his happiness.

"The end has come, Don Franco."

Mockingly says Salvatore. Enrico had gone to find Raffaelle, who had agreed to come only because Enrico had assured him Franco himself had told him Salvatore had the confession recorded. The reporters were ready and entered with Enrico and Raffaelle. Enrico couldn't believe it and with tears in his eyes, he asks Franco.

"Is it true Salvatore has the confessions of various crimes recorded in his possession?"

Enrico asked heaven for Franco to say no, but Franco says.

"It is true."

Enrico closed his eyes and looked around and saw that all the workers looked at him in amazement. They realized Enrico was an undercover detective. He saw Adriana looked at him and cried.

"Do you know these crimes will cause imprisonment and the arrest is immediate?"

"I know, and I just hope you do your job without consideration or mercy."

Enrico dried his eyes and said.

"You don't leave me any other alternative. I would love a more pleasant ending."

"I would not change this ending for anything in the world. I finally feel liberated. I can now die in peace."

Enrico asks Salvatore. "Do you have the evidence?"

"Yes! I never let them go off my hands. Here they are."

Salvatore gives the tapes to Enrico and Enrico passes them to Raffaelle, who is still stunned by what happened.

Enrico says in tears. "Can you stand up?"

"Yes, with a lot of pain, but I can."

"Then do it." Enrico ordered.

Franco stands up and Enrico puts the handcuffs on him and tells him.

"Franco, you are under arrest for murder."

Franco laughs and tells him.

"Where do you get such a thing? You arrest me without even checking the evidence."

The pictures were one after another. The picture of Enrico's face with his mouth open, the one of Raffaelle who could not help laughing and that of Salvatore in total shock.

"Yes, the tapes have the confession. Listen to it."

Franco says. "I do not deny that the tapes contain the confession, but I demand you listen to it."

"Very good." Enrico says.

Luigi hands him the tape recorder and puts the tape on, turns up the volume and everyone listens to Salvatore's voice.

"Yes, I lied to imprison you. I know you did not kill Venancio. I also lied about the witness and forced you to plead guilty, but as you well know, the end justifies the means. I do not regret it, that is nothing."

Enrico felt as if a train had passed over him. Raffaelle was laughing hard.

Salvatore screamed. "That is fake."

Franco says. "He gave it to you himself. He also has the film where the same thing will come out but with an image, analyze it and verify its authenticity."

Enrico puts his hand on his head and sits down. "God help me!"

Enrico tries to get a grip on himself. He stands up. Enrico looks at Raffaelle, who cannot stop laughing.

"Chief Raffaelle, please behave yourself. This is not a comedy show."

"Excuse me, cousin, today it is my turn to enjoy the scene."

Enrico tells Salvatore. "You have one minute to explain what happened."

Salvatore, nervous and out of control, says.

"He invited me to confess his crimes. He confessed. I recorded them. Then we had lunch together, and I called you. I told you I had the confession recorded. We had lunch together. We drank some wine. He wanted to poison me. He tied me to a chair and later released me. That is all."

Enrico asks Salvatore. "Is that your voice?"

"Ah, ah, ah." Salvatore couldn't speak.

Enrico yells at him. "Is that your voice? Yes or no?"

"Yes, it's my voice, but I didn't mean that."

Raffaelle explodes with laughter again.

Salvatore points to Franco and says.

"He is a cheater. That was obtained without my consent. It is not valid in court."

Enrico asks him. "How can it be without your consent, if you were in front of the camera and the microphone?"

"Because they had turned it off and given me the tapes." Salvatore responds.

Enrico stands in front of Franco and tells him. "Don Franco, you have two minutes to give me your version."

"Salvatore heard I have little left to live, and he kept calling every day, asking for a meeting. His obsession is so great that when I die, he will no longer have a reason to continue living. I agreed to meet him, so he would stop calling me. He told me he wanted to make a pact with me, because if I died, he could not clear his honor, so he would rather die with me. I saw him emotionally unstable. I tried to convince him, but he insisted on committing suicide with me. I invited him to lunch and when I saw he had not changed his mind, I told him if he confessed what he had done to me, then I would take the poison with him. He confessed to the camera and microphone, which I never thought he would. He then told me he had fulfilled his part, and I had to fulfill mine. He brought out a bottle of wine, served two cups, and asked me to finish the pact. He told me the poison will act quickly and we would not suffer. I saw he was totally crazy. He was really going to poison himself. I hit his hand before he took the poison, and he went totally crazy. I thought he was having seizures. Luigi had to tie him to the chair so he wouldn't hit himself during his seizures. He then recovered, and we released him. You can take the bottle and the cups. He is the only one who touched them."

Raffaelle couldn't stop laughing. Franco tells Raffaelle.

"I am glad you are laughing. That is good for the soul, but can you tell your cousin the handcuffs are cutting off my circulation?"

Enrico jumps and says. "Forgive me, Don Franco."

Enrico removes Franco's handcuffs and, while he is taking it off, he whispers in his ear. "You're a son of a bitch".

Franco looks at him and says.

"From the first time I saw you, I knew you were the ideal man to close this case once and for all."

Raffaelle bursts into laughter again. Enrico looks at Luigi and sees he had a smile on his face. Enrico whispers in Franco's ear.

"Laugh, because today is my last day in the department. You are going to pay for this one with interest."

Enrico stands in front of Salvatore.

"Salvatore, you are under arrest for perjury."

Salvatore screamed. "No! He confessed. Listen to the tapes. I am innocent. The reporters took Salvatore's pictures on handcuff, begging for mercy."

Franco asks Enrico. "What happened to me now?"

"I will take all the evidence. It will be analyzed and presented before a judge who will determine if Salvatore committed perjury by lying under oath in court on more than one occasion. Then the judge will dismiss your case and only when the judge signs it you will be a free man again. So, don't die this week."

"Do you want to see me free?" Franco asks him.

"No! I want to kill you."

Once again Franco monopolized the headlines of the country "The real criminal goes to jail." "The island celebrates, their hero was innocent." "Scandal in the investigation department, forces top officials to resign." The news spread like wildfire on the island. The people took to the streets and wanted to burn down the police station, demanding they hand over Salvatore. Raffaelle knew only Franco could prevent a catastrophe. Raffaelle hurried up the hill and implored Franco to come with him to avoid a bloodbath.

"Don Raffaelle, you heard what Enrico said. I can't leave until the judge dismisses the case."

"That hell with the judge. My men are in danger of being killed as we speak here. I take responsibility."

Raffaelle forced Franco into the car and hurried to the police station. The protesters stopped throwing stones and calmed down when they saw Franco. Franco stood in the car and spoke to the people.

"I thank you for your loyalty and trust in my innocence, but this is not the way to go. Justice sometimes takes time. It comes and when it comes, it is a reason to celebrate, not for violence."

They all started screaming. "Long live, Don Franco".

Franco goes to speak again when Ronaldo, the crazy old goat herder, screams.

"The island is celebrating. Let's take Don Franco around the town."

The people went crazy and Raffaelle realized the only way to drive the crowd away from the police station was to drive Franco through the town as if he was the Pope. Raffaelle drove Franco for two hours to every corner of the island. People came out of their houses and threw flowers at him. Raffaelle drove the car, laughed, enjoyed, and greeted the people as if he was part of the parade. Upon returning to the complex, Franco could no longer bear the pain in his spine. He was crying out for pain pills.

Maria's family is having breakfast in the villa. Six days had passed since their re-encounter. Patricia had improved a lot. She was pronouncing words and moving her right arm. Don Pedro says.

"Maria, we must return home."

"Father, what is the problem?"

"The factory is closed, and the house is alone."

"You told me your only client is Valentino. Are you going to continue working with him?"

"Is not that. There are people who depend on that work."

"You told me Valentino owns the factory, too."

"Yes, he owns fifty percent."

"Well, let him take care of the factory. I need you here. I have to take care of Mother Patricia, and all this business has to be supervised. I can't do it alone."

"I promise you I will be back soon."

Maria asks her mother.

"Mom, aren't you going to say something to dad?"

"Yes, of course."

"Well tell him."

Angela continues eating, and without looking up, says.

"Pedro, we will wait for you here."

"Pedro furious says. You come with me. I need you."

"Why, so I can cook and take care of you?"

"Angela, you are disrespecting me!"

"No Pedro, I am telling you the truth. You don't need to go back so soon. You don't need money, because Valentino gave you enough money to last for a long time."

Young Pedro says.

"If you want next week, I will go with you. You sell everything and you can come live with us. I am going to college soon and you cannot leave all these women alone."

Pedro feels pressured and drops the subject. The young man says, today I am going to Ancona to pay the university fees and I will use the money from the Swiss university scholarship. Maria and her parents look at each other but say nothing.

"Remember to bring your grandmother's medicine."

"Yes mom. Do you need anything else?"

"No, son. God bless you!"

Angela asks Maria. "Will you ever tell him about Franco?"

Maria cuts her off abruptly. "Mother, that name in this house is forbidden!"

Angela answers. "You look so much like your father that you are hurting yourself."

"I am immensely proud to be like him." Replies Maria.

Don Pedro makes a proud face.

That afternoon, young Pedro arrives and greets everyone like he usually does.

"Mom, I have always said you have a very strong temperament. You allow yourself to be carried away by your impulses instead of coldly analyzing before judging."

"What are you talking about, boy?" Maria asks.

"Do you remember you almost hit me twice for not agreeing with you?"

"I do not know what you are talking about." Maria replies.

"Here you are. I leave it for you to read."

The young man gives her three newspapers with Franco's headlines on the front page. Maria takes them and reads them. She sits down and says nothing. After reading the three newspapers, she stops and says.

"Son, pack your suitcase. We're going on a trip tomorrow!"

"What did you say?"

"You heard me."

"But, what happened?"

"We are going to take Mama Patricia to a specialist doctor."

"Why didn't you tell me about it before?"

"Because I just got the appointment this afternoon. We can't miss it, so hurry."

The young man goes to his room to pack his suitcase and Angela and Pedro ask her.

"What is happening, Maria? What doctor are you talking about?"

Maria shows them the newspapers. Pedro and Angela are speechless.

Angela says. "God forgive us!"

Maria says. "I could not forgive myself if Franco dies and his son does not get to know him."

"Go Maria, we stay. We will take care of Patricia."

"No mom, Patricia is going with me. She is my responsibility. Dad, you are in charge of everything. If, by any chance, Romulo appears around here, you sign all the documents. You tell him all this is yours and if he does not leave immediately, you will call the police."

Pedro asks. "The documents Valentino gave you?"

"Yes, those documents."

"Do not worry, I know what to do."

Maria arrives at the port of Ischia and calls for a taxi.

"Where do you want to go, lady?"

"Please to the hill complex."

"Don't waste your time. That place has no vacancy. People make reservations three months in advance."

"Please take us there."

"Miss, do you have a reservation?"

"No!"

"Then I can suggest another place."

"I told you, the hill complex. Do you have a problem with that?"

"Don't be rude! I told you so, because you will waste your time and money."

"It's my time and my money. Don't worry."

"Oh, my God! What a temperament! It is your money. I don't mind taking you there."

"Well, it doesn't seem like it." Replies Maria.

"Mom, calm down, please. You are very aggressive. The taxi driver just wanted to help us."

Maria was extremely nervous. The last time she was on the island, she was another person. Then, she had the sweet and kind character of her mother, but now she had the strong character of her father. Thanks to that strong character, she had survived all these years.

"Mom, isn't that the place of the mobster you hate so much?" Asks her son.

The taxi driver just had started the engine when he heard what the young man said to his mother. The taxi driver turned off the engine, opened the door and yells. "Get out of my taxi!"

"What's wrong?" Asked Maria.

"Are you deaf? I said get off my taxi now."

"Explain yourself! What is going on?"

"You have called Don Franco a mobster. How dare you call a mobster a person who has been unjustly held prisoner for many years? He, selflessly, using his own money, has done for us more than any government for this island. That man is a saint. A lack of respect to Don Franco is a lack of respect to all of us."

"Please don't be offended. The boy does not know what he is talking about."

"I just said to get that hell out of my taxi."

"My God, you are the one who has a temperament. That's fine, we get out."

"You are really something. Look who's talking about temperament." The taxi driver replies.

They get out of the taxi, and she tells her son. "We are going to take another taxi, but please don't open your big mouth again."

Maria arrives at the complex and sees a long line at the reception. Maria pushes the wheelchair to the front and people protest.

"Lady, the line starts in the back! Hey, don't play deaf!" But Maria ignores them and says to Guido.

"I need to see Don Franco."

Guido is so busy he doesn't even look at Maria and with his mouth full of cookies, he answers.

"Don Franco is busy in his office. He cannot receive anyone."

Maria does not answer him and pushes the wheelchair towards Franco's office. Young Pedro follows her and says,

"Mom, didn't you hear? He can't see us now?"

Maria doesn't answer him.

"What does the doctor have to do with this man?"

Maria continues to push the chair. They are in front of Franco's office when Guido and the security chief rush in, yelling.

"Hey! Where do you think you're going? Stop right there."

Maria tells Pedro. "Open the door."

"No mother. We can't do that."

Maria yells. "Open the damn door!"

The young man opens the door and Maria enters with Patricia in the wheelchair and Pedro next to her. Guido and the security officer rush to the door, but he can only see the backs of Maria, Patricia, and Pedro. Guido says,

"Don Franco, I tried to stop them, but they didn't listen."

The security manager says.

"I am going to take care of this right now. The three of you will learn to respect private property. Either you get out on your own feet or mine will be pushing you in the back."

Franco is standing from his wheelchair. It seemed as if he has seen not one, but three ghosts.

"It's okay Guido. I'll take care of them." The man who was talking to Franco says. "As I was telling you, Don Franco."

Franco responds. "Not now. We'll talk another day."

"But, Don Franco, you told me you need this in a rush."

"Well, I have another rush now. It will be another day. Thanks for coming."

The man stands up, annoyed, and glares at the newcomers.

Maria tells him. "What happened? Don't you know what is another day?"

The man leaves and Franco still did not come out of his astonishment. Maria and Franco stare at each other and both don't know what to say. Young Pedro breaks the silence and says.

"Excuse me, sir. We came for my grandmother's medical visit. My mother is very nervous because we are late for the appointment."

Franco answers him, but without looking at him. He keeps his eyes fixed on Maria.

"It's better late than never, although I would have preferred you to bring your grandmother many years ago."

"No, sir. It wasn't necessary. Grandma had this problem a few months ago."

Maria interrupts him and says. "Pedro, enough of stupidity and give your father a hug."

The young man was shocked, he turns and asks.

"What did you say, mom?"

"Yes, he is your father."

The young man turns, still with his mouth open, trying to assimilate what his mother had told him. He sees Franco in front of him with open arms.

"Come, my son, you are the best news I have received in my life."

Franco hugs his son and cries like a child. Maria approaches Franco, and crying, tells him.

"Forgive me. I have been very unfair to you."

Franco hugs her and responds. "There is nothing to forgive here, but a lot to celebrate."

Franco yells.

"Guido, tell the kitchen that there is a party today. Maria and my son have returned."

Guido comes over and says.

"Doña Maria, forgive me. I did not recognize you."

The security director does not know what to do. He is like a dog with the tail between the legs. He says.

"I said that as a joke. I hope I didn't offend you."

Franco asks his son. "How are you, son?"

"Fantastic. Imagine a week ago I found out that I had another grandmother and a grandfather. Now, I just found out I have a father. I would like to finish this today."

"What do you mean, son?"

"Show me, my brothers and my sisters."

Franco tells him. "On my side, there is nothing to show."

Maria responds. "And neither on mine."

Franco sits in his wheelchair and goes over to Patricia.

"So, you are the competition?"

Patricia laughs, it was the first time Patricia laughed. Franco asks Maria. "Who is this beautiful lady?"

"She is Mother Patricia. She is the angel who welcomed me when I ran away from home. She took care of me, supported me, and she is my business partner."

"In that case, you are just as important to me. Can I call you Mama Patricia?"

Patricia, with tears in her eyes, raises her right arm, touching Franco and shakes her head in approval. Franco gives a cry of joy and says.

"Let's all get out of here; we have to celebrate. At that moment, Enrico enters the office dressed in his class A uniform which had several decorations on his chest.

"Where do you think you are going?"

Enrico yells at Franco, in a military manner.

"Did you forget you are my detainee?"

Maria is horrified. She can't believe that the horrific scene will repeat again.

Franco understands Enrico does not know what had just happened. Franco says. "Enrico, please."

Enrico looks at him and orders.

"Let it be clear to you. I am Officer Enrico. Come here now."

Enrico throws some documents on the table and yells at Franco.

"Sign here. Didn't you hear me? I said sign here."

Franco is sweating, he is pale and hardly can speak. Somehow, Salvatore had recorded his confession and now he was going to prison for the rest of his life.

Franco does not even read the document. He just signs it and hugs Maria.

Enrico pulls out his handcuff, and Franco is about to faint. Maria hugs him tight, and tells him. "I will never let you go."

Enrico yells again. "Look at me Franco, it is over."

Franco let go of Maria and stands in front of Enrico. He looks at Enrico and tears run down his cheeks.

Enrico spoke in a loud voice.

I want to inform you that with that signature I officially closed the hill case and finished my work in the department. You are a free man."

Franco stands, hugs him, and tells him in the ear.

"Son of a bitch, you got me good."

"No, you still owe me."

"I thought I have to go in front of the judge."

"Yes, but it must be in front of the judge who sentenced you. After what happened at the police station, the judge is afraid the people are going to lynch him at the courthouse."

Enrico takes two uniforms from a bag, one of a health inspector and one of a cook. Enrico asks Franco.

"Choose one of the two."

Franco says." You don't have to quit your job."

Enrico looks at Franco and, with an intimidating face, asks again.

"Which of the two?"

Franco asks him. "Would you like to be the head of security? You have all the qualifications."

"After today, I never want to see a gun in my life."

"I don't know what to tell you. If you can't decide, let Adriana decide for you."

Franco tells Enrico. "Look, he's my son."

Enrico responds. You old scoundrel portraying yourself as a monk and with scattered children everywhere. By the way, you cannot deny him. He looks just like you."

Enrico tells Pedro. "Boy, tell your father to take you out for a walk. He is already a free man. I want you to know you are the luckiest young man in the world for having this father. You cannot imagine how he made me suffer. Today he pays me back the first one, but there are many more to come."

Franco tells Enrico. "Please, can you take out the bag that is on top of that closet?"

Enrico takes out a black bag and hands it to Franco. Maria had kept quiet all this time. She approaches Franco and tells him.

"I want to ask you something, and I understand you if you do not want to answer."

Franco answers. "I also want to ask you something and I understand that if you do not accept it."

Franco opens the bag and takes out all the pictures he had kept of Maria. Those pictures were torn into pieces. Maria had torn them before leaving the complex. Maria sees the pictures of her and remembers that fatal night when she tore the pictures and cursed him.

Franco asks her. "Please, tell me what you wanted to ask me?"

Maria drawing strength from deep inside of her and so ashamed she could not look Franco in the eye, she says.

"Can you forgive me?"

Franco had in his hands the engagement ring that Maria left with the broken pictures.

"Yes, I forgive you. And would you marry me?"

Maria couldn't believe what she was hearing. She lifts her head and sees Franco holding the ring in his hand. She jumps out of happiness, hugs, and kisses Franco.

"Yes yes! This time you won't escape me."

The scene moves everyone, and Enrico says.

"Wait, this Saturday I'm getting married. You have delayed my wedding three times; I will not delay it one more time for you."

"No Enrico, we will have the weddings together."

Franco went out with Maria, Patricia, and his son to tour the complex. Passing through the kitchen, they saw Enrico dressed as a cook.

"Enrico, you already decided?" Franco asks him.

"Yes, Adriana and her mother say I have no vocation to go from bar to bar and restaurant to restaurant. They say my place is right here in the kitchen with them."

"I congratulate you. Now you will have your mother-in-law as your supervisor."

Enrico looks at him and says.

"Don't you make fun of me. Yours is yet to come."

That Saturday was a holiday on the island. The two weddings were celebrated on the hill and all the churches bells tolled when the priest pronounced them husband and wife.

The people gathered on the outside of the hill. They celebrated in style. All the residents at the back of the hill were guests of honor, including Ronaldo, the crazy old goat herder, and his two dogs. Vittorio and his wife were present, but his son Alberto did not attend because he had left for America.

Raffaelle shows up at the wedding and Franco tells him.

"Hi Raffaelle, it's nice to see you."

Enrico tells Raffaelle. "Cousin, I knew you would not fail me and attend my wedding."

Adriana asks him. "Are you really cousins?"

Raffaelle responds. "Yes, we are distant cousins. So distant, I don't know who the hell was his mother from."

Maria's parents were present at the wedding. They apologized and thanked Franco and Valentino for everything they did for them.

The governor tried to attend the wedding, but the people prevented him from entering.

Franco, despite having enough money to live the rest of his life wherever he wanted, stays on the island of Ischia. The beauty of the Island, its simple and charming people voluntarily kept him captive for the rest of his life.

END.